All H...

Charly Cox

San Diego, California

Canelo US
An imprint of Printers Row Publishing Group
9717 Pacific Heights Blvd, San Diego, CA 92121
www.canelobooksus.com

Printers Row Publishing Group is a division of Readerlink Distribution Services, LLC. Canelo US is a registered trademark of Readerlink Distribution Services, LLC.

First published in Great Britain in 2019 by Hera. This edition originally published in the United Kingdom in 2021 by Hera Books.

Published in partnership with Canelo.

Correspondence regarding the content of this book should be sent to Canelo US, Editorial Department, at the above address. Author inquiries should be sent to Hera Books, Unit 9, 5th Floor, Cargo Works, 1–2 Hatfields, London SE1 9PG, United Kingdom, www.herabooks.com.

Publisher: Peter Norton • Associate Publisher: Ana Parker
Art Director: Charles McStravick
Editorial Director: April Graham
Production Team: Beno Chan, Rusty von Dyl

Cover design: The Brewster Project
Cover images: Depositphotos, Unsplash

Library of Congress Control Number: 2021953463

ISBN: 978-1-6672-0861-9

Printed in Faridabad-Haryana, India

28 27 26 25 24 1 2 3 4 5

For Kevin and Timothee,
for your love, unflagging support, and faith in me

and

For all the police, military, and first responders out there,
risking your lives day in and day out.
Thank you for being willing to sacrifice everything for us!
You are appreciated.

PART ONE

Chapter One

The woman didn't feel right. She wasn't getting enough oxygen, and she was certain she was being smothered. Sharp spasms tore through her stomach with every breath she attempted to take, and what was that in her mouth? Her entire body felt weighed down, as if a ton of rocks had been substituted in place of her comforter. Not to mention the fact she was so cold that even her bones seemed to be chattering.

Wherever she was, it wasn't in her nice, cozy bed, covered in her warm, comfortable blankets and surrounded by her down-filled pillows. She tried to open her eyes, but they refused to cooperate for more than a second, and even then, she was surrounded by darkness. She reached out her arm – it was so heavy, like someone had infused her blood with liquid steel – to grab onto something, though she didn't know what.

She really needed to sit up and figure out where she was, but when she tried, she realized she couldn't separate her legs. The tightness in her chest magnified as she tried to remember if she'd been in an accident. A brief image of fists raining down on her body as a foot kicked out in anger flashed in her mind, and an overwhelming sense of dread made her go numb.

She whimpered as memories flickered, coming at her in lightning speed. She squeezed her eyes shut, hoping to escape this nightmare, praying sleep would drag her back under.

–

'Are you sure no one will find us back here, Jack?' the young woman asked the man she'd met a few nights ago at the bar her cousin owned. Having moved here only a few months earlier, she wasn't too familiar with the area, but she knew they were somewhere up in the Jemez Mountains, far from any of the hiking trails she'd seen along the way. They'd left his X-Terra at a campsite and were trekking 'just a short distance' off the road. His 'short distance' gauge and hers were apparently not in sync because it felt like they'd been walking an hour already.

'Positive. Relax, babe. I come out here all the time to hike. I've never seen anyone out here, ever,' he assured her. The young man stopped and looked into his date's wide eyes. 'But you're the first girl I've ever brought up here. You're special, Trinity.' He brushed her hair to the side and leaned in to kiss her.

It wasn't true, of course. He'd brought plenty of women up here. He told them all they were special.

He found his lucky spot in a small copse of trees and released Trinity's hand so he could pull the knapsack off his back and set the small cooler down. After he cleared some brush away, he unzipped the large compartment of his bag and pulled out a heavy wool blanket which he laid on the flattest part of the ground, securing all the corners in case the wind picked up. He glanced up at the sky and thanked the heavens it was such a nice day, even up here in the mountains. When everything was the way he liked it, he pulled out a bottle of wine, pouring a little into two plastic cups.

Jack handed Trinity one of the cups and situated himself in the center of the blanket, legs stretched out. When she simply stood there looking unsure, he tugged gently on her hand, encouraging her to sit next to him. When she did, he moved her hair away from her neck and kissed the silky soft spot below her ear.

'Relax, Trinity. We don't have to do anything you don't want. You know that, right? We can just chill on the blanket,

3

watch the clouds, and talk.' As he spoke, he rubbed soothing circles on her back.

Within a short amount of time, Trinity had drunk two glasses of wine and was on her third. 'You're not doing a very good job of keeping up with me here, Jack.'

'Ah, but I'm the one who's driving, remember?' Jack poured more wine into her glass even though it was still half full.

Trinity giggled nervously and took another sip. With just a hint of slur in her words, she said, 'If I didn't know better, I'd say you were trying to get me drunk.'

'Now, babe, I wouldn't do that. I just want you to relax a little.' She wasn't drunk yet, but she'd finished off those other two glasses rather quickly, so she must be feeling pretty buzzed. He didn't *really* want her completely inebriated; he didn't want to take *advantage* of her – he wasn't a jerk. He wanted her to enjoy this as much as he would, but still, he let her continue drinking. While she was busy taking another sip, he slipped his hand under her shirt.

It didn't take much longer before Jack was able to coax Trinity to lie down 'to get more comfortable.' Still, he didn't rush things. He continued stroking her arms, her belly, brushing under her breasts, but never quite touching them. He teased her mouth with kisses, not giving in to her obvious desire to deepen those kisses. No, he wanted her completely ready because there was nothing worse than a girl backing out at the last minute.

He felt her resistance slipping away, so it surprised him when she suddenly pushed him off her and sprang into a sitting position.

'What's the matter, baby? Come back down here,' he coaxed.

'What's that noise?' Trinity looked around her wildly, then back at him, eyes wide. 'Do you hear it?'

Jack sat up and strained to hear whatever had spooked her but heard only the breeze. 'It's just the wind blowing through the tops of the trees. It always sounds like cars on the highway. It's o –'

4

'No, not that!' Trinity cocked her head. 'That! Listen. It sounds like… I don't know… like someone else is out there.'

He sat up and laughed, nestling his nose into her hair. 'Baby, trust me. There's no one else out here.' He tried to ease her onto her back again. 'Let's just…'

Trinity pushed him away. 'No. Seriously, Jack, listen. Just be quiet a second.' She kept her hand up to ward off further advances.

Jack swallowed his irritation and did as he was instructed – he listened. He still didn't hear anything. It was probably just birds singing in the trees or some type of animal stomping through the brush, something intent on leaving them alone as long as they left it be. Regardless, he sure as hell wasn't going to tell her that because he didn't want her freaking out about other kinds of wildlife lurking about. He moved his legs and winced a little. His pants were too tight. He groaned. He was so close.

Then he heard the sound, too. It was a strange noise, unlike any animal he'd ever heard. It was more of a… muted gurgling, almost.

He listened more closely to get a better idea which direction the sound was coming from. East. It was coming from the east. He stood to get a feel for how far away the person was – and he was suddenly convinced there was definitely a someone, not a something, out there. He held his hand out for Trinity and pulled her up but released her as she struggled to re-hook her bra and untwist her shirt. When she finished, she stepped forward and squeezed his arm with a grip tighter than he would've thought she was capable of.

'You hear it too, don't you?' she whispered.

Jack nodded. He put his finger to his lips and tilted his head. There it was again. He glanced at Trinity, walked over to his knapsack, and pulled out the hunting knife he always carried with him, a gift from his father. He cringed at Trinity's gasp.

'What the hell is *that* for?'

'Relax,' Jack said. He felt like he used that word with her a lot. 'It's for protection, just-in-case. I always carry it. I never

5

need it, so I don't even think about it being there. Until times like now.' He saw the wariness in her face and knew she was unsure whether or not she believed him, but he ignored that because right now, he was glad he never left home without his Ka-Bar. The sound came again. Trinity tucked herself closer to his side.

'Stay here,' he ordered. 'I'm going to take a look. It might be a wounded bear or something.' He didn't believe that for a second, and he'd already forgotten about his plan not to mention wild animals. 'I'll be back in a minute.'

'You're kidding, right? I'm not staying here. No freaking way. I watch horror movies; I know what happens to the person who stays behind. Yeah, not gonna happen. I'm coming with you.'

He started to argue, to tell her she'd be safer here, not to mention she'd be closer to the truck in case she needed to make a quick getaway – no one else was ever up here, so he kept his keys hidden under the back seat's floor mat – but instead he nodded. He didn't really want to be a hero anyway. Not his style. 'Yeah, okay. Sounds like it's coming from over that way. Just stay behind me – and run if I tell you to. Okay?' He didn't want to *be* a hero, but he wanted to sound like one. Trinity nodded, and the two set off to find out what was making the noise.

They walked quietly into the trees, pausing every few seconds to listen. As they moved, dry vegetation crunched under their feet, twigs snapped, and the wind rustled the leaves. Birds chirped, and squirrels raced up trees. A woodpecker drummed somewhere off in the distance. All the various sounds of nature made it difficult to tell if they were still going the right way. They paused again, straining their ears for any tell-tale sign they were on the right path. Jack searched left and right, looking for – he didn't even know what he was looking for.

'Do you still hear it?' he asked. She shook her head and squeezed him tighter. He stared at his arm. It was beet red from where her fingernails dug into his skin. Half-crescent moon shapes covered his forearm. He nonchalantly removed her hand and pushed her a little further behind him. He felt her latch onto the waistband of his pants.

Waving his knife in front of him, Jack inched forward, Trinity close on his heels, both hoping to uncover the mysterious sound and both hoping to find nothing at all.

They had just turned left into a small grouping of trees not far from their picnic spot when Trinity jerked to a stop and screamed. The sound was so shrill, Jack winced, wanting to cover his ears. A jackrabbit bolted from the bushes and ran in the opposite direction, startled birds scattered from the treetops, and a chipmunk scurried into the brush. Jack didn't blame them; he wished he could run, too.

He crouched and brought his knife up in a defensive motion, rotating his body left and right. Trinity pointed down, her other hand covering her mouth. She continued screaming, but the sound was more muffled. He moved her to the side so he could see what she was pointing at.

An arm, red and covered in wounds, stuck out of a natural trench covered with sticks and leaves, resembling a grave that someone had forgotten to finish filling in. They'd almost tripped over it.

'Shh. Stop screaming,' he hissed at Trinity. When she finally pulled herself together enough to stop the unattractive sound coming from her mouth, Jack whispered, 'I'm going to look. Wait here.' Trinity nodded, but she kept hold of his pants and inched forward with him. He figured that since her body quivered so much, she probably couldn't feel his own body trembling.

When he was close enough, Jack moved the top limb out of the way and poked the arm sticking out. Nothing happened. He crept closer. He started to uncover some of the brush, moving more quickly as he did. Then Trinity was helping him move the twigs and leaves, both of them glancing every few seconds at the arm. Jack didn't know what he expected it to do, but still, he couldn't look away for long. He'd probably watched too many zombie movies.

Tangled yellow strands of hair began to show through the pile of colorful, damp leaves. *Lank* was the word that came to mind. When the gurgling noises stopped, Jack worked more quickly, tossing handfuls of leaves behind him, and then finally shoveling with his hands.

Trinity had stopped helping and moved back, her hands again covering her mouth, her eyes so wide, he thought they'd pop out of the sockets. His hand hit something solid. A woman's head. Her eyes were closed, the parts of her body that showed covered in bruises. Jack worked frantically to uncover the rest of her.

It wasn't long before he realized the woman was nude. Cuts, deep and long, covered her entire body. Her face was red, along with a myriad of other colors, and swollen. Her wrists and ankles were purple and raw, the skin torn in several places. *Jesus*, Jack shuddered.

The abrasions on the woman's wrists reminded him of the wolf that had been snared in one of his father's steel traps. The wolf had gnawed almost completely through its front paw trying to get loose when his dad, using a long-handled lever for just such a case, carefully sprung the steel trap, releasing the wolf. The wounded animal had looked back at Jack and his dad as if to thank them before limping off. And just as he had back then, Jack held his breath, scared of what might happen next.

He looked over to Trinity, and then wished he hadn't. She was facing away from him, throwing up. He averted his eyes, not knowing where to focus. He fought against the instinct to look at the body again, but it was like a train wreck; he couldn't stop himself.

One of the branches brushed Jack's leg, snagging on his jeans, and he glanced down to move it away. He shrieked, jumping back. The hand sticking out of the brush was clasped onto his pants.

The gurgling sound started again, and he jerked his gaze back up to the woman's battered face. Her swollen eyes were small slits but open now, staring vacantly right at, or rather through, him, reminding him of his blind uncle who 'stared' directly at people though he couldn't see.

Embarrassingly, a small scream burst from his throat before he could stop it. His heart took off at a gallop, and he sucked in so much oxygen, he became light-headed and was afraid he might faint. He slowly backed away. Not paying attention to what was behind him, he tripped over a tree stump and stumbled, falling, his legs splayed in front of him. One foot touched the woman's outstretched arm, and he scrambled backwards.

Jack had forgotten all about Trinity until she was suddenly by his side, trying to help him up. The woman's arm twitched, touching the exposed part of his leg where his jeans had inched up, and a gurgled sound escaped her throat. Shaking, he leaned in to try to make sense of the woman's incomprehensible babble. A breath of sound escaped her lips, and this time Jack understood.

'H-h-help me!'

Chapter Two

Four days earlier – Monday, March 25, 3:30p.m.

'We, the jury, find Lucas Bloomfield guilty on all charges.'

Cheers and sobs alike erupted throughout the hot, stuffy courtroom as soon as the words left the foreman's lips, and as the judge banged her gavel and called for order, Detective Alyssa Wyatt felt as though a granite boulder had been lifted from her shoulders. Though she had never really doubted the district attorney's ability to get a conviction, there had been times over the years when she'd been unpleasantly surprised by the unpredictability of a jury.

Watching Bloomfield's cold, impassive face as the verdict was read, she couldn't help but think of her own family's tragedy all those years ago when she was only nine years old.

But when the couple in front of her turned around and mouthed 'Thank you,' Alyssa knew this was why she'd come today. For these parents, and for their daughter, who Bloomfield had stalked for weeks, finally following her back to her apartment where he spent hours torturing her before stabbing and leaving her for dead. Somehow, she'd survived that brutal attack and had managed to call 911.

Several witnesses had described seeing a black pickup truck in the area in the days before the attack, and with the help of security cameras placed around the apartment complex, Alyssa had been able to zoom in and get a license plate, enabling her to track Bloomfield to his home on the West Side. The second he saw them, he bolted out the back, but Alyssa was ready, taking him to the ground by shooting 1200 volts through his body. From the evidence they obtained inside his house, the young woman wasn't his first victim, but Alyssa made sure she was his last.

Through the grapevine, she'd heard that HBO had offered the woman and her parents a lucrative sum for their story. The parents had informed them that their daughter's suffering was not for sale and to never call again before hanging up on the caller.

Someone tapped her arm, and Alyssa turned to her left. Her partner, Cord Roberts, leaned his head toward the exit, and Alyssa nodded, giving the parents' shoulders a squeeze as she stood to leave.

Outside, she shooed a stray cat away as she, Cord, and her favorite forensic artist, Liz Waterson – who had rendered the sketch that led to Bloomfield's arrest – walked down the steps of the county building.

Liz's satchel containing her sketch pad, charcoals, pencils, and facial recognition catalog thumped against her back as she slowed her pace to match Alyssa's. Years ago, someone had asked Liz why she always had 'those things' with her, and she'd said, 'I'm superstitious that way,' and left it at that. Now, she swiped an imaginary check mark in the air and said, 'One less pervert roaming the streets.'

'Unfortunately, there's never a shortage of them out there,' Alyssa said as Cord nodded his agreement.

'Sadly, that's true,' Liz replied, before moving ahead. 'I'll catch you two later. I'm off to the cemetery. Thirty-seven.' She waved before trotting down the rest of the steps and heading in the opposite direction.

Every year on her sister's birthday, Liz announced the age her sister would've been and placed flowers on the grave. Five years ago, just as Cord was signing on as her partner, Alyssa had solved the mystery of Liz's murdered sibling. Unknown to her family, an ex-boyfriend of Amelia's had started coming back around.

When she rebuffed him, his explosive temper had taken over, and after beating her, he shot her in the face point blank.

It had taken Alyssa less than a week to determine who Amelia's killer was and arrest him. Shortly after the man's conviction, Liz requested to be transferred to their precinct. Alyssa wished it hadn't been under those circumstances, but she was grateful to have her on their team.

Before heading the one block to the designated parking garage for officers and courthouse officials, Alyssa pulled out her phone and turned the sound back on. When she saw the blinking blue light, she opened her texts to find a message from her husband, asking how things had gone.

Guilty on all charges, she replied before catching up to her partner who waited at the corner.

'Wish you and Sara could've come to Holly's party,' she said, switching gears from professional to personal. 'It might've been easier to ignore Mabel if you'd been there. I swear that woman could drive Mother Teresa to drink if she was still alive.' *That woman* was Alyssa's interfering mother-in-law who never passed up an opportunity to let her daughter-in-law know how she felt about her.

'Sorry, Lys. Had a ball game to play. You know how it goes.'

'Still wish you'd been there. Then you'd see once and for all I haven't been exaggerating about her all these years.'

'Never thought you were,' Cord said. 'At least you can be grateful you don't have to deal with her every Sunday anymore.'

'True. Yet, she still finds a way to make my Land of Enchant-ment a House of Horrors.' Alyssa grimaced, remembering the days when Mabel had insisted on spending Sundays with her beloved son and grandchildren. Now, however, both Holly and Isaac were teenagers with busy schedules, so the Sunday ritual had thankfully gone by the wayside. Still, the time spent with her husband's mother came all too frequently for her taste.

But she tolerated it because Mabel was the only grandparent her children had. Brock's father had died before Holly was born, and her own parents… well, even if they had been alive, there was no telling what kind of grandparents they'd have been. Would her children, like her, be nothing more than a daily reminder of Alyssa's mistake?

She slowed as they came to one of her favorite cafés situated next door to the parking garage. 'I need coffee. Want some?' she asked, already reaching for the door.

Predictably, her partner shook his head even as he reached around her to hold the door. Chivalrous to the bone. 'No, thank you. I'll never understand how you ever manage to sleep with all that caffeine running through your veins.'

As they waited in line, Alyssa continued where she'd left off. 'Did I tell you Mabel mentioned buying that vacant house on our street so she could be closer?' She winced, remembering the panic she'd felt at that prospect.

'You ever consider she gives you such a hard time because she knows *you* don't like *her*?' Cord asked, reaching out to steady an inattentive twenty-something girl who nearly collided into him as she texted on her phone and then had the audacity to glare at him as if it had been his fault instead of hers.

Alyssa ignored the people around her and stared at her partner like he'd suddenly grown two heads. 'What? Just, *what*? Haven't you been listening? She has *never* liked me. Ever. Seriously, the woman wore all black to our wedding! If people didn't know better, they would've thought they were attending a wake!'

'Maybe black's her color.'

Her response was to roll her eyes. 'She's rude and undermines everything I say.'

'I don't know what to tell you, my friend. You know the saying, though – kill 'em with kindness.' Cord winked.

'Sure, that'll work. Not.' Now at the front of the line, she paused long enough to place her order, a grande black coffee, no room for cream, and a decaf passion fruit tea for Cord, though he hadn't asked for it. 'I know it was Holly's birthday, but, Lord Almighty, I didn't think that party was ever going to end!'

Cord leaned against the counter as Alyssa watched the barista make three fancy coffees before finally pouring her brew. Her mouth salivated. The poor kid behind the counter barely had a chance to set the cup down before she snatched it up and took a careful sip. Her eyes nearly rolled to the back of her head as she let out a sigh of contentment.

'Ever consider that addiction of yours might cause a health issue somewhere down the road?' Cord asked as they headed back outside. It wasn't the first time he'd posed the question to her.

And her answer was the same as always. 'Nope. So, do you want to take a stab at what she got Holly for her birthday? Even Brock 'bout lost his mind,' she said as they made their way up the ramp to where Alyssa's car was parked. 'Isaac, on the other hand, suddenly became the most attentive brother on the planet when he saw what his grandmother got her. He was tripping all over himself trying to please his sister. If I hadn't been so pissed, it would've even been funny. Go ahead. Guess.'

'A yacht? A Lamborghini?' Cord volunteered.

Alyssa shot her partner what both her kids called 'the mom look.' Paired with her 'detective look,' it could bode danger for the person on the receiving end. 'Be serious. Plane tickets to Europe this summer with any friend of her choice. All summer. Any friend. That's what.' Alyssa, trim, athletic, and solid at five foot three, had a six-foot-four attitude when she was good and angry, and this weekend, she'd definitely been good and angry.

Cord choked on his tea, and his eyes widened comically. 'Seriously? How can I get your mother-in-law to adopt me?'

'You can have her,' she muttered under her breath.

Cord laughed. 'Just kidding, but seriously, didn't the woman ever see *Taken*, that movie where girls are kidnapped *in Europe* and set up for human trafficking?'

'Exactly my point. We already told her no when she suggested it two months ago. She "just wants to give her first grandchild the experience of a lifetime," ' Alyssa mimicked her mother-in-law. 'We even explained – well, *Brock* did because she sure as hell wasn't listening to me – that we weren't comfortable with the idea of Holly traipsing around Europe by herself. Her solution was to get two tickets so she wouldn't be alone.'

Her Chevy Tahoe in sight, Alyssa pressed her key fob twice to unlock the doors. Before Cord slid into the passenger side, he glanced up and then cleared his throat in a way that told her whatever he was about to say, she wasn't going to like.

'Holly *is* eighteen now. Maybe it's time to let her get some life experiences under her belt.'

She was right. She didn't like it. She glared at her partner over the hood of the car. 'Life experiences? Why does she need to go to *Europe* to get life experiences? She can get them just fine here in New Mexico.'

What Alyssa didn't mention was that she knew, if push came to shove, that Holly was now legally an adult and could venture anywhere she liked with whomever she liked, with or without her parents' permission. Of course, since she was still living under their roof…

Alyssa opened the door and slid into the driver's seat. As soon as Cord climbed in, she said, 'You know what, forget I brought it up.' She knew his silence was less capitulation than it was speculation. Either way, for now, the subject was closed.

She turned the ignition and shifted into reverse just as her phone rang, the car's built-in Bluetooth flashing the caller's name. Foot on the brake, Alyssa pressed the button to answer the call.

'You're needed for a missing person's call,' Ruby, the squadron's no-nonsense secretary said before Alyssa could issue a greeting. Once upon a time, there'd been a secret pool placing bets on Ruby's age. Nobody had won because she'd found out, and there'd been hell to pay. Getting on Ruby's bad side was never a good idea. It had been said that the cops in her precinct would rather face a gunman than a pissed-off Ruby.

'Joe and Tony are already there, taking the initial report. Husband reports wife was missing when he came home from work. Name's McCormick, Rafe and Callie.' She rattled off an address and then snapped out, 'Are you getting all this down, Detective?'

Alyssa could picture the woman looking down her bespectacled nose as she barked out information.

'I've got it, Ruby,' Cord answered. 'And we're on it.'

'Good,' was all she said before she ended the call, making both of them chuckle. Not even Cord's charming personality could melt Ruby's outer shell. *Warm* was definitely not a word one would use to describe the grandmotherly-looking secretary. It was a clear case of deceptive appearances.

'Well, I didn't really want to do any paperwork today anyway,' Alyssa said as she released the brake and headed to the McCormick residence.

Chapter Three

Callie opened the shower door, steam billowing behind her. Absently, she pulled a towel off the heated towel rack – something she didn't know existed until she'd married Rafe – thinking of all the things she needed to get accomplished today. She considered writing a list, not that she necessarily needed it; she just felt more of a sense of achievement when she could mark things off. In fact, there were times when she made her list, did something that wasn't already on it, then wrote it down simply so she could cross it off. Oh well, she thought. There were worse things in life than being obsessive compulsive.

As she stood there debating whether or not to pen her To-Do list, she heard Scorpions singing 'Wind of Change,' and she scrambled to answer the phone before it went to voicemail.

'Hello?' she said breathlessly.

'Busy?' her husband asked.

Did he sound irritated, or was it just her imagination? 'Just got out of the shower. Why?' Sometimes Rafe called just to chat, but, more often, he needed her to do something.

'I called the service shop to have your transmission looked at. You have an appointment at nine. Can you make that?'

Callie glanced at the clock sitting on her nightstand. 8:07. If she hurried, she could make it. She stifled her frustration that Rafe rarely considered what her schedule may be like before he made appointments for her. Sighing, she reminded herself he was only trying to be helpful, even if it was mainly because he

17

was tired of hearing her nag about the trouble with her car. For weeks, an awful grinding and clunking sound could be heard under the hood.

If only she'd paid attention when her father had tried to teach her about vehicles, she might've been able to figure it out herself. Growing up, she understood her family couldn't afford to take their cars somewhere else to be repaired, but as a teenager, she couldn't be bothered to learn. And even though she could now afford simply to buy another vehicle, like Rafe urged her to do, she liked her Jeep. 'Sure. I can make that. I'll just move some things around,' Callie said.

'Good.' He paused then added, 'I tried calling you earlier, but it went straight to voicemail.'

This time, the accusation in his voice was clear.

'I was either in the shower or talking to Terrie.' She pulled her phone away from her ear long enough to see that she had, indeed, missed a call. 'Well, I need to finish getting ready so I'm not late.' She hesitated a beat before adding, 'Thanks for calling the shop for me.'

'No problem. See you tonight.'

'See –' Rafe was already gone. 'All righty then,' she said, setting the phone on the sink. Before she donned her skirt and blouse, she stood in front of the mirror, examining her body from various angles, frowning as she did, unhappy at the few extra pounds she'd packed on. Even though Rafe hadn't specifically said anything about it, she felt like he looked at her differently. 'It's not entirely my fault I've gained a little weight,' she said to her image. 'With all the charity boards Rafe wants me on, it's not like I have as much time to hit the gym.' Where they'd first met nine and a half years ago. Theirs had been a whirlwind romance with him treating her to fancy dinners at fancy restaurants with menus that didn't bother to display prices – places which, in her world, existed only in movies. And before she'd known what was happening, they were married.

She feared the concept of further change in her body was the main reason behind her husband's refusal to discuss the possibility of her becoming pregnant. Before they'd married, they'd agreed on waiting five years before trying. That time had elapsed by an additional four plus years.

Callie shook her head. She didn't have time to ponder why her husband suddenly clammed up when she brought up the subject of adding to their family of two. Before her emotions could get away from her, she slapped on some eyeshadow and mascara, then dried and brushed her long, unruly hair before tying it back into a low ponytail.

After another quick peek in the mirror, she deemed her appearance good enough, and grabbed her purse, making sure to slip her e-reader into the pocket. She wanted to have something to do while she waited for her vehicle to be serviced. Unlike Rafe, she was unable to sit for more than fifteen minutes without having a book to read or a puzzle to solve.

In the garage, she climbed into her Jeep and started it, wincing at the sound that escaped from beneath the hood. She was glad it was a short drive to the dealership's service station.

–

Five minutes after she arrived, Callie handed her keys to the service technician and went to the lobby, prepared to sit for the next hour or so. So far, she was the only customer inside. She spotted a freshly brewed pot of coffee sitting in the corner of the room and helped herself to a cup. Taking a small sip to test its bitterness, she nodded in approval. It was better than most service station coffees. Even so, she added a liberal amount of sugar and cheap powdered creamer to improve the taste.

On her way back to her seat, she stopped to peruse the various magazines strewn about and decided she really didn't need to read about '15 Ways to Please Your Man' or 'The Top Ten Things Your Man Wants You to Do, But is Too Afraid to Ask.' Really? Who supplied this stuff?

She glanced around the little room, but saw no newspapers in sight, which was good because she was on a self-imposed media strike, refusing to read or watch what was going on in the corrupted world around her. Some days, she even refused to watch the weather channel, something that irritated Rafe. As Callie made her way across the lobby, she glanced at the television in the corner, recognizing the current morning show as one she used to enjoy. She sat in a chair furthest from the mechanic's workshop but closest to the window. She set her purse and bottled water in the seat next to her, settled in, and grabbed her e-reader, ready to continue the romantic suspense story she'd started late the night before while Rafe watched some reality show he was currently addicted to.

She'd been reading for approximately ten minutes when another customer, an older man, walked into the room. He looked to be in his late sixties and was hunched over, wearing a red flannel shirt and worn jeans with holes in the knees and frayed edges on the hems. He reminded her of the cranky neighbor she'd had as a child. She watched as his eyes wandered the room before he chose the chair next to her.

There was a small table separating the two of them, and Callie wondered why in the world the man would choose to sit practically on top of her when there was plenty of available seating. Slightly annoyed, she went back to reading.

She jumped when the man suddenly exclaimed, 'I don't believe it. No one wants to work at anything anymore. If it ain't easy, just give up.' Callie glanced up to see if he was speaking to her or merely talking out loud. Since he was staring at the television, she turned to look. Someone had changed the channel and turned up the sound, but she'd been so absorbed in her story, she hadn't noticed.

The news anchors, or whatever they were called, were discussing yet another celebrity couple who had announced they were splitting up after nine years of marriage, but who still loved each other and would remain steadfast friends.

Callie had no interest in these particular stars, so she simply smiled at the man and returned to the story in her hand, hoping he would take the hint and leave her alone.

'I mean, don't these people realize marriage takes a little bit of effort? Don't you agree?'

It was obvious she wasn't going to get out of this conversation so, sighing, she turned to the man. 'Yes, marriage isn't an easy venture, but my husband and I have always worked hard at ours,' she said while playing with her two-carat, pear-shaped wedding ring. *Though it seems like one of us tries harder than the other,* she thought.

To her dismay, her comment allowed the man to jump into a conversation about the disastrous marriages that had befallen the country in the last half-century. Callie listened politely while glancing down surreptitiously, noticing that he wasn't wearing a wedding ring himself. Of course, not all married couples had a double-ring ceremony, but it was fairly uncommon not to. And not all men wore their rings. In fact, her father had rarely worn his, afraid he'd get it caught on one of his woodworking machines.

While the man droned on, she began to suspect he was lonely and just happy to have an attentive audience. He was certainly friendly, the type she never wanted to sit next to on a long plane ride. When she was in the air, she wanted to lose herself in sleep or a novel – not in the life story of a passenger she'd likely never see again.

'Would you like me to get you another cup?' The man interrupted her thoughts, pointing to her now empty Styrofoam cup.

'What? Oh, that's kind of you, but no, thank you. I've had my limit of caffeine for today. I've got my water here,' she said, holding up her bottle.

'You probably like that fancy stuff they got on every corner anyway,' he said before launching into a commentary about how shameful it was that so many large companies were running mom-and-pop shops out of business. She almost confessed that Rafe owned a couple of those fancy coffee shops. Instead, she accepted she wasn't going to get any further reading done, and not wanting to run her battery down, she closed her e-reader and gave her almost-full attention to the talkative gentleman. She was in for quite the friendly conversation, like it or not.

As he spoke, she noticed certain details. For instance, he wore a buzz cut, hinting at a possible past military career, and spoke with a slight accent, though she couldn't quite place it. His voice was smooth and warm, grandfatherly almost. She was still trying to place his accent when she realized he was asking her a question.

'I hope that's not too forward?'

She blinked. Forward? She'd obviously tuned out more than she realized.

'I said I like that color.' He nodded toward her blouse. 'It looks good on you, especially with your hair color. Blondes have more fun, right?' He winked, then added, 'I always liked when my wife wore blue.'

'Um, thank you,' she said, feeling awkward. She scooted herself further into her chair, hoping she wasn't being obvious about it. As she did, the man's words sank in: *liked, wore.*

Past tense.

The man started to twist the ring that wasn't on his finger before realizing what he was doing. 'I work a lot with my hands and had to take my ring off. I still forget it's not there.'

'My dad used to do the same thing,' Callie assured the man.

When a minute passed in silence, Callie began to hope he was finished, but then he bounced right into another story, content to carry the conversation himself.

She was relieved when the door jingled and three more customers, two elderly gentlemen and a younger man, entered the lobby. After checking in with the receptionist, the two older men took seats on the opposite side of the room, close to the television in the corner while the younger man randomly grabbed a magazine, and after taking a quick sweep of the seating situation, sat where he could easily see everyone, and proceeded to read. She hoped her new *friend* would include them in his dialogue so she could continue reading. Nope, no such luck.

Finally, after more than an hour and a half of very, God help her, detailed conversation – some of it excruciating in minutiae – the service technician announced her car was ready. Callie stood and gathered her belongings. Before she could make her way to the counter, the man also stood.

He grabbed one of her hands in both of his and shook it vigorously. 'It was so nice to meet you. It was kind of you to listen to an old man's rambling.' The man turned a little red, and she felt guilty for wishing he'd stop yammering.

'It was a pleasure listening to you,' she lied. 'Have a great day.' She walked to the counter and paid her bill, waving to the man one last time before walking out the door. As soon as she got in her car and drove away, she pushed the weird conversation to the back of her mind and focused instead on the things she wanted to get done.

She never noticed anyone staring at her intently as she left.

Chapter Four

Alyssa locked the car and whistled at the opulent beauty of the two-story red brick house in front of her. The McCormicks lived in one of Albuquerque's finer upper middle-class neighborhoods. This one happened to be one of the more recently developed ones, so everything was bright and shiny and new. 'Nice landscaping,' she said as she and Cord walked up the paved pathway to the front door.

She admired the vibrant reds, yellows, and pinks of the rose bushes, so much like the ones her mom had grown before tragedy struck. In a raised bed, tulips popped up from the soil. The trees were already sprouting new leaves, and various flowers, along with the roses, were in early bloom, making the air heavy with the flowery perfume. Spring was in the air.

The front door of the house was already open, so the two of them entered the foyer without knocking. Potted plants adorned every corner, clustered together in groups of three. Suspended from a hook on the wall was a twirling red chile emblazoned with the saying, *Mi casa es su casa*. Cord nudged Alyssa and nodded toward the windows.

'Would you look at that view? I could definitely get used to seeing that every day.' The back of the house boasted a large window, making a natural picture frame for the backdrop of the beautiful Sandia Mountains, capped with what little snow the area had received this year and which hadn't yet melted off. It made for a stunning contrast to the already greening valley.

To the right was an equally impressive view of downtown. The reflection from the glass made everything seem larger. 'And that, my friend, is why it's called the Land of Enchantment,' Cord murmured.

'It's certainly one of the reasons we stay here,' Alyssa agreed as she eyed the assortment of photographs and framed artwork that adorned the walls on either side of the windows. She refused to think of the other reasons she lived in New Mexico instead of her home state of Indiana.

Eager to abandon that train of thought before it derailed her, Alyssa approached a young officer who looked up from snapping pictures. She leaned around him to see what he was photographing, and when she saw it, she poked Cord and pointed to a rather large indentation in the wall near the base of the stairs. What appeared to be blood was splattered there, as well as nearby on the floor.

'How's the new baby, Joe?' Alyssa greeted him, noticing the exhaustion in the man's eyes.

Officer Roe paused in what he was doing and glanced up. 'Colicky. Anthony's in the living room, interviewing the husband.' He pointed in the general direction and returned to what he was doing.

'It'll get easier,' Alyssa assured him. When he responded with a grunt, she smiled.

Following the sound of voices, she rounded a corner into a grandiose living area connected to a wide open and quite gorgeous kitchen. With her training, she was able to mentally record several details with just a glance. She felt a tiny twinge of envy, wishing she owned a kitchen like this – not that she'd have much time to utilize it. Suspended from the high ceiling were copper-bottomed pots and pans. An arrangement of herbs and spices hung in wicker baskets above a stainless-steel sink, filling the room with a slight herbal scent. Granite countertops and cherry cabinets completed the room. Dotted throughout the house were what Alyssa liked to think of as Southwestern décor requisites: a Kokopelli plaque, along with other fetishes, a howling coyote statue, and the colorful pottery that could be found almost anywhere one went. She herself had many of the same types of things, though her own collection seemed far less expensive than the McCormicks'.

The living room was open to, but not part of, the kitchen and gave the space a welcoming feel. Along one wall, near a fireplace, was a red leather sofa where a dark-haired man in his early to mid-forties sat stroking a beautiful dog, an Alaskan Malamute, if her guess was correct. She and her brother had owned one when they were kids. She'd always thought she'd get another when she was older but had never gotten around to it. Even her children had stopped pleading for a dog. With everyone's schedules as hectic as they were, they just didn't have the time required to devote to a pet.

On the mantle above the fireplace were several framed photographs. One of the silver frames had been taken down, leaving a clean spot in the light dusting of the wood. The picture now sat on a glass coffee table. Alyssa took a quick look. The woman in the picture was petite and quite stunning with her long blonde hair and striking green eyes. In the photo, she wore a brilliant yellow strapless summer dress that made her eyes stand out even more than they already did. Hanging off one finger was a pair of matching strappy yellow sandals.

Officer Anthony White, whose name aptly described his pasty color, wrote something in his notebook as she and Cord approached. Hearing their footsteps, the man on the couch looked up expectantly, or maybe a more accurate description would be *hopefully*. She wasn't sure which, and probably it was a little of both.

When he saw Alyssa, the man did a double take, and even though he continued to stare, the frightened gleam in his eyes reappeared, and he rubbed the back of his neck before running his hand through his already ruffled hair.

'Here are Detectives Wyatt and Roberts now,' Officer White nodded his head toward them. To Cord and Alyssa, he said, 'Mr.

McCormick just finished a rundown of what transpired from the time he arrived home to the time he contacted the police.' He ripped off a sheet of paper and handed it to Cord who briefly scanned the page.

'Thanks, Tony,' Cord said. 'We'll take it from here.'

Alyssa waited for Officer White to leave the room before she began. 'Mr. McCormick? I'm Detective Wyatt. We understand you think something happened to your wife. Why don't –?'

'I don't *think* something's happened to my wife; I *know*. Didn't you see the foyer when you came in? And I've already told the other two everything I know,' Rafe McCormick interrupted.

'We understand, and we apologize, but we really need to hear your account firsthand for ourselves, make sure nothing gets left out in the retelling of events.' Cord's voice was simultaneously full of compassion and authority. 'Oftentimes, when people are distraught, little details are overlooked or omitted the first time through. Sometimes one little detail is all we need to locate a loved one.'

Aiming a weary look at the detectives, Rafe McCormick released a deep breath and ran his hands over his face. Voice heavy with exhaustion and worry, he began. 'When I got home, I was on my phone dealing with an issue from work, so I didn't notice right off that my wife's car was gone.'

Alyssa interrupted. 'Where do you work?'

'I own The Espresso Grind cafés,' Rafe said, his eyes shifting to the other room as Roe and White discussed the dent in the wall. Though they spoke quietly, their words still carried.

Alyssa drew Mr. McCormick's attention back to her. 'Do you normally arrive home from work around the same time every day?'

He nodded. 'Yes. We open the stores at five every morning, so I'm frequently there by four-thirty, so I can leave again before rush hour traffic hits.'

She nodded. 'I see. Please go on.'

'As I was saying, I hadn't noticed Callie's vehicle was gone until I finished my conversation and yelled for her like I always do. When she didn't answer, I thought maybe she was across the street with our friends, but when I went back through the garage, I realized her Jeep wasn't there. I decided to grab a drink before I called to check where she was, and that's when I noticed her lunch on the counter... and I realized the house hadn't been cleaned, either.'

Alyssa let her gaze sweep around the room. It looked clean to her.

'Callie has a touch of OCD, and she always cleans on Mondays, whether the house needs it or not. Afterwards, she lights scented candles because the chemicals in the cleaning supplies give her a headache. Those damn things give *me* a headache. But, as you can see for yourselves, none of her candles have been lit.'

Cord glanced at Alyssa, eyebrows arched. Obsessive compulsive disorder or a need for perfection? Alyssa had a tendency to lean towards perfectionism herself, so it was a trait she well understood.

Her memory transferred her back to her childhood where she'd tried to become the model daughter in order to make up for the most destructive, life-altering mistake she could've ever made. It didn't matter that she was only nine...

Cord coughed, effectively snapping Alyssa back to the interview where she belonged – not in a past that would never change.

She refocused her attention on Rafe McCormick.

'My wife has an aversion to her routine being interrupted and *hates* dirty dishes on the counter, much less food left out. Anyway, that's when I realized the dogs were still outside – Callie knows I don't like to leave them out there when we're not home – so I opened the patio door to let them in and noticed they were acting a little strange.'

'Strange how?' Alyssa asked.

Rafe McCormick took a deep breath and tangled his hands in the dog's fur. It was a good thing the dog didn't seem to mind because it looked painful. While he worked on regaining his composure, Alyssa studied the part of his hands and forearms that were visible at a glance. There were no obvious signs of a struggle. Which could mean something or nothing at this point.

'They were whining and kept running from the kitchen to the front of the house and back again, like they wanted me to follow. So, I did.' He swallowed. 'That's when I saw Callie's phone. My wife *never* goes anywhere without her phone. She won't even go to the mailbox without it. Hell, she takes it to the bathroom with her. It's like an extension of her hand,' Rafe whispered, almost to himself.

Alyssa and Cord exchanged glances. Why would his wife take her phone *everywhere,* including the bathroom? Was she afraid her husband would discover an affair? Some other secret? She nodded as her partner jotted down *get phone records.*

Mr. McCormick looked up. 'Did you see the foyer?'

'We did.'

'Callie's phone was on the floor, the screen broken.' He looked up, his eyes pleading with theirs. 'And then I saw the hole in the wall and the blood, and I knew…' His legs began to shake. 'I knew something bad had happened. And I called you guys.'

At that moment, a Pekingese waddled out from beneath a table and jumped onto Mr. McCormick's lap. Alyssa watched as he lowered his face to rest against the small dog. She thought he might be trying to wipe away the tears that had sprung up in his eyes. Real or for the detectives' benefit?

She glanced at Cord, glad he was taking notes. The two of them had a well-oiled system where Cord took down inform-ation while she concentrated on observing behaviors and other details. They would compare written and mental notes later.

She'd loved working with Ellie, her last partner, before she had moved to southern New Mexico, and had been concerned that it would take a while to get used to working with someone new – and for someone to get used to working with her. But her worries were for naught because Cord's naturally laid-back personality was the perfect complement to her well-known caffeine-riddled one, especially when his low-key, teddy bear-like approach encouraged witnesses and suspects alike to place their trust in him. On the downside, she never got to play 'good cop' to his 'bad.' With her take-charge attitude and naturally suspicious nature, it always backfired. They didn't even try anymore.

Now, Cord scanned his notepad and said, 'Earlier, you mentioned you thought your wife might be at a friend's house?'

'Yes, that's right.'

'Can I get their names?'

Rafe cleared his throat, moved the small dog to the couch, and pressed the heels of his hands over his eyes, clearly aggravated.

'Mr. McCormick – may I call you Rafe?' Alyssa asked. At his nod, she continued. 'We understand you're upset and worried about your wife. We know it's frustrating having to recount what you've already given in a statement to Officers Roe and White. But you also need to understand that we need as much information as possible. We don't ask questions we don't presume are important.' If she sounded impatient, it's because she was, but if the man wanted his wife found, she didn't have time to sugarcoat things.

'We want the same thing as you, to locate Callie,' Cord added, his tone much friendlier than Alyssa's.

'Terrie and Richard Mitchell.'

'These are your neighbors? Your friends across the street?' Cord clarified.

Rafe nodded. 'We met when Ranger got out one day and ended up in their yard.'

Hearing his name, Ranger placed one paw on his owner's leg and laid his head down. Rafe ruffled the dog's mane.

'When did you last see your wife?' Cord asked.

'This morning before I left for work,' Rafe said, 'and I talked to her this morning when I made the appointment at the dealership for her to get her car worked on.' He tilted his head toward the ceiling and said, 'I tried to talk her into just buying a new car, but she liked that old Jeep of hers. Anyway, she called me when she left the shop sometime before eleven to let me know she was headed home.'

'What time did she take her car in, and what dealership?' Cord asked.

'Her appointment was at nine at MCM near the freeway.'

Cord jotted it down.

'What else can you tell us about your wife's daily routines?' Alyssa asked. 'Does she work? Who are her friends?'

'She doesn't have an out-of-the-house job. She occasionally does freelance copy writing, but that's pretty sporadic these days. She's on the board of library advisors, and she volunteers for several national and local charities.'

'Which ones?' Alyssa asked.

'Race for the Cure, The Cancer Society, American Heart Association, that kind of thing. I don't remember all of them. I'm sure I can get you a list if you need me to.' Steepling his hands, he added, almost as an afterthought, 'She'd just started talking about volunteering for the neonatal unit at the new hospital.'

'What about friends? Does she have any standing lunch dates?' Cord asked.

'Not standing. She likes to get together with a couple of the girls from yoga once in a while for coffee or a walk in the park. Mostly she's a self-professed homebody.'

She was involved in an awful lot of things for a homebody, Alyssa thought. 'You mentioned your wife was interested in helping out in the neonatal unit. Do the two of you have children of your own, Mr. McCormick?'

A haunted look fell like a curtain across his face. 'No. No kids.' His next words were a whisper of sound. 'She would've made such a great mom.'

Alyssa zeroed in on the fact that he'd used the past tense. She shot a sideways glance at her partner and saw that he'd noticed, as well.

'What else can you tell us about your wife? Has she mentioned any strange phone calls, someone she might've upset intentionally or unintentionally?' Cord asked.

Rafe chuckled lightly. 'No strange calls that I'm aware of, and if Callie has any enemies, I'll eat my hat. If anything, she makes friends with the strangest of strangers. She's a good person, detectives. Better than I'll ever be, that's for sure.'

Three and a half hours later, after the police technicians had searched through the entire house, including the garage and downstairs, Alyssa and Cord thanked Rafe McCormick and assured him that they would do everything they could to find his missing wife.

By the time the techs and Officers Roe and White left, Mr. McCormick's hair stuck out every which way from running his hands through it, not to mention he looked strung out and ready to collapse. While she remained sympathetic to the man's anguish, Alyssa couldn't help but tire of the fact that nearly every time he answered a question, he posed one of his own, although it was always the same one. 'Shouldn't you be out there *looking* for her?' Once again, she had to shut down the memory that her family had once been the ones in Mr. McCormick's shoes, the ones demanding the police act immediately. *Different time, different life,* she reminded herself.

To Rafe, she explained, 'There's clear evidence of a struggle, and we'll be getting right to work on this.' What she didn't say was that they would also be looking into the McCormicks' relationship, among other things.

As it turned out, Alyssa didn't have to say it because Rafe McCormick told her as they were leaving, 'I know you have to look at the husband first, so get it done so you can find my wife. Please.'

'If you think of anything else, don't hesitate to call, anytime, day or night,' Cord said, handing him one of his cards while Alyssa did the same.

Rafe took the cards, already bending them in his agitation, but he said nothing as he led them to the door.

Outside and out of Rafe's earshot, Alyssa said, 'His hands were clean, no recent scrapes or scratches, no signs of a struggle. So, if McCormick is involved in his wife's disappearance, he either cleaned up well, or he's not the one who caused the damage in the entry.'

'Yeah, I had the same thought. And it's possible, if he is responsible, he may not have any wounds – or visible ones anyway. Regardless, we still need to have a look into their relationship, see if there were financial or marital troubles. And I'd like to get my hands on Callie McCormick's cell phone records to see why she kept it with her at all times. What was she hiding?'

'Agreed! Before we head out, let's try the neighbors, the ones McCormick thought his wife might be with,' Alyssa suggested just as her stomach grumbled loudly, reminding her she hadn't eaten since around noon. A quick peek at her watch told her it was nearly eight o'clock now.

Across the street, Cord knocked on the Mitchells' door and waited. When it was apparent no one was home, or no one was answering, they walked back to Alyssa's SUV and climbed in.

Alyssa made a mental note to try the Mitchells first thing in the morning. They needed some insight into the McCormick family dynamics, though her gut told her the husband had had nothing to do with whatever had happened. Still, her instincts had been wrong before. And when it came to husbands and wives, the closest suspect was often the guilty party.

'You grabbed the notes from the officers canvassing the other neighbors, right?' she asked as they pulled away from the curb, even though she already knew he had.

Cord flipped open his folder and rustled some papers. 'Got 'em right here. Roe said he'd write up a report and put it on your desk before he headed home tonight.'

Alyssa acknowledged the comment with a nod. They still had a long night ahead of them.

And she couldn't help but be aware that Rafe McCormick's night would likely be longer.

Chapter Five

A few minutes after she left the dealership, Callie left a message for Rafe to let him know the technician had addressed her initial concern, as well as fixed a few other minor issues with the car. When she got home, she parked in the garage, and then went inside, automatically hanging her keys on the wooden key rack, ignoring her yapping dogs as she set her things down.

First things first, Callie thought. She was ravenous, so she'd eat before she cleaned the house. She briefly considered putting off her Monday chores until tomorrow, but she knew she wouldn't. Looking at the dirt and dog hair would drive her batty, and she'd end up sweeping and mopping anyway.

Besides, after she cleaned, she could relax with the story she'd been trying to read earlier. She always felt less guilty for reading if she did something productive first.

Her mind made up, she stared out her kitchen windows. It had been an unseasonably warm winter, and only a little white remained on the mountain, but she enjoyed looking at the diamond-like sparkle of the snow reflecting off the mountain-side, so she decided to take advantage of the low winds and eat on her back patio.

She made herself a tomato sandwich, grabbed a snack bag of wasabi peas, and a glass of water and went outside. She set everything down on the table and petted her two dogs to help calm them.

'Hi, Ranger. Hi, Sassy. How are my good dogs? Do you want a treat? You do?' Callie watched her Alaskan Malamute

35

and Pekingese run in excited circles upon hearing the word *treat*. It was amazing how high Sassy, the Pekingese, could jump when she really wanted something. She laughed as they bumped each other out of the way in order to get the first tasty morsel. Rafe was always frustrated with her for giving the dogs snacks when she was trying to calm them down because it never failed to have the opposite effect.

She broke one steak-flavored treat into small pieces for Sassy, and after watching Ranger sit and shake, fed him two. The dogs relaxed, and she rubbed their heads before sitting down to enjoy her own lunch.

'Go on now. It's my turn to eat.' Both dogs wagged their tails and lay down, placing their heads on their paws as they looked hopeful that she would drop her human food on the ground. She laughed as Ranger army crawled closer. Placement was key to snatching up any droppings.

She had just taken a few bites of her sandwich and was munching on a handful of wasabi peas when someone knocked loudly, using the old-fashioned brass knocker they'd installed on their wooden door, and then rang the doorbell, which had the unpleasant effect of riling her dogs. Why did people do that? *Knock or ring the doorbell, one or the other. Not both,* she muttered to herself.

Ranger and Sassy jumped up, turned in circles, tails wagging ferociously, and looked at each other as if to ask, '*Who's here? Can we play?*' She put her hand out, palm down, giving them the signal to stay and be quiet. They plopped down, their tails brushing the cement in anticipation of visitors who might play with them.

She peered at the clock hanging on the patio wall beside the window and wondered who it might be. She had a package coming, but that wouldn't arrive until later in the week. She hoped it wasn't the new neighbor, who had a propensity for popping in and asking for bizarre things. 'Whatever happened to asking for a cup of sugar?' she'd complained to Rafe after one odd request for half a cup of flour, egg white alternatives, and gelatin.

She considered not answering the door, but recalled how, not too long ago, there was a rash of break-ins not far from here. The thieves would knock on someone's door, and if no one answered, they broke in and robbed the people blind. Not willing to risk it, she knew she wouldn't wait to see if the unannounced visitor would simply go away.

She walked through her kitchen, setting her glass and partially eaten lunch on the counter near the sink. As she passed through the front room with the large window, she tried to see who was at the door. Sometimes after knocking or ringing the doorbell, people – like her new neighbor – peered into the window. It was something that puzzled her and frustrated Rafe. 'Who does that?' Rafe griped every single time.

But now, seeing no one through the glass, Callie approached the door, and as was her habit, peeked through the peephole.

She didn't know the man standing at the door, though he looked vaguely familiar. He was dressed in business attire and holding something in his hand. Maybe she'd seen him around the neighborhood, peddling whatever he was here to sell. She groaned. Just what she needed – a salesperson. She was never good at getting rid of them, and she always felt guilty saying no, afraid if she didn't purchase something, it would be her fault if the person ended up in the poor house – a state of living she never wanted to return to and would never wish on anyone else. Inevitably, she ended up with lots of things she didn't want or need and would never use. It drove Rafe nuts. Longing only to return to her solitude, she opened the door instead.

–

'Hi,' Callie said through the locked screen door. She knew it was no real protection against anyone who really wanted in, but it still gave her a moderate sense of security.

The man appeared embarrassed. 'Hi. I'm sorry to interrupt you. I was hoping I could have a few minutes of your time.' He looked at Callie expectantly.

Actually, no, you can't, is what she wanted to say. 'Sure, I have a few minutes. How can I help you?'

The man let out a breath and let his shoulders relax. 'Thanks. I'm not here to sell you anything, by the way. Really.'

Well, that's a relief, Callie thought. Outwardly, she laughed lightly and said, 'Oh, okay, good.' As she waited for the man to continue, she took in his appearance and decided he looked harmless enough. Still, one could never be too careful – just look at Ted Bundy. Besides, while this guy seemed safe, there was something just weird enough about him that it set her ick-o-meter swinging. Maybe it was the nervous way he smiled or the way his eyes kept shifting or something else… but there was definitely something.

'I'm new to the area. I just moved here from Minnesota. My house is around the corner,' the man said, pointing.

Um, okay. 'Welcome to Albuquerque. The weather's much nicer here,' she joked. 'Of course, that's just my opinion.' She knew this also annoyed Rafe – he thought she was too friendly to the people who came to the door, telling her it only encouraged them.

The man chuckled and ran his hand over his face. 'Yeah, I'd have to agree on that point. Shoveling snow in Minnesota is not a good time.' He looked away, blushing, then turned back and continued. 'So, um, I was driving around, checking things out, kind of getting a feel for the area…' He paused again, looking like he'd rather be doing anything else except standing there.

From a young age, her parents had instilled in her the importance of unfailing politeness, telling her that just because they were poor didn't mean they had to be rude, and now that need to be kind to strangers reared its head as she watched the poor guy shuffle from foot to foot, feeling sorry for him. 'And how can I help you?' she finally asked, since she was pretty sure he hadn't knocked just to tell her about his move.

The man inhaled deeply and blurted out, 'My car broke down.' He nodded down the road to a blue car. It was too far away to tell what model it was. 'This is so awkward.' He glanced at Callie then the ground, kicking at the leaf that had blown under his shoe. Looking back up, he said, 'I was hoping you could recommend a good tow company and give me the number… Umm… and let me borrow your phone. I left mine charging at home. I didn't expect to be gone more than a few minutes. But I also didn't know my car was going to die. I tried some of your neighbors, but either nobody's home or no one's answering.' He stared at Callie hopefully.

Why didn't he just run back to his house to get his phone?

As if reading her mind, he said, 'I forgot to put my house key on my key ring, and the garage door isn't working, so… yeah.' He shook his head and shrugged. 'I figured I'd worry about how to get back into my house later. I keep wondering what else can possibly go wrong today.'

Callie sincerely wished she didn't have such a compulsion to always answer the door or a ringing phone. But, she did, and as much as she regretted it and wanted to say she was sorry, but no, she couldn't help, she knew she wouldn't turn this man away any more than she would've declined to purchase something from him if he *had* been a peddler. Instead, she said, 'Sure. Let me just grab my phone. I'll be right back.'

She turned to go, but stopped when the man said, 'Thanks. Um, do you mind if I wait inside?' Little alarms went off in her head. She might be friendly, but she wasn't stupid.

She gave a regretful smile, hoping he wouldn't be offended. 'I'm sorry,' she said, 'but I'm afraid my dogs might bite you.' It was a white lie, but it sounded better than the truth – that she was scared to let him in, and her dogs were more likely to lick him to death than bite him. She was somewhat happy to help, but letting a strange man into her house was pushing it a bit much.

The man's face turned red. 'Of course. I'm sorry. Again. You don't even know me. I'm still getting used to living in a town

39

where not everyone knows you and your entire family. I'll just wait here while you get your phone. I really do appreciate your help.'

'Okay, I'll be right back.' She considered closing the main door, but didn't want to appear rude, so she left it open. Besides, the screen door was still locked. She grabbed her phone from the kitchen and walked back to the front door. 'I keep one of the tow company's number stored on my phone because I never know when I might need it. Let me just find it.' She scrolled through her contacts until she found what she was looking for. 'Okay, here it is. Anytime Towing.' She reached for the door, saying, 'I just love their slogan: *Don't use your hands when you can just use our tows*. So clever. But they really are good and fast, and reasonably priced. I happen to know that from experience. So, here ya go.' She was still talking as she opened the door to hand the man her phone.

'Thank you,' he said as he reached for it. But instead of grabbing her phone, he grabbed her wrist, first yanking, then pushing and throwing her off balance. That was when the first pain shot through her arm. The man twisted it, shoving her back through her own door. Scared yet not comprehending what was happening, Callie stared at the man's hand.

Chapter Six

Cord walked into their shared office – or more accurately, their shared cubicle space – carrying two steaming cups of coffee. He'd called thirty minutes earlier to let her know he'd be running a little late.

'Tell me that's a double shot, strong, and I'll be your slave for the day!' Even though she'd already had two cups that morning, Alyssa's mouth watered.

'Yeah, that's what you say every time, and I'm still waiting,' Cord laughed as he set down her coffee. 'And a double shot vanilla latte, no foam, extra whip for me.'

'You know, I didn't get my run in this morning, and I might not have been such a crank if you'd just told me you were going to be late because you were stopping to pick up my special brand of poison. Speaking of which, how can you stand to drink that sweet stuff? And what's the point of no foam if you're just going to fill that space up with whipped cream? Blech!' She shuddered dramatically.

Cord lifted the lid off his cup and stuck his lips into the whipped cream, making him look like a clown. He licked the cream off his mouth, and said, 'I'd tell you I don't know how you can drink that sludge with no sweetener, but I know you'll just tell me you don't need any sugar when you're already sweet enough.'

Grinning, Alyssa said, 'That's right. I keep telling you I'll stir your coffee with my finger, and that'll add all the sweet you

41

need.' They laughed at their familiar banter and then got down to business, pulling out the file on the missing McCormick woman.

'Not that I expected to get that lucky, but no one's reported an abandoned car matching Rafe McCormick's description of his wife's Jeep. No witnesses, no calls, no leads. Nothing. How does someone just vanish with *no one* noticing anything? We don't know if we're looking at a robbery gone bad, or something else, something worse.' Alyssa tried not to think of her family's own devastating end to their tragedy, reminding herself that Callie McCormick was an adult, not a child.

She mentally shook her head and tapped her fingers against the file. All the McCormicks' neighbors claimed to have been busy or not home during the time Callie was likely taken. Nobody saw anything out of the ordinary. The myth that every neighborhood had a nosy old neighbor lady keeping an eye on everybody's business was truly just that – a myth.

'By the way, I was able to get ahold of the Mitchells this morning before they left for work. So, whenever you're ready, we can head over there,' Cord told her.

Alyssa pushed her chair back and stood, snatching her coffee and the keys to the Tahoe. 'Why didn't you just lead with that? What are we waiting for? Let's go.'

On their way out, they waved to Hal, an officer loved and respected by all. Rookies weren't the only ones who flocked to him for advice. Alyssa had been known to bend his ear more than once, and he was always one of the first people she requested for her team.

'Go get 'em, Detectives,' he said as he rolled past them in his old-fashioned wheelchair.

Alyssa smiled. 'Thanks, Hal.'

–

The woman who answered the door at the Mitchell residence was petite with short blonde and red-streaked hair.

'You must be Detectives Wyatt and Roberts. Please, come in.' Alyssa and Cord stepped inside and waited as Mrs. Mitchell quieted her barking dogs and opened a door off the side of the formal dining room, telling the person on the other side, 'Richard, the detectives are here.' A tall man, similar in stature to Rafe McCormick, walked out and shook their hands.

'Detectives. I'm Richard Mitchell. Rafe called last night to tell us what's going on, so we were expecting your call. In fact, if you hadn't contacted us this morning, we would've reached out to you. If there's anything my wife and I can do to help…'

'Thank you,' Alyssa replied as Cord nodded his thanks.

'And thank you for rearranging your schedules to meet with us today,' Alyssa added. She noticed Terrie Mitchell staring at Cord. She was used to it. Cord was tall, about six foot two, and looked like he worked out at the gym two hours a day. His black hair, combined with his vivid blue eyes outlined with ridiculously long lashes, gave most women pause. It was rare to encounter a woman who did *not* do a double take. Thankfully, her partner wasn't like a lot of men who looked like walking gods. In fact, more often than not, he was embarrassed by the attention his good looks brought – not that he didn't use it to his advantage when he needed to.

'How well do you know the McCormicks?' Cord directed the question to Mr. Mitchell.

'Why don't we go sit in the living room? We'll be more comfortable there,' Mrs. Mitchell offered. 'Would you two like a cup of coffee?' Cord declined, but Alyssa accepted, having left her own cup in the car. After settling onto the brown suede couches, Richard responded to Cord's question.

'We go Jeeping and camping and get together for dinner and barbecues when we can. The women,' he leaned his head toward his wife and pointed as if they could all see the McCormick house, 'hit it off right away. Sometimes Rafe and I think they share the same brain.' Everyone laughed, helping to break up the tension. Like waiting to speak to the principal,

43

no one liked talking to the police, even if they were innocent of wrongdoing; it was human nature to be nervous.

Terrie Mitchell smiled. 'We met when their dog, Ranger, got out and dug up my flowerbed. Callie was mortified. In fact, when I came home from work the next day, she'd replaced all the ruined flowers. I knew then we'd be great friends.' Her eyes misted over, and she shook her head sadly. 'I hope you find her soon.' Mrs. Mitchell clasped her husband's hand in her own, her grip tight enough to turn her knuckles white.

'Can you tell us a little about Rafe and Callie's relationship? Did they have any recent fights about anything? Money? Jobs? Anything you can think of?' Alyssa asked.

Richard wrinkled his forehead, a confused look on his face. Terrie, on the other hand, shook her head. 'No. They kind of have the perfect marriage, you know? They do almost everything together. But, come to think of it, Callie did mention the other night that she was frustrated Rafe hadn't looked at her car yet. I guess it'd been making a funny noise for a few weeks.'

'Did they argue about it?' Cord asked.

'I don't know if *argued* is the right word, really.'

Alyssa waited, but Terrie didn't expand on her comment. 'Mr. McCormick said Callie was involved with several charities. Do you know what they were? Was it something she enjoyed doing?' Alyssa purposely changed the topic because the switch often threw people off-balance, making them forget to be careful if they were hiding something.

Terrie sat up straighter, and she peeked at her husband, before glancing back at the detectives. 'Well, to be honest, I've always gotten the impression that Callie does those more for Rafe's sake than her own. He likes her to be involved because it looks good for his company, or at least that's what she told me once. He owns The Espresso Grind cafés.'

The Espresso Grind was one of the more expensive coffee houses, and Alyssa allowed herself to splurge there only occasionally, usually after wrapping up a particularly difficult case.

Alyssa noticed Terrie glance at her husband again, one eyebrow raised, as if asking his opinion – or permission. He shrugged.

Cord noticed the exchange, as well, prompting him to remind them, 'Mrs. Mitchell, anything you tell us could potentially help us locate your friend.'

'Well, lately, Callie's been making sure she doesn't volunteer on Rafe's days off – he doesn't like it. But that's not the only reason. She's been wanting to have a baby, and she's been working on trying to convince him. But I guess he's just not interested right now. Though, according to Callie, they've already waited several years longer than they had planned.'

Interesting that Mr. McCormick hadn't mentioned that yesterday, Alyssa thought. 'Would you say this was a sore spot in their marriage?' she asked.

'I don't know if it was a sore spot in their marriage, per se. But I do know Callie had noticed she'd gained a little weight, which she thought bothered Rafe, and she suspected he wasn't prepared for her to lose her figure like that in pregnancy. Those were her words. Personally, I suspect it may have more to do with the fact that he's ten years older than her and doesn't want to start a family this late in life. On the other hand, Callie's thirty-three now, and she was afraid she was getting too old to have a baby. So, she started becoming somewhat insistent. But she said every time she brought up the subject, he shut it down or clammed up. It was really starting to get to her. So much so, that she was considering quitting her birth control without telling him.'

Cord jotted something down in his notebook, then piped up. 'Did you ever witness the two of them argue about it?'

'No,' Terrie and Richard both answered at the same time. Then it was Richard's turn to reconsider his answer and look to his wife for guidance. She nodded, and he began. 'Well, not about that. Something else, and it was just once. Rafe and I were outside shooting the breeze one day. Callie was gone, but when she got home and walked over to give him a kiss, he kind of shoved her away. She smelled like cigarette smoke, and he kind of flipped out.'

'When was this?' Cord asked.

Again, Richard looked at his wife. 'Maybe a month or so ago? Maybe not quite that long. I really don't remember. I'm sorry.'

'That's okay. You said Mr. McCormick "flipped out." What do you mean by that?'

'Well, he ranted for what felt like a full five minutes but was probably only thirty seconds or so. His face was red, and he was yelling about how inconsiderate she was, smoking behind his back, knowing how he felt about that kind of thing…' Mr. Mitchell paused to explain, 'His dad died fairly young from smoking, I guess. Anyway, when he finally stopped to take a breath, Callie explained she hadn't been smoking, that the chairman of the charity had been. She said that since their meeting had been at his residence, she couldn't exactly ask the man not to smoke at his own house.'

'Rafe made her quit that charity, immediately. I don't remember which one it was, though,' Terrie added. 'Do you, honey?' Mr. Mitchell shook his head.

Alyssa and Cord questioned the Mitchells for another fifteen minutes before Alyssa finally stood, indicating the interview was over. 'Thank you for your time. We'll let you know if we have any more questions for you. In the meantime, please call if you think of anything, no matter how insignificant you think it might be.' Like they had with Rafe McCormick, they each handed their cards to the couple.

'Of course. Anything we can do to help,' Richard said, reaching for the business cards.

As they walked to the door, Alyssa noticed Terrie Mitchell looking at her in an odd way. 'Mrs. Mitchell, is there something else you'd like to tell us?'

Terrie looked embarrassed. 'No. I'm sorry. I know I'm staring; it's just, well, you remind me of Callie in a way. Again, I'm sorry. But we'll call if we think of anything.'

-

Back in the car, Alyssa waited until they'd pulled away from the curb before she said, 'Sure doesn't sound like the perfect marriage to me. You?'

'Nope,' Cord agreed. 'Makes me wonder if Mr. McCormick maybe got tired of being harassed over a baby. Maybe decided to do something about it? Or maybe he just wasn't willing to share his wife with another person, even if that person was his own child.'

'Maybe after we speak to the MCM folks, we'll pay another visit to our distraught husband,' Alyssa said.

Chapter Seven

The moment Callie saw the red marks on her arm from the man's squeezing fist, her fight or flight instinct kicked in, and she started to shove back. He was barely taller than she was, maybe five foot eight, and so she was surprised her shove didn't so much as faze him, as if he didn't even register her touch. Her heart beat rapidly as she gazed up at the man's face.

The look in his eyes halted her movement; they were no longer those of a friendly, embarrassed gentleman, but those of a very frightening man. Again, she tried to release his grip so she could escape. Why hadn't she listened to her inner voice trying to warn her something was off when the man had asked if he could wait inside? Oh God, what was he going to do? Her lungs seized, and she started gasping, trying to bring in more air, which proved fruitless because the man sucker-punched her in the kidney and shoved her all the way back into her house. He slammed her door shut, the sound echoing throughout the downstairs. He turned to lock her door, the click deafening in its loudness.

The shove caused her to fall hard against a wall, hitting her head. When the man turned back to her, she tried to wrap her mind around what was happening. Her eyes watered, though she didn't know if it was from fear or pain or a combination of both. Wetness trickled down her arm, and she risked a glance, wincing at the pain in her head as well as her back. Blood trailed down her arm, but she couldn't figure out where it came from.

So many thoughts raced through her mind, she barely registered her barking dogs. Unlike most dogs, they didn't bark at every passer-by or visitor; they only barked when some type of commotion upset them, and right now, they were making quite a ruckus outside. She prayed someone would hear and come over or… or just call the police. Did people do that? Call the police over barking dogs? Probably not. Most just grumbled and complained. Maybe her crazy neighbor would drop by to request some oddball thing – but that would only put her in danger, too. Callie would have to save herself.

The man glanced in the dogs' direction, and then back at Callie. He watched her, observing, a Taser in his hand.

'Don't you know it's rude not to invite people in when they come calling?' the man said now.

In some distant part of her mind, she noted his voice had changed. It was more gravelly, rougher, like a two-pack-a-day smoker.

She heard a choking sound and realized it was coming from her. She was always irritated in movies when the females simpered and whined for someone to rescue them. She wanted to scream at the screen, 'You're not helpless, you idiot! *Do* something, anything.' However, in the space of a few minutes, she had turned into the clichéd, naïve, whimpering female she so abhorred.

'I have money and jewelry. You can have it all; I'll tell you where it is. Please.'

The man leered at her. 'You think I want your money? I don't care about your money or your stupid jewelry. I want you.'

Fear coiled low in her stomach. Frantically looking around for something, anything, she could use as a weapon, Callie summoned the courage to stand, her legs wobbly. As she steadied herself with a hand on the wall, the man punched her again, this time in the stomach. Pain exploded in her abdomen, stars blinking in front of her eyes, and she was afraid she was going to puke or pass out.

49

She was still doubled over, clutching her middle and gasping for breath when the man grabbed her hair and yanked her erect. His cruel smile never reached his dead eyes. He twisted her hair and whispered quietly, 'Do I have your attention now?'

Somehow his whisper was scarier than if he had spoken in a regular voice. 'Y-y-yes,' Callie cried. She couldn't stop shaking, and the tremors sent shockwaves of pain through her stomach muscles.

'Good. Now, I want you to listen carefully and do everything I ask. No questions, no hesitation. Do you understand? Nod once if you do.'

'Y-y-yes,' Callie nodded with as much movement as she could, considering he still had ahold of her hair.

He twisted the handful of hair even more tightly and slapped her at the same time, snapping her head back so forcefully her teeth made a loud cracking noise from the impact. 'Did I tell you to speak?' he growled menacingly. 'No, I did not. I told you to nod once if you understood. You will not speak unless I tell you to speak. Now, let's try this again. Do you understand my instructions? Nod once if you do.'

She let her head fall forward in a nod, tears streaming down her face, her fight or flight instinct abandoning her as quickly as it had arrived. Her cheek was already going numb. Shallow breaths came quickly as panic bubbled up inside her chest, rendering her all but immobile.

'Here's what we're going to do. Are you paying attention?' He waited for her slow nod. 'We're going to get into your car, and we're going to drive. Well, I'm going to drive; you're going to be a little, let's say, incapacitated. But just so we're clear, you're not going to attempt an escape or do anything else foolish. If you're lucky enough to get someone's attention, I will kill you both. Nod if you understand.'

She nodded, her eyes wide. She didn't think her terror could escalate any higher than it was, but when she realized the man's intent was to *kidnap* her, where things could only get worse, her pulse spiked. 'Pl-pl-please… why are you doing this?' she stammered. She understood her mistake before the words were fully out of her mouth; she didn't need the second punch and yanking of her hair to remind her she'd spoken without permission.

She remembered reading somewhere that if a potential kidnapper tried to take you somewhere, you just did not go. You always, always fought. Chances were the perpetrator wanted an easy target and would run off if a person put up resistance. What no one mentioned was this situation – what if the attacker wasn't in a public place? What if someone was in her own home when attacked? What then? Another cry escaped. *Oh, please, I'm not ready to die.* She shivered.

She was jarred back into reality when the man released his hold on her hair and twisted her arm high behind her back. He whispered in his deadly voice, 'Remember what I said. Do not try to run or scream for help. And you should know that the more you struggle, the more you fight me, the worse things will be for you later. I swear I'll make you beg for death before I'm finished with you.'

Callie believed his words were not an empty threat, and she tried not to vomit when he pushed up against her, forcing her to feel his obvious excitement. 'So, please, do think about whether or not you want to fight back.'

She noticed the dogs had stopped their frantic barking and now clawed at the glass door. Though she was beyond terrified, she was glad she'd left them outside. There was no telling what this man was capable of doing. She glanced at the front door and, despite his warning, considered making a run for it. But she knew she wouldn't get far, and even if she did manage to make it to the door and get outside, someone else might be killed coming to her rescue, and she didn't want that on her conscience. She didn't want to give this monster a reason to become more violent. She could only pray she'd find a way out of this.

'Where are your car keys?'

Was she supposed to talk or point? 'I-I… they're hanging… by the back door.' She moved her eyes in that direction, scared to move her head. The man dragged her along, yanking her when she stumbled. He snagged the keys off the wooden peg.

She wanted to weep, to scream, to cry, to howl with rage as the man forced her elbow upward, twisting her arm even higher behind her back as he shoved Callie toward the garage.

Chapter Eight

Tuesday, March 26

They'd just left the Mitchells' residence when Cord's phone rang. 'Roberts.'

'Detective, Joseph Roe here. Called MCM like you asked, and talked with Mark, the manager over there. He had his secretary pull yesterday's invoices. Said it looks like Mrs. McCormick was there for approximately ninety minutes, give or take, while her transmission, radiator, and a few minor things were worked on. Said he'd be more than happy to meet with you this morning, if you have the time.'

'Thanks, Joe. We'll head that way right now.' Cord relayed the message to Alyssa who made a U-turn at the intersection and headed in the opposite direction.

As soon as they pulled into the parking lot of MCM, Alyssa received a text from Isaac.

Going to Trevor's after school to play video games. That cool?

She found a place to park and then replied.

Yes, but let your dad know, and be home for dinner.

Even as she typed it, she recognized the irony in demanding her fourteen-year-old son be home for dinner when more than half the time, she herself struggled to make it.

Cord waited until she was finished and had placed her phone in her pocket. 'Everything okay?' he asked.

'Yep, just Isaac checking in,' she said.

'Let's do this then,' he said as he got out of the vehicle and headed for the entrance.

Inside, she and Cord approached the front desk where a brass name plate indicated that the woman behind the counter was Aubrey Brown, Customer Service Specialist. They waited as she ended her call and typed something into her computer. Finished, she smiled at the detectives. 'Sorry about that. Thanks for waiting. Welcome to MCM. How can I help you two today?'

'Detectives Wyatt and Roberts with the Albuquerque Police Department. I believe Mark's expecting us,' Alyssa said.

'Of course. Let me grab him for you.' Aubrey pushed back from the computer and jumped up, teetering a little on her high heels before she caught her balance. Alyssa barely resisted the urge to roll her eyes. High heels might make a woman's legs look sexy, but in her opinion, they were highly overrated.

Leaving behind a wave of perfume that assaulted the senses and nearly made Alyssa's eyes water, the receptionist disappeared into the garage area.

A few minutes later, Aubrey reappeared with a middle-aged, well-dressed man sporting a haircut that seemed more suited to a teenager. As he approached, he held out his hand to shake theirs and introduced himself. 'Mark Jacobs. I'm the service department manager. Why don't you two follow me so we can chat with a little more privacy?'

Without waiting for a response, the manager turned and headed back the way he'd come, leading the detectives through the garage area before ushering them into his office. 'Please, have a seat,' he said waving his arm.

Definitely someone who was used to being in charge, Alyssa thought as the man grabbed a file from his desk and opened it. More often than not, they had to ease people's natural fear of speaking to the police before they could get down to business, so she appreciated being able to get right to it without first filling the space with idle chitchat.

'Okay, after Officer Roe called, I had Aubrey check yesterday's invoices.' Mark ran his finger over the page in front of him, nodding as he did, and then glanced back up. 'Like I told the officer on the phone, it appears Mrs. McCormick was here approximately ninety minutes, and in that time, there were only a few other customers.' He closed the file and pushed it over to the detectives and added, 'Aubrey said she specifically remembered Mrs. McCormick because it was a slow morning, and when Mrs. McCormick arrived, she was the only one in the waiting area until another customer came in and started up a conversation with her. Said that Mrs. McCormick appeared friendly, but it was somewhat obvious she didn't really want to engage with the man. Said she kind of felt bad for her.' He reached out a finger and tapped the file. 'Figured you might want to speak to him – Mearl Leroy is his name – so I had Aubrey print out his phone number and address for you.'

'We would like to speak to him – and anyone else here during those same ninety minutes, including anyone working yesterday,' Alyssa said.

'Already in there, too,' Mark said. 'In fact, anyone who was working yesterday is here today, and I've already put them on notice that you might be needing to ask them a few questions. Told them they were to stop whatever they were doing in order to assist.'

Appreciating the manager's take-charge attitude, Alyssa opened the manila folder. A copy of Callie's invoice sat on top, and a quick peek at the time stamp confirmed when she'd arrived and when she left. She situated the file so Cord could see it, too. 'Appreciate you having this ready for us,' she said.

'No problem. Anything to help.' Mark shifted his gaze back and forth between Alyssa and Cord and said, 'Now, Officer Roe mentioned you wanted to have a look at our surveillance videos?'

'Yes. We can get a search warrant here, if it'll help,' Cord said.

Alyssa really hoped the manager wouldn't require one because she didn't want to wait if they didn't have to.

'Not necessary. Already spoke with the owner, and he said to cooperate any way we could. In fact, I've already loaded the records, so if you'll move over here, I can get out of your way.'

Alyssa was grateful for the owner's willingness to accommodate them and wished everyone they interviewed would be this cooperative.

'I've forwarded the video to about five minutes before Mrs. McCormick came in, but if you need to go back further, just hit this button here,' Mark leaned over and pointed to the keyboard. 'And if you need to pause or forward, it's these two buttons. I'm going to step out now, but if you need me for any reason, just use my phone there and call the front desk. Aubrey's extension is hashtag one.'

'Thank you,' Cord said. He waited until Mark closed the door behind himself before he reached over and tapped *play*.

Happy to let him navigate, Alyssa scooted her chair in closer. 'Think they have popcorn here?' she joked. Video surveillance footage was virtually guaranteed to be dry and boring, and it was one of her least favorite aspects of investigating, but it was a necessary evil in her line of work. And this, at least, was only a couple of hours' worth.

Cord laughed even as his eyes stayed fixed on the screen. Within five minutes, Callie could be seen entering the waiting area, just as Mark had said. She approached the desk and, after checking in and handing over her keys, walked directly over to the coffee pot where she poured herself a cup and tested it.

A woman after her own heart, Alyssa thought and watched as Callie then picked up a magazine, shook her head, and set it back down before finally settling into a seat near the front window. As she observed Callie McCormick, she was struck by how attractive she was. And though Terrie Mitchell had said her friend and neighbor had gained a little weight, to Alyssa's eyes, she looked, well, normal.

It was as if Cord read her mind. 'Well, she's not a stick figure, but certainly no need to start looking into the latest fad diet,' he remarked.

'Just had that same thought myself.'

Every once in a while, either Alyssa or her partner would comment on something in the video, but so far, all they could truly say was that Callie McCormick seemed content to sit and read. In fact, it wasn't until Mr. Leroy, a wizened old man in scuffed blue jeans, walked in and chose the seat right next to her that either detective caught a glimpse of any show of personality at all.

Mrs. McCormick was irritated. And Alyssa didn't blame her one bit. Why would the man choose to sit practically on top of her when there were so many open chairs?

'Odd. Most people tend to search for the space farthest away from other individuals,' Cord observed as he studied Mearl Leroy.

'Right. Which leads me to say: Mrs. McCormick's much nicer than I would've been,' Alyssa commented.

Cord chuckled. 'That's probably true. But, remember, you're the one who said it.' A couple more minutes passed before he stopped the video once more, his head tilted to the side. 'I can see why Mrs. Mitchell said you remind her of Callie. There is a slight resemblance, don't you think? I mean, it might be more obvious if your hair was still blonde.'

Trying to be objective, Alyssa mimicked her partner, and cocked her head first to one side, then the other as she studied the woman onscreen. Except for the shape of their faces – what people described as heart-shaped – she didn't really see a likeness. 'She's taller than me.'

'That she is,' he said, still staring at Callie McCormick.

'Hey!' True or not, she didn't need her partner to agree.

Eyes wide, he swung his gaze her way, hands in the 'I surrender' position. 'Not that there's anything wrong with your height,' he amended, having learned the hard way that her size was no joking matter.

On his second day on the job, he'd called her *shorty*. Every cop within earshot had stopped what they were doing, and in a move that looked like a choreographed dance, stepped away from him. Astute detective that he was, he'd picked up on his mistake instantly. And spent the next week trying to make up for it, finally succeeding when he brought in a package of some of the most expensive Guatemalan coffee he could find and placed it in front of her.

'Still,' Cord said now, steering away from the dangerous topic of height, 'I can't place my finger on it yet, but there's definitely something about Callie McCormick that makes me think of you.'

'Maybe,' Alyssa allowed before she reached around her partner to hit *play*. Distracted by Cord's observation, she found herself studying the missing woman's features more than paying attention to the interaction between Callie and the man sitting beside her, thus requiring her to rewind the video several times before she finally muttered, 'This is ridiculous. There's nothing to see.'

'Too bad there's no audio here,' Cord said. 'I'd like to know what they're talking about.'

'No kidding,' Alyssa agreed. 'Appears to be more of a mono-logue than a dialogue, though.'

'Ain't that the truth,' her partner said, nodding. 'Our girl doesn't seem to be offering much to this conversation, does she? All I see is the man's mouth constantly moving.'

'He's certainly excited about whatever he's on about, if his flailing arms are anything to go by,' Alyssa said.

A short time later, two older gentlemen and a younger well-dressed man entered the frame. The two elderly men – Mervin Wallace and Hunter Jenkins, according to the file – paused briefly before choosing seats closest to the flat-screen mounted on the wall. The third man – Larry Wilkins – grabbed a magazine and sat where he had a clear view of the front desk, as well as the entire lobby.

The tedious monotony of staring at the screen was getting to her, but Alyssa forced herself to pay close attention. 'I could really go for some coffee right now,' she muttered. From the corner of her eye, she saw the phone sitting on Mark's desk. Aubrey was #1.

And then as if she'd conjured her up, the receptionist was pushing open the door. She seemed startled to see the detectives still there. 'Oh,' she said. 'Um, Mark sent me up to see if you two needed anything. Coffee? Water? Soda?'

Whatever reason Aubrey had for being in her boss's office, it wasn't to offer them refreshments, Alyssa thought. But it was a quick recovery, and frankly, she didn't care. She'd even forgive her for infecting the small office space with that overwhelming scent of perfume – did the woman bathe in it?

'I'd love a coffee, please. Black.' Her stomach rumbled out a sound that Alyssa swore was a thank you.

Aubrey bobbed her head up and down. 'Detective Roberts? Anything?'

'I'd love a bottled water, if you have some available.'

'We do. I'll be right back. So sorry for the interruption,' she said as she backed out the door.

'Apology unnecessary,' Alyssa assured the woman.

Less than two minutes later, Aubrey was back. She set the drinks down and left without a word.

Alyssa handed Cord his water and snatched up the coffee, taking a drink before setting her eyes back on the screen. 'Other than Mr. Leroy, no one seems to be giving our missing woman more than a passing glance,' she said now.

After guzzling half his water, Cord aimed one finger at the video. 'I hope when I'm that age, I still look that fit. If I hadn't seen his face, I'd have thought that body belonged on a much younger man.'

'Hmm,' was all Alyssa said as she stretched her arm across her partner's chest so she could grab the file sitting there.

Finally, ninety-four minutes into the recording, Callie McCormick looked up at the receptionist, gathered her belongings and stood, relief evident on her face. Mr. Leroy jumped up, as well, and shook her hand. Then he watched as she approached the desk, signed something, folded some papers, exchanged a few words with the technician who'd entered the waiting area, and turned to go.

One last wave to Mearl Leroy, and she was gone.

One hour and thirty-seven minutes later, after Wallace, Jenkins, and Wilkins had all left the shop, Cord hit *pause*. 'What do you think?'

Alyssa rubbed her temples and twisted the kinks out of her neck. 'I think we have a chat with the mechanics on duty yesterday.'

File in hand, Alyssa jabbed at the first name on the list. 'You want to go grab him, or shall I?'

Cord was already heading out the door when she yelled, 'Oh, while you're at it, do you mind grabbing me another coffee?' Her partner's answer was to shake his head in disbelief. As long as he returned with her drink of choice, he could do whatever he wanted.

Chapter Nine

Evan Bishop was upstairs in his kitchen, whistling while the evening news played in the background, replaying today's events back in his mind. Even though he hadn't gone to MCM with the intention of taking anyone, he had donned his disguise before leaving the house, always prepared in case he discovered *The One*. The last two he'd chosen had been sorely disappointing, disgusting him in their unceasing whimpering and lies. His patience for training them was in short supply, and so he'd had to get rid of them far sooner than he'd planned – which was probably why, in the last couple of weeks, that familiar desire to find the *real* one had resurfaced, eating at his mind with such ferocity, at times it almost drove him mad.

Then he'd seen *her*. And a flash of a memory struggled for a stronghold in his mind, but as quickly as it had come, it disappeared. These flashes had been occurring with more frequency, and he'd come to view them as a sign.

As he had watched her, every flip of her blonde hair, every time she blew her bangs off her forehead, had made him more certain that he had to have her. But it was when she laughed that the unmistakable itch between his shoulders really began to burn, and he knew if he didn't scratch it, it would only grow hotter until he did. It was just her bad luck that she'd been in the wrong place at the wrong time.

When a technician addressed her by name, he repeated it quietly. Callie McCormick. He liked how it rolled smoothly around in his mind. Obtaining her address had been a stroke of luck, a little bit of genius, and a matter of process of elimination.

After she'd left, he'd had to fight the battle warring within: impatience gnawing at him to follow versus the logic that dictated he needed to behave normally. While he waited, he filled his mind with fantasies of how she was the one. When the mechanics finally finished, he forced himself to make small talk with the technician who handed him his keys, to smile at the dim-witted receptionist behind the counter, and above all, to obey the speed limit on his way home – getting pulled over would only cause further delay. But the second he pulled into his driveway, he locked the car, sprinted into his house and grabbed a small kit that held everything he needed, and then ran to catch the bus that would drop him off near Callie's house.

Getting her to open the door had been ridiculously easy. Keeping himself from lunging at her had been hard. But he was patient. Many of the women he'd taken over the years had an aversion to appearing inhospitable, even if it meant endangering their own safety, and making them so much more vulnerable.

The woman downstairs was no different. He'd recognized the look on her face as she considered whether or not he was dangerous. And when he'd smiled, it was because he'd been thinking, *Yes, yes, I am.*

Women could be so stupid sometimes. It made that moment when they realized they'd made a monumental mistake that much sweeter. And Callie McCormick had not disappointed. The gamut of emotions that played across her face when he'd forced his way in – the shock, the terror, the confusion, the tears, and finally, the resignation – had fed the hunger surging inside him.

And as she opened the hatch of her vehicle, he'd plunged the drugged needle into her neck and tossed her inside, securing her hands and feet before covering her mouth with duct tape.

Snapped back to the present by the sound of moaning and movement coming from his basement, he cocked his head to listen. The sedative must finally be wearing off. He'd probably given her more than he should've, but he couldn't risk having her wake before he got her here – that had happened with the last woman, and he learned from his mistakes.

Unfortunately, that meant he'd had to carry her, and unconscious, she was dead weight.

Inside, he'd ripped the duct tape from her hands and feet, replacing it with manacles he'd purchased online. He removed skin when he tore the tape from her mouth. That would smart when she woke. He smiled. Sometimes it was the little things.

Now, the moaning grew louder, so he picked up the soup he'd made and walked toward the basement. Never let it be said he wasn't a gracious host.

Chapter Ten

'It's been almost twenty-four hours since Callie McCormick was first reported missing and twenty-eight since she left a message on her husband's phone.' Alyssa paced the front of the room as she addressed her team, all of them feeling the pressure to locate the missing woman.

'Albuquerque can't afford for this case to go national, Detectives.' Captain Guthrie Hammond had intercepted them as soon as they'd entered the precinct this afternoon after leaving MCM. He was five foot eleven, but his muscular bulk and barrel chest made him appear larger and more intimidating, especially when standing in an already crowded space. 'We're still reeling from the Lucas Bloomfield case. And now that he's been convicted, he's going to be front and center on all the news stations again, which means so will our great city. Tourists are going to start thinking Albuquerque's not a safe place to visit.' He'd bored holes into them with his stare. 'Get this wrapped up. Yesterday,' he ordered as he turned around and stormed away.

'What does he think we're trying to do?' Alyssa grumbled. Behind his back, he was referred to as Captain Hothead, and she tended to agree.

'Just doing his job,' Cord replied, already heading to the conference room they'd long ago established as their own. 'I'll round up Roe and White. You track down Liz and Hal, and we'll meet back here in,' he peeked at his watch, 'say, thirty?'

'I'm found,' Liz Waterson said, overhearing the comment as she rounded the corner. 'Not sure what services I can offer yet, unless you have a witness who saw our girl snatched?'

'Don't I wish,' Alyssa said. 'But an extra pair of eyes and ears never hurt,' she added, 'if you've got the time.'

'For you, I'll make the time.' The forensic artist headed inside the conference room and set her bag down, claiming her spot.

Hal was easy to find. He was in the break room, offering his sage advice to the newest, freshest-faced member of the police force. In for less than three months, the rookie had already had a gun pulled on him – twice. Hal was the natural choice to seek out in this instance, in great part because several years ago, he'd been shot by a strung-out junkie, paralyzing and forever confining him to the wheelchair he was in.

Legend had it that Hal's wife, in her worry over his depression, had handed him his service revolver one day, telling him she loved him, but that he was merely *breathing and not alive*. She cried and told him how sorry she was for the hand that he'd been dealt, that they all had. She told him she didn't want him to die, no one did, but she couldn't stand seeing him like this anymore. It was time to make a choice.

According to Hal, he'd weighed the heaviness of the gun in his palm and almost pulled the trigger that day until he saw the photo collage his wife had laid on the nightstand for him to see. It contained pictures of all their happiest moments – their wedding day, a picture of each of their three children on the day they were born, and his police academy graduation. In every single photo, Hal said he was wearing a smile as big as the day. He'd clicked on the safety and started living again.

Now, he wasn't only everyone's favorite go-to guy, he was also a master at getting people to spill their guts. 'People just trust a guy in a wheelchair,' he'd remarked one day when Alyssa had marveled at his ability to crack in twenty minutes the suspect she'd been grilling for four hours.

Add that to the man's other remarkable skills – like research – and he was one of the strongest assets in the entire precinct.

Fifteen minutes later, everyone had been rounded up, and as the team trickled in, Alyssa shot off a text to Brock.

> Looks like I might not be home for dinner. Team meeting. Hammond's breathing down our necks. Also, don't forget Holly is going to Sophie's to work on their senior project.

Less than thirty seconds later, she had a response.

> Thanks for the reminder. Don't forget to eat. See you when you get home.

God, she loved that man. She pushed aside the guilt that swamped her every time her job got in the way of family time, but this was the career path she'd chosen. And she was damn good at it. Brock, Holly, and Isaac all knew that, but it didn't stop the knot from forming in her stomach every time she had to miss a dinner or sporting event. She did her best… but sometimes she fell short.

When everyone was settled, she handed out copies of the invoices Mark Jacobs, the MCM manager, had secured. 'Cord and I watched the surveillance footage from MCM today.' She glanced up, 'Thanks again, Joe, for setting that up.' His head fell forward in acknowledgement, and she continued. 'We've already spoken to the four technicians on duty yesterday when Callie McCormick was in. For now, they're in the clear, but still on the table.'

Alyssa walked over to the white board and chose a red marker. 'This is what we know,' she said, drawing a rudimentary timeline across the middle, jotting down the events from when

Rafe McCormick first called his wife to inform her of the car appointment to Callie arriving at the dealership, to her calling her husband to let him know she was on her way home, and finally the call from Rafe McCormick reporting his wife missing.

'Now,' she replaced the red marker with a blue one and wrote: *broken phone, dented wall, blood splatters.* She stepped aside and continued. 'Aside from these things, what else do we have?'

From a compartment he had on the side of his wheelchair, Hal removed a pile of papers. 'I checked into the McCormicks' financials like you asked. Steady input, automatic outputs. Nothing there to send up a red flag.' As he spoke, he slipped copies across the table to the rest of the team. 'Called a few of the neighbors who the police canvassed last night, but none of them had much to say about Callie or her husband. Seems like most of the folks on that street keep to themselves. No neighborhood barbecues on this block. I'll keep digging.'

Cord took over from there. 'Thanks, Hal. Liz made copies of our notes from the surveillance video. They're in that packet in front of you. If you have any questions after looking things over, just ask. Until then, we'd like to locate Mearl Leroy, the man who engaged Callie McCormick in conversation while she waited for her car.'

Liz interrupted, fingers poised over the keyboard on her tablet. 'Suspect or person of interest?'

'Person of interest,' Alyssa answered. 'Right now, we'd like to find out what they discussed in that waiting room.'

'In fact,' Cord piped in, 'as of this hour, we have nothing in the way of suspects, so let's be careful not to throw that particular word around. We don't want to spook any potential witnesses. Apart from the person who took her, the individuals we want to speak to are just possibly the last people who saw her.'

Alyssa jumped in. 'Joe and Tony, you try to hunt down Hunter Jenkins, Mervin Wallace, and Larry Wilkins and find out what you can. Their phone numbers and addresses are in those papers. Hal, you keep digging for anything you can find that might give us a lead. Maybe run a quick background check on the employees from MCM, specifically the ones who worked yesterday, if only so we can clear them.' Her gut told her none of the mechanics, the manager, or even the receptionist had anything to do with this case, but she needed to be able to officially check them off the list. She continued, 'But for now, let's keep our main focus on these three, and let me know what you find.' She tapped the names of Leroy, Jenkins, and Wallace. 'Liz, could you help out on that front and check with the technicians about that partial print lifted from Callie McCormick's phone?' At the forensic artist's nod, Alyssa said, 'Great. Cord and I will head over to Mearl Leroy's place right now, and then we can reconvene here at seven o'clock tomorrow morning. Or tonight, if we need to. Either way, make sure you keep me in the loop.'

After everyone headed out to take care of their assignments, Cord pulled out his phone. 'Let me call Sara to let her know I might be late. Don't want her to hold dinner. And then we can head over to Mr. Leroy's.'

'Sounds good,' Alyssa said, then grabbed her empty cup and went in search of a refill.

Chapter Eleven

Monday, March 25, 6:30p.m.

Callie opened her eyes, disoriented. Her head was heavy, as if someone had placed a weight on her forehead. Her tongue was thick, and her mouth felt like it was stuffed with dirty cotton balls. She gathered what little moisture she could garner and licked her lips. The movement hurt.

Cold air blew down on her, and she shivered as goosebumps popped up all over her body. Where was she? A sharp pain shot through her temples when she shook her head, trying to clear it. She reached up to rub warmth back into her arms but couldn't.

She blinked her eyes several times, trying to remove the gritty sensation. It felt like someone had poured sand into them, and they drifted closed once again, refusing to stay open. With effort, she finally forced her eyes open and slowly turned her throbbing head.

Everything was muted, unfamiliar. She knew this wasn't her room, but she had no idea where she was. Her heart raced, and her breathing was ragged as she struggled to remember. Moving just her eyes, her gaze swept the dimly lit room, landing on a large shadowbox mounted on the wall. Inside was a variety of necklaces and other jewelry and what appeared to be…

And that fast, her memory returned. Bile forced its way up her esophagus, greeting the whimper that careened from her throat.

As her head whipped from side to side in denial, she realized she was naked, her wrists were handcuffed, secured to a chain around her waist, and her legs were shackled to two posts centered on the footboard of the bed she was in.

Thousands of fire ants ran along her nerve endings, causing even her toes to tingle.

Her whimper became a sob, and then she screamed.

When the door at the top of the stairs opened, the scream died in her throat, and she snapped her neck in that direction, causing a wave of nausea to wash over her. She struggled against her bindings, sucking in a sharp gasp as pain shot through her stomach where she'd been punched.

'Glad to see you're finally awake.' The man descended the wooden stairs, carrying a small, rusted kettle.

Afraid to look at him, and afraid not to, Callie's teeth chattered as her body convulsed.

The man grabbed something leaning against the wall below the shadowbox before stopping at the foot of the bed to check her bindings. When he was satisfied they weren't loose, he moved to her right side and set up a television tray, the kind she used to love using at her grandpa's house before he died. He placed the pot on top.

'Welcome, Callie.'

How did he know her name?

The blood pounding in her head made it difficult to think… she remembered thinking when she had opened her front door that he looked familiar, but she still couldn't figure out where she'd seen him before. A mewling sound gurgled up from her chest.

'Nothing to say? Cat got your tongue?' He laughed at his own joke. 'That's okay for now. You'll be talking soon enough. Sorry about the lips. Taking duct tape off is like removing a Band-Aid – you gotta be quick. My name is Evan, by the way.'

His gaze roved her body, stopping at the juncture between her thighs. Callie swallowed as she suffered through his degrading examination, but when he reached out his hand to touch her, she instinctively tried to raise her shackled arms in an attempt to protect herself.

Anger flooded his face, and as he raised his fist threateningly, she forced herself to remain immobile, even while he touched the strawberry birthmark above her left hip, stroking it the way a lover might. Tears streamed down her face as she tried to picture a green, grassy meadow with bright yellow dandelions, and butterflies flying about.

However, this time her method for conquering stress and fear abandoned her as she wondered: Was this where he raped her? Would he kill her then? How would he do it? Slit her throat? Shoot her? Or would it be more painful than that? Or would he just continue to rape her until there was nothing left of her but an empty shell?

But then he stopped and smiled at her like they were old friends catching up. 'Well, you must be parched and hungry. That sedative is a killer when it comes to dry mouth. I brought you some soup; it's tomato. I hope you like it,' he said, approaching her like he might a trapped and wounded wild animal. She fought down the hysterical laughter that bubbled up inside her. Because she was the epitome of a trapped and wounded wild animal.

The man placed some soup on a spoon and held it to her mouth.

Was he drugging her again? In an odd way, she hoped he was because then she could pass out and forget this was happening. She opened her mouth, allowing the man to place the soup in her mouth. It was tepid but tasty, surprising her. It seemed wrong and out of place that it would actually be good.

'Do you like it?'

Callie tilted her chin downward, afraid to speak. The slap across her face stunned her. Something wet landed on her arm. Red splattered her chest and the plastic mattress sheet where the soup sloshed over the rim of the bowl.

'Did I tell you to nod? No. I asked you a question, and I'd like a verbal response. I went to a lot of trouble to make this soup for you. Now, I'll ask again – do you like it?'

71

Her vision blurred from the tears that fell in streams down her cheeks, and she whispered a soft, 'Yes.'

'Good. Now, let me explain a few things. While you are in my company, you will do *anything* and *everything* I ask as soon as I ask it. When I'm not here, you can scream all you like. No one'll hear you, and you'll only strain your throat, but please, be my guest. Get it? My guest?

'I'm going to be honest, so pay close attention. While you're here, I'm going to cause you pain you never knew was possible. But it's for your own good. Until you learn.'

Learn what? Callie was sure, whatever it was, she didn't want to know the answer.

'If, at any time, you attempt an escape, I promise you *will* regret it. I'll make killing you take such a long time, you'll do anything to get me to end it for you.' Her gaze immediately went to the shadowbox on the wall.

The man set the bowl down and moved the table near the wall before returning to the bed. While he spoke, he checked the bindings around her wrists. Convinced things were as they should be, he turned to leave.

Callie felt her heartbeat in her throat. On an intellectual level, she understood there were people like this in the world – those who enjoyed, relished even, causing pain to others. She'd read about them in the newspaper, online, and seen them on the news. She always shook her head, thinking how sad it was, but, like many people, was secretly relieved she wasn't the victim. She used to think that what she was now experiencing happened only to other people, or in books and movies. The sickening realization hit her that, to someone else, she *was* the other person.

'Please,' she pleaded, not caring that he hadn't given her permission to speak. 'My husband has money. We'll give you anything you want. Please, just let me go.'

Her captor seemed amused by her suggestion, and he cocked his head as he studied her. 'But I already told you: I don't want your money, or your jewelry. I just want you. To listen to you beg for mercy. Beg for the opportunity to please me.'

'Please, I'm… I'm… pregnant,' Callie lied, willing to say anything.

The man laughed. 'Is that so? Well, I wouldn't let that concern you, if I were you.' Then, without warning, he whirled back and punched her, laughing at her horror-struck expression. She immediately felt the swelling in her cheek.

'You just never know when something is going to hit you,' he said before returning upstairs.

The quiet closing of the door was incongruous with what was happening to her. When she heard the lock click into place, she wept, the wracking sobs jerking her body which sent shockwaves of pain coursing through her as her wrists and ankles pulled against the bindings.

–

Evan stood at the top of the stairs and listened. Tears were always exciting. It meant they were scared and willing to obey, that he had control. And the soup always threw them.

Gotta keep 'em on their toes.

Chapter Twelve

Alyssa shook her head as she approached Mearl Leroy's house. A perfectly edged and trimmed lawn adorned either side of the sidewalk, but it was the hedges bordering the front porch that were cut into neat poodle shapes that amused her. When she reached the large wooden door, she reached out and rang the doorbell.

From the corner of her eye, she saw a curtain move. She turned her head and watched as an older man flicked the curtain back and peeked out. She jostled Cord with her elbow, and they both lifted their hands and waved. The curtain fell back into place, and loud footsteps made their way to the door.

When a face appeared in the little glass window, Alyssa held out her badge for the person inside to see. The door cracked open, the chain lock still firmly in place.

'Mearl Leroy?' Alyssa asked.

'Who wants to know?'

'I'm Detective Wyatt, and this is Detective Roberts. We're with the Albuquerque Police Department. Are you Mr. Mearl Leroy?'

'I am.'

'We'd like to talk to you for a few minutes, if that's okay.'

'Don't tell me that crazy old bat next door called again about me leaving my trash can too close to her driveway. I've told her a million times if I've told her once that it's still on my property.'

She interrupted the man before he could really get rolling on his rant. 'Mr. Leroy, we're not here because of the... crazy

74

old bat… next door.' She smiled. 'But we do need to ask you a few questions about a case we're working on. Do you mind if we come in? We'll try not to take up too much of your time.'

Alyssa thought Mr. Leroy resembled an owl when he wobbled his head back and forth between her and Cord, trying to decide whether or not he should allow them into his house. Finally, she cleared her throat. 'Mr. Leroy?'

'What kinds of questions?' The man closed his door slightly to lift the lock, then leaned in, pushing the door further open, but didn't invite the detectives in.

'We'd really like to talk to you inside, if you don't mind. Never know who's lurking about, listening,' Cord took over, intentionally cocking his head toward Mr. Leroy's nosy neighbor's house.

Mr. Leroy regarded them carefully before relenting. 'Okay, come on in. Excuse the mess. I've been spring cleaning. Just finished scrubbing my basement,' he pointed to a closed door. 'Why don't you all come on into the living room?' He led the way without waiting to see if the detectives were following.

Alyssa shrugged her shoulders at Cord and followed the old man into his living area. The room was dark and dreary. Mr. Leroy picked up a poodle that'd probably seen better days – literally. The gray cloud covering its eyes told her it was probably blind.

'Curly Lee here's deaf and going blind,' Mr. Leroy said as he gently set the aging animal down into a soft dog bed. 'He was my late wife's pooch, really; I prefer bigger dogs that are actually dogs, if you know what I mean.'

Deaf and blind – that would explain the lack of barking and reaction on the dog's part. 'I certainly do know what you mean,' Alyssa said. She looked around the sparsely decorated room. A tattered brown couch, a scratched coffee table, and the dog pillow took up most of the area. To the left and right of the couch were two mismatched end tables with some of the ugliest orange and green lamps she'd ever seen. They had to be from the seventies.

75

The nicest things in the room were the russet-colored curtains covering the windows. They were made of a heavy fabric and did a great job of shutting out the outside. There were few pictures on the walls. She'd been in hotel rooms that felt more lived-in.

A large flat-screen television was mounted to the wall, and what must be hundreds of DVDs lined a shelf. Various novels decorated the coffee table as if the man couldn't pick just one book to read. From the looks of it, he liked his mysteries and horror stories.

To Alyssa's thinking, the house was a little on the creepy side. When Cord raised his eyebrows in his trademark *What the hell* look, she knew his thoughts ran similar to her own.

'You live here alone, Mr. Leroy?' Cord began.

'Yes, I do. My wife died six years ago next month. Heart attack. But I'm sure you didn't come to talk about my wife, so I ask again, what is it I can help you with, Detectives?'

Cord pulled out a picture and handed it to the man, watching his expression. 'Have you seen this woman?'

Mr. Leroy took the picture from Cord's hand and stared at it. He kept his head down, not hiding his nervousness. 'Yeah. She's the woman who was on the news this morning, the missing woman.' He looked back at them.

'Is that the only place you've seen her? On the news?'

'No, no. I met her at the MCM service station yesterday. We were both getting our cars worked on, and since we were the only two there for a while, we started talking. Since you're here, I assume you already know that.'

'What time did MCM finish working on your car?' Cord asked.

'Oh, I guess it must've been around eleven thirty or so. It took longer than I expected, and I was pretty hungry when I left. I remember thinking I could still beat the lunch crowd if I wanted to stop at Blake's and grab a hamburger.' He peered directly into Alyssa's eyes, making her feel a little uncomfortable.

'You maybe think I had something to do with this woman's disappearance? I can tell you all I did was talk to her.'

Since he'd addressed his comment to her, Alyssa asked, 'What did the two of you discuss?'

Mr. Leroy looked away sheepishly. 'You know, I chatted with her for a long time. She was awfully nice, letting me talk her ear off.' He peered down at the picture, back up, then down again, running his finger along the photo. 'She looks different in this here picture. Her hair's longer or something. I don't know; I can't quite put my finger on it.'

His gaze went from the picture to Alyssa and back again. 'Sorry. We talked about the celebrity couple who's splitting up, the one that's all over the news. That and dogs. I told her how I used to train police canines. That's about it.'

In Alyssa's opinion, a man who trained canines for the police force should have something adorning his lawn besides poodle-shaped hedges.

'Did Mrs. McCormick,' she nodded her head to indicate the picture still in his grasp, 'mention anything about going somewhere, meeting someone?'

Mr. Leroy looked confused. 'No, no. Why would she?' His face turned red. 'Besides, I did most of the talking. It was… nice… to have someone listen to me ramble. It's been so long since my wife –'

Alyssa interrupted. 'If you knew Callie McCormick was missing, why didn't you call the police immediately and let them know you'd spent time speaking with her?'

'I'm not sure I follow. What was I supposed to say? It's not like I knew her; she was just someone I passed the time with while my car was being fixed. You people would never get anywhere if everyone who ever spoke with a missing person called to report it.'

Cord reached out and took the photo back. 'Alright, well thank you for your time. We just need to eliminate people from our list.'

'I hope you find her soon. She was a real nice lady.'

At the door, Alyssa reached for the handle and then stopped. 'One more question – you wouldn't happen to have your receipt from Blake's, so we can verify the time you were there?'

Mr. Leroy shuffled his feet. 'No, I don't believe so. I paid with cash and tossed the receipt. Guess I didn't know I was going to need it for an alibi.'

'No, I guess you wouldn't know that, would you?' Alyssa said as she opened the door and stepped outside. The door clicked behind them as they moved off the porch into the bright sunlight.

At the car, she climbed into the driver's seat and waited for Cord to close the passenger door before speaking. 'I don't know about you, but that house gave me serious heebie-jeebies. Did you see those hideous lamps?'

'Yeah, that they were. Other than needing a major update on furniture, what's your take on this guy?' Cord asked as he snapped his seatbelt into place.

She started the car and pulled away from the curb before responding. 'He has an apparent love for the macabre, wouldn't you say? Those movies? *Saw, Halloween, Psycho, Insidious, The Last House on the Left*…That's a little… sinister, I'd say.'

'Having a taste for horror movies doesn't mean he's guilty of anything. Just shows he likes the dark and mysterious. I did find it weird, however, that he got all choked up about his wife's death but didn't seem to have any photos of her lying around – at least nowhere I could see,' Cord said.

'Yeah, I caught that, too. But, aside from a dark, creepy vibe and a haunted house feeling, I really didn't get a clear read on the man himself. Unfortunately, I think you're right. Mearl Leroy might be a little unnerving and bizarre, but it doesn't make him guilty of anything.'

Cord leaned in to turn up the radio. 'So, we keep looking, but we don't mark him off our list yet?'

'Exactly.'

Chapter Thirteen

Tuesday, March 26

Callie's legs had fallen asleep, and she struggled to stretch them, startled when she couldn't. She tried again, but then something sharp poked her foot, and her eyes swept down to her feet. She screamed when she saw someone — no, not someone — HIM — standing at the foot of the bed with a fireplace poker, repeatedly jabbing her in the foot. Fierce pain ripped through her legs, and that's when she realized he was also burning the soles of her feet. The poker was hot, as if it had recently been pulled from a fire. On instinct, she tried scrambling backwards to get away…

Callie jolted awake from a nightmare-plagued sleep, slamming her back into a reality she literally couldn't escape. Not a nightmare. A memory. Sometime during the night, her captor had come in for the simple pleasure of torturing her, or so it seemed. 'So, you don't try to run,' was his reasoning when she'd asked why he was burning her feet and begged him to stop.

Her brain categorized every searing pain. As a teenager, she'd been in a terrible car accident and spent weeks in the hospital. At the time, she thought nothing could feel worse than that. She was wrong. Her right cheek was still tender from his punch, and the abrasions on her wrists and ankles burned where she'd torn her skin as she'd yanked them in her attempt to get away from his torturous game.

Why was this happening to her? Unable to choke it back, she felt panic begin its familiar trek up her throat until an intense pressure low in her stomach forced its way to the front of her mind, giving her a new focus; she really needed to pee.

Her gaze swept the room, searching. Aside from a dim light down what she assumed was a hallway, the room she was in was dark with no windows to tell her if it was still night or the next day.

And no way to escape.

Once more, her eyes landed on the shadowbox. She squinted as her brain tried to make sense of what it held. When it did, she squeezed her eyes in denial, a scream bubbling up from deep in her chest, threatening to choke off her air.

The door opened at the top of the stairs, and her screams turned into a keening, pleading wail when she noticed the man holding something in his hands. 'Oh god, oh god, oh god,' she whimpered even though she couldn't tell what it was he held. Just imagining whatever it was caused violent tremors to course through her body. He ignored both her cries and shaking as he grabbed the TV tray and set his things on it.

'Hello, sleepy head. I'd ask if you had a restful night, but I already know the answer.' He cocked his head and gave her a strange look. 'Do you know you talk in your sleep?'

Heart threatening to pump through her breastbone, Callie struggled to remember the rules. Her *no* was a whispered plea, and she was only mildly relieved when she saw him nod his head in approval.

'Well, you do,' he continued. 'Several times I thought you'd woken, but maybe you were just having bad dreams.' He looked at her expectantly.

Tears blurred her vision as her eyes glued onto his every movement, trying to brace herself for whatever he was going to do to her.

'I used to have bad dreams, too,' he said conversationally as he lifted one of her feet, inspected it, and then repeated the same thing with the other. 'They go away eventually.'

When he reached for something on the table beside him, she cried, 'Please, no.'

He froze for just a moment before returning to what he was doing.

When she felt a warm dampness on her feet, she realized the man was tending to the wounds he'd inflicted during the night, muttering to himself as he worked. She clenched her teeth and struggled to breathe against the sharp, burning sensation that flowed from the tips of her toes to the top of her head.

When he finished, he said, 'There. That should help.' His eyes narrowed. 'Don't you have something to say to me?'

Her mind raced until she realized what he expected.

'Th – th – thank you.' Her teeth chattered so violently, it sounded like a jackhammer in her brain.

He nodded in approval. 'That's a good girl.' He walked around the corner into the dimly lit hallway and pulled a chair over to the side of the bed. 'Now, I know you have questions. You asked them in your sleep. So, let's start with *why you*. I suppose the answer is, *why* not *you*? Give it a day or two, and I think you might find I'm not unreasonable at all. All you have to do is obey me.'

At his words, her eyes darted again to the shadowbox on the wall. He followed her gaze and smiled at her like he was proud, though it was unclear if he was proud of her or himself. 'Do you like it?' He stood and walked over so he could pull it down.

When he held it in front of her face, she gagged, her mind recoiling at the tiny, framed pictures of bound and beaten women. Spots swam in her vision as she realized that, dear God, she wasn't his first victim. Lord help her, she didn't want to know what had happened to them. The urge to look away or close her eyes grabbed at her throat, but she was too terrified to move. Each niche held various items along with the photographs – necklaces, earrings, and other jewelry. With each item was a braided length of blonde hair. Seven of them.

But when she saw the niche where a discolored yet otherwise well-preserved dismembered hand rested beside a jar that held an actual eyeball, the vomit she'd tried so hard to hold in gushed up and out, spraying her captor, who leaped back in shock and rage. At the same time, her bladder released, the strong scent of ammonia drifting up to greet the odor of terror as she flooded the plastic cover beneath her. The dark look that overtook his face prepared her for the coming slap.

One hand reached out and squeezed her jaw, tightening his fingers when she cried out. He twisted her head and forced her to look at what she'd done. 'Filthy! Disgusting!' he roared, his spittle landing on her. 'I will *not* tolerate this type of behavior. I should shackle you face down into your own filth.'

'I… I'm sorry,' she choked out.

The man released her and reached into his pocket. When she saw what the item was, her gaze flew to the stairs, but even before the thought of escape could fully form, she knew there was no way, especially with her damaged feet.

Key in hand, he inserted it into one shackle and then suddenly stopped, and since Callie was watching that, she was unprepared for the punches to her chest and stomach. She gasped, trying to get enough air into her lungs.

'That's in case you think you can escape me.' He was still yelling when he unlocked the manacles and dragged her from the bed, her body hitting the floor with a thud. She screamed as her bloodied, raw ankles scraped against the rough carpet. He didn't stop until he reached a very utilitarian bathroom. It had a sink, a lidless toilet, a shower stall with no door or curtain, and nothing else. He thrust her into the shower and turned the water on.

Needles of icy water hit her tender skin, but she was in too much pain to try to scramble out of its path – even if she could.

Lost to the fire lighting up every one of her nerve endings, Callie didn't know if it was an hour or a minute later when he turned off the spigot, and dragged her over the lip of the shower floor and back into the bedroom where he used his foot to send her the rest of the way. For one blessed second, Callie thought he was leaving when he turned away, but all he did was throw the cloth at her that he'd used on her feet.

'Clean this mess and get back in the bed,' he ordered.

But she couldn't force her muscles or mind to obey, and she collapsed the rest of the way onto the floor, her body curling into a fetal position. 'Please,' she begged, 'please, I can't. What did I ever do to you? Please, let me go.'

She passed out from the kick to her kidney area, welcoming the blackness as it closed her in its arms.

Chapter Fourteen

Wednesday, March 27

Creaking, groaning pipes and a blast of obnoxious noise – what her son referred to as music – alerted Alyssa that it was time for Holly and Isaac to get up and ready for school. She smiled gratefully when Brock placed her first cup of coffee in front of her, bending down to kiss the top of her head before reaching for the remote to turn on the early morning news.

A photo of Callie filled the screen.

'…your help in locating Callie McCormick, who was last seen Monday morning at the MCM Jeep service station located on Eagle Ranch Road. Callie's husband, Rafe McCormick, owner of The Espresso Grind cafés, has offered a substantial reward for any information leading to the safe return of his wife. You can see the full interview tonight at 10:00.

As soon as the reporter moved onto the next story, Alyssa reached over and muted the sound.

'Did you know about the reward?' Brock asked.

'Yeah. I don't know how much it's going to help, but we'll take anything we can get. Even if it means initially having to wade through hundreds of false leads first.' She didn't need to remind her husband that the odds of finding Callie alive reduced with every ticking second.

At the sound of the shower turning off, Brock changed the subject. 'By the way, Mom called. Her stomach's bothering her again, so she won't make it to dinner tonight.' He winked at his wife. 'Try not to be too devastated by that news, okay?'

If she was being completely honest, she'd already forgotten Brock had told her Mabel had called Monday evening to invite herself over. 'I'll do my best,' she said just as Holly walked into the kitchen, pulling up short when she saw her mom.

'Do your best for what?' she asked as she opened the refrigerator and pulled out the orange juice. She poured a glass, looked at the time, and then said, 'I'm surprised you're still home. Shouldn't you be at the precinct by now?'

Behind her daughter's shoulder, Alyssa saw Brock's smile widen, and she bit back her own. 'Not until seven, and I haven't seen much of you and your brother lately, so I figured I could go in after I see your bright, shining faces.'

The rest of the conversation was interrupted by Isaac's heavy, tired footsteps as he plodded his way into the kitchen. Like his sister, he did a double take at seeing his mother still there. Unlike Holly, he didn't speak, heading straight to the cupboard for strawberry pop tarts – the only kind there should be, according to him – and only after he had devoured them did Alyssa attempt to speak to her son, knowing better than to try to have a conversation when he wasn't fully alert or firing on all cylinders, which didn't occur until after his morning sugar buzz. She smiled. If either of her children was going to have her penchant for coffee, it would be this one.

'Good morning.'

'Morning,' Isaac said, his voice still groggy. 'How come you're still here?'

She was beginning to feel a little unwelcome in her own home, Alyssa thought grumpily. So, instead of answering her son's question, she looked at Holly and said, 'Dad told me you got that internship at the Labs that you applied for. I'm so proud of you, baby. When do you start?'

Holly, a miniature version of her mother, though she stood a couple of inches taller – something she pointed out as often as possible – grinned. 'Not 'til the end of June, and it's only for a month, but it'll get my foot in the door, at least.' She hesitated.

'I could still go to Europe for a few weeks. It wouldn't be the whole summer, but…'

Isaac suddenly perked up as he looked expectantly at his parents, hope and excitement etched over every feature.

'Dad and I are still discussing that.'

'Whoop whoop,' Isaac yelled before Brock shot him a warning glance. 'What?' he mumbled. 'Can't I be excited for my sister?'

'Yeah, that's what it is, excited for *me*. Has nothing to do with hoping you'll be the *friend* I choose to go with me,' Holly said sarcastically, rolling her eyes at her brother. 'As if.'

Alyssa caught her husband's eyes, both quietly agreeing not to inform their son – yet – that, even if Holly was allowed to go – and that was still a big if – there was no way she was allowing her not-quite-in-high-school, fourteen-year-old son to traipse along unchaperoned in Europe, of all places. Good lord, it was more than five thousand miles away! Despite being an adult in the eyes of the law, her eighteen-year-old daughter did not count as a suitable guardian in this case.

Isaac opened his mouth to argue.

'Your mother said we were still discussing it,' Brock cut him off, ending the conversation. Then, locking eyes with his wife, he pulled a large white envelope from behind the enormous Winnie-the-Pooh cookie jar and set it in front of Holly. 'Besides, I think your sister might have some more good news to share.'

Bewildered, she cocked her head to one side and said. 'I do?' Then: 'Is that from Cornell University?' Her hands shook as she fumbled to open the letter. 'What if it's a rejection?' Holly bit her lower lip, reminding Alyssa how her own little brother used to do the same thing whenever he was anxious or excited. She shook her head, refusing to allow sadness to interfere with this moment.

Isaac, still irritated at his sister's comment regarding her plus one to Europe, rolled his eyes. 'Only one way to find out. Why don't you open it?'

When she still hesitated, Alyssa went to stand by her daughter and draped her arm around her shoulder. 'Come on. We'll do it together.'

It was difficult to say whose hands trembled more. The envelope finally opened, Holly slid out the top piece of stationery. She handed it to Alyssa. 'You read it. I can't. Just break it to me softly if it's bad news.'

'*Congratulations! The selection committee in the College of Engineering has approved…*' That was as far as she got before her entire family erupted into cheers and her oldest child threw herself into her arms.

Isaac forgot he was annoyed with Holly and thrust his fist across the table. 'Pound it, sister!'

Beaming, she tapped her brother's fist with her own before they both pulled their arms back and opened their hands wide to mimic an explosion. 'Boom!' they cried out in unison, laughing.

'My turn,' Brock said, moisture in his eyes as he pulled his daughter into his chest. 'Would you look at that? My little girl's going Ivy League. So proud of you, baby.'

'Oh my gosh! I need to tell Grandma.' She turned and headed down the hall to grab her phone. Alyssa knew the second Mabel answered because Holly squealed.

She smiled and nestled her head against her husband's chest as he drew her in. 'Thank you for not showing her last night. I would've hated to miss that.'

Brock's answer was to tilt her head up and kiss her softly.

And Alyssa was able to forget, for a few precious minutes, about Callie McCormick and the dangerous world they lived in.

-

Thirty minutes later Alyssa was still smiling as she walked into the conference room. She was so happy for Holly. Her lifelong dream of getting into one of the Ivy League universities had once seemed far-fetched, but she had worked hard to achieve her goal, and she'd done it.

She was checking her phone when Cord walked in, followed by the rest of the crew. As soon as Hal wheeled his chair in, closed the door, and joined them around the table, they got down to business.

Alyssa started with Joe and Tony. 'Tell me what you've got.'

Tony pulled out a sheet of paper and slid it over to Alyssa. 'Mervin Wallace lives with his sister in a condominium up in the Heights. Volunteers his time at the homeless shelter and to various veterans' administrations throughout the county.'

Alyssa's eyebrows shot up, but guessing her thoughts, Tony shook his head. 'Never met Callie. Different charity. I already checked.'

Disappointment dug in deep, but she listened as White continued. 'Wallace was at the dealership because his sister, who he described as "a meddlesome, nagging old fool who always thinks she knows what's best for him and his life," was ill, and he'd offered to take her car in for her. Unless Hal uncovers something in the background check, for now he seems clean, at least as far as this case is concerned.'

'I'll take it from there,' Joe said, mimicking his partner by sliding his report over to Alyssa. 'Hunter Jenkins. Lives in a small, one-bedroom rental house in the South Valley. When we got there, he invited us right in. He remembered seeing a woman in the waiting area but didn't take much notice of her other than she was talking to her father.' He paused. 'He assumed Mearl Leroy was her dad. And as far as Mr. Wallace goes, Jenkins said he'd never met him before Monday when they both dropped their vehicles off at the same time. In fact, he said he was planning to walk over to the McDonald's for some hotcakes, but when they told him his car wouldn't take too long, he decided to wait.' He closed his file. 'After I spoke with him, I asked for his landlord's number, and he gladly rattled it off for me, and then told me where she lived, even invited us back if I had further questions. According to his landlady, Mr. Jenkins wouldn't kill a fly, much less kidnap a woman.' He glanced around the room. 'I added that last part, not her. Anyway, she said he was in and out a lot, never had a lot of visitors, and was a good renter.' Joe's face reddened as he added, 'Strange-looking dude, but for now, appears he's on the up and up.'

In other words, they still had nothing. Alyssa nodded and moved on. 'Hal?'

'Well, as much as I'd like to tell you I have the smoking gun and the silver bullet, I don't.' Before continuing, he laughed at Liz's horrified expression. 'Got to find the humor in life, or you're bound to lose yourself.' Then he looked back to the detectives. 'What I can tell you is this: the young man Larry Wilkins happens to be a private investigator.' He grinned. 'Turns out the receptionist's husband suspected his wife was having an affair with one Mark Jacobs, so he hired Wilkins to check it out.'

Well, that explained Aubrey's surprise when she'd unexpectedly walked into the manager's office only to find the detectives still there.

'Anything else?' Cord asked.

'Still waiting for the McCormicks' phone records, so not from me,' Hal answered.

'Technicians are still backed up, so nothing yet on the prints lifted from the crime scene, either,' Joe added.

'What about a DNA profile from the blood found on the wall and floor near the stairs?' Tony asked.

'Probably still a little too soon to tell whose it is, but Hal, do you mind calling the medical examiner's office and checking on that for me?' Alyssa asked.

'Consider it done,' Hal said, writing a note to himself.

'I heard Ruby griping up front,' Liz said. 'Guess people are calling in hoping to cash in on that reward.'

Alyssa winced. 'Yeah, Ruby all but threw these,' she lifted a stack of memos in the air, 'as soon as I walked through the door.'

She shared a few of them with the others. 'So far, we've got three people who've seen Callie cross the border into Mexico, another who was positive she'd seen her heading into Canada with a man who was definitely not Rafe McCormick. One witness claims he performed plastic surgery on Callie so she could escape her abusive spouse.' The next one made her laugh out loud. 'Gladys here swears she watched, and I quote, "the missing woman get sucked into a spaceship." End quote.' She tossed the memo onto the table.

It was Liz's turn to laugh. 'If only we were in Roswell instead of Albuquerque, that would have to be moved to the top of the list.'

Alyssa read one more. 'And this one here wishes to remain anonymous until an arrest is made and the "money collected." But he would like us to know he's a psychic and believes this is all a ruse set up by Callie's husband in order to distract creditors from his deep financial troubles.'

'Already discredited,' Hal piped in.

'Okay, well, since we still have to follow up on these, no matter how far-fetched, I'll let you handle this one, Hal.' Alyssa divvied up the rest of the memos, keeping a couple for her and Cord. 'Let's keep digging,' she said, her voice somber. 'Let's find Callie and bring her home. Keep in touch today and let us know how things are going.'

Chapter Fifteen

Wednesday, March 27

Bishop, still seething about yesterday, descended the steps, a bowl of oatmeal in one hand, a bedpan in the other. He'd been so furious when he'd finally dragged Callie back onto the bed that he'd left the house so he wouldn't have to listen to her constant screams. He'd hoped that starving her would shut her up. She was turning out to be another huge disappointment.

'Please, tell me why you're doing this to me!'

'Because I can,' he said coldly as he set his items on the tray, and without another word, inspected her feet. When she flinched, he dug his fingernails into the raw skin of her ankle, causing her to cry out.

'You don't seem to be very grateful to the person feeding and taking care of you,' he said, shoving the small plastic tub roughly beneath her. This always disgusted him, but it needed to be done. 'You might as well use it. You won't like the consequences if you make another mess.'

He was glad when she finally urinated, and he carefully removed the bedpan and went around the corner to the bathroom he'd installed himself and washed his hands. When he returned, he grabbed a chair he'd placed at the foot of the bed and set it up next to the side.

'I thought today you might want me to give you another chance. You must know by now that I'm not going to let you go, so really, it's up to you how much you want to suffer.'

He followed her gaze as it swung to the shadowbox. 'You want to talk about my mementos? Okay, then.'

Once more he grabbed the box from the wall. He pointed to one of the pictures. 'This was Mary.' He tapped the braid. 'This was her hair. I realized right away she wasn't right, so she only lasted a day.

'This,' he pointed to another picture, 'was Alice. This is her necklace.' He stared down at Callie. 'She kept telling me she'd give me all her jewelry if I just let her go. So, I did – by slitting her throat and dumping her in the river – and I kept her jewelry and her hair.'

He laughed when tears sprang to Callie's eyes, but when she closed them, he jerked her head around. 'Look,' he ordered.

'This,' he tapped the glass on a picture, 'is Debbie – no, I mean, Denise. She tried to claw me with those perfect finger-nails, so I cut off her hand before I killed her. I even let her choose which one.'

He moved on to another braid, this one with a bright blue ribbon weaved throughout. 'Sandra. She bored me. I don't even know why I thought she was the one.'

He paused before he moved onto the last item, opening the latch on the back of the box so he could remove the glass jar containing the eyeball. He held it directly in front of Callie. When she squeezed her eyes closed, he ordered her to open them. 'Meet Rhonda.' He sighed as he remembered her. 'I really thought she was it. She did everything I told her to do. It only took her one day to stop crying and begging.' His eyes darkened. 'I was going to reward her, but when I unlocked her chains, she attacked me and tried to escape. I cut out her eye because she'd looked at me with deception.' He watched Callie's reaction.

He barely made it out of the way before she retched all over again.

Chapter Sixteen

Wednesday, March 27

Evan Bishop fumed, his fists pummeling Callie's body wherever they landed, hitting harder the more she screamed. How could he ever have thought she was *the one*? Stupid! Stupid! Stupid!

A flash of memory – two little boys, huddled in a corner – there and gone before he could blink, had him halting his fist mid-air. And when he did, he glared at the woman in his basement. 'I thought you were different,' he seethed. 'But, you're no better than the rest. A deceitful, dirty liar.'

Get rid of her.

The voice in his head was so loud, he actually turned to see who had spoken. Then it came again: *No time like the present,* and he knew what he needed to do. Without a word, he swung away and headed upstairs.

Too beaten and broken to wonder why he'd left so abruptly, Callie watched Evan take the stairs two at a time, leaving the door cracked open behind him. The idea of escape barely flitted through her mind. Even if an attempt had been possible, she could barely lift her head, and she was certain her ribs were cracked, every breath shooting splinters of agony through her.

Overhead, she heard him pacing, his footsteps sounding like gunshots. *Weak*, he had screamed over and over as his fists battered her, and ashamed, she prayed to die right now, this minute. She was so tired of fearing what would happen next only to realize that reality was far worse than anything she could imagine. Each time the door opened, each time the monster appeared, he brought more torment. And after seeing the man's mementos...

A door slammed, intruding in her thoughts, and when silence fell, she knew she wasn't really ready to die yet. They had to be searching for her. She could survive this. She strained to hear; the silence was worse than the pacing. Had he left her to die chained to the bed? Or was he preparing an even worse torture for her? Immediately, her mind conjured up the eyeball floating in liquid, and dry heaves racked her body because there was nothing left for her to give.

–

Plan in place, Evan organized everything in a neat, orderly fashion: midazolam, syringe, scissors, two rubber bands, shovel, tarp. Whistling as he worked, he wondered if he should've held onto Callie's Jeep a bit longer. But it was dangerous keeping it around, and besides, it wasn't like he could use it to dump her body. Too many chances for someone to spot. No, he'd done the right thing in getting rid of it. The police would be looking for her vehicle, not his.

He'd take her to the mountains. Even if someone found her body, there was a good chance the coyotes, wolves, or even the mountain lions would have gotten to her first. In a world where DNA was king, he wasn't afraid that forensic science would be able to identify who she was. Knowing her identity wouldn't help the authorities much. After all, bones couldn't talk.

Finally, satisfied he had everything he needed, he filled a syringe with sedative, frowning when he realized he didn't have as much as he thought, as his last order hadn't yet arrived. He shook his head. No matter. What he had would get the job done, he was sure of it. Besides, now that he knew what he needed to do, he was too impatient to wait.

Scissors and rubber bands came next.

When he stood back, a smile spread across his face. He was ready.

-

He sang as he came down the stairs, and all Callie could do was watch, wondering what he had in store for her now. When he reached the bed, the light from above glanced off something in his hands. She blinked when she realized they were scissors. At first, she didn't understand. Then she saw the malicious gleam as he stared down at her, and suddenly, she did.

A great shuddering sob escaped her as she struggled against her bindings, ignoring the stabbing pain. When he grabbed hold of her hair, she jerked her head to the side in an effort to dislodge his grip, but in her weakened state, her efforts were no more irritating to him than a buzzing mosquito. Still, she continued fighting and pleading. 'No, no, please no. Please, I'll do anything. I'm sorry I got sick. Please just give me another chance,' she cried.

Then a fist crashed into her face, and she heard as much as felt the bone in her nose break. Viciously, he twisted her neck to the side, using his elbow to hold her cheek to the bed as he tugged and yanked at the back of her head. Blood gurgled in the back of her throat, nearly choking her, and cutting off her sobs.

Then he released her, stepping back, her limp, blonde hair in his fist. She watched, numb, as he set the scissors down and calmly pleated the length of hair into an uneven braid. Defeated, she squeezed her eyes closed, hoping if she stopped fighting, he'd kill her fast. She wondered how he'd do it. At the sound of tapping, her eyes flew open again, and she saw the syringe filled with a light-colored liquid seconds before the needle was jammed into her neck.

'Time to say goodnight and goodbye, Callie,' was the last thing she heard as he depressed the plunger.

Followed by her last thought: *At least it'll be over.*

Chapter Seventeen

Wednesday, March 27

Frustrated and hungry, Alyssa said, 'Flip you for the honor of getting to be the one who returns Hammond's call.'

'Tell you what, you give the good captain a holler, and I'll buy lunch before we head over to visit one Josephine Graffe, our latest in the long line of callers who are one hundred percent positive they've spotted Callie McCormick crossing state lines.'

Her eye-roll told him exactly what she thought of that. 'Coward,' she muttered, already placing the call.

'Hammond here.' The voice on the other end was gruff and sounded every bit as irritable as she felt. She was about to make his day worse.

'Captain, it's Alyssa. I –'

'Yeah, I know who it is. What've you got?'

'We just finished chasing down a couple of leads. And we're about to –'

Hammond interrupted. 'I don't need to tell you again, Detective, how important it is that you solve this case promptly. Fire from the mayor's getting hot on my neck. Call me when you have something concrete. And Alyssa?'

'Yes, sir?'

'Make it fast.'

'Yes, sir,' she repeated and tossed her phone onto the dash before leaning forward and resting her head on the steering wheel. 'I'm trying to like the man, Cord, I swear. But, does he actually understand how an investigation works? He didn't even let me tell him why I called.'

'Why don't we discuss it over green-chile–smothered enchiladas and chips and salsa?' Cord said.

Alyssa sat up, a smile on her face. 'And margaritas?'

'Later. I promise.'

She started the car and backed out. 'I'm holding you to that.'

'I have no doubt,' Cord retorted.

Ten minutes later, they pulled into the parking lot of her favorite Mexican restaurant, and fifteen minutes after that, their food was delivered. No sooner had she taken a huge bite, than her phone rang. She swallowed, green chile and cheese hanging off her chin. 'If that's Hammond, I'll scream,' she said. She glanced at the screen.

'Captain?' Cord asked.

'Not a number I recognize.' She took a drink of water to ease the sting of hot cheese burning her throat, and then answered. 'Detective Wyatt.'

'Detective Wyatt, this is Officer Cutler from El Paso. Is this a good time?'

El Paso? 'Sure.'

'We got a stolen car down here we think you may be interested in. It's a 2014 Jeep Grand Cherokee, registered to a Rafe and Callie McCormick there in Albuquerque. I called your precinct, and someone named Ruby gave me your number.'

Alyssa sat up straighter. 'You found Callie McCormick's car?' she asked, getting Cord's full attention. She scribbled invisible lines in the air and then put one finger in her ear to block out the noise from the lunch crowd, nodding as her partner yanked a pen from his pocket before searching for something to write on. He settled on a napkin, thrusting both in front of her.

'We did,' said Officer Cutler. 'We caught a young buck trying to cross the border into Mexico with it. He was acting squirrely so border patrol ran the plates and came back with a hit. We're holding the kid until he makes bail. It looks like that might be a while.'

97

'What's this kid's name?'

'License says Manuel Gomez. Ring any bells for you?'

'Manuel Gomez.' Alyssa repeated, eyebrows arched at Cord to see if the name meant anything to him. It didn't. 'No, but like Texas, that's a fairly common name here in New Mexico. Did he say how he came to be in possession of McCormick's vehicle?'

'Swore his uncle gave it to him a few months back. He kept changing the wheres, whens, and whys, but when we informed him he was driving a stolen vehicle, his story changed. Instead of his uncle, he said he'd gotten a call from a pal who'd told him where he could find a free and clear car, keys already in it. All he had to do, the guy said, was move the vehicle out of the States.'

'Don't suppose he shared his pal's name?' Alyssa asked as she scribbled down notes.

'Clammed up right quick when we asked. But he did say his pal heard about it from another party. Insisted he didn't know names, just that his pal claimed it was an anonymous call.'

'Of course. Anything else you can tell me?'

'Yeah, one more thing. We've had a sudden surge of violence down here, so our technicians are a little backed up at the moment. It could be weeks or even months before our guys can go over it, and since the vehicle's stolen from there, it might be faster if we transfer it back to Albuquerque so your techs can run a fine-tooth comb over it.'

'Okay, thanks. I appreciate the call. As soon as I get the okay, my partner and I will head down. Mind if we ask for you when we get there?' She glanced at the time. 'It's eleven forty-five now, so it'll be around four thirty, five when we get there, depending on how quick we can get the travel approval.'

'Yep, you've got my number. Just let me know when you get here.' Cutler rattled off the address of his precinct, and then hung up.

Before Alyssa ended the call, Cord was already on the phone with the captain filling him in and clearing the cost, so Alyssa flagged down the waiter to request the bill. Still on the phone, Cord whipped out his credit card and thrust it into the waiter's hand before the man could walk away.

Two minutes later, they were out the door. She fished her phone back out, and as soon as Liz answered, she said, 'We're on our way to El Paso. Details later. Can you follow up on a new lead that's probably not a lead at all?' she asked.

'Yep. Give it to me,' Liz answered.

'Mrs. Josephine Graffe left a message this morning telling us she was certain she'd witnessed Callie McCormick heading into Colorado. According to the caller, Callie was alone, her hair framed into a bob, and appeared happy,' she said.

'Right. Address? Phone number?' Liz asked. After Alyssa rattled off the information, she said, 'Okay, I'll let you know what I find out.'

'Thanks, Liz. I appreciate it.' Next, she called Brock. 'You're on speaker,' she said when he answered.

He laughed. 'Thanks for the warning. I'll refrain from spilling any state or personal secrets. What's going on?'

She filled him in. 'Needless to say, I'll be late getting home tonight. Tell the kids I love them,' she said before hanging up.

A long drive and countless hours of questioning later, it was evident Manuel Gomez had nothing to do with Callie McCormick's disappearance. Furthermore, Alyssa's gut told her he was telling the truth about how he came to be in possession of Callie's vehicle. In other words, they had her car, but nothing else. They were no better off than they were before they'd left this afternoon.

Exhausted and discouraged, she spoke with Cutler before heading back, making arrangements for the Jeep to be returned to Albuquerque so their own technicians could go over it.

Due in part to breaking a few speed limit laws along the way, Alyssa walked in her door close to midnight and peeked in on Isaac and then Holly before heading to her own room and climbing into bed next to Brock.

Chapter Eighteen

Thursday, March 28

The next morning, the house quiet except for the faint sounds of the shower running in the master bathroom, Alyssa grabbed her favorite coffee mug – a Mother's Day gift featuring a photo collage of Holly and Isaac in various goofy poses – and poured her first cup of the day. She was walking to the table when she heard Holly's alarm go off. A quick peek up the stairs showed a light glow beneath her daughter's bedroom door. *She must have an assignment she needs to finish.* Proud of her work ethic – she'd needed it to get her internship at the Labs, as well as getting accepted into Cornell – Alyssa couldn't help but worry Holly was working too hard. 'You're only young once,' she frequently told her daughter.

Upstairs, she heard the water shut off, followed by the rustling sounds of Brock getting ready for work. Ten minutes later, her husband, hair still wet, joined her in the kitchen with his own cup of coffee. 'What's Holly doing up so early?' he asked.

As if summoned, they heard their daughter's door open, and the clap of her feet as she bounced down the stairs, seeming to hit every creaky step along the way and sounding far too loud in the stillness of the morning. 'Guess we're about to find out.'

As soon as she walked into the room, Holly smiled. 'Good morning. I set my alarm early so I could talk to both of you before you left for work.'

Brock and Alyssa exchanged glances, and when he simply shrugged, she asked, 'What's up, sweetie?'

Her daughter tipped up on her toes then fell back onto the balls of her feet before repeating the movement. She was nervous about something. Again, Alyssa caught her husband's eyes, a question in her own. Again, he shrugged.

Finally, Holly settled, and blurted out, 'I was just wondering if you and Dad had decided anything yet. You know, about the Europe trip. Grandma called last night,' she said by way of explanation.

Damn Mabel, Alyssa thought, her good mood evaporating. What had started out as a pleasant surprise at seeing her daughter before she headed to the precinct, she was afraid, was about to turn into a rather *un*pleasant discussion.

Careful not to let her irritation at her mother-in-law show, she said, 'I've already told you Dad and I haven't decided. We're both very busy. Your father's working on getting the construction bid for the new hospital wing downtown, and I'm a bit embroiled in a missing person's case at the moment.' She tried to control her words, but it was too early for this. She already knew this conversation wasn't likely to end well.

She was right.

Holly made a show of checking the time on the microwave. 'You have twenty minutes right now, before you go to work. And like Grandma said, I'll need time to get ready.'

Teeth clenched more in frustration with *Grandma* than her daughter, Alyssa said, 'Yes, but it is the end of March, and the trip will be the first week of *June – if you go.*'

'You're also forgetting, Holly, that Grandma purchased *vouchers*, not tickets. So, the date is irrelevant at this point,' Brock added.

And then Holly did it – she pulled the age card and threw it down like a gauntlet. 'I'm eighteen. Legally, I can do anything I want, and you guys can't stop me. So, really, getting *permission* to go to Europe is just a courtesy.'

Though she'd been expecting it, Alyssa narrowed her eyes and carefully set her cup on the table. 'Be careful, Holly, before you draw that line in the sand. Yes, you're eighteen, though right now you're acting more like a thirteen-year-old who's been told she can't attend an adults-only party. But, even though you're legally an adult, you are still living in this house.'

Holly matched her mother's narrowed gaze. 'I could always go live with Grandma,' she snapped back.

A thunderous clap reverberated through the room as Brock's hand slapped down on the counter. 'Enough! We are tabling this discussion before one of us says *something else* we will regret.' To Holly, he pointed upstairs. 'Go. Because I can tell you, right now, with your attitude, I'm not feeling too charitable about anything, much less allowing you to go. And yes, I did say, allow.'

The urge to argue brewing in her eyes, Holly abruptly snapped her mouth shut, turned around, and stormed up the stairs, which was how they knew their raised voices had woken Isaac. His 'oomph' as his sister shoved past him filtered all the way into the kitchen.

'I probably shouldn't have told her she was acting like a thirteen-year-old,' Alyssa said, both hands cradling her head. 'But she blindsided me. Us,' she corrected.

'That she did. I'll call Mom today when I get a chance,' he said through gritted teeth.

At the mention of her mother-in-law, Alyssa gulped down the last of her coffee, pushed back from the table, and saw her son standing hesitantly in the doorway. She waited for him to say something, but when he stayed quiet, she walked over and pecked him on his cheek. 'Morning.' No sense in saying 'good' when it obviously wasn't. Then, holstering her gun, she kissed her husband, and said, 'Guess I'll head into the precinct early.'

—

An hour later, Alyssa sat at her desk, one hand absently rubbing circles around her right temple, as she stared blankly at the open file in front of her. With her free hand, she grabbed her coffee, raising it halfway to her lips before realizing it was empty and set it back down. She tapped the paper on her desk. 'I don't think seven is too early to call Mr. McCormick, do you?'

'Not if we want to inform him about his wife's car before the media gets wind of it,' Cord answered. He studied her for a minute. 'Still thinking about your argument with Holly, huh?'

Eyes closed, she mumbled, 'That obvious, huh?' To each other's surprise, they'd both pulled into the parking lot within a minute of each other, and one look at her face, and an 'uh-oh' from him was all it took before she admitted what had brought her in before six a.m.

'Kind of, yeah.'

'Well, hopefully,' she touched the screen on her phone to check the time, 'in twenty-one minutes and forty-seven seconds, this damn headache will be gone, and I'll be able to focus.'

But, twenty-five minutes later, her blood still pulsed rudely in her temples as she called Rafe McCormick.

When he didn't immediately answer, Alyssa didn't know whether to hope he would or wouldn't. She was mentally preparing a message to leave when he finally picked up.

'Hello.' The voice on the other end of the line was hoarse, desperate, and hopeful all rolled into one confusing breath.

'Mr. McCormick, this is Detective Wyatt. I'm calling —'

'Did you find Callie?' This time there was no mistaking the optimism in his words.

Alyssa's head tipped back as she stared at the ceiling, noticing the dirty tiles that were probably dropping all kinds of bacteria into the room. Could this day get any worse? And it was only seven a.m. 'I'm sorry to say we haven't, but —'

'Then what happened? Why are you calling?' Rafe demanded.

I'm trying to tell you if you'd let me complete a sentence, she thought before immediately feeling guilty. The man's wife was missing. He had every reason to be on edge. 'We've located your wife's car. It was down in El Paso, and the ELPD have agreed to transport it to Albuquerque so our technicians can look it over. It should be here sometime this morning.' She decided not to mention that the likelihood of the techs going over the car today was slim to none. No need to frustrate him more than he already was.

Quiet filled the air for so long that if it hadn't been for the simple fact she could hear Rafe breathing into the phone line, she would've thought he'd ended the call.

'El Paso? As in Texas?' He sounded confused. Then: 'What about Ca–Callie?' he asked, this time, fear coating his words.

Alyssa inhaled deeply and exhaled slowly. 'We're still looking.' She closed her eyes against the increasing pressure in her head, answering the best way she could. 'I assure you, Mr. McCormick, we're doing everything we can to locate your wife. We're following every lead that comes in.' *Including alien abductions and investigating 'suspected' shady financial deals with the mob.* 'These things take time.' As soon as it came out of her mouth, she regretted it, knowing she'd made a mistake but unable to take it back.

After explicitly reminding her that 'the police worked for him' and that 'his taxes paid their salaries,' and to 'do what they were effing paid to do,' Rafe ended the call.

Alyssa set her phone aside. 'Well, that went swimmingly,' she muttered. 'Tell me the day can only go up from here,' she begged.

'I would, but I don't want to lie to my best partner,' Cord said. 'Come on. I'll buy you another cup of poison before we attack more of these.' The ever-growing pile of 'leads' had been nicknamed 'Nemesis' and had been sorted into piles of *good, maybe,* and *no way* before being divvied up between the team members. Alyssa could've hugged Hal when he volunteered to contact the *no ways* in an effort to cut down on time they considered wasted.

That evening, still battling a headache now accompanied by a stomachache, Alyssa finished drying off the counter and folded the dish towel. Tired, frustrated, and just plain angry at life in general, she stared out the window. She'd arrived home at six thirty to a chilly reception from Holly, who immediately returned to her room after dinner. Brock was still working, massaging the numbers for his latest construction bid, and Isaac and his best friend, Trevor, were busy playing some complicated computer game she didn't understand.

Adding to her discomfort regarding her family's sudden chilliness was her inability to get anywhere with the McCormick case. Their technicians now had Callie's Jeep, but they had told her it could take several days before it worked its way up their very lengthy line. No amount of begging or whining budged the boys in the garage. She may have understood, but she didn't have to like it.

A bottle of red wine sat on the counter beckoning her, and she decided to indulge herself. But just as she reached for a glass, her phone rang. She cursed. Couldn't one thing go her way today?

Answering without checking the caller ID, she tried but failed to keep the snip out of her voice. 'Hello?'

'You'd better get back here quick,' Cord said. 'Some hikers came across a partially buried, barely alive female in the Jemez. I think it might be our girl.'

'How did you find out?' Alyssa asked, already moving to the gun safe where she'd automatically stored her weapon when she got home.

'Sara got caught up at the hospital with that wreck up on Nine Mile Hill, so I decided to go back and grab the McCormick file to see if I could figure out what we're not seeing. Call came in as soon I got there. Ruby passed it on to me.'

'On my way.'

She grabbed her keys and went into the living room where Isaac and Trevor were each sprawled across opposite ends of the couch, feet up on the coffee table. She didn't have time to be aggravated. 'I've got to head out again.' A distracted wave indicated her son had heard. 'Let your sister know if she ever comes out of her room.' This earned a thumbs-up, and then she was out the door, calling Brock as soon as she was in the car to let him know she wasn't sure when she'd be home.

Hope replaced irritation as she ignored the posted speed limits, squealing into the parking lot of the precinct in record time.

Chapter Nineteen

Thursday, March 28, 7:00p.m.

People jumped when the door slammed open, announcing Alyssa's arrival. Cord, interrupting the officer speaking to him met her partway across the room. 'I'll fill you in on the way. I'm driving.'

For once, Alyssa didn't argue about being the passenger. 'Where are we headed?'

'Rust Presbyterian Hospital.' Outside, he grabbed her arm. 'I'm this way.' When they reached the car, Alyssa had barely climbed in and buckled up before Cord hit the gas so hard, they both jerked forward, making her issue a silent prayer of thanks for seatbelts.

Pulling out of the parking lot, he took the corner too sharply, and she reached up to grasp the handle above the door to keep herself from bouncing around too much. 'Tell me what you have,' she said.

Cord flashed his lights at a slow-moving vehicle. 'All I know so far is a young couple found a badly beaten female, partially buried up in the Jemez Mountains, off the main trails. Said they were hiking when they practically tripped over a woman's arm sticking out of some brush.'

Alyssa raised her eyebrows, skeptical, and said, '*Hiking*? Is that what we're calling it these days?'

The faintest of smiles tipped the corner of Cord's lip up as he concentrated on passing a moving van. 'Yeah, well, hiking, making out, that's not really the point. Anyway, they started pulling leaves and twigs and branches off her.' He paused. 'She was nude.'

Alyssa closed her eyes. She would *not* think about her own past right now.

Cord swallowed before he added. 'And apparently bound at the ankles.'

'Christ,' Alyssa muttered. 'Why do we think it's Callie McCormick?'

'It might not be, but the description fits, despite all the cuts and bruises. Height and eye color match. Blonde hair, but with a large chunk apparently hacked off.' He risked a quick glance at her. 'Strawberry birthmark on her hip.'

'Has Mr. McCormick been notified?'

'Not yet. I thought we could call on the way. Plus, I wanted to let you know first.'

Alyssa nodded even though her partner couldn't see the movement. 'Who called? If they were deep in the mountains, they couldn't have had cell service.'

Cord navigated a turn before answering. 'They didn't. The couple, Jack Henderson and Trinity Davis, hightailed it back to their vehicle, and the second they had reception, called it in to the Jemez police.'

'You're telling me they found a barely alive beaten woman, and they *both* left her there – alone? Are you freaking kidding me?'

'It makes sense from a civilian's point of view,' her partner countered. 'They were both too freaked out to stay behind. Think about it. Wouldn't you be? And Henderson had absolutely no problem taking the officers back to the site. Said he hikes there all the time.' Alyssa didn't miss the emphasis on the word *hikes*.

'Turnaround time?' She asked.

'Total turnaround from finding the body to getting her to the hospital was a few hours.'

'So, they found her early this afternoon then?'

Cord nodded. 'Sounds like.'

'What's her condition?'

She knew she wasn't going to like his answer when he remained quiet. Finally, he said, 'Critical. It's not looking good.'

That made her decision both easier and more difficult. Normally, standard operating procedure dictated a uniformed officer be sent to the family's home – like they had when her family had suffered their loss – but in this instance, she was afraid they didn't have time. 'Let me notify Rafe McCormick. He has a right to know and to see her, especially if it might be his last chance to see her alive.' The words caused her throat to swell, and she swallowed several times before she trusted her voice to make the call.

'What if it's not her?' Cord asked, though she detected from his tone that he was pretty sure it was.

'Then he has hope for another day,' she said.

Unlike that morning, the phone was answered immediately, and she dove in, head first. 'Mr. McCormick, there's a slight chance it might not be her, but it's possible Callie's been located.' She held the phone away from her as he shouted out questions she couldn't understand. 'We don't know anything yet. Detective Roberts and I are headed to the hospital right now... Rust Presbyterian in Rio Rancho. Are you familiar with the area? ... Okay, we'll see you there. But, Rafe,' she addressed him by his first name to get his attention. 'Please brace yourself.'

'Well, that's done,' she said as she put her phone in the center console. 'Any ideas on how long she'd been there?'

'No telling. A couple of officers said she was dumped in a natural trench formed by all the rains this past fall.' Cord looked over at her. 'Hospital requested a couple of extra officers be on hand so they could post guards. No one's taking any chances at this point.'

'That's probably for the best,' Alyssa said. 'Where are the hikers now?'

'Jemez police interviewed them and sent them on their way after getting their contact information. We can talk to them when we finish up at the hospital.'

Thirteen minutes later, Cord swung into the hospital's parking lot. A car pulled out of one of the spaces near the front doors, and he whipped around the corner to stop a Ford Escape from beating him to it. The driver blasted his horn and gave him the one finger salute, shouting obscenities.

Alyssa stepped out of the car and flashed her badge. It was getting dark, but with the parking area lit up like a stadium, it was still light enough to see. The driver sped off. 'Hmm. Guess he had a change of heart,' she said. She heard the chirp of the remote as Cord locked the SUV's doors, and then they walked briskly into the hospital.

They approached the information desk situated in the center of the huge lobby and held up their badges. 'The woman found up in the Jemez?'

The blue-haired lady didn't need to look in the system to point the detectives in the right direction. Ever since the brutalized woman had been brought in, it had been all any of the volunteers could talk about.

Chapter Twenty

The beeping sounds and strange, medicinal odors nauseated Alyssa. That combined with the stark white walls and the continuous *beep, beep, beep* of the machines made her antsy, sending her reeling back to a time when she was still desperately trying to atone for the biggest mistake of her life.

She tried not to fidget as she and Cord stood in the corner and out of the way in the room with the person they believed to be Callie McCormick. The woman was hooked up to every conceivable contraption possible. Needles and tubes stuck out everywhere. Two nurses checked the woman's vitals and pushed some buttons on one of the monitors. The wet suction sound of the respiratory machine turned Alyssa's stomach.

It was hard to tell if the woman really was Callie – battered and beaten, she was nearly unrecognizable as a human. When they'd first approached the nurses' station, Alyssa had overheard some of the orderlies discussing fractured cheekbones, a broken wrist, cracked ribs, dehydration, and innumerable other issues.

They'd only been there a few minutes when a doctor, her red hair streaked with gray twisted into a severe bun, walked in.

Alyssa stepped forward. 'Doctor, I'm Detective –' The doctor ignored her outstretched hand and walked over to her patient. Alyssa's arm dropped back to her side as she moved back into the corner to wait.

'How's our patient doing? Any changes?' The doctor addressed the nurses.

'Nothing. Vitals are still weak, and her blood pressure is low. Her bandages have been changed, except for the ones on her feet which we are about to do, but those infected lacerations are still oozing. The swelling in her knee has gone down slightly, but the gouge in her thigh is red and hot to the touch.' The nurse – Ellen, according to her ID badge – looked uncomfortable as she stared at the detectives for a moment. Even though she knew they shouldn't be in the room, Alyssa held the woman's gaze until she turned away. 'After we palpated the abdomen to check for the possibility of a ruptured colon, we ordered that ultrasound you requested. The results should be on your computer by now.'

A look passed between the two before the doctor grabbed a clean pair of sterile gloves from the box mounted on the wall under the television and then pulled back the bottom corner of the sheet covering their patient. She used a metal instrument to peel back one of the bandages covering the woman's left foot, and beside her, Alyssa felt Cord recoil when he saw the damage.

Without looking up, the doctor addressed them. 'Detectives, you're going to need to step out while we examine my patient.' Then to the nurses, she said, 'Let's keep her as comfortable as possible and give the antibiotics time to kick in and bring this fever down. Right now, we need to tend to her feet and that broken nose. We'll proceed from there.'

Alyssa and Cord remained where they were.

'We have privacy laws for a reason, so unless you were able to miraculously obtain an unidentified woman's family's permission, I don't know how you two were even able to talk your way in here,' the doctor said with a cool voice as she finally faced them, 'but you will step out for a few moments.' She held up her hand to halt Alyssa's argument. 'Look, I know you want answers; we all do. I'll come talk to you as soon as I'm finished here. But right now, my priority is my patient.'

Cord grabbed Alyssa's arm before she could annoy the doctor. 'I saw a vending machine around the corner.'

Before the door closed, Alyssa overheard the doctor's softly spoken words. 'Well, young lady, we're going to do all we can, but you're going to have to do your part to help us help you, okay? Don't let whoever did this to you win.'

The door clicked behind them, but instead of heading for the junk food dispenser, they went into a special waiting room reserved for family members of intensive care patients. They found a couple of chairs far enough away from other people so they could talk without accidental or purposeful eavesdropping.

Cord leaned over, hands between his knees, head hanging low. 'Who *does* that to someone else? *Why?*' He sounded tired, almost defeated.

Almost exactly how her parents had sounded when… She shook her head, not allowing herself to be transported back to that dark place. Right now, she had a job to do, and the woman lying in that hospital bed had obviously been through hell and deserved Alyssa's full attention with no distractions. 'It doesn't matter how many years I do this, it always comes back to me questioning humanity.'

Nearly twenty minutes later, they heard a commotion outside near the nurse's station, and the two of them sprang up and headed out in time to see Rafe McCormick shove a technician out of his way as he barreled through the ICU doors, a security guard right on his heels.

'Sir, you can't be back here,' one of the nurses yelled.

Rafe ignored the man and skidded to a halt when he spotted Alyssa and Cord. 'Where is she? I want to see her!'

Cord grabbed a passing nurse, flashing his badge. 'Is there an empty room where we can talk privately to this man?'

'I don't want an empty room! I want to see my wife!' he shouted.

Alyssa spoke quietly, using a soothing tone in an attempt to calm Rafe's escalating anger. 'We don't know one hundred percent that it's her,' she said, even though she was as positive as she could be that it was. 'As soon as the doctor comes out to speak with us, we'll have you go in and ID her.'

'Why do I have to wait for the doctor?' he asked as he turned away. But when the security guard blocked his way, he turned back around. 'What the hell?'

'Mr. McCormick – Rafe – I know you're anxious to see if that's Callie, but,' she looked him straight in the eyes, 'you need to prepare yourself. The woman in there is in bad shape, and it won't be easy to see. Do you understand?'

Rafe flinched as if she'd slapped him.

'Excuse me?' A voice interrupted, and all three of them turned to see the doctor standing there.

'Detectives, I'm sorry I can't apologize for my earlier abruptness. Preserving our patient's integrity is of the utmost importance right now, whether she's aware of it or not.' She angled her body towards Rafe. 'And you are?'

'Rafe McCormick. That's my – I believe that's my wife – in there.' His face was two shades paler than when he'd arrived, and Alyssa had an urge to put her arm around him, to lie and tell him everything would be okay.

'I'm Dr. Homa,' she said as she extended her arm, shaking each of their hands with a firm, no-nonsense hold, and then nodding her head down the hall, she added, 'Why don't we go somewhere we can speak a little more privately?' At a door marked 'Employees Only,' she swiped her card to unlock the door, then stepped inside and waved them in.

'Thank you for taking the time to talk to us,' Alyssa said. 'I'm Detective Wyatt, and this is Detective Roberts.'

'Before we discuss anything, I'm going to need Mr. McCormick to positively ID our patient, and then if she proves to be his wife –'

'Callie. Her name is Callie,' Rafe whispered.

'And then if it proves to be Callie, we'll return here where we can speak in more depth.' To Rafe, she said, 'Sir, I overheard the detectives warn you about the condition of the woman lying in that hospital bed, but I need to reinforce that. Do you understand?'

After a long hesitation, Rafe, his body trembling, his eyes telegraphing fear, nodded.

'Then please follow me.' Before they went in, the doctor opened the door, blocking their view as she asked the nurses to leave for a few minutes in order to give them a little more privacy. 'Ready?' she asked Rafe.

'I'm ready.'

The three of them held back as Rafe approached the bed, his footsteps heavy and loud in the enclosed room. And, even though they'd suspected – *known* – it was Callie lying on that bed, the way he lurched forward, sobs clawing their way out of his throat as he lovingly and carefully caressed his wife's face, was all the confirmation they needed.

Alyssa felt the weight of it on her shoulders. 'Mr. McCormick, we need you to verbally confirm or deny that the woman lying in that bed is your wife, Callie McCormick.'

He didn't stop touching his wife's face. 'It's her. It's my Callie.' Then quietly, he asked, the words sounding strangled as they emerged, 'Was… was she… did they rape her?'

Dr. Homa stepped up and gently placed her arm on Rafe's. 'No,' she said firmly. 'But if you don't mind, I'd like to discuss her condition elsewhere. I'm a firm believer that our patients can hear us, subconsciously or consciously, even in a state such as your wife's.' When he resisted, she assured him, 'I promise to be as quick as I can so you can return to her as soon as possible.'

With a gentle kiss to Callie's forehead, Rafe agreed, and the four of them found their way back to the 'Employees Only' room once again, but this time, the doctor placed a 'Conference in Session' placard on the hook hanging outside the door. She glanced once at Alyssa and Cord, but then focused her attention on Callie's husband.

'Mr. McCormick, before we begin, I'll need your permission to speak freely in front of the detectives.' He agreed, and she continued. 'First, I'm sorry for what you're going through, but I'm going to shoot straight here.' She gestured and said, 'I've been on my feet all day, so if it's okay with you, I'd like to sit.'

Once everyone was situated around the table, she began. 'This is always the toughest part of my job, being honest and upfront with families. That being said, I don't want to tell you there's *no* hope, nor do I want to offer *false* hope.' Dr. Homa's eyes held steady as she said, 'Mr. McCormick, recovery is not looking promising. We're doing all we can, of course, but you saw her. We don't know how long she'd been in the elements, but we can estimate from her body temperature when she was brought in that it was likely anywhere from twenty-four to forty-eight hours, and some of those would've been in freezing overnight temps.'

She waited while everyone grappled with this bit of news. Then she said, 'You saw the blunt force trauma to her head and face, and the cuts and lacerations covering her body, especially her wrists and ankles where she was obviously… held in bondage… but I am afraid these are only a small part of what we're dealing with.'

Quiet sobs shook Rafe's body, and Dr. Homa slid a box of tissues over to him before she asked, 'Do you need a moment?'

He shook his head, the movement weak, and waved a trembling hand for her to continue.

'Most of her ribs are bruised, and some are cracked. The burns on her feet are badly infected, and we've started her on a very heavy regimen of antibiotics.' She paused, 'Does your wife have any allergies we should be aware of?'

'Mushrooms, but no medications.'

'Then we should be safe on that front. To continue: from the needle marks in your wife's neck, there's a strong possibility she was drugged. We should find out when the blood tests come back.' She paused to give everyone time to process what she'd said so far before she resumed, this time looking at the detectives. 'This is one of the worse cases of torture I've ever seen, and that's saying something.'

Dr. Homa removed her glasses and rubbed her eyes wearily as if she was struggling with what she was about to reveal.

When the doctor's voice softened, Alyssa's stomach tightened. How much more could Rafe McCormick handle before he completely broke down?

'I told you your wife wasn't raped, Mr. McCormick.' When his head shot up, eyes wide, she held up her palm. 'No, no. She wasn't. I didn't lie about that. But I am afraid to tell you that she lost the baby.'

A collective gasp bounced off the walls of the small room. 'Baby? My wife wasn't pregnant, Doctor.' The bewildered expression on his face was testament that he was being truthful.

If Alyssa hadn't been watching, she might've missed the slight drooping of Dr. Homa's shoulder.

'It's entirely possible your wife was unaware of her condition as yet,' she said. 'But, when one of the nurses felt an unusual hardness in her abdomen, I ordered an ultrasound, and the pregnancy was confirmed. The blood tests will back that up.' A heavy sigh preceded the doctor's next words. 'I'm very sorry, but I want to prepare you for the very real possibility that your wife may not wake from this ordeal, and even if she does, we don't know what kind of damage her brain has sustained.'

What Alyssa heard in the unspoken words was that, even if Callie survived, she may never be the same, mentally, emotionally, or physically. As the impact of that hit, failure filled her, magnified tenfold when Rafe finally collapsed onto the table, his enraged howls full of heartbreak. Before she could stop it, the memory of her mother's anguished cries, so similar to Mr. McCormick's, flashed through her mind.

When he finally lifted his head and stood, his movements slow, he said, 'Thank you, Doctor. I appreciate your candor. Now, unless there's more,' he choked on the last word, 'I'd like to go be with my wife.'

'That's all for now.' When he reached the door, Dr. Homa stopped him. 'I'm sorry, Mr. McCormick. But, despite the bad news, I swear we will be doing *everything* possible to keep your wife alive and get her healed.'

Rafe's head fell forward in acknowledgement, the only indication he'd heard, before he left the room.

As soon as the door closed behind him, Alyssa thanked the doctor.

She pushed back her chair and stood. 'You can thank me by catching whoever did this.'

'That's the goal,' Alyssa said, just before the doctor was paged over the loudspeakers.

PART TWO

119

Chapter Twenty-One

It was breaking all over the late-night newscast that Callie McCormick had been rescued from the Jemez Mountains, her body stumbled upon by hikers. Outraged, Evan pounded his head into the wall several times for making such a sloppy mistake. He knew it was the midazolam, that the amount he'd injected her with hadn't been enough to kill her.

This was all her fault! If she'd behaved the way she should've instead of constantly crying and begging, he wouldn't have had to get rid of her at all. He could even have forgiven her for her disgusting messes.

He should've tossed her in the river like he had the last one. Evan shook his head. No, that had been risky. Far too many potential witnesses with the growing homeless population down there. Besides, *should've* didn't matter. He hadn't, and now he had to live with the fallout.

You never were that smart. His adopted father's voice intruded in his thoughts, and his footsteps faltered, fingernails digging into his skin.

The voice was right. If only he'd taken the time to properly bury her, he knew she would've suffocated to death before ever being discovered. But anger had clouded his judgement every time he looked at her, the vomit still on her chin where it had dribbled that last time. So, instead of using the shovel he'd brought with him, he'd stumbled upon that trench far back from any of the regular hiking trails, tossed her in, and concealed her body with leaves and broken limbs from nearby trees, beating her once more for making him do this.

He resumed pacing and forced himself to think. There was no possible way she could lead the police to him. She couldn't identify him even if she could describe him. Besides, according to all the news reports, she'd been unconscious and in critical condition since she was brought in.

What if she wakes up, you fool! What then? This time the voice was so loud, he half expected his father to be looming over his shoulder, even though he knew that was impossible. He'd made sure of it.

For just a second, he considered breaking into the veterinarian's office down the road and stealing some of their pentobarbital, the medication they used to euthanize animals, and then sneaking into the hospital and administering a fatal dose to Callie. This time, he'd make sure he got the job done. He'd double what was needed. He'd triple it.

What about the police guards, and that husband who hasn't left her side since he arrived?

Frustrated with the voice as well as his carelessness, Evan pummeled his head with his fists and then chewed at his nails until they bled. Ever since that very first girl, he'd been meticulous, perfecting his technique along the way. 'Where were you then?' he shouted into the empty room, the pulsing behind his eyes threatening a severe headache.

And even though he fought against it, he couldn't help but remember that first time.

Ready for a change, he had decided to leave the muggy, humid, mosquito-infested Midwest. Uncertain where he wanted to go, he drove aimlessly, stopping whenever something drew his attention. During one of these stops he saw her. She walked past him with the sparkly bangles jingling on her wrists and long, blonde, braided hair bouncing against her back, and he felt a spark of something that was there and gone in the blink of an eye.

He approached her to talk, rage overtaking him when she blew him off, like courteousness was a foreign concept. Without thinking, he grabbed her, jamming his finger into her side as he dragged her along. She sucked in a breath and opened her mouth to scream, and he jabbed her harder, 'Make one sound, and I'll blow your bloody insides out all over this sidewalk!'

Unsure what had come over him; he knew only that he had to teach her a lesson for acting as if he didn't exist. But when they reached his car, he hesitated. He couldn't just shove her in the backseat, and he didn't have any rope, so he couldn't tie her up. Besides, that would look suspicious. His hesitation cost him because she began screaming and flailing her arms, scraping her wicked nails down the side of his face as she did.

Scared and taken off-guard, he punched her hard enough to knock her out, her head making a sick thud as it hit the cement. He left her there as he sped off, his heart racing, driving until he reached Tijeras, New Mexico, where he was forced to make a pit stop for gas, food, and tires. Something about the small village drew him in, and so as he waited for his car, he explored, and in doing so, knew he'd arrived at his destination.

Several weeks passed, and he stopped worrying about that girl, about being caught.

He got a job at a feed supply store in the canyon, and with that salary, along with the money left to him by the man who'd raised him, he purchased a lot and built his house.

Shortly after he'd moved in, he crossed paths with his second victim. Instantly drawn to her in a similar way as the first one, he planned his attack this time. Tuesday nights were slow, and he offered to stay and lock up for the night. Just before closing time, like clockwork, she came in.

She never knew what hit her.

Each night, he descended into his basement to tell her about the investigation, watching the terror as it played across her face. It made him feel powerful – even more so when the mystery of her disappearance remained unsolved, due in large part to the fact that the relatively safe village of Tijeras wasn't a big enough community to warrant closed-circuit surveillance cameras. And the feed store was a small, family-run *business that had been around for sixty years and had never seen a need for 'spying' on its own employees and customers. In the end, it had all been a matter of denying she'd ever been there that evening when the police came to question him, leading them to believe something had happened to her along the way.*

Eventually, frustrated when she refused to behave the way he imagined she would, he killed her.

He was wiser now, so although it was all Callie's fault, the fact was, he'd still screwed up. But the likelihood of anything coming from it was slim, and dwelling on it changed nothing. He'd just have to watch the morning news for any updates.

Chapter Twenty-Two

Friday, March 29

Alyssa slapped the button to shut up the annoying alarm. When continuous hitting didn't quiet the obnoxious sound, she cracked open one eye. Her cell phone screen was lit up with an incoming call. So, that was why she couldn't stop the incessant buzzing – because it was her phone. She checked the time – 5:37 in the morning. She'd only been home from the hospital two hours, asleep for one and a half.

The ringing stopped before she could answer, so she flopped back down. Brock's arms came around her, pulling her back into his chest. 'Who is it?' he mumbled sleepily.

She started to tell him she didn't know when the ringing started back up. 'Jus' ignore it,' her husband suggested groggily.

'Can't. Might be important,' she responded while simultaneously picking up the phone and swinging her legs to the floor so she could sit up. 'Hello,' she said around a yawn, wiping sleep from her eyes.

'Detective Wyatt?' The voice on the other end sounded exhausted but familiar.

She stood and moved away from the bed. 'Yes, this is she. Who's calling?'

'Detective, this is Dr. Homa. From Rust Presbyterian Hospital. I'm afraid I have some bad news for you. Callie McCormick succumbed to her injuries early this morning, about an hour after you and your partner left. Her husband was with her, which is a small comfort. He's still here now. He didn't answer when I asked if there was anyone I could call for him, so I'm contacting you as the lead investigator on this case.'

Alyssa felt a rush of anger at the unfairness of it all as she quietly closed the bedroom door so as not to disturb Brock. 'I know you said it was a strong possibility, a probability even, but I'd hoped you were wrong, that she'd be strong enough to overcome what happened to her.'

'As we all did. However, the strain on her body was more than she could handle, and there was some internal bleeding after all. Combined with the midazolam found in her system, she really didn't have much of a fighting chance.'

'Mid – what?'

'Midazolam. It's a very powerful drug that's often used as an anesthetic. We discovered it when the blood tests came back from the lab. To be honest, Detective, with the amount she had in her system, I'm amazed she wasn't dead when they brought her in.'

'How would someone get their hands on something like that, Doctor?'

'Well, now, I imagine that's something for you and your partner to figure out.' A heavy sigh drifted over the line. 'Though I can tell you this: with the internet and dark web and all those other frightening things out there, people can get their hands on just about anything they want with very little effort on their part.'

She was right about that. 'Thank you for the call, Doctor. I'll get dressed and head back over there right away. One more thing; do you know when she'll be sent over to the medical examiner for an autopsy?'

'Yeah, about that. Her husband pitched quite a fit, saying she's been cut up enough. I explained the purpose behind it, that his wife died from an egregious attack committed against her, and that the police are going to need to gather any evidence they can to catch the person who did this to her. He still didn't like the thought of it, but he said he did understand.'

Alyssa sighed, already feeling the beginnings of another headache. 'Okay, thank you again.'

'You're welcome. If you need to, please have me paged when you arrive. I should be here a few more hours at least,' Dr. Homa said before hanging up.

Alyssa wanted to throw her phone. Damn it. *Why, Callie, why couldn't you hold on at least long enough to tell us who did this to you?* she whispered as she walked down the hall. In the bathroom, she splashed water on her face. When she looked at her reflection in the mirror, she cringed. Her hair was a tangled mess, and mascara was smeared under her eyes because she hadn't bothered to remove it last night before collapsing into bed.

When she called Cord to break the news, his reaction was much the same as hers. After she hung up, she traipsed back upstairs to brush her teeth and take a quick shower. Fifteen minutes later, she was in the kitchen. She poured a cup of coffee and allowed herself a few small sips before heading out the door, the weight of failure heavier with every footstep.

–

At 6:42a.m. Alyssa greeted Cord in the hospital parking lot. 'I was able to get ahold of Liz and Hal. They said they'd head in and put a fire under the lab technicians to move Callie's car up the priority chain and dust it for prints. Hal's planning on contacting the medical examiner again to see about any potential DNA left at the scene. Were you able to get ahold of Tony and Joe?'

'I was. They said they'd meet up with the rest of the team.'

At the entrance, she said, 'I feel like we've overlooked something obvious that could've saved Callie McCormick.'

Cord placed his hand on her arm and held her back, pulling her out of the way of two elderly volunteers making their way inside. 'Lys, you know you can't think that way. You're the one who taught *me* that. Remember?'

She nodded.

'Besides, that's not going to help Mr. McCormick right now.'
Her shoulders dropped. 'No, you're right.'

They navigated the elevators and halls back to the intensive care unit, where they were told by the desk that Callie had been moved to the morgue. Just as Alyssa was about to request Dr. Homa be paged, she spotted Rafe coming from the room where his wife had died. He was hunched over, his hands hanging limply at his sides, as he stared at the floor instead of where he was going.

Despair and desperation were feelings she was once married to, and though she wished she could offer advice that would help him heal, she knew it was a road he would have to navigate in his own way.

'Mr. McCormick,' she said softly as she and Cord approached. His head jerked up, surprised to see them there. 'I'm so sorry.'

Red, puffy eyes drilled into the detectives, his voice breaking as he said, 'Yeah, well, if you'd done your job, you wouldn't have to be sorry, now, would you?' He knocked her shoulder as he moved past, seeming to shrink into himself with every step he took.

His words turned her stomach into a knot as nausea worked its way up her esophagus. She knew she deserved his reproach. She had failed. Reluctantly, she followed him through the doors, Cord beside her. In the elevator, Rafe leaned heavily against the wall, simply staring ahead with wet, dull eyes when he realized the detectives wouldn't be waiting for the next car.

Silence, like a damp, wool blanket, weighed heavily in the enclosed space, and Alyssa wanted to fill the air with promises of retribution and justice. But speaking now would likely ignite the flame burning inside the pressure cooker that was Mr. McCormick.

Seconds after the elevator doors opened, it exploded anyway when the three of them were greeted by a crowd of reporters shoving microphones into their faces, eager for the best angle and soundbite. Cord's arm shot out to separate the waves of bodies crushing in as Alyssa ordered everyone back.

But he was too late. A reporter she didn't recognize had pushed his way to the front of the mob of media vultures, stopping just shy of Rafe.

'Sir, is it true that your wife died from the torture she sustained? Can you tell us what you're feeling? Is it true she was raped? Tell us –'

Rafe's fist came up. At the same time, Cord used his full height to shove the offender away, a breath before Rafe's knuckles could make contact with the idiot's face.

His face mottled, nostrils flaring, Rafe snarled. 'Keep them,' he swung his arm wide towards the reporters, nearly hitting two who were dumb enough to stay too close, 'out of my face, and find the asshole who killed my wife and baby. Think you can manage at least that much, *Detectives*?' His fist, still clenched, rammed the space between the elevators. Shaking his hand, he stormed off, shoving anyone unfortunate enough to be in his way.

Every single second of it was caught on camera. Alyssa could already see the viral video that it would become, playing on every news outlet around the nation, as well as every social media site. In other words, this was about to turn into a circus.

The grieving husband no longer available, the reporters turned to Cord and Alyssa. 'Detectives, do you have any idea who did this?'

Yes, of course. It's just police procedure to let the bad guy get away with murder. 'An official announcement will be issued from the department later today,' she said, before forcing her way through, ignoring the shouted questions chasing after her.

'Damn vultures,' she muttered under her breath.

Chapter Twenty-Three

Friday, March 29

'We have breaking news this morning. Let's go ahead and cut over to Rust Presbyterian Hospital where Gabrielle Sanchez is standing by. Gabrielle, we understand that Callie McCormick has died? Is that right?'

'Yes, that's correct. We received an anonymous tip early this morning that Mrs. McCormick was unable to recover from the trauma inflicted upon her person. As you know, Callie was the wife of Rafe McCormick who owns The Espresso Grind cafés and who recently offered a $25,000 reward for information leading to his wife's safe return. We're waiting to speak to Mr. McCormick –'

A loud commotion behind her interrupted the reporter's words. The cameraman zoomed in. A reporter was shoved back before a man's fist could plow into his face. 'Keep them out of my face and find the asshole who killed my wife and baby. Think you can manage at least that much, Detectives?' The man punched a wall before storming off.

Evan hit pause on his DVR. *Baby?* He rewound and hit play. '... find the asshole who killed my wife and baby.' So, she really was pregnant.

Immediately, his body felt lighter with the release of tension that came with the knowledge of Callie's death. He was still processing his good fortune when another reporter shouted a question to the female detective, the cameraman zooming in on her as she tried to move past. A buzzing began in his ear, making it difficult to hear as another flicker reached out and grabbed him by the throat. *One little boy, staring at a basement door...*

His eyes glued on the detective, he shook his head to clear it and moved closer to the television as if by doing so, he could be closer to *her*. She was short and athletic-looking with long auburn-colored hair pulled back into a ponytail. As she pushed through the throng of people, she snapped a rubber band around her wrist. His head tilted to the side, he watched her, curious about the strength of the spark she'd elicited.

An overpowering need to know about her swamped his thoughts. But first he needed to drive into Albuquerque. The shops near the main police station on 4th and Roma were great places to pick up on rumors surrounding breaking news. And as soon as Gabrielle Sanchez cut back to the studio, he jumped into his car and headed downtown where, in a spur of the moment decision, he whipped into The Espresso Grind, his heart thumping wildly at the knowledge that he would be just another face in the crowd.

Inside, customers and employees alike huddled together in groups, already whispering about the tragedy, exchanging theories ranging from too close to home to outright ludicrous. Several times, he had to battle his urge to tell someone what he *knew*.

And then someone mentioned *her*, the female detective. *Alyssa Wyatt*. Like he had with Callie, he rolled her name around in his mind. It wasn't as smooth as Callie McCormick's, but it still drew him in. He made his way to the counter where he ordered a coffee he didn't really want, but it got him that much closer to the person talking about his interview with the detective.

'Of course, I didn't mind talking to her as long as I got to ogle her partner. That man was yummier than a hot fudge sundae on a summer day.'

Annoyed, Evan bit back the urge to snap at the man to get back to the detective. But, once on the topic of the hot partner, neither individual seemed inclined to discuss anything else. So, he left his untouched coffee on the counter and walked outside, ignoring the barista as she yelled after him that he'd forgotten his drink.

Outside again, standing on the sidewalk, he was drawn to the tall, adobe building that housed the main police station a mere block away. Warmth infused his blood as he fought the impulse to waltz in and look around. *Are you stupid? Is that it?*

He froze, looking around, realizing he was standing on the steps leading into the station. He'd been so focused on the possibility of seeing *her*, he hadn't noticed he was moving. He remained where he was until he spotted three officers heading his way. He turned and walked back down the steps, forcing himself to walk normally back to his vehicle. He drove to two more cafés before he bored of hearing the same gossip and headed home, anxious to learn more about this Detective Alyssa Wyatt. As he drove, he softly sang her name as if it were the lyrics to his favorite song.

In the privacy of his own home, he booted up his computer, forcing himself to begin with the detective's partner. He typed in the man's name, and a few clicks later, discovered all he cared to know. Cord Roberts, married three years to his high school sweetheart, no kids and no social media accounts he could find, though his wife had a private one. One article featuring his heroic efforts to save a young girl from jumping included his photograph, and he understood why the guy in the coffee shop had been so over the moon; Roberts looked like he should model for *GQ* magazine.

Palms clammy, he finally moved on to Alyssa Wyatt. His pulse accelerated and sweat dripped off his forehead as he entered her name in his search engine. None of the other women had elicited such a powerful response, and he was anxious to know about her.

Forty-two minutes later, he thrust his mouse away from him. Finding information on the detective outside of her cases was difficult, and his temper bubbled just below the surface, one click away from boiling over.

He stood and paced, mumbling to himself. And then it came to him, and he rushed back to his computer, navigating to a site he'd learned about long ago. He typed in her name, city, and state, leaning in closer as he waited for the results to appear. Less than one minute later, multiple prospects popped up, and he scrolled through, deleting any whose names were not a match or whose ages weren't close. That left him with two possibilities, so he opened the first one, paid the fee for the full report, and waited for the page to load. And hit pay dirt on his first try. A phone number, address, aliases used, something he assumed was a maiden name, and several possible relatives flashed in front of him. Disappointed no photo accompanied the information, he closed out the window and opened another, this time typing in *Alyssa Archer*. Thousands of results filled his screen, and methodically, he began opening and scanning each one.

Until one caught his attention. Eagerly, he clicked on the article, sitting on the edge of his chair as he began to read.

Chapter Twenty-Four

A sharp knock on the conference room door was all the warning they had before it opened. To everyone's surprise – and Alyssa's immense relief – Ruby walked in, pushing a cart filled with sandwiches from Jason's Deli, cookies, a platter of fruits and vegetables, along with coffee, sports drinks, and bottled water. If she'd thought she could get away with it, Alyssa would've hugged the normally grumpy lady.

'Ruby, you're just a gem,' Hal said as he rolled over to the cart, earning himself a glowering eye-roll from the precinct secretary.

'Well, that's original,' Ruby groused. 'Certainly never heard that one before.'

Rounds of gratitude were uttered as the tray was attacked with gusto. Cord, bless him, grabbed the coffee carafe, poured her a cup, and set it and the entire carafe in front of her. He knew her so well. Why did she ever think she'd miss her old partner, Ellie? Ellison had never indulged her passion for caffeine.

Carefully, she moved the files to the side so she wouldn't make a mess on them. After everyone else had grabbed some food, she approached the cart and randomly grabbed a sandwich, chips, and kiwi. But when she went to take a strawberry, an image of Callie and her strawberry birthmark filled her head, her shoulders dropping as she was reminded of her failures.

The day had begun with Callie's death, and had seemed to go downhill from there. As soon as she and Cord had left the hospital, Alyssa's phone had rung. It was one of the lab techs calling to let her know the partial fingerprint lifted from Callie McCormick's shattered phone had been unusable. *Of course. Why should anything go her way so she could solve this case?* she thought sarcastically.

For the next five minutes, no one spoke as everyone shoveled food in. Finally, Alyssa turned to Hal. 'Before Liz continues with what she was saying, I'd just like to know if you really do have a death wish.' At his blank look, she cocked her head toward the closed door.

Hal laughed. 'Oh, you mean Ruby? I'll get that woman to smile one day if it's the last thing I do,' he said.

'Yeah, well, it just might be the last thing you do if you're not careful.' Alyssa turned to Liz. 'Go ahead with what you were about to say.'

'Before she does, I'd like to tell you we finally got Callie McCormick's cell phone records, not that it does us any good,' Joe interrupted. 'Most of the calls are to and from the charities she volunteered for, the Mitchells, and her husband. Same for text messages.' He pushed the document over to Alyssa. 'In other words; there's nothing there that might help us.'

'Thanks, Joe. Okay, Liz. Go on.'

Liz looked to Hal, and he nodded for her to go ahead. 'Well, like I was saying before Ruby came in, there was something about Callie McCormick's picture that was making my neck itch. I tried to blow it off as something as simple as a similarity to someone I'd sketched in the past. And then it hit me, the reason why she looked so familiar, and I called Hal to help me do some research. Hal?'

He swallowed his food and washed it down with his sports drink before he began. 'Do you remember back about fifteen years ago, that woman in the canyon who went missing?' He pulled out the newspaper article that had featured the case back then and slid it over to Alyssa. 'Evelyn Martin, twenty-five years old, headed to the Old Country Feed Store in the canyon like she did every Tuesday night. Except this time, she never returned home, seemingly disappearing into thin air. Her car was found abandoned on Route 66 with a flat tire, and her purse and phone were missing.'

Liz chimed in. 'When the police pulled her phone records, she hadn't called anyone, so their forefront theory was that someone happened along and offered to give her a ride.'

Hal picked up again. 'Shortly after she was reported missing, there was a hard rainstorm which washed away any potential evidence, including footprints. Case went cold after a year when all leads trickled and then stopped altogether.'

He thumbed through some papers in front of him. 'I took the liberty of pulling the original police report and requesting the file from that investigation, including a list of every suspect questioned and cleared.' He passed that along the table, as well.

When it reached Joe, he grabbed it, walked to the copier that had been brought into the room earlier, and made copies for everyone.

'It wasn't my case, but I remember it, though I'm not sure how it pertains to Callie McCormick or her death.' They'd met up with the rest of the team as soon as they left the hospital, and Alyssa was beginning to feel the effects of functioning on less than two hours' sleep.

Liz chimed in. 'Look at her description: petite, long, blonde hair.'

Alyssa pursed her lips, one eyebrow raised, as she glanced sideways at Cord. She had an idea where her favorite forensic artist was going with this, and her fatigue made her want to shout, *We're wasting time!* 'I assume you'll make your point soon?'

Hal handed another photograph over to Cord who studied it before passing it to Alyssa, his face revealing nothing.

'Jill Lawry went missing ten years ago,' Hal continued.

Alyssa nodded. 'Also, not my case, but I remember her. Still unsolved, correct?'

This time, Liz nodded eagerly as she said, 'Yes. But her body was found somewhere up in the Sandia's a few months after she was murdered.'

Cord jumped in. 'Let me guess: long, blonde hair, petite, young?'

'Look, I know what you two are getting at, but there are an awful lot of young women with long blonde hair in the Southwest.'

'Hold up,' Hal said. 'There's more.' He rustled through his pages and pulled out a stack of newspaper articles and photographs, tossing them into the center of the table. To Anthony, he said, 'Mind laying those out?'

As Officer White did as he was asked, Hal rattled off names. 'Mary Terra, Alice Winslow, Debra Hyatt. All went missing. None of them found. All of them –'

'Young, long-haired, blonde...' Alyssa interrupted, her stomach tight as she could no longer deny an emerging pattern. Still, what her teammates were suggesting was...

'Not to mention they all share the same heart-shaped facial structure,' Liz said, causing Alyssa to shift her eyes quickly toward her partner as she thought back to how he had commented on the resemblance between Callie and herself, and how she hadn't really seen it, aside from the heart-shaped face.

Liz was still speaking, so she forced her mind back to what her teammate was saying. 'Hal and I ran a state-wide search to see if there were other similar cases,' Liz said. 'In Cloudcroft, Rhonda Dupres and Sandra Jackson went missing within two months of each other. I called down there – did you know your old partner, Ellie, has been promoted to the entire southern district's cold case files?'

Alyssa nodded. 'I'm aware. Go on.'

Liz spoke faster as she became more excited. 'I spoke with Ellie, and she pulled up their electronic files. She said the resemblance between the women was so strong, they could've been sisters.'

'I think I remember that one, too,' Tony said. 'I was in Cloudcroft on vacation when Sandra went missing. I called you about it, remember, Joe?'

Joe scratched his head. 'Is she the one whose bones were found a few years back not far from your dad's cabin?'

'That's the one.' Tony stood and scanned the photos now scattered in the middle of the table.

A clicking sound filled the air as Cord used his laptop. A few minutes later, he turned it around for everyone to see. A collage of the women's pictures filled the screen, including Callie McCormick's. Two – now three – of the women pictured had been found dead, bound, badly beaten, and tortured. None of their killers had been caught. If what Liz and Hal proposed was correct, that meant there were at least eight women who'd been killed by the same person.

Her brain shied away from the reality of what they were looking at, but she couldn't escape what was right in front of her. But thinking and admitting it were two very different things. Verbalizing it was like willfully bringing on a bad omen.

It was Cord who did it. 'Think it's time we call the captain in. If there's *any* possibility we have a serial killer on our hands – one who's been getting away with it for at least fifteen years – we need to get on this quick.'

A sour, acidic taste in the back of her throat, Alyssa stood. 'No time like the present,' she said, noticing her teammates' faces; a mixture of relief they weren't the ones having to break the news to Captain Hothead and empathy that she was. Each step closer to Hammond's office made the pressure behind her eyes pulse.

Just outside his door, Cord came up beside her. 'You forget we're partners; you don't have to do this alone,' he said.

The captain's door was open, and Alyssa tapped on the glass before walking in. Cord followed, closing the door behind him.

Hammond's eyebrows shot up as he stood and walked around his desk, making the room smaller. 'If we need privacy, I'm not going to like whatever it is you're here to tell me.'

137

Alyssa wondered if it was a conscious or subconscious decision on the captain's part to intimidate by shrinking the amount of available space in a room. Not wanting to be in there any longer than necessary, she cut to the chase. 'We don't have concrete proof yet, but we may be looking for a serial killer.'

She kept her mouth shut as the captain spit out a string of colorful curses. When he'd finished, he said, 'Serial killer is an awful big label to be throwing around, so you'd better have good reason.'

When Cord handed him a copy of the images he'd shown the team, Hammond studied the pictures while they took turns detailing what the team had uncovered. He glanced up, eyes drilling first into Cord's, then Alyssa's before stating the same objection Alyssa had put forward earlier. 'Awful lot of young, blonde-haired women in Bernalillo County.'

'The victims were scattered throughout several counties, not just Bernalillo, sir,' she said. She moved so she could see the women's faces. 'These two,' she tapped on the images of Rhonda Dupres and Sandra Jackson, 'went missing in Cloud-croft in 2013. Rhonda's body was never recovered, though, according to the report Hal dug up, blood found at the scene of her disappearance indicates foul play. Of course, her family insists she had everything going for her and no reason to up and disappear.' She moved her finger over. 'Sandra Jackson's body, or rather, her bones, were discovered in 2016. You might recall; it was on the news.

'Jill Lawry lived in Valencia County, but her body was found in 2009 – that was just before you moved here, I believe – in the Sandia Mountains, not too far from the Sandia Cave.'

'Sandia Cave? Isn't that the back road through Placitas up to the Crest?' Hammond asked, moving back behind his desk where he stood near the window looking out to downtown.

'That's the one,' Alyssa said, almost adding he should drive it and visit the cave soon since he'd lived in Albuquerque nearly ten years now. But then she looked at his bulky frame and decided maybe it wasn't a good idea to suggest the captain crawl around in a dark, enclosed cave.

'Christ,' he swore as he tapped his steepled fingers together. Finally, he said, 'There's enough there to explore, I'll admit that. But not enough to go public and create mass hysteria,' he decided. Then, glaring at the detectives, he said, 'I don't like thinking there's been a serial killer lurking about on my watch.'

Alyssa fought the urge to roll her eyes. *You think we do?* 'Trust me, sir, neither do we.'

'Grab anyone else you need for your team, and then I suggest that you catch this person. Preferably yesterday.'

As if that wasn't everyone's primary goal. 'Yes, sir, we're working on it.'

Hammond waved them out. 'Work harder,' he demanded, just before he slammed the door behind them.

'Well, that went well, I think,' Alyssa muttered.

Chapter Twenty-Five

Friday, March 29

Lips pressed together, Evan wrestled with his emotions as he reread two of the articles he'd found, shaking his head. His brows pulled in and he rubbed the middle of his forehead as flashes of memory swam in and out of focus. *Two little boys huddled together. A floor – the kitchen? – blood everywhere. Pain, so much pain.*

–

Friday, August 12, 1983

Grim Discovery Found at Home that Burned to the Ground – Neighbors are Asking: Could it be the Missing Children?

Upon entering the burned-out shell of a home located on Ohio Street, firefighters stumbled upon nearly a dozen bodies in several enclosures in the basement of the home. Due to the size of the remains, the bodies are believed to be those of young children – which leaves families here wondering – could these be the remains of some of the missing children?

Police and firefighters search for answers to the startling and grisly discovery they encountered while attending to a fire that broke out in the Ohio St. neighborhood Friday night around eleven p.m. According to witnesses, the home was already fully engulfed in flames by the time emergency crews arrived on the scene.

Captain Joe Harvey reported that rescue workers, despite believing that 'no one could've survived flames that hot,' searched through the rubble for possible survivors who may have been home. *Harvey refused to comment at this time as to what may have caused the fire.*

The home belongs to the Brim family but is currently rented out to truck driver Carl Freeman, who was not believed to be home at the time of the fire and could not be reached for comment.

Police are asking the community for help in locating Mr. Freeman, but Sheriff Ryan Daniels stressed, 'Mr. Freeman is **not** a suspect at this time. Right now, we just want to make sure he's safe and ask him some questions.'

—

Evan ran his palms over his head as he repeatedly paced from one end of his kitchen to the top of his stairs. Several images fluttered in his mind, but the one that flashed most was that of two little boys huddled together.

One hand reached up to pull at his ear while the other scratched at his cheek. He wished his father was here so he could ask him… what? What could he ask him? He didn't even know.

Back in the kitchen, too fidgety to sit, he remained standing as he read the second article.

—

Tuesday, August 16, 1983

Ohio Home a Torture Chamber?

As investigators continue to delve into the mystery of what exactly happened at this Ohio Street home, more disturbing information is coming out.

Police have uncovered what appears to be a torture chamber in the basement of the deceptively serene-looking home found on this quiet Ohio street in Indiana. Lead detective, Glenn Reed, said, 'In all my years as an investigator, I've never seen anything like this. These children, if that's who they were, were kept chained inside tiny little enclosures in the basement. It appears there was a slot for food and water to pass through, but not much room to move around. I've seen dogs that've had bigger spaces.'

Police and neighbors are wondering how something like this could have taken place in this small community without anyone noticing or suspecting. Authorities warn it could still be several weeks before the identities of the bodies are known, but they are working as quickly as they can.

We tried to get a statement from the Archer family since this discovery follows so closely on the heels of little Timmy Archer's body being discovered, but they declined an interview, saying they 'just want to be left alone to grieve.' The question, however, begs to be asked; could Timmy Archer have been one of Carl Freeman's victims, also?

—

Eyes burning with unshed tears, Bishop threw the offending pages across the room with a howl. Full of manic energy as he teetered on the edge of a mental cliff, he snatched his keys and went for a drive.

Chapter Twenty-Six

Just before nine o'clock on Friday night, Alyssa sat on her couch surrounded by old newspaper articles, punishing herself as they brought up the same feelings of rage and inadequacy she'd felt in the past when she couldn't save her brother, and now magnified by her failure to save Callie. And if Liz and Hal were right, they weren't the only ones she'd failed.

One hand covered her mouth as she stared down at the image of Timmy playing outside on his bike. Gently, her finger traced down his face, remembering when this picture was taken – it was his first time without training wheels, about a month before he was kidnapped. Visible beneath the picture were the articles that had given her nightmares for so long, their blurbs a nonstop neon light flashing in her memory.

June 1983: Four-year-old LaPorte County boy fifth to go missing in two months. Families fear for the safety of their children. What are authorities doing to stop these kidnappings? How are the authorities protecting the people of these small towns?

August 1983: Badly decomposed body found partially buried in the woods. Authorities are trying to determine how long the child's body had been in a location that was thoroughly searched by both officials and volunteers.

August 1983: The body found dumped in the woods has been identified as that of Timothy Archer, aged four. Although the body was badly decomposed, his parents were able to identify him by his clothing, Chicago Bears baseball cap, and the bike found near his body.

Alyssa sank deeper into her chair, the familiar pressure building in her chest as she repeated the same mantra she'd been repeating for nearly thirty-six years. *You were just nine years old; it wasn't your fault.* But with her wounds reopened, and the scars torn apart, she was plunged back to that day when her life was irrevocably changed; the day Timmy was ripped from their lives, murdered by a child killer who was never found and never brought to justice.

-

The humidity was high, and the mosquitoes were swarming, thick as the pea soup she hated. She was so thirsty. She yelled to Timmy that she was going in to get some grape Kool-Aid and asked if he wanted any. He told her no; it wasn't strawberry. She told him she'd be back in just a minute. She was wrong. Inside, she washed her hands, then splashed cold water on her face to cool off. She poured a small cup of Kool-Aid and gulped it down before pouring another.

When she finally came back out five, maybe ten minutes, later, Timmy was gone. At first, she thought he was hiding. He liked to hunker down in the bushes or in the trees or around the corner and then jump out and scare her. Once, he even hid under the porch steps, and when she walked by yelling his name, he grabbed her ankle, tripping her.

As she fell to the ground, she accidentally kicked him in the nose, breaking it, she was sure. There was blood everywhere, and both of them were in hysterics.

Alyssa shook her head, trying not to drown in the memories, but in a tidal wave, they dragged her back under, holding her hostage as they crashed over her.

They had screamed for their parents who had come running around the corner, stopping dead in their tracks when they saw the mess. Alyssa remembered thinking at the time that her parents looked like a cartoon, the way they skidded to a halt. On the way to the hospital, Alyssa, through tears and hiccups and in between begging Timmy not to die, explained what had happened.

Luckily, Timmy's nose had not been broken, but he had required eight stitches for the clobbering it took.

She'd thought Timmy would have learned his lesson from that incident, but no, he continued with his pranks, delighting in new and inventive ways to scare his big sister.

So, on this fateful Saturday in June, at the beginning of their summer break, Alyssa went searching for her baby brother, trying not to be irritated. After all, she was nine now, too old for playing hide-and-seek with a four-year-old. It was just exasperating. She tried the new grown-up word on her tongue. She'd heard Timmy's preschool teacher use that word to describe his in-school antics, and though Alyssa didn't know what it meant, she knew it sounded like a smart word – and she used it every chance she got.

She used it in different ways as she scoured the yard and street for Timmy. Spaghetti for dinner? Exasperating. Wash your hands before eating? Exasperating. No dessert unless you clean your plate? Waaaay exasperating.

Twenty minutes of wiggling around under the crawl space, in the cellar, and looking up in the trees turned up no Timmy. Alyssa forgot about her new fun word; she was beginning to get scared for real. Could he have ridden his bike down the trail and landed in the water? Did he fall somewhere and hit his head? Had Jason found him and somehow taken him? (She knew she wasn't supposed to watch scary movies, but her babysitter let her watch Friday the 13th because she was so busy making out with her boyfriend that she didn't want to take the time to put Alyssa back in bed.)

Alyssa, really frightened now, finally decided she needed to tell her parents Timmy was gone.

Mama and Daddy searched what seemed an awful long time, no one wanting to believe it wasn't just another of Timmy's pranks. Anxious but trying to remain calm, Mama finally called the police to report Timmy missing.

The police came to the house and questioned Alyssa repeatedly, getting all their facts straight, they told her. She was afraid she would be in trouble for staying in the house too long, but the nice policeman told her she didn't do anything wrong. But if she hadn't gone inside, would Timmy be gone now? She didn't think so.

Two officers stayed in the house and talked to the family while two others searched the nearby woods beyond the house. No Timmy, and not even Timmy's bike. It was as if he had turned into a ghost and vanished into thin air. One minute he was there, and the next he was gone. Poof.

And as scary as that was, it wasn't until Alyssa looked into her daddy's eyes that she became truly alarmed that something was definitely wrong, something very bad had happened. Something that would change their lives forever. Her big, strong daddy who could fix anything and make everything better sat on the couch, shaking, tears in his eyes, shock on his face. She watched her parents sitting on the very edge of the sofa, rocking back and forth, looking lost, as they listened to the officers drone on about procedures that didn't make sense to her little mind.

At one point, Daddy went to the mantle and pulled down a picture frame. He pulled out a picture of Timmy and handed it to one of the officers. Alyssa thought Daddy looked like a robot, his movements were so mechanical. The officers took the picture and wrote down Timmy's physical description along with what he was wearing, and the make and color of his bike.

Nearly six weeks later, it was Timmy's Chicago Bears baseball cap the hikers first noticed.

They hadn't wanted to believe the body was Timmy's, but his clothes, his cap, and the bike found nearby made it difficult to deny. She watched all her mother's hope drain away at the realization that her little boy would never be coming home again. Alyssa watched the light and happiness that was her mother dissolve, leaving in her place a walking shell of a woman.

Before Timmy's body was found, Mama swore she didn't blame Alyssa, that it wasn't her fault. She told her that every night after Alyssa took her bath, when she tucked her in. But it didn't matter what Mama or Daddy thought because she knew her little brother would still be here if she just hadn't gone in for the Kool-Aid. If she had only insisted on Timmy playing in the backyard. If only, if only, if only.

It never occurred to her that Mama blamed herself.

As a teenager, Alyssa would think of the day of Timmy's funeral as the day they physically buried Timmy and emotionally buried Mama, who was distant and emotionless. Anger and blame would have been easier to handle. Instead, it was like living with a zombie. Mama couldn't be bothered to care about anything Alyssa did or didn't do. Daddy was only slightly better.

Within a week of Alyssa graduating high school, Mama died – the doctors said it was a heart attack – and two weeks later, Daddy followed suit, leaving her truly lost and alone.

–

The memory crashed over her like an avalanche, burying her, and leaving her just as cold, each mental image of Timmy sawing away at her composure. She leaned her head back wishing she had some ibuprofen as she fought back her stampeding emotions.

She didn't realize Brock had returned from the store until he sat down beside her. She cocked open one eye, and God bless the man, he had his hand out, palm up, holding three Advil. A glass of water resided in his other hand.

'You're a miracle-working mind reader, you know that, right?' She sat up and popped the pills in her mouth, swallowing them down with the water.

He indicated the pile surrounding her. 'Want to talk about it?'

'Not particularly.' A fuzzy green blanket was draped over the back of the couch, and she pulled it onto her lap, the chill in her heart making the rest of her cold, as well.

'When you weren't home in time for dinner, I made a plate for you. Let me go heat it up. I'll be right back,' he said, already standing.

Guilt creeped in and jumped on the pile to join regret and grief. 'I can heat it up myself,' she said.

Brock pushed her back. 'I know you can. But, so can I. Be right back.'

She didn't argue. Brock was a good husband, good father, hard worker, fierce and loyal. All the things her father had once been. She gave herself a mental shake as she struggled not to fall back into the memories.

She smelled the lasagna before she saw it. Her mouth salivated, and her tummy grumbled right on cue. The microwave dinged, the silverware jingled, and then the most mouthwatering food she'd seen in days was placed in front of her. She sank her teeth into a cheesy, gooey bite and moaned in pleasure when her taste buds exploded with excitement.

Brock laughed. 'I'm glad you like it,' he said as he sat beside her, rubbing small circles on her back as she ate.

Halfway through, she slowed, feeling satisfied but not yet full. 'I may have to keep you awhile longer. Who needs Will Smith anyway?' She leaned into him and kissed his whiskered cheek. 'I love you,' she whispered.

'I know.' Again, he waved his hand over the pile of papers. 'Since Holly is at Sophie's and Isaac's at Trevor's, I'm going to ask again. Do you want to talk about things?'

'No. Yes. No. I don't know. It's not like Callie McCormick is the first victim I've had die, but for some reason, I can't shake the feeling that I failed her.' Her voice cracked, warning her husband she was on the brink of an emotional collapse.

He continued massaging, moving his hands up to her neck and shoulders. 'Is that why you have all this out?'

He knew her so well, she didn't need to answer.

'This wasn't your fault,' Brock said, and Alyssa wondered if he meant Timmy or Callie. Either way, he was wrong.

'Did I ever tell you I saw the crime scene photos?' The words were out before she knew she was thinking them.

Her fists tightened, as did her posture when he wrapped his arm around her and leaned them both back, gently pushing her head into the crook of his neck. 'Tell me now,' he said softly.

'They weren't the actual crime scene photos. And I wasn't supposed to see them. Shortly after Timmy's funeral, I took out the trash for my dad. The newspaper was soggy and covered in potato peels, kind of shoved deep into the corner of the garbage bag, like someone was trying to hide it.' She paused for a moment. As an adult, she marveled at the metaphor of feeling like trash that had been shoved aside. At the time, though, she was just curious.

'I made sure Daddy wasn't watching.' A sad laugh escaped. 'I should've known he wasn't. Neither of them watched me again, though Dad pretended for a bit. Anyway, I knew Mama wouldn't be watching because she wouldn't even get out of bed to take a shower most days.' She closed her eyes, letting it all play back as if she were living it all over again. 'There was a grainy picture, and at first, I wasn't sure what I was seeing. Then I realized it was a picture of the spot where Timmy had died – or at least where he was found.'

Her tears went unnoticed until the taste of salt touched the corner of her lip a second before Brock's thumb wiped it away. Unable to go on with the unbearable guilt crushing her from the inside out, she closed her eyes and cried as the thought that several missing women might be connected to one killer added to the sheer weight of what she could only see as failure on her part to save not only Timmy, but now Callie, as well.

Chapter Twenty-Seven

Alyssa stood at the stove, her nose stuffy from a night of crying, the past couple of days replaying on a continuous loop in her brain. More than once, she was snapped back when the sizzling bacon grease splattered her arm. The third time it happened, she turned the heat down, and walked to the sink to run cold water on the burn. At the same time, Holly slid up to her and put her head on her mom's shoulder.

'I'm sorry I was such a brat the other day. It wasn't fair, especially since I know you've got this case… I heard she died. I'm sorry about that, too,' she whispered.

Alyssa turned and hugged her daughter. 'Thank you. And I'm sorry, too. I shouldn't have told you that you were acting like a thirteen-year-old.'

Holly stepped back and grinned. 'No, you shouldn't have. But, I kinda was, wasn't I? And you don't need to answer that, by the way.' She tilted her head toward the stove. 'Want some help with breakfast?'

'I'd love it,' Alyssa said, her heart swelling. God, she loved her kids. Sure, they could be typical teenagers once in a while, but overall, she was blessed with wonderful, courteous children. She'd keep 'em.

Picking up the spatula that her mom had tossed down, Holly said, 'I'm surprised you're not at the precinct.'

'I'm going in later, but I'll work from home for a while first. I was hoping to have breakfast with everyone this morning, but

Dad had to run to the office to grab his files on that construction bid and won't be back until later, so I guess it'll just be you and Isaac.'

As if on cue, her son came stumbling into the kitchen, serious bedhead exploding around his face.

'Good morning, sleepyhead,' she greeted him.

Something resembling a grumble Cookie Monster could be proud of and a *good morning* spilled from his mouth as he opened the cupboard and reached for a pop tart. She ruffled his hair on the way to refill her coffee cup. 'In case you didn't notice, we're working on a bit of a better breakfast here than those things,' Alyssa said.

Isaac popped his first course of breakfast into the toaster, turned the knob to 'dark' and slumped at the table while he waited. He wiped sleep from his eyes as he answered. 'I'm a growing boy. I can eat both.'

When the pop tarts were ready, Alyssa deposited them on a plate before adding eggs and two slices of bacon. She repeated the same for Holly without the pop tarts, and set both plates down, along with freshly squeezed orange juice.

Both Holly and Isaac thanked her, and as they ate, she poured herself another cup of coffee. 'Aren't you having any?' Holly asked, eyeing her mother's mug. 'How many cups does that make?'

Sometimes Alyssa thought her daughter and her partner got together and planned attacks on her caffeine addiction. 'I'm not hungry right now; my stomach's a little queasy,' she admitted. When Holly gave her mug a pointed look, she laughed. 'It's not because of the coffee. And besides, this is only my third cup.'

'Yeah, third cup of your tenth pot,' Holly deadpanned.

Coffee-addiction guilt trip aside, Alyssa felt lighter as she sat at the table with her children, glad she'd chosen to take the morning off. She needed to regroup if she was going to be at her best. And Callie McCormick deserved her best. The names of the other women flashed in her mind. *You don't know they're victims of a serial killer yet.* She pushed the thought aside for later as Isaac rinsed his plate and placed it in the dishwasher. 'Don't forget I'm staying at Trevor's tonight. They're releasing *Days of Doom* at midnight, and Mrs. Lewis said she'd take us to wait in line.'

Holly chimed in. 'And I'm staying at Sophie's. After the dance tonight, we're gonna grab some pizza and watch movies the rest of the night, okay?'

Possible serial killer was like a neon sign blinking on and off in her head, and Alyssa's natural instinct was to tell both her kids to cancel their plans. 'I remember. But you make sure you text me the minute you leave the dance and as soon as you get to Sophie's. And you,' she turned to her son, 'don't *you* forget you promised Dad you'd help him clean out the shed tomorrow. So, if you stay up all night playing video games, you've still got obligations here at home.'

'Yeah, I know,' he grumbled.

Shortly after Holly left and Isaac finished his shower, the front doorbell rang. It was Trevor. 'Hi, Trevor,' Alyssa said when she answered the door. 'I thought you guys weren't getting together until later.'

'Hey, Mrs. Detective.'

Trevor's mom insisted he call her missus, so Trevor compromised by calling her 'Mrs. Detective.'

Her youngest offspring stumbled down the stairs five minutes later. 'Mom, we're going to hang here awhile first, okay?'

'Sure. So, Trevor, how's the new baby brother?'

'Loud. And smelly. I don't get how all the girls that come around are like *Oh my gosh, I just love that new baby smell.* I must be missing something. And, holy… sh… man, does that kid have a pair of lungs! I have to sleep with earplugs in.'

Isaac grabbed his friend's arm. 'Dude, let's go play *Before Doom*.'

Later that evening, the house quiet with both kids at their slee-povers and Brock at a company baseball game, Alyssa brushed her hair back into a ponytail and yanked on her favorite comfort clothes – a pair of sweats and a Notre Dame sweatshirt – and went back downstairs.

In the kitchen, she poured herself a glass of wine, singing the famous Jimmy Buffet song 'It's Five O'clock Somewhere' when the guilt seeped in. *You spent seven hours at the precinct with your team poring over past case files, trying to connect the dots; you're entitled to this,* she thought. Then, grabbing her drink and the files she'd brought home with her, she went into the living room, shoved the furniture out of her way, spread everything out, and got lost in trying to find the missing piece to the puzzle. She read the interviews of the individuals questioned in Evelyn Martin's disappearance. Al and Margaret Garcia, in their eighties, had owned the Old Country Feed Store for sixty years at the time. When Alyssa ran a search of their names, she discovered both had died of old age approximately one year after Martin's mysterious disappearance. Their son Miles ran the place now, and though he'd helped out, he was in Bora Bora during that time period, an alibi verified by police.

Julia Vincente also had an airtight alibi as she'd been at the hospital visiting her newborn grandson. That left Robert Ortiz, Evan Bishop, Chris Peterson, and Benjamin Benton. According to the report, Ortiz, Peterson, and Benton had gone home early that evening since things were slow, leaving Evan Bishop to lock up on his own. On the surface, their interviews didn't show any glaring irregularities, but she decided her team needed to visit the four men again, if for no other reason than to check them off the list of potential suspects. She wrote notes to herself as she went along.

She didn't know how long she'd been hunched over studying the items sprawled all around her, but her back was beginning to protest, cracking as she stood to stretch her muscles. Arms raised high above her head, she went up on her tiptoes before bending at the waist, her ponytail tickling her nose, to let her fingers sweep the floor. *Oh, that feels good*, she thought. She stayed that way a few seconds before standing again.

After a few minutes of stretching, she grabbed the remote control off the end table, and ignoring the myriad of movie channels her family subscribed to – even though no one was ever home to watch them – she went straight to the music stations, picking an alternative rock station and turning the volume down low.

In the kitchen, she switched from wine to orange juice and grabbed a bag of pretzels before heading back to work. As she passed the front window, she got that niggling, itchy feeling people claimed to get when they thought someone was watching them.

She circled around to the sofa and nonchalantly peeked out the front window. Other than a few cars parked along the sidewalk, no one was in sight. She watched a few more minutes before letting the curtain drop back into place. Fifteen minutes later, she couldn't shake the feeling, so she went outside, looking up and down the street, but saw nothing that would cause this certainty that she was being watched. She'd just gone back in when she heard the garage door.

'How was the game?' she asked when Brock was inside. He rarely got to attend due to his busy schedule, but anytime he could snatch the opportunity to watch Albuquerque's minor league baseball team play, he jumped on it.

'Fun. Isotopes won by two runs,' he said as he hung his keys on the hook near the entrance to the garage, then kissed her. 'Hmm. You taste like oranges. Did you relax at all, or have you spent all evening poring over your cases?'

'What do you think?'

'I think you spent the day pondering how you can finally leave me for Will Smith. Am I right?'

She laughed. 'Yes, but after twenty years of marriage, I felt I owed it to you to break it to you in person first.'

'Well, that's awfully nice of you.' He made a show of looking around the room before he tugged her into his arms, engulfing her in a hug. 'Since we don't seem to have any kids around to demand our attention, what do you say I try to convince you to stay with me a while longer, hmm?'

Alyssa closed her eyes and tipped her head to give Brock better access to her neck. 'Mmmm… I think I owe it to us both. Will can wait,' she murmured, her eyes shifting to the living room where her case was still sprawled out. Then she pushed aside her guilt and allowed her husband to lead her upstairs.

Chapter Twenty-Eight

For the second day in a row, Evan found himself outside Detective Alyssa Wyatt's home. Friday night, he hadn't known where he was going until he was parked across the street a couple of houses down from hers in front of a vacant home. Around six thirty, two teenage boys emerged with a soccer ball which they kicked back and forth as they walked. It was too dark to get a good look, and he couldn't tell which one was the detective's son. They hadn't gone far when they stopped, and one of the boys pulled a phone out of his pocket, checking the screen before answering. After a short exchange, he said something to the other boy, and they turned around and headed back to the Wyatt residence.

A few minutes later, a young girl emerged, heading for a white Honda Civic parked in the driveway. He rolled down his window, straining to hear. 'Just get in. Dad says Mom doesn't want you walking right now,' she barked out, obviously irritated at having to play chauffeur. The boy holding the soccer ball asked a question he couldn't quite make out. 'I don't know. Probably something to do with the case she's working on,' the girl said, cutting off the boy's reply by slamming the driver's door. Ten seconds later, the three of them pulled away, the girl doing a double take when she spotted him sitting there. Heart thundering, he smiled and looked down, hoping he appeared busy. For an instant, he considered following. But it wasn't them he was drawn to, so he stayed.

Nearly two hours later, he had just turned the ignition when headlights lit up the interior of his car. He slid down in his front seat until she passed, recognizing the detective as she exited her car, the light from her garage acting as a temporary spotlight. As the garage door rumbled closed, he tried to cling to the image of the little boys, this time with a hulking shadow hovering over them. Fear, stark and real, vibrated off him in waves.

When her husband left shortly after Alyssa arrived home, he climbed out of his car and found himself partway up her walkway when he realized what he was doing. The magnetic pull to continue to the door was difficult to ignore, but he managed to break away. Knowing the urge would only grow the longer he sat here, he headed home.

This afternoon, knowing he was playing with fire, he'd driven over again, leaving his vehicle at the park one block away, then walking the rest of the way, just another man out for a stroll. From the shadows of the trees decorating the lawn of the vacant house, he observed the Wyatt residence. Was she home? He was tempted to cross the street and peek in the window... but he'd done that once, a long time ago, and he knew not to make that mistake again. Still, the urge for just a glimpse clawed at his insides.

And then the front door opened, and the detective stepped outside, looking around, as if she'd heard his wish and was granting it, looking for *him* as he was looking for her. His feet moved forward.

Ever heard the saying 'curiosity killed the cat, boy'? That what you're trying to do, huh? Get yourself killed?

His father's voice brought a flash of memory that breached the edges of his mind, and he fell forward, almost tripping over an exposed tree root. He froze, immobile until he heard a car's engine draw closer and then pull into Alyssa's drive. As soon as she went back inside, he bolted.

Chapter Twenty-Nine

Monday, April 1

Monday morning, Alyssa and Cord pulled up in front of the McCormick residence. Procedure dictated they check in on the surviving family members of violent crimes, and so they'd called ahead to let him know they were on their way, surprised when he agreed to see them, especially after his verbal assault at the hospital. While they waited for the door to be answered, she looked around. The yard that was immaculately taken care of one week ago was now unkempt, with unmown grass and weeds sprouting in the rose garden, as if they, too, mourned the loss of their caretaker.

The door opened to a shell of the man they'd first met. Dark circles colored the skin beneath Rafe's eyes, scratches covered his arms, his hair hung in greasy clumps around his head, and he appeared to have lost even more weight since when they'd seen him on Friday. Without making eye contact, he waved his arm, ushering them inside, as if words would cost too much of the energy he didn't have to spare. They followed him into the living room, the once bright room barely resembling the space they'd seen the first time they were here.

All the windows were covered with light-blocker shades, blocking the stunning views of the city and mountains, and except for the dim light shining in from the kitchen, the room was shrouded in darkness, giving it a tomblike feel.

Against her will, Alyssa was transported back to the time when her family home resembled this one, full yet empty and devoid of love or laughter when, at one time, that was all there was. A noise from outside drew her back in, and her gaze flew to the back door where the dogs pawed at the screen and whined to be let in. The shade on the sliding glass door was partially open, allowing Alyssa to get a glimpse of the animals.

Rafe barely lifted his head as if even that was too much for him to handle. 'Excuse me,' he said as he walked over to let the dogs in. Their slow, lumbering gait told her even they missed Callie.

'When will I be able to get Ca – Callie's body so I can plan…' Unable to finish his question, his body sagged forward as if suddenly weighed down by a load of bricks.

The smaller dog – Sassy, she thought its name was – approached Alyssa and then stood on her hind legs as her front paws clawed at her pants. She reached down to pat the dog's head.

'I think you remind her of Callie,' Rafe whispered. 'Because you kind of look like her, except for your hair, of course.' Tears pooled in his eyes as he said, 'Callie was also… softer… than you. Her personality, I mean.'

Alyssa caught her partner's eyes as Rafe's knees buckled, and he collapsed into a nearby chair, his sobs bouncing off the walls. When Ranger nuzzled up to his master in an effort to comfort, he buried his face in the dog's mane. A few seconds later, Sassy abandoned Alyssa and leaped into the chair with Rafe.

'She wanted a baby so much, but I wouldn't even discuss it.' His words were muffled, and Alyssa had to strain to hear.

When he sat up again, his arms wrapped around his middle, eyes swollen, voice hoarse, he said, 'I was afraid she'd leave me if we had a baby. My mom left my dad right after I was born, and my grandmother left my grandfather after my father was born. So, I shut her down every time she brought it up. Even though it wasn't true, I let her believe it was because I'd be embarrassed if she got fat with a child,' he choked out. Then, his voice grew quieter. 'Terrie told me Callie talked about going off the pill

159

behind my back. I guess she must've done it after all.' Finally, he looked up, his eyes shifting to their wedding picture on the wall. 'All those times I envisioned her leaving me if she was pregnant – none of them ended like this.'

A tightness squeezed her chest, and all Alyssa could think to say was, 'I know it doesn't mean much right now, but I *promise* we will catch the person who did this.' She ignored the warning glance Cord shot her. She knew she shouldn't make promises she may not be able to keep, but she couldn't stop herself. Besides, she vowed she would not fail Rafe or Callie McCormick again. 'And we'll let you know when the medical examiner has finished with –'

'With Callie,' Cord interrupted, and she knew he was afraid she'd say 'body.' She shot him a look that could pass as irritation or thanks. Even she wasn't sure which she meant.

'What about her car? Will I be able to get that back?'

'Our techs are processing it today.' She avoided mentioning that they'd started on Friday, having moved it up the list due to Callie's murder. He didn't need to know that. He just needed to know they wouldn't rest until his wife's killer was found. And neither would Alyssa.

A few minutes later, Rafe walked them to the door, his gait halting and forced. Before stepping outside, Cord reached out and touched the man's shoulder, giving it a light squeeze. 'If you don't mind, we'd like to know when you have Callie's service. If it's okay with you, we'd like to attend.'

What Cord didn't say, Alyssa knew, was that not only did police officials attend funerals out of a sense of courtesy and duty, but also because it was well-known that perpetrators frequently attended gatherings conducted in honor of their victims.

Rafe's head dropped forward in what they took as agreement.

–

Back at the precinct in the conference room, Alyssa snapped the hairband on her wrist, twisted her hair into a messy ponytail and yanked it out, just to turn around and whip it back up, lost in the black tunnel of this mystery. For the fifth time in as many minutes, she glared at the clock – 1:42. She'd been staring at the pieces of this puzzle for nearly three hours now, moving headlines, images, and files around the massive table, trying to fit them in with the Callie McCormick case. It was frustrating that not a single person who'd been interviewed in any of the cases showed up more than once. *Because that would be too easy, giving us a place to start,* she thought sarcastically. If there really was a serial killer, there *had* to be a link, aside from hair color and the relative youthfulness of each of the women. In fact, of all of them, Callie, at thirty-three, was the oldest by eight years.

The door banged against the wall, making her jump and reach for her gun. 'We might have just caught a break,' Cord said, out of breath.

'Jesus, Mary, and Joseph, you scared the hell out of me.'

'Did you hear what I said? We might have something.' His phone rang, and he pulled it out to see who was calling. He sighed impatiently and answered. 'I'll call you right back,' he said without so much as a hello to the person on the other end of the line.

His abrupt dismissal of the caller got her attention more than his words did, and her fingers gave her wrist a rest from the continuous snapping of the fabric-covered rubber band.

'What've we got?' she asked, locking her hands together to keep them still.

'Our techs lifted a nice fingerprint off the McCormick vehicle. We're running it now. Hedge should be calling us any minute.'

The balloon of hope in her chest deflated. 'That print could belong to anyone, including but not limited to Manuel Gomez or his cousin. Or any number of people who've come into contact with the Jeep since it was discovered. In fact, it could belong to Callie herself, or even Rafe.' She returned to snapping her hair band.

'I knew you would say that because I thought the same thing. But call it intuition or gut instinct or whatever, but I think we just caught our first break.'

The look she shot him was a cross between annoyance and amusement.

'Don't look at me like that. I'll concede your point. But, Alyssa, according to the techs, except for Gomez's prints, that car was so clean, you could eat off the floor mats. Be doubtful if you want, but I think we're closing in.'

'Well, I guess we'll find out soon, won't we?' She picked up her empty mug and refilled it with the last of the coffee, setting the carafe down with a dull thud.

'I don't know why you even bother using a cup,' Cord said.

Without turning around, she flipped him off.

Five minutes later, they were still waiting for the call when Joe and Tony swung in, having finished up with the second interview with Mearl Leroy, the man who'd chatted with Callie at the service station.

Alyssa took one look at Joe's exhausted face and Tony's amused one. 'What happened?' she demanded.

'I could be wrong, but I think it's pretty obvious Mearl Leroy did not kidnap nor murder Callie McCormick,' Tony said.

Joe glared at her and Cord. 'I thought you said Mr. Leroy gave you the willies? I thought that was why, as senior detectives, you sent us out for the second interview.'

'He did, and we sent you out for the second interview because we were busy meeting Rafe McCormick,' Alyssa said.

'Well, unlike you, this time, it was all we could do to extricate ourselves from his company before he brought out a photo album of him, his wife, and every. Single. One. Of. His. Dogs. The man was starving for attention, and he latched onto our company – well, mine because *someone* had to take a call outside – even if it meant being interrogated by the police.' He glared at Tony's smirking face.

Tony shrugged. 'What? It was a police call.'

Alyssa interrupted before the two could snipe at each other. 'Why didn't you just tell him you had to go?'

'I tried. Then I felt bad, and I –'

He was cut off by the sound of Cord's phone. 'Hedge, talk to me, my man.'

Alyssa didn't bother to pretend she wasn't on pins and needles waiting to hear what Hedge had discovered.

'Prints belong to a Hunter Jenkins.'

Bill Hedge had such a booming voice, co-workers joked he wouldn't need a microphone to speak to an auditorium full of people, so Alyssa heard before Cord could hang up and tell her.

'Hunter Jenkins,' Cord said. 'There's got to be a logical explanation.' His earlier excitement was nowhere in sight. 'Remember when we watched the security footage how I remarked that I hoped to look that good when I was Jenkins' age?' He waited for Alyssa's nod, then continued. 'He was fit, but fit enough to incapacitate Callie McCormick and kidnap her? Maybe he touched her car on his way into the lobby?'

Alyssa shuffled some papers around, running her finger over the page until she saw what she was looking for. 'It says work began on her car at 9:08 that morning. Hunter Jenkins arrived long after that.' She looked up. 'Logical explanation or not, we need to have another talk with Mr. Jenkins.'

She grabbed her keys and followed Cord out.

Chapter Thirty

Monday, April 1

Watching the detective's house had become an obsession. When he woke at four thirty that morning, bathed in sweat, his body shaking from the nightmare that had woken him Friday, Saturday, and again Sunday night – a little boy crying, as a blazing fire lit up the night sky – Evan told himself he would just take a quick stroll around the block this time, but when he saw her back out of her garage around 5:45, a dangerous idea began to take shape in his mind, and instead of leaving, he found himself at the back of the vacant house where he was pleasantly surprised to see someone had left the door unlocked. Inside, he planned.

At precisely eight o'clock, he made sure no nosy neighbors lurked, and then exited the house. Playing the part of an old man, he stopped frequently to 'rest.'

He walked to the end of the block and back. The street and neighboring houses were quiet. In front of the Wyatt residence, he paused to 'catch his breath,' in case anyone was watching. Then, slowly and carefully he moved to the block wall separating Alyssa's house from her neighbor's. He unlatched the gate, cringing when the rusty hinges squeaked. When the opening was wide enough for him to squeeze through, he made his way into the detective's private backyard. Three large, mature trees lined each of the back walls, effectively blocking out prying eyes. Heart fluttering, he inched toward the back door where he pulled out the little tool kit he carried with him at all times, though he rarely had use for it. After studying the lock, he grabbed one of his tools, and less than a minute later, he was inside.

-

His pulse beat frantically as forced himself to remain still, barely breathing, looking with his eyes only as he counted to three hundred before he finally allowed himself to take a careful step forward.

Finally, he was in the kitchen where everything seemed to be in its place. No dishes cluttered the counter, not even a coffee cup, and a newspaper lay neatly in the center of the table. The only indication that anyone had used the kitchen that morning was the aroma of coffee lingering in the air. He inhaled deeply, enjoying the scent, and a long-ago memory tried to wiggle its way into his mind; an old man throwing his mug against a wall, shattering it as a dark liquid ran down, staining it. He paused as he tried to pull on the strings of the memory, but when it was clear it wasn't returning, he continued his exploration.

The formal dining room housed a long wooden table, covered with a cream-colored doily. Two candelabras and a plastic cornucopia adorned the center. Six chairs and six place settings finished the look.

Separating the formal dining room from what appeared to be a game room was a soft leather couch. Along one wall was a gaming console complete with a television and a dozen video games lined up haphazardly on a shelf. He read a few of the titles, recognizing none of them. He ran his fingers over a shelf overflowing with DVDs, stopping on the one titled *Primal Fear*. On impulse, he slipped it inside his jacket pocket.

Next, he went around a corner and entered a foyer. To the right was a great room with leather furniture surrounding an enormous flat screen television. The entertainment center below held another assortment of DVDs.

He licked his lips and rubbed his hands together as he entered a narrow hallway. To the left was a large laundry area with a half bath across from it. At the end stood a doorway, which he assumed led to the two-car garage.

On the right was a set of closed French doors, and he wondered if they led to an office. He had just taken hold of the handle when he heard the unmistakable sound of a garage door opening. His heart thudded painfully against his rib cage as a cold sweat broke out over his entire body.

Frantic, he swung around, looking for a place to hide. He remembered the coat closet he'd passed and hurried to it. He yanked open the door and pushed aside dozens of jackets and sweaters before quietly closing the door behind him. Risking the use of his penlight, he stepped carefully over a slew of athletic gear, noticing as he did that the closet was a deep one with a little opening in the back. He headed for it, ducking as the space became smaller the further in he went. It was just a little extra storage space under the stairs, but the Wyatts had very few things back there, so he hunkered down.

Even if whoever was home opened the closet, they would likely never see him. Still, he caressed the Taser he carried with him. For a moment he allowed himself the fantasy that it was the detective. This time his heart quivered in excitement that lasted until he realized it was Alyssa's husband who'd come home unexpectedly.

Brock was on the phone when he walked into the house. Though the voice was muffled, Evan could still make out Brock's end of the conversation. 'No, no. I'm sure I left it on my desk this morning. I'll just grab it and race back to the office. If they get there before I do, try to stall them.' Brock laughed. 'Well, yeah, you could always try that dance – or you could just offer them some coffee and tell them I'm on my way.'

Evan heard a lock rattle and a door open. Brock's muted voice barely carried through then, and it wasn't until he heard the office door close that he was able to make out any more of the conversation. 'Got it! Be back in the office in fifteen minutes – twenty, tops.'

When he heard Brock's voice again, he was talking to himself. 'Okay. What else? Locked the back door, wrote a note to remind the kids to be more careful, so guess that's it.'

Evan waited until he heard the garage door close before venturing back out, wiping his sweaty palms down the length of his pants. Curious, he checked the office door, but, as he suspected, it was locked. Not wanting to take the time to pick it, he moved on to the main family room where he lingered, looking at pictures of a happy family. There were the requisite grades K-12 collages for both kids. The girl's was completed, but there were several years of photos yet to come for the boy who strongly resembled his father with his sharp cheekbones, brown, wavy hair, and dark eyes. The girl, however, looked like her mother, only with light-colored hair. A quick flash of a young girl braiding her hair in the kitchen made him knock over one of the pictures, catching it as it tumbled into his hands. Carefully, he replaced it, lining it up perfectly with the clean spot in the barely-there dust.

A wedding picture of the detective and her husband stood center stage with several smaller photos surrounding it. It looked to have been a lavish and joyous affair, though not everyone in the photos was smiling. A woman in black, hiding in the background, wore a huge scowl.

He had just decided to move on when his eyes were drawn to a photo of a much younger Alyssa, perhaps around the age of seventeen. He reached up and pulled the picture down. She posed on a large lawn with lots of green trees in the background. The picture didn't appear to have been taken in Albuquerque. He studied the area surrounding the detective, vaguely aware of a tingling on the back of his neck.

An urge to shatter the glass and its frame and cut the photo into hundreds of pieces surprised him. With shaking hands, he returned the frame to its spot and headed upstairs, the feeling of anger staying with him.

On the second floor, he paused in the first doorway. It was a typical boy's room, decorated with sports trophies, numerous posters of various athletes, a laptop, and dirty clothes strewn everywhere. Clothes, books, and movies exploded from every available surface onto the floor. The only clear spot in the entire space was a shelf designated for video games and their components. The kid even had his own bathroom, and after peeking inside, he could see why no one would want to share the space.

The next room was the girl's, and it was as clean as the other was filthy. Everything was organized and in its proper place. Like her brother's, this room held a laptop, but it also included a variety of books. In the bathroom, he sniffed various lotions and perfumes before he opened the medicine cabinet to find more of the same.

He continued. Outside the master bedroom, he ignored the buzzing in his ears and, opening the door, entered the world of Alyssa Wyatt's most personal, private domain.

Much later, in the privacy of his own home, he stood in one of his spare rooms, picking through his bounty. He lifted the bottle of jasmine and lavender lotion he pilfered from a basket resting on Alyssa's vanity to his nose and inhaled, breathing in deeply as the scent washed over him. He ran the scarf through his fingers, enjoying the sensation.

Silky. Soft. Pink. Feminine.

This time, he was positive Alyssa Wyatt was the one he'd been waiting for all this time.

Chapter Thirty-One

Monday, April 1, 2:15p.m.

South Valley traffic was touch and go due to construction, and Alyssa wanted to scream for people to get out of her way.

Finally able to turn and get out of the crush of vehicles, she expertly navigated through the neighborhood until they reached the quaint adobe home nestled between two juniper trees. As she and Cord approached the front door, Alyssa noticed the house was dark and quiet, bringing up the possibility that Jenkins wasn't home.

Alyssa knocked loudly as Cord stood to the side, observing the perimeter. When there was no answer, she knocked again, this time yelling out, 'Mr. Jenkins, this is Detective Wyatt with the Albuquerque Police Department. Open up!' When there was still no response, Cord cocked his head to the side of the house and mouthed, 'Backyard,' waiting for her nod before he stepped off the porch to check around back. He returned a few minutes later, shaking his head.

A white-haired lady approached, and Alyssa turned to speak to her.

'He's not here,' the woman said, her voice raspy from too many years of smoking. 'Mr. Jenkins moved out a few days ago. Was almost never here anyway.' She pulled a pack of Camels out of her tattered gray smock nightgown, leaned forward, and lit up.

'Are you his landlord?' Alyssa asked.

'Was,' the grizzled-looking lady nodded as she took a huge drag off her cigarette, then blew a series of smoke rings into the air. 'Eunice Jones, but you can call me Neecy. Everyone does.'

'Neecy, did Mr. Jenkins leave a forwarding address or another way to contact him?' Cord asked, stepping outside onto the sidewalk in front of the house.

Neecy peered up at Cord, cigarette dangling from her fingertips. 'Well, aren't you a fine young thing? I've got a grand-daughter… if you've got a hankering.'

Alyssa choked on her laughter as she watched Cord blink rapidly, a flush spreading up his neck. Recovering quickly, he winked at the old lady, 'That's a mighty sweet offer, thank you, but I'm already taken.' He lifted his left hand, flashing his white gold wedding band. 'Now, about Mr. Jenkins. It would certainly be helpful if he left you a way of contacting him.'

'No, he didn't leave no word. And I didn't ask for one. Mr. Jenkins always kept up the place real good when he did show up, never complained, and took care of all the repairs himself. Never even asked for reimbursement, he didn't. And he done gave me three extra months' rent in cash 'fore he up and took off. Figured there weren't no reason for a forwarding.' She grinned up at Cord, showing off yellowed, crooked teeth. 'If you wasn't married, and I was just a wee bit younger, forget my granddaughter, I might oughta have snagged myself husband number four.'

Alyssa snorted, enjoying the way Cord shuffled backward, looking at the car the way a man lost in the desert would look at water. In fact, she'd seen him be less afraid in police standoff situations. Taking pity, she refocused the woman's attentions on the matter at hand. 'Is there any way you can let us in to have a look around, see if maybe he left anything behind that might give us an indication of where he might have gone?'

Neecy extracted a key from the same pocket her cigarettes were in and mounted the steps slowly, wiggling the doorknob as she unlocked the door. 'It's a little tricky,' she said by way of explanation, then shoving the door inward, she motioned them inside. 'Go ahead and see for yourselves, but I can tell you already, there's nothing there. It's my policy to do a walk-through with my renters before they leave. Mr. Jenkins left it as spotless as it was the day he moved in. Matter of fact, if I didn't know no better, I'd suspect he never did… move in, I mean.'

Eunice Jones was correct. The house had been cleared out, a fine layer of dust the only thing remaining. 'Do you mind if we check the other rooms?'

The old lady gestured down the short hall. 'One bedroom, one full bath, laundry in the garage.'

It took less than five minutes to confirm what they already knew. There was nothing here that would assist in locating Hunter Jenkins' whereabouts. Outside again, Alyssa thanked the woman. 'Thank you for your time, Neecy.' She pulled out a card and handed it to her. 'If you do hear from Mr. Jenkins, could you please let him know we need to speak to him?'

Eunice took the card, and then with an expectant look on her face, held her palm out for Cord's card as well. Reluctantly, he handed one over. Alyssa half expected to see the woman latch onto him. But when the landlady doubled over, coughing, she was more frightened the old lady was about to expel a lung. When they were sure she would be okay, Alyssa gave one last wave and climbed into the driver's seat of her SUV.

Cord stared straight ahead. 'Well, that was a bust *and* scary!' A shudder shook his body, and once again, she had to bite back laughter.

'You mean you're not going to pack up and leave Sara right away?'

If the pinched expression on his face was anything to go by, he was not amused. 'I'm going to call Hal and see if he can work his magic; find out if he can get a bead on where Hunter Jenkins might've gone.'

Serious once again, Alyssa nodded. 'In the meantime, I want to head back to the precinct and watch the security footage from

MCM again. I don't like what my gut tells me this disappearance might mean.' She was quiet for a second, then said, 'It's hard to picture him kidnapping someone… but stranger things have happened.'

'Let's not jump ahead of ourselves. There could still be a logical reason Hunter Jenkins' prints were found on Callie McCormick's vehicle,' Cord said, though even he didn't sound convinced.

Alyssa was quiet for several moments, chewing on her thoughts, as she expertly maneuvered through traffic. Finally she said, 'I haven't seen Hunter Jenkins' name in connection with any of the other missing women, so if it turns out he *did* have something to do with Callie McCormick's death, then it's possible her murder wasn't at the hands of a serial killer.'

'Are you saying you no longer believe there's a link?' Cord clarified.

'No, I still believe there's something there, just maybe Callie's not a part of it. After all, she was older than the other missing women by eight years. All the others were a few years apart in age,' she said. She couldn't explain it, even to herself, but she really hoped Callie's murder wasn't connected to the other women.

A minute ticked by before Cord poked a hole in her theory. 'Just because he didn't appear on the other lists doesn't mean he wasn't there.'

–

At home later that night, Alyssa was wiping down the counters after eating celebratory slices of strawberry rhubarb pie to congratulate Brock's winning proposal for construction on the new hospital wing. He was explaining how his bid, though slightly higher than some of the others, had pulled ahead to earn the contract.

'Uh-hmm,' she murmured, lost in her own head. *What had caused Hunter Jenkins to clear out? Could the old man truly be capable of kidnapping and murdering Callie McCormick?* Was it also possible he was responsible for the disappearance and murders of at least seven other women? When she'd left the precinct, Hal was still there, digging into the man's background. With a little luck and a lot of perseverance, maybe they'd have something soon.

'And then the aliens dropped in and speared their prisoners with their laser eyes, and everyone lived happily ever after,' he said.

'That's good...' she blinked rapidly. 'Wait, what? Who lived happily ever after?'

Brock walked over and removed the washcloth from her hand and draped it over the sink. 'While you've been cleaning the same spot for twenty minutes – it's clean now, by the way – I was discussing when work should begin on the project. What's on your mind? And if you scrub that spot any harder for much longer, there won't be any counter left,' he said in response to her protest that she wasn't quite finished cleaning up as he pulled her into the living room where he dropped into the loveseat and dragged her down beside him.

She snapped the rubber band on her wrist. 'I'm sorry. I should've been paying attention. You've worked hard to snag this deal.'

He laid his hand on tops of hers to stop her compulsive rubber-band snapping. 'I know you can't discuss specifics, but do you want to talk about what you *can* share?'

Thundering footsteps interrupted anything she was about to say as both her children flew into the room, Holly collapsing into the recliner which forced Isaac onto the sofa. 'You knew I was going to sit there,' he grumbled.

Holly shrugged and grinned. 'Beat you to it. That's what happens when you're too slow.' Then she turned to her parents. 'So, no one bought the Zeller house, did they?'

Something akin to panic reached in and grabbed hold of her insides, and Alyssa shot an anxious-ridden look at her husband, instantly tense. Had Mabel changed her mind and purchased the vacant home a couple of houses down? Frowning, he shook his head, and relief made her exhale loudly. While her children might be thrilled if her mother-in-law lived that close, the thought alone had Alyssa on the verge of hyperventilating. 'Not that I know of, why?'

Her daughter shrugged. 'No reason, really. It's just I've seen someone over there the last few days. He was parked in front of the house Friday night when I was headed to Sophie's, and I thought I saw him coming from the Zellers' yard yesterday and this morning, too when I left for school. But I didn't see the guy's car, so it's probably nothing.' She smiled at her mom. 'Paranoia from my mom's career choice must be rubbing off on me.'

'Better paranoid than dead,' she said, her standard reply when either of her kids accused her of being paranoid. But as soon as it was out of her mouth, she wished she could take it back as an image of first Timmy's then Callie McCormick's body flashed in her head. She tapped her husband's thigh. 'That reminds me, we really need to get that security company out to fix the alarm. I haven't had time to contact them. Do you think you could give them a call tomorrow?'

'I can probably do that,' he said.

To Holly, Alyssa said, 'Maybe someone's just looking at it, but next time I'm home and you see him, will you let me know?' If someone *was* purchasing the vacant house, she wanted to know who. She may not speak to her neighbors regularly, but she knew them all by name.

'Sure,' Holly agreed. 'Well, I'm going to binge-watch *Big Little Lies* since there's no school tomorrow.'

Before she could go, Isaac scooted to the edge of the sofa and cleared his throat. 'I have something to tell everyone since you're all here,' he said. The sudden seriousness in his voice alarmed Alyssa, and she found herself searching for her husband's hand.

'What is it?' she asked. When he refused to look at them, she pasted on a reassuring smile. 'Isaac?'

174

Still avoiding his parents' gaze, he mumbled, 'You remember that girl I liked and asked out to the dance about a month ago?'

'April?' Alyssa clarified.

Hands clasped in front of him, he said, 'Yeah, that's her.'

'Oh-kay. What about her?' Alyssa's palms were beginning to sweat.

'Well, um, so, um…' Isaac stood and began pacing. Finally, he stopped, took a deep breath, and blurted out, 'You're going to be grandparents.'

Alyssa and Brock both exploded off the loveseat as she felt the world drop out from beneath her. 'What?'

And then it was Isaac's turn to explode, only in laughter. 'April Fool! Get it? April? And it's April Fools' Day? Oh my god, you should see your faces right now.' By then, he was doubled over in laughter, even as his mother slapped him and his father collapsed back onto the loveseat.

One look at her husband's face, and Alyssa couldn't tell which was the more prominent expression: relief or pride that his son had just pulled off a classic prank.

She grabbed the nearest throw pillow and aimed it at her son's head as he easily ducked to avoid it. 'Brat, go to your room. And never give me another heart attack like that again. Until you're at least twenty-five!'

Still laughing, Isaac and Holly bumped fists as they went back upstairs. 'Good one,' she said to her brother as they left the room.

Later, as she climbed into bed beside her husband, Alyssa felt twin twinges of guilt: that she'd been able to mentally set aside her case for a brief amount of time and feeling shame that she'd done so. It was a double-edge sword she frequently cut herself on.

Chapter Thirty-Two

Tuesday, April 2

Weighed down with six hulking bags of groceries, Alyssa wrestled with the doorknob before finally turning it enough to bump the door the rest of the way open with her hip. Much like her father before Timmy's death, she was of the ilk who refused to make more than one trip from the car to the house. She could always find a way to lug it all in two arms on one try, and the kids often took bets on how many bags she could carry and how many things would crash to the floor before she could safely heft the items to the counter. Eggs breaking or jars shattering were bonus points. To date, she'd not had so much as a dropped jar of pickles or a crack in an eggshell.

Since schools were closed for an In-Service Day for teachers, and she was driving herself, Cord, and Hal crazy as they waited for a call back regarding a hit Hal had received on Hunter Jenkins, she'd decided to grab some groceries. Because it was such a dreaded chore in her household, it wasn't uncommon to completely run out of everything before someone finally caved. She figured it was her turn and she needed to get out of the precinct before someone cuffed her and tossed her in a cell. Or more specifically, before Hal did. After an hour of snapping the rubber band on her wrist, and asking him if he'd heard anything back yet, the normally patient man had had enough, and he'd even gone so far as threatening to run her over with his wheelchair if she didn't 'get out now.' One look at his irritated face, and she believed him, so she told him where she was going and made him promise to call her the second he heard back.

She walked to the foot of the stairs and yelled up. 'Isaac? Are you home?' She already knew Brock and Holly were out since both their cars were gone. When she didn't get a reply, she figured Isaac was with one or the other, so she returned to the kitchen to put things away, disappointed because she would've appreciated the help, and her son's company would've helped keep her from going crazy while waiting for information.

She'd just finished putting the canned goods in the pantry and separated the mass packages of chicken and pork into more suitable family-sized portions when she thought she heard shuffling footsteps above her. She stopped whistling and listened, shrugging it off as house-settling noises when it remained silent.

She was labeling her freezer storage bags when she heard boards creaking overhead, even louder than before. Isaac must be home after all. He'd probably fallen asleep with his head-phones on, listening to mind-numbing lyrics he insisted *she just didn't get*, and hadn't heard her calling for him.

Before walking to the foot of the stairs again, she washed her hands of the raw meat she'd been handling. She labeled the Ziploc bag with the date and contents and stuck it in the freezer, then yelled, 'Isaac?' No answer. She tried again, louder this time. 'Isaac!' The creaking stopped.

How many times had she told him blasting his music like that would rupture his eardrums, rendering him deaf? Apparently, not often enough.

Exasperated, she headed upstairs and stalked to her bedroom door, which was shut. *Odd*, she thought. *What could he possibly be doing in there?*

She pushed the door open and jumped back, letting out a little yelp when it was pulled from her hand.

'Ahh! Jeez, Mom! You scared the crap out of me!' Isaac screeched as he stumbled backwards.

Her hand covered her pounding heart. 'I scared you? You just shaved a good five years off my life! *What* are you doing in my room, and why didn't you answer when I hollered for you?'

Isaac fixed his baseball cap and pulled both earplugs out of his ears, letting them dangle around his neck. Alyssa could hear the grating noise emanating from them all the way across the room. 'I never heard you yell for me. When was that? And why are you even home?'

She looked at her watch then back at her son. 'Maybe fifteen minutes ago. I yelled several times. And I'm home because I picked up some groceries. I'm heading back after I finish putting things away.'

Her son's cheeks turned a slight shade of pink and he mumbled, 'Sorry. I didn't hear you.'

'Yeah, I kind of gathered that.' She looked pointedly at his iPod and said, 'I don't doubt in the least little bit that you didn't hear me. As loud as you have that garbage blasting in your ears, I'd be surprised if you heard an explosion right outside your room. How can you even understand what they're saying? Are they even singing – and I use that term very, very loosely here – in a language you understand?' She shook off her irritation and said, 'Never mind, it doesn't matter. I need to get back downstairs and finish putting the groceries away.'

His face filled with glee as he followed her out of the bedroom. 'You bought food? Score! Did you get –'

Interrupting his inquiry, she repeated. 'So, *why* were you in my room in the first place?'

'Um. I fell asleep in there.'

'You don't have a bed of your own? Last I checked, you still had a queen-size pillow-top in your room. It may be hard to find, mind you, under all that mess, but you definitely do have one. I specifically remember paying for it and lugging it up the stairs.' They entered the kitchen and Alyssa said, 'Wash your hands. You can help me finish up here.'

Isaac rolled up his sleeves, squirted soap into his hands, and obediently cleaned up. 'I thought I heard Dad or Holly come home earlier because I thought I heard the door beep. When are we getting the alarm fixed? Anyway, no one came upstairs, and Dad didn't yell up for me, so I figured I was hearing things and went back to my room.'

'It was probably a beeping in your brain telling you to turn your music down,' Alyssa replied in a snarky tone.

'Ha ha, very funny, Mom. Do you want to hear this or not?' he grumbled.

'Actually, I think it *was* funny. It was a rather clever comment, if I do say so myself. But I'll shut up now. Please. Continue.'

Isaac rolled his long-lashed green eyes, so much like her brother's had been.

'Don't roll your eyes at me; they'll stick that way.'

'I thought you weren't going to interrupt anymore,' Isaac said, raising his eyebrows at her.

'Oops. You're right. Sorry. Not another word until you finish, I swear. See? Locked up tight.' She turned the pretend lock on her mouth and threw the imaginary key behind her.

'Anyway,' he continued, 'I went back in my room and about, I don't know, ten or fifteen minutes later, I thought I heard Dad walking around in your room. I was surprised he didn't let me know he was home because he always does, you know. I had to ask him something, so I went to your room, but he wasn't in there. I figured the house was making those creepy settling noises again, and I started to go back to my room when I realized Dad forgot to turn off the TV.' He put the packaged meat she handed him into the meat drawer of the freezer.

He continued, 'I went to shut it off, but then that funny insurance commercial came on – you know the one where that guy breaks in? So, I watched that, and then some show came back on, and I stood there watching it a few minutes. *Raiders of the Lost Ark?* For an old movie, that one's pretty good. Anyway, before I knew it, I was kicked back on your bed. Next thing I know, I'm waking up and you're scaring the hell – heck – out of me.'

'Well, at least you remembered to turn the television off.'

'Nah. It was off when I woke up. I must've rolled over on the remote or something.'

'Hmm. Well, tomorrow's laundry day, so guess you can wash my bedclothes along with yours, and get that dirty, sweaty, teenage boy stink out,' she teased as the two of them finished storing the rest of the freezer items. 'Did you just roll your eyes at me again?' she asked in mock anger.

'I don't know. Did it look like this?' Isaac asked comically, giving a dramatic repeat performance. 'If so, then yes, yes, I did.'

Alyssa couldn't help but laugh. She snapped his leg with a wet towel. 'Brat,' she said.

Her phone rang, and she snatched it off the counter. Cord. 'Tell me,' she said by way of greeting.

'Hunter Jenkins was arrested for a petty misdemeanor in Michigan over twenty years ago for shoplifting a candy bar. The judge let him off with a warning since it was his first offense,' her partner said.

She heard more in the silence that followed than what he'd said. 'There's more. What is it?'

'Thing is, Hunter Jenkins died earlier that year in an ATV accident.'

'So, you're telling me that someone else has assumed Hunter Jenkins' identity?' Alyssa asked.

'It's possible,' Cord said. 'I know this isn't what you wanted to hear – none of us did. But for my money, I'm thinking we're finally moving on the right track with this guy, at least for the McCormick case.'

She closed her eyes and took a deep breath. 'Damn it,' she muttered. 'Well, the alias throws a monkey wrench into the works, but I agree that we're on the right path because innocent people don't assume someone else's identity unless they're hiding something.'

'Before you hang up, I wanted to tell you Lynn Sharp came by looking for you.'

The only reason Alyssa could think of for the medical examiner wanting to speak to her would have to be in regards to the McCormick case. 'Why didn't she just call me?'

'She was already here for something else, so she decided to try her luck and drop in. She found a hair that didn't belong to Callie McCormick, as well as enough skin cells beneath the fingernails that she thinks there's a good chance she can extract a DNA profile. But she said it could still take a while to get the results back. In other words, patience is key here.'

'In other words, don't be myself. Is that what you're saying?'

'You said it, not me,' Cord said.

Patient or not, her pulse quickened at the news. This could be the break they'd been hoping for. 'Okay, I'll finish up here and head back. Should be there in less than twenty.' When she hung up, she automatically checked to see that her gun was still holstered, and then grabbed her keys from the wall hook.

'Um, Mom, do you think you could drop me off at Trevor's on the way? I'd walk, but, since you're heading the same direction…'

'Sure, get your things, and let's go,' she said as he sprinted up the steps to grab his phone to text his friend he was on the way.

Chapter Thirty-Three

Tuesday, April 2

Thunk. Thunk. Thunk. Evan allowed the steady pattern of his shoe hitting the wooden floors to help calm him. He checked his alarm system for the third time since walking through his front door a little over an hour ago.

That was close. Way too close. Closer even than when Alyssa's husband had come home unexpectedly. How was he supposed to know schools were closed today? When he woke this morning with that familiar burn in his stomach, he knew he wouldn't stay away, despite the risk that returning presented. The harder he tried to convince himself it was too dangerous, the more impassioned he became to see her, to touch the things she loved, the place she slept.

After being caught off guard yesterday, he decided to wait until late morning. Discarding his usual disguise, he pulled on a pair of running shorts and a tank top, becoming a regular guy out for his morning run.

When he rounded the corner to Rancho Blanco where Alyssa lived, her husband was just leaving. The detective's car was already gone. He waved as Brock Wyatt drove by, watching until he saw him turn right out of the neighborhood. When he reached the vacant house, he veered left and ran into the backyard.

There he waited ten minutes to make sure the coast was clear before hurrying over to Alyssa's house where he slipped through the gate and entered the house through the back door.

He wasted no time exploring the downstairs again. His aim was upstairs. He trod quietly down the hall past the children's closed rooms where the door to the master bedroom stood ajar. Eyes bright, he wet his lips and re-entered Alyssa Wyatt's most private domain.

His focus was so complete, the voices didn't register right away. When they did, he spun around, looking for any place to hide. A nervous titter escaped when he realized the sound was nothing more than the television mounted on the wall above the dresser. He found the remote control and turned the volume down, making a mental note to return the level to twenty-two before he left.

He entered the bathroom first, opening cabinets, picking things up and replacing them exactly how he'd found them. He wasn't looking for anything in particular; he just enjoyed touching the detective's things... and her not knowing it made his hands tingle.

He peered behind the bedroom door and went through the closet, touching her clothes, but resisting the temptation to take anything else. His fingers trailed over her silky negligees draped around padded hangers, and he rubbed some of the silkier ones across his stubble, becoming aroused as he did.

Near the bed, he stared at yet another framed photo of Alyssa and her husband. That familiar tug was back, tickling his memory, and tying his stomach in knots. *She's the one.* This time the voice wasn't his father's but his own. Squatting down, he opened the bottom drawer of her nightstand, rattling the knocker-type knobs. Inside was an old leather photo album, and he had just pulled it out to look when a rustling sound came from down the hall. He stood so quickly, the resulting head rush made him dizzy, and he stumbled back, kicking the open drawer.

'Dad?'

A deer caught in the headlights, he fought against a rising panic, using one hand to pinch his lips between his thumb and forefinger. What was the kid doing home? When cushioned footsteps made their way down the carpeted hall, his heart beat erratically inside his chest.

'Dad? Can you help me with something?' the boy asked, his voice growing louder with every step closer.

I told you curiosity killed the cat, his father's voice cackled in his ear. Evan squeezed his eyes shut to tune him out and then turned in a circle. He couldn't go in the bathroom or closet – what if the boy came in there looking for his dad? He looked down at the album in his hand and then at the floor. Mere seconds before the kid walked in, he closed the drawer and slid under the bed. In the back of his mind, he was able to appreciate – and be amazed – at how dust-free it was under there. Who cleaned under the bed?

'And don't forget to clean under your bed. Don't just shove all your toys under it!' This was a different voice, an unfamiliar one, nice, and Evan wanted to cling to it, but then the boy was in the room.

'Dad? Dad? Hmm. Guess you're not home.' The kid chuckled to himself. 'I've got to stop watching scary movies. Keep hearing things go bump.' Then: 'If I'm talking to myself, does that make me crazy? Nah – only if I answer. Wait! I just answered myself. So, I guess Holly's been right all along; I am certifiable.' Another snicker, then, 'Wait, crazy people think they're sane, so if I think I'm crazy, I must be alright. So there. How's that for logic?'

You wouldn't think you were crazy if you looked under your mom's bed, little boy, Evan thought. He almost laughed out loud, blowing his cover.

From beneath the bed, he could just make out the bottom of a pair of ratty gray sweats. To his annoyance, the kid stopped moving toward the door. *What now?* The kid barked out a sharp laugh. 'Man, I love that commercial,' he said.

Evan watched the boy shuffle backwards, and then he felt the mattress depress as he sat at the foot of the bed. He knew when

184

the kid moved into the middle, not just because of the noise, but because the box springs lowered so much, they briefly brushed his back. The volume on the television went up, drowning out any other noise.

His breathing shallowed as claustrophobia threatened to choke off his air, and he forced himself to take several deep but quiet breaths to calm his galloping heart. He wiped his forehead against his sleeve to remove the sweat dripping into his eyes, listening to the squeak of the headboard as the boy shifted against it. A tickle on his leg distracted him, and he rubbed against the carpet in an effort to alleviate some of the discomfort.

Two distinct thumps and the closing of the bedroom door startled him, and he almost cried out when he hit his head on the bottom of the bed. At first, he thought the boy had finally gone, but then a deep sigh sounded above him, and he realized he was just settling in, getting more comfortable.

Cautiously, he wormed his way to the other side and peeked out. The boy had thrown his shoes across the room, where one of them had hit the bedroom door, causing it to close the rest of the way. The other had left a faint dirt mark on the wall.

Evan's pulse hammered in his brain, and he lowered his hand to the Taser in his pocket. He lay quietly as the boy watched some movie. What to do?

Time ticked by slowly, and he fought back the insane urge to kill the kid and be gone already. He brought his wrist close to his face to check the time on his watch. Close to three hours had elapsed since he entered the house.

He was considering his options when he became aware that something had changed. He closed his eyes and concentrated. It finally came to him – the boy had fallen asleep. What he was hearing were the soft snores of the teenager above him.

A solution opened up. If he moved slowly, he could crawl from beneath the bed, tiptoe to the door, and get the hell out of this house. Worst case scenario, the kid woke up, and he had to Tase him. Or kill him. He hoped it wouldn't come to that.

He listened for the boy's deep, even breathing indicating he was still fast asleep. Just as he was about to make his move toward the door, another sound filtered up to his ears – the garage door. Someone else was home.

Once again, sweat trickled into his eyes as his heart hammered. *Think,* he ordered himself. If it was the daughter, he'd take the boy out first, then surprise the girl.

Cautiously, he crawled out from underneath the bed, slowly coming to his feet, hoping none of his bones would creak and pop as they were wont to do at times. He paused to look down at the boy, noticing he had one earbud in while the other had fallen to the pillow. He backed away and inched slowly across the room, checking occasionally to make sure the kid still slept.

'Isaac? Are you home?' It was *her*, the detective! Wild-eyed, he turned to look at the boy, who stirred slightly but didn't wake. Evan's neck jerked from the closed door to the bed and back again as he considered what to do now. He still hadn't decided when the boy rolled over, forcing Evan to dive for cover beneath the bed once more just as the boy's socked feet hit the floor. Her son yawned loudly and moved to pick up his shoes, sitting on the floor to put them on, then standing as the detective yelled again.

The boy reached for the door just as his mom turned the handle and pushed it open. Both of them screamed. But it was *her* scream that he realized he wanted to hear again. His pulse picked up speed, and he found it hard to concentrate. The sound of her voice, different from when he'd heard it on the television, triggered something inside him, and he knew that she was the one he'd been searching for all along. All the others were no more than practice for the real deal.

He exhaled slowly and unclenched his fists when the detective and her son left the room, neither of them ever suspecting the danger they were in.

Remaining where he was, he dug his fingers into the carpet as he ran his palms over the soft texture, allowing the rhythmic movement to calm him as he contemplated his choices. Though he wasn't prepared yet, he could take the detective now. He'd have to kill the boy, though, because he'd be a witness. He didn't relish the idea, not wanting to follow in his father's footsteps, but he'd do it. On the other hand, as an officer of the law, she would have a gun, and he knew she wouldn't hesitate to shoot him, especially in the act of protecting her son. Despite his father's voice constantly reminding him differently, he wasn't stupid, and knew the chances were slim that he'd come out the winner in a battle between his weapon and hers.

Then her phone rang, jolting him into action. He crawled from beneath the bed and over to the vent where her voice was so clear it was almost as if he were standing next to her. His spine stiffened when she mentioned the shoplifting arrest. It had been so long ago, he'd forgotten all about it. Out one evening when Carl was preoccupied in the basement, he'd run across a group of boys in an abandoned field sitting on all-terrain vehicles smoking pot and drinking beer. When he approached them, the apparent leader of the bunch had glanced up with a 'What's up, man?'

'Not much,' he'd said. When the guy offered him the joint they were sharing, he thought *why not* even though he'd never done drugs before, and took a drag, choking so hard he was afraid he would pass out. Everyone had laughed, but they kept handing the joint to him, and with each hit, he coughed less. The more stoned the guys got, the chattier they were, and that's how he'd learned their names. No one had asked his, and he never offered.

Then a month or so later, Carl was busy yet again, and Evan had snuck out, stealing the truck. He'd been driving aimlessly about an hour when the munchies overtook him, and knowing there was nothing back at the house, he headed into town where he stopped at a gas station. When he thought the owner wasn't looking, he swiped a candy bar, a bag of chips, and a Pepsi – and was promptly busted. No matter how much he begged, the old man wouldn't cut him any slack and held him there until the police came.

When two officers showed up and asked for his identification, he invented a story about how he'd lost it, and then lied about his age, saying he was eighteen and then offered up the first name that popped into his head – Hunter Jenkins. How was he supposed to know the kid had died from an ATV accident after he'd met him? After his release the next morning, he was afraid to go home, fearing Carl's rage. But he'd lucked out because Carl had been so preoccupied that he'd never even realized Evan – or his truck – was gone.

He was dragged away from his memory as he listened to Alyssa tell the caller she was heading back to the precinct, and then the boy asked for a ride to a friend's house before rushing upstairs and thundering back down.

He waited until he heard the garage door close before he went downstairs, sneaking out the same way he'd come in. After peeking around the corner to ensure no one was lurking about, he jogged to the park where he'd left his vehicle, thinking about how close he'd been to the detective. When he reached for his keys to unlock the car door, he realized he was still gripping the album he'd taken from her nightstand drawer.

Chapter Thirty-Four

Tuesday, April 2

Two stoplights before she was back at the precinct, Cord's name popped up on her Bluetooth screen. 'I'll be there in less than two minutes,' she said. 'I'm stopped at 6th Street.'

'Might as well hang a right and head to the McCormick's neighborhood. Ruby just took a call from a neighbor who's been out of the country since March twenty-fifth,' Cord told her.

'The twenty-fifth is the day Callie went missing. What did the caller say?'

'Vance Normandie says he remembers seeing an unfamiliar car when he left for the airport that day but didn't think much of it until he returned and was going through his stack of mail and collection of newspapers his son had set on his counter. When he read the news that his neighbor's wife had been murdered, he remembered and called as soon as he could.'

Alyssa put on her blinker and changed lanes. 'Okay, I'm headed that way now.'

'Do you want me to meet you there?'

She thought about it for just a second. 'No, I'll take this witness's statement, and then I'll stop in and check on Mr. McCormick. Why don't you and the others see what else you can find out about the man claiming to be Hunter Jenkins? Also, maybe see if his description fits any of the other suspects in the other cases. If this is an alias, he could have others.'

'I'd caution against telling Rafe about the possible DNA until we have something concrete,' her partner said.

She rolled her eyes though he couldn't see it. 'Good bit of advice. Since it's my first week on the job, I probably wouldn't have thought of it myself.'

Cord ignored her sarcasm. 'Glad to be of assistance. I'll see you when you get here.'

They ended the call, and Alyssa maneuvered through traffic until she could get on the freeway. Nearly twenty long minutes later – did Albuquerque have to have construction on every major roadway at the same time? – she pulled up to Mr. Normandie's house, three doors down on the opposite side of the McCormick residence. As she got out of the car, her eyes were drawn to Rafe's yard. Her heart felt like a five-pound weight had been added to it as she noticed the yard which was still overgrown with weeds.

Before she could ring the bell, the front door opened, and a tall, sixty-something man wearing a plaid shirt and well-worn blue jeans stepped out. 'Detective Wyatt?' he asked.

Alyssa stretched her hand out to shake his. 'Yes, sir. Mr. Normandie, I presume?'

'Vance is good. Thanks for coming so quickly. Come in, come in.'

Alyssa followed the man inside. Green, leafy potted plants lined every wall, and several ferns hung from hooks on the ceiling, their vine-like leaves draping low and making her feel like she was walking through a tropical jungle in the Amazon. She half expected to see a few snakes slithering around on the floor.

'Can I offer you a cup of coffee? Hot tea?' Vance asked as they passed the kitchen on their way to a large open great room complete with a massive gas fireplace surrounded by one of the most beautiful oak mantles she'd ever seen.

She declined, anxious to hear about this mysterious vehicle. 'No, thank you. Mr. Normandie – Vance – I was told you saw an unfamiliar vehicle the day Callie McCormick went missing, is that correct?'

The man launched into his story, and Alyssa mentally groaned. He was the kind of person who, when asked if it was snowing, would talk about the clouds, the barometric pressure, and the temperature all before saying no. As he launched into an account of his trip to England, she cut him off. 'I'm sorry, Mr. Normandie, but as lovely as that trip sounds, I need to know what you saw.' She pulled out her notebook and a pen, purposely portraying every clichéd television detective she'd ever seen.

'Right, right. Of course. Well, like I told the lady on the phone, I was heading to the airport, and there was a blue Toyota Camry parked almost in front of my drive. I almost hit it backing out, and it bugged me, so out of habit, I checked the license plate.'

'You don't happen to recall what that was, do you?' She expected not, since more than a week had passed.

'I sure do. It was a vanity plate from the state of Minnesota. LETITSNW.'

'LETITSNW? Oh, Let it Snow,' Alyssa said, writing it down. 'Did you see anyone around the car?'

'No, no. I was running a little late.'

'Do you remember what time it was then?'

Vance stared at the ceiling as he tried to remember. 'I don't recall the exact time anymore, but it had to have been between eleven and eleven twenty, as I needed to be at the airport by eleven thirty, and I recall thinking I was going to be fifteen to twenty minutes late, depending on the traffic.' He glanced back at Alyssa and asked, 'Does that help?'

'It does, thank you,' she answered.

He twisted his neck from side to side cracking it loudly, causing goosebumps to pop out on her skin. 'Too bad about Mrs. McCormick. She was a friendly sort. I'd talk to her every now and again when she was out walking her two dogs or working in the rose garden out front.'

He stopped just shy of asking if they had any leads, but Alyssa saw the curiosity in his eyes. She closed her notebook and put her pen away. 'Thank you for calling, Mr. Normandie. I'll be in contact if we need any more information. Likewise, if you think of anything else, please don't hesitate to call.'

He escorted her back through the jungle to the front door, watching as she crossed the street to the McCormick residence. At the front door, her hand hovered. Was she making a mistake coming here? She remembered one of the officers who'd shown up several days in a row after Timmy's body was found, to check in on her family, and later, to check in on her. She ignored the knocker and opted for the doorbell.

Just as she was about to give up, the door opened. Rafe McCormick's eyes were red and swollen, his hair hung in clumps, and his red sweats hung off his frame. He resembled a prisoner on death row, and she supposed, in a way, that's exactly what he was, at least until he found a way through his grief, which he wouldn't be able to even begin to navigate until his wife's body was returned to him. Dangling from his left hand was a half-empty bottle of vodka.

'Mr. McCormick? I was in the area and wanted to check in on you. Can I come in?'

Vacant eyes stared straight ahead. His voice hollow and gravelly, he said, 'Is Callie ready?' His words slurred, and he had to try twice before he got the question out.

'No, I'm sorry, not yet. But soon,' she promised, wondering why she felt so compelled to offer hope when she shouldn't. As he stood swaying in the door, a strange mixture of scents wafted out the front door, and she recoiled. It smelled like… sweat, dirty socks, lavender, citrus, and pine all rolled into one. She peeked around his shoulder and saw flickering shadows on the wall, and she realized all the 'damn candles' Callie had so loved and he'd so hated were lit. Combined with his body odor and the alcohol seeping through his pores, it created a ghastly aroma.

'Have you found out who did it yet?' he asked then.

'We've got some promising leads,' she said, being honest, yet somehow misleading. They didn't know what kind of information the DNA profile would return, and they needed to chase down whatever details they could about Hunter Jenkins before talking to Rafe about him. 'Every investigation is like a tree branch. Every lead branches off into another which branches off into more.'

Rafe nodded, though she wasn't sure he really heard, especially when he said, 'I've got to get back now,' before stepping back and closing the door in her face.

Slowly, her footsteps leaden, Alyssa returned to her car and called Hal with the license plate, asking him to run it and tell Cord she was headed back to the precinct.

An hour later, she walked into the conference room where Hal and Cord watched the wall where they'd projected the MCM security footage so they could re-watch it without being crammed around one small computer. Specifically, they wanted to study Hunter Jenkins' movements again, hoping they'd reveal some sort of clue. As soon as she entered the room, her partner hit pause and swiveled in his chair at the same time Hal rolled his chair around to face her. The identical scowls on their faces made her want to turn right back around. Immediately, her gaze went to the frozen image on the wall. Obviously, she wasn't going to like whatever they were about to tell her.

Maybe because he drew the short straw or perhaps because he was the one who'd garnered the information, Hal was the one to break it to her. 'Minnesota license plates belong to an elderly couple, Herman and Faith Gilbertsen, who were here visiting their new great-grandchild who happens to live next door to one Mr. Vance Normandie.'

Like a balloon on a hot day, she deflated. *So much for that branch leading to another,* she thought. She took a deep breath. It was her job to lead this team, and she couldn't let negativity cloud the issues. 'Then we keep digging. Each dead end is bound to bring us closer to the right road.' She tilted her head toward the wall. 'What've you got so far?'

Cord snagged a chair with his foot and rolled it over. 'Just started, so you didn't miss a thing. Liz, Joe, and Tony commandeered another conference room, and they're running a fine-tooth comb over the other missing women's cases to see if there's any connection to Hunter Jenkins.'

'Okay, that's good.' She ignored the offered chair, choosing to stand. Disappointment and drive were battling for first place in her head, so she closed the door and leaned against it as Cord hit play. Suddenly, her back stiffened. 'Pause it!' she ordered, moving over to the wall.

'How far?' Cord asked.

'Fifteen seconds should do it. Okay, play and watch.' Just before the video got to the same place, she said, 'Get ready. There.'

'He's walking to the desk. We've already seen that,' Cord said, confused.

But Hal got it. 'Yes, but look how straight he's standing – not at all hunched over like he was when he first arrived.'

Alyssa smiled. 'Hal, if I wasn't happily married…' Her finger tapped the image. 'That, too, but, look at what he's doing here.'

They'd missed it before, but Hunter Jenkins leaned across the counter as he peered casually over the desk. He said something to the receptionist who threw her head back and laughed, and a few seconds later, he hobbled back to his seat, once again hunched over. He said something to Mr. Wallace before he pulled out his phone.

'We didn't see it before,' Alyssa said, 'because Hunter Jenkins, at first glance, appears to be a man on the last leg of his journey on Earth. Maybe he acts feeble so he's less intimidating, making it easier to lure in his victims, and he just forgot for a second? Didn't Ted Bundy do something similar?' she asked. She studied the man on the screen, and then said, 'Can you zoom in for a closer look at what's on Aubrey's desk?' Her nerves tingled the way they did when she was onto something. She didn't know what this meant yet, but her gut told her they were branching out onto the correct limb now.

Hal's fingers flew across the keyboard and Cord joined her at the wall, as if by being closer, they could reach out and nab Hunter Jenkins from the screen. 'Tell me when to stop.'

'Right there. What do you see?' she asked. Though the magnified image was blurry, it was still identifiable.

Cord whistled. 'Callie McCormick's invoice.'

'Callie McCormick's invoice,' Alyssa repeated. 'Hal, go ahead and hit play.'

'What the hell?' This time it was Hal who hit rewind.

When she saw what he had, she inhaled so fast, she choked. As Hunter Jenkins returned to his seat, for a split second, his lips turned down, and when he looked up, his gaze sweeping over Callie McCormick, anger flashed briefly across his face before he turned his attention back to Mervin Wallace.

It was there and gone so fast that if they hadn't been watching so intently, they would've missed it – again.

'Despite what's in front of me, I'm having a difficult time wrapping my head around the idea that Hunter Jenkins not only may have kidnapped and killed Callie McCormick, but that he may also be a serial killer,' Cord mused.

'The mind's good at seeing what it wants and ignoring the rest,' Alyssa said. 'But my gut tells me once we locate Mr. Jenkins, we'll also find that string we need to pull to unravel this case. So, let's get busy.'

Chapter Thirty-Five

Tuesday, April 2

In the kitchen sobbing, face turning blue, snot dripping from his nose, stood the new Boy. That's what all the new ones were called – Boy.

Evan remembered being scared his first time, too, so he put his arm around Boy and whispered, 'Don't cry. It'll make him mad.' But that just made Boy cry harder and louder. 'Please,' he begged… But it was too late. Carl stormed into the room. Familiar with his adopted father's rage, Evan grabbed Boy's hand and backed up until they hit the door leading to the basement, sliding down as Carl advanced.

'Shut him up, or you'll both end up down there!' he roared at the same time he leaned in and slapped Boy across the face.

His arm around the little boy's shoulder, Evan's head bobbed frantically, his stomach crawling up his throat. He hated the basement. He waited until Carl returned to the living room and turned the volume up on the television before he risked standing and urging Boy up. 'You have to be quiet before he makes us go to the basement.'

'Wh – what's in the basement?' Boy stuttered.

Evan shook his head. He didn't like to think of it. Besides, Boy would surely find out soon enough. Otherwise, he wouldn't be here. He pulled on Boy's arm and leaned his head. 'This way,' he whispered as they tiptoed past the living room. In his room, he lowered his voice even more, 'Why did you get sent here?'

Boy wiped his sleeve across his nose, his voice quivering with every word. 'My mommy didn't want me anymore. Little boys are too hard, so she just wants my sister.'

Evan nodded. 'That's what happened to me, too.'

This time, Boy's sobs came so fast and hard, Evan was afraid he'd die from not breathing. And Boy hadn't even been to the basement yet. He would really not be able to breathe down there.

'How old are you?' He didn't know why he asked, but he did.

'I'm four.'

Maybe because Boy was younger than him, Evan decided right then he'd help him, so he scooted over and patted his shoulder, watching his open door to make sure Carl wasn't standing there listening. 'It'll be okay. We'll go talk to your mommy together, all right? And then she'll see you won't be too hard at all.'

Boy hiccupped. 'For really?'

Evan nodded, his little mind made up. 'For really! Carl – Dad – falls asleep,' he pointed to the clock, 'when the small hand is on the two and the big hand is on the six. He doesn't wake up until both hands are on the three.' And then they had to go to the basement, but he didn't tell Boy that. 'But we have to be very quiet until then,' he added.

When the time came, Evan tiptoed into the living room to check that Carl was really asleep, and then motioned for Boy to follow, putting his finger to his lips. In the kitchen, he grabbed some bologna and two warm bottles of pop. He didn't know how long it would take to get to Boy's home, and he wanted to make sure they had something to eat. Boy wanted to take some chips, but Evan was afraid to open the squeaky cupboard, so he shook his head. He couldn't reach the bread, so they'd have to leave it.

'Ready?' he whispered.

But when they turned to go, Carl was standing there, his left eye ticcing furiously. Neither of them had heard him get off the couch.

Evan recognized that tic, and he was even more scared than he had been on his first day.

Especially when Carl grabbed the knife off the butcher block and dragged it across Boy's throat, making a hideous smile where there shouldn't be one, ordering Evan to stand still as the blood sprayed his face. And when Evan closed his eyes, Carl cuffed his ears, making them ring. 'This is your fault, so you watch!'

Bathed in sweat, pulse thundering, heart galloping, Evan jolted upright, jerking his head around as he tried to remember where he was. Slowly, as his surroundings became clear, he realized he was in his own home, not back in Bar Harbor, Michigan.

He wiped his mouth and grabbed the bottle of water off the coffee table, guzzling it down in one fast chug, then lowered his head between his knees, fighting off dizziness. The flashes he'd been having – two little boys huddled together in front of the basement door. How old had he been at the time, five, six? Older? It was hard to say. The years all seemed to meld together.

On the other hand, he clearly remembered having to eat his dinner as he stared at the gaping gash of Boy's throat. Carl left the body in the middle of the kitchen as a reminder, and only when it started to stink and attract flies did he get rid of it, ordering Evan to have the mess cleaned before he returned. Or else the basement. If Evan closed his eyes, he could still smell and taste the coppery, briny flavor of the blood, and he gagged thinking about it now.

The more he watched and obsessed over the detective, the more detailed his nightmares became as the memories were becoming clearer. Suddenly he was glad Callie McCormick was alive when she was found because if she hadn't been, he might not have been watching the news, and he would've missed seeing the detective. Everything was falling into place the way it should.

He stood and went into the kitchen where another flash stopped him in his tracks. *'You don't want me to kill you, too, do you?' Carl asked. 'I don't want to slit your throat like I did to Boy there, but I'll do it if you ever do something like that again.'*

Evan heard the words as if Carl was sitting beside him right now. And as he had then, he dug his nails deep into his forearms to stop himself from shaking. He'd understood all right. And never again did he make the same mistake. Not even when their screams echoed from the basement. In fact, he learned if he hid in a closet and covered his head with a pillow, he could pretend they weren't there. But the truth was as long as *they* screamed, Carl left him alone, didn't make him descend those dark steps where he'd be forced to do those things he didn't like. Those things that hurt and made Carl make strange, scary noises.

As he got older, Carl, a harsh teacher who lashed out at every mistake, taught him to read, write, and do math since he wasn't allowed to go to school, which was just as well since they were constantly moving. So, he learned. And not just about academics.

When he turned ten, Carl used him to lure the new Boys. It was distasteful, but he'd come to understand he was too old for his dad's particular tastes now, which freed him up to do what he pleased, as long as he didn't leave the property. Or at least as long as he didn't get *caught* leaving.

Until eight or nine years later, when Carl got sick, cancer eating away at him, rendering him useless, unable even to go to the grocery store. One day, Evan, who had taught himself to drive a year earlier, was cruising around the water when an idea sparked, and he sped the rest of the way home, not even caring if he got a ticket. Impatiently, he waited until dark, then dragged his weak, bedraggled father down to the old fishing boat, and rowed out before he dumped the old man into Lake Michigan. Carl tried to fight the inevitable, but he was feeble, so Evan sat back, detached, and watched as he listened to his dad's pathetic whimpers, begging Evan to save him. When Carl finally disappeared beneath the water for the last time, Evan rowed back to shore.

At the house, he located the key for the safe tucked into the back corner of Carl's closet and opened it. Stacks of money filled the chamber. He counted it. $63,413. The old man had hated banks, didn't trust them, so every time he got paid for whatever job he held at the moment, usually being a trucker or handyman, he stashed the money in this safe.

Evan divided the money into three suitcases and lugged it all out to the truck. He took nothing else. Not a toothbrush, clothes, or food. He was ready for a change, and though sixty grand wasn't enough to last a lifetime, it would go a long ways in getting him out of the Midwest.

As he remembered that day, Evan smiled. All that had led him here to Alyssa. And as he raised the scarf he'd stolen from her house and inhaled deeply of her scent, his eyes ran across the photo album. Curious, he grabbed it off the table and opened it.

Chapter Thirty-Six

Tuesday, April 2, 9:00p.m.

Alyssa grabbed a towel to wrap around her body as she stepped from the tub replaying the day's events in her mind. After watching the way Hunter Jenkins had reacted to Callie McCormick, they'd called in the rest of the team, and then she'd called Brock and begged off from dinner at his mom's house. 'We still have too much to do. Do you mind if I skip out this time?' she'd asked, not mentioning the words *serial killer*. And though she was telling the truth about work, they both knew, truth be told, she could've said she had to pluck her eyebrows, and that would've been just as effective at getting her out of seeing Mabel.

She and Cord had spent all morning and most of the afternoon trying to locate the people interviewed in Evelyn Martin's disappearance while Joe, Tony, Liz, and Hal divided the workload of the other missing women's cases. To her surprise, three of the individuals they were looking for were still employed at the Old Country Feed Store, and with their assistance, they were able to get contact information on two others. The only person they'd been unable to locate was Evan Bishop.

'He doesn't work here anymore. Hasn't for about eight, maybe ten years,' said Miles Garcia, the new owner of the store.

'Do you know how we can get ahold of him?' Alyssa asked.

'Nope. He was a bit of a recluse even when he worked here. He'd come in, do his job, and then leave. He never went out with any of the others, never came to the holiday parties or gatherings. Don't get me wrong. He was real friendly, and the customers liked him. He just kept to himself is all. None of us even knew where he lived, I don't think, but you can go ahead and talk to the others, in case I'm wrong. Honestly, if I didn't run into him at the market every once in a blue moon, I'd think he moved away.'

Then later that afternoon when the team reconvened to discuss and share information, Alyssa's phone had chimed an urgent email alert, so she'd taken a break to see what it was. The background checks on Larry Wilkins, Mearl Leroy, and Hunter Jenkins had come back. She skimmed the pages and then shared it with her team. 'Larry Wilkins is exactly what he claimed to be. His record is clean, not even a speeding or parking ticket to mar things up. Mearl Leroy is retired military with a few minor run-ins with the law in his early twenties. Aside from that, there's nothing that stands out as a red flag. And as for Hunter Jenkins, they didn't have much to go on, but they did verify his name came up as deceased.'

Something had been bugging her all day, and she'd looked over to Cord. 'I'm going to see what our techs can dredge up on Evan Bishop since he's the only person related to the Evelyn Martin case that we haven't been able to locate.'

'Good idea,' he'd said.

She shot off an email to the techs, and then the team went back to work, poring over the cases, trying to connect dots where there were none, and bouncing ideas and theories off one another. The entire time, Alyssa's mind was trying to figure out if Hunter Jenkins was a serial killer who could be responsible for more than Callie McCormick's murder, or if they were following a false trail.

By eight o'clock that evening, after hitting yet another meta-phorical brick wall, she was frustrated, sore, and plain pissy, especially after Cord cut off her caffeine supply because she hadn't eaten when the others had ordered pizza. The entire team moved back, allowing plenty of room for when Alyssa lost her mind. 'I *have* eaten recently,' she growled as she made to move around him, literally baring her teeth at him when he blocked her path and crossed his arms across his muscular chest, eyebrows raised in a dare as he refused to budge. Did he think she wouldn't use her Taser on him? Because her hand was already inching that way. How had she ever thought he was courteous, the jerk.

'Crackers,' he said snarkily, 'do not count as eating. You either eat – there's still a slice of veggie pie over there – or we call it quits for the night and start fresh tomorrow morning.'

Alyssa glared at everyone's exhausted faces and then relented. 'Fine,' she said, grabbing a few things, 'but when I get home, I'm drinking coffee.' And then she'd walked out.

Now, as she stood in front of her mirror, still foggy from her steamy bath, she used her blow dryer to clear a small circle and thought about the connection her teammates, specifically Liz, had made, that several of the victims looked like a much younger *her*. She grabbed her favorite brush and dragged it through the tangles in her hair. Objectively, she could see why Liz thought that, but personally, she wasn't convinced.

You remind me of her.

Terrie Mitchell's words rang in her mind, and she shook her head. Like she had told the others, there were lots of young, blonde women in New Mexico, and besides, she was unnaturally auburn. As she worked the knots out, she replayed her conversation with the medical examiner who'd come by after speaking to Captain Hammond regarding another case.

'I know Cord already relayed this information to you, but I wanted to speak to you myself. Now, I don't want to get your hopes up,' she said, 'but, in addition to the dirt embedded in Callie McCormick's nails when she tunneled her hand through her shallow grave, we've also got skin cells. That, in addition to several foreign hairs tangled in with her own, could give us enough for a DNA profile. I've already sent the samples off to the lab.'

Callie, we're getting close, she whispered. *We're going to find Hunter Jenkins or whoever did this to you and make him pay. I promise.* She repeated the vow as she twisted her hair up and grabbed for her favorite clip to hold it in place. 'Dang it, Holly. You have your own clips; why do you insist on stealing mine?' she said to her absent daughter. Irritated, she reminded herself she was grateful for the kind of relationship with Holly that allowed her to borrow her mother's things. She'd missed out on that aspect of growing up because Timmy's murder had drowned her mother's most basic ability to care about anything, including Alyssa. When she and Brock married, she had vowed if she ever had a daughter of her own, she would keep the lines of communication open, no matter what. Still, she wanted that hair clip.

She settled on a rubber band instead, finished putting her hair up, and went into the bedroom to put on her most comfortable pair of pajamas just as her family arrived home. Even if the slamming door hadn't shaken the whole foundation of the house, it would be hard not to notice everyone was here, considering her children were currently trying to outshout one another. With a groan and a muttered *Mabel*, she made her way downstairs.

'*I'm* not only the oldest, but I'm also Grandma's first grand-child, so obviously, the car would go to me!' Holly shouted.

'So what? It's not my fault I'm the youngest. Besides, I'm her only grandson, and you don't even like sports cars or racing, so why would you even care?' Isaac yelled back at his sister.

Brock was leaning against the counter, legs crossed, crunching an apple. She kissed his cheek, stole the fruit from his hand, and took a bite before handing it back. She inclined her head toward her children and mouthed the words, 'Your mom's *car*?' Her mother-in-law drove a beautiful but flashy yellow Camaro. Alyssa thought it made her look ridiculous. Her mother-in-law thought it made her look cool. 'Yep,' he said.

Alyssa shook her head and nipped the heated argument before it got completely out of hand. 'Grandma hasn't kicked it yet, so there's really no need to argue about who gets her car, now, is there? Besides, maybe neither of you will get it.'

Both Holly and Isaac turned their dispute on her, speaking over one another until she was forced to draw on the 'mom death glare,' shutting them both up. They knew that look, and they knew not to argue when she gave it. Holly walked by her, and Alyssa remembered her hair clip. 'Holly, don't forget to put my brown hair clip back in my bathroom, please.'

Holly turned in the doorway. 'What are you talking about? I don't have your brown hair clip,' she said, her voice surly.

'Well, it's not in my bathroom, and I'm sure neither your brother nor father took it, so, my deductive reasoning and detective skills tell me that leaves you.'

'Well, I didn't take it, so your deductive reasoning must be rusty. Maybe *you* lost it somewhere.'

Everyone stared at Holly like she'd grown a third eye in the center of her forehead. Alyssa religiously put things back where they belonged. *It only takes five extra seconds,* she always said whenever someone said they'd put something back 'later.' Standing her ground, Holly muttered, 'What? It could happen.'

Alyssa sighed. She was tired, and the last thing she needed to be fighting about was a hair clip. 'Will you just look? You might've even shoved it into your gym bag without thinking.'

Holly shrugged her shoulders, 'Okay, but it won't be there because I didn't take it.' She turned on her heels and walked away.

Isaac started to trail after his sister when Alyssa noticed his face was red and flushed. She put her arm out to stop him and settled the back of her hand against his forehead. 'You're a little warm. Are you feeling okay?'

'Everyone was coughing and hacking at Trevor's. It was gross. Maybe I caught a bug there. Can I go now?'

'Sure,' she said, letting her arm fall back to her side.

A few seconds later, two doors shut loudly enough to indicate teenage displeasure without actually slamming the bedroom doors. They'd learned early in life that slamming doors was not worth the trouble it caused.

'Do I even want to know how that conversation got started?' she asked Brock.

'Mom,' he said, and that was all she needed to hear.

His mother had a penchant for causing strife between her only two grandchildren. She liked to hear them argue over who loved her the most. It was like a game to her, a kind of power trip even. 'Of course. Why didn't I think of that?'

'I don't know,' Brock replied, grabbing onto the tie of her pajamas to pull her to him. 'Why didn't you?'

'So, what'd I miss for dinner?' she asked.

At his grimace, she laughed. 'Meatloaf? Really?' He wrinkled his nose, and she laughed harder. Mabel insisted that her son loved her homemade meatloaf when in reality, he could barely stomach it… and refused to break her heart by telling her. 'I'm so sorry I missed that.'

'Yeah, I'm sure you are. On a different note, did you get anywhere on your case?'

Reminded of her disappointment, she admitted, 'Not far. And Cord cut off my caffeine,' she grumbled, still irritated, even if he'd been right.

'Jerk. Want me to beat him up for you?' Brock pulled her into his arms where she settled her head against her husband's solid chest.

'Hmm. It's an idea. Can I get back to you?' She felt his nod, and she smiled. 'He said I had to eat first, that crackers weren't considered food.'

'He's right. But I'll still kick his ass if you want,' Brock said.

'Thanks,' she mumbled into his frame as the words *serial killer* and *resembles you* blasted through her brain. 'And I think our leads are finally starting to branch out now. It's just a matter of finding which limb to go out on first.'

'You'll get it, babe. You always do.'

Chapter Thirty-Seven

His chest heaving as he tried to calm his galloping heart, Bishop observed the wreckage he'd created in his blind rage. Vein pulsing in his temple, he jerked open the utility closet, nearly ripping the door off its hinges, grabbed a broom, and swept up the splintered glass littered with the news articles about Alyssa Wyatt. Just thinking about her made him howl, an unnatural growl echoing off his walls, and he threw the broom across the room. After seeing the photo album, he'd read them again, this time with a new understanding.

His gaze was drawn to a trickle of blood trailing down his arm where he'd gouged himself. Tremors shook his body as he moved over to the sink to clean his arm. When he finished, he walked into the living room, his fists clenching and unclenching at the sight of his shattered lamps.

Shattered – just like his life. His fury almost blinded him as he began the process of picking up the broken pieces. Shards of glass were embedded in the couch and the furthest recesses of the room.

It all made perfect sense now. In order to survive, he'd forced his life before Carl to the darkest recesses of his mind, but now that they were back in the open, the memories swamped him like thousands of tiny gnats on a hot summer's day.

He'd been riding his bike in front of the house when Alyssa went inside for some Kool-Aid. She left him there alone to fend for himself against the bad man. He was only trying to help the old man in the wheelchair.

It was a sunny day, and the mosquitoes were thick, but Timmy wanted to play outside anyway, and since all his friends were gone for the summer, he begged his sister to play with him, but she refused.

'I'm braiding my hair,' she said as he watched, mesmerized as her fingers magically twisted her hair into a long pleat. She'd been practicing doing it by herself since she was nine now.

And then Mama came in, and he put on his sad face and said, 'Mama, 'Lyssa won't play outside with me. She says she's too old.' He looked down at the floor and scuffed his shoes against the tile.

Mama put her hands on her hips. 'Lys, it won't kill you to play outside with your brother for a while. Why don't you go ride your bikes or something?'

'I don't want to play with him. I'm too big now,' Alyssa whined.

Mama placed one finger against her lip, tapping as she thought about it. Then she said, 'Yes, I can see that. You're right. So, why don't you go change your clothes and grab some garden gloves? You can help Daddy and me weed, mow the lawn, rake the leaves, and mend the fence.'

Alyssa hated yard work, just hated it. And Mama knew it, too. She heaved out a huge breath and glared at her little brother. 'I'll play with Timmy.'

Mama looked surprised. 'Oh. Well, I guess it's your choice. I just thought you were too old.'

Timmy ran over and threw his arms around his sister's waist. 'We're going to have so much fun, just wait and see!'

'One hour. We'll ride our bikes for one hour, not a second more, okay?'

Timmy nodded and ran out the door, Alyssa close on his heels.

Overheated from riding in the hot sun, she stood in the shade of a willow tree and watched him for a while before she hollered, 'Timmy, I'm going to get some Kool-Aid. Do you want some?'

'Is it strawberry?'

'No, grape.'

He wrinkled his nose. 'No way,' he said. As soon as the screen door slammed, rattling the glass at the top, Timmy rode from one mailbox to another in front of his house and his neighbor's even though he wasn't supposed to leave the yard.

When he heard someone call out, he stopped and looked around. A man in a wheelchair was sitting on the sidewalk in front of his friend's house and waving for him to come over. Timmy looked over his shoulder to the house and then the backyard. His sister hadn't come back out, and Mama and Daddy were still busy, so he got off his bike and laid it on the ground.

He knew he wasn't supposed to leave the yard, but he was also supposed to be polite because it was the right thing to do, Mama always said. Besides, he was pretty sure this was the same guy who'd lost his puppy by his preschool a few days ago.

'Hi,' the man said. 'My puppy ran under that blue van there, and I can't get him out. Can you help me?' He pointed down the street.

It was the same man. He should buy a better leash. 'I'm not 'posed to go that far or talk to strangers,' said Timmy. 'I'll get my daddy, and he can help.'

'Oh, well, it's just my puppy might get away if I don't hurry.' The man sounded so sad.

Timmy was conflicted. He didn't want to get in trouble, but he didn't want the man to lose his puppy either. He looked at the man, then at his house, then back at the man. He sure wished his sister was here. She'd know what to do because she was nine now.

If he hurried, he could get the puppy and be back before anyone knew he'd left the yard. 'Okay, I'll help, but we have to hurry.'

The man smiled. 'Thank you. What's your name anyway?'

'Timmy. Timothy Evan Archer,' he said proudly.

'Well, Timmy, Timothy Evan Archer, my name is Carl. Now, we're not strangers.' Carl reached out and shook Timmy's little hand, then pointed to the blue MBC plumbing van. 'I think I saw Spot — that's my puppy's name — go under that van. He might be by the back tire. Can you check for me?'

Timmy knelt down to peer under the van, but the man said, 'I don't know if you'll be able to see him from there. He's a sneaky little bugger. You might have to go behind there to look.'

'Okay,' Timmy said as he stood back up and walked toward the open back door of the van. And then something covered his mouth and nose, and he suddenly felt very tired. Just before he passed out, the man stood and threw the wheelchair and Timmy's bike into the back of the van.

When he woke, he was tied to a bed. He tried to lift his head, but his body felt like those heavy bags of dry cement Daddy used to make the patio. He was scared, and the bed was wet beneath him where he'd peed his pants. He started to cry. 'I want my mama,' Timmy sniffled.

'Well, now, I'm afraid your mama doesn't want you.' The man, no longer in the wheelchair, came through the door, and Timmy screamed. 'That's why she asked me to take you,' he said, speaking over Timmy's cries.

But Mama loved him; she said so every night when she tucked him in and read him a bedtime story. Even when she was mad, she told him she loved him. Voice shaking, Timmy stammered, 'My mama lo-lo-loves me; she to-to-told me so.'

The man removed Timmy's shirt and wet pants, leaving him naked. 'Well, you see, Timmy, your sister – that was your sister outside with you, right?' When Timmy nodded, Carl said, 'Why did she go in the house and leave you outside?'

'To g-g-get a dr-drink of Kool-Aid.'

Carl stared down, his scary eyes making Timmy shudder. 'She didn't really go in for Kool-Aid, Timmy. She went in so I could take you. You're too much trouble, and your family never wants to see you again.'

Spasms of sadness and fear raced through him. Why didn't they want him anymore? What had he done wrong? Was it because he wanted to play outside? And what about Daddy?

Carl touched Timmy's face, and then moved his hands down his body. 'Pretty soon you won't even remember your old family.' And then he'd put him in the shower and taken him to the basement.

The next day, he told him his new name would be Evan. And every day when Carl hurt him, he reminded him that his family no longer wanted him, that Carl was his dad now. It wasn't long before Timmy began to disappear, and he forgot his first family altogether.

Other Boys came and stayed in the scary basement, too. Some only stayed for a little bit, and some, like Evan, stayed for a long time. Then one day, Carl unlocked his cage and told him they were leaving. The other little boys watched with wide, frightened eyes as Carl dragged him by one arm up the steps. Outside, he tossed him in the truck where he landed hard on the floorboard. They drove to the end of the road, and then he stopped and jumped out, ordering him not to move, and Evan knew to obey. Pretty soon, a loud explosion rocked the truck, and then Carl jumped back in and hit the gas.

They passed lots of firetrucks on their way out of town.

He let the memory wash over him, reigniting his rage. Spittle formed in the corners of his mouth and his nostrils flared as he now turned his attention to his basement. It was still intact; he hadn't used it since Callie McCormick. He cleaned it anyway, scrubbing every surface, including the walls, until his fingers were raw. He had new plans for this room, and those plans included Alyssa Wyatt. And she would come to him because he was going to do to her what she'd done to him.

Chapter Thirty-Eight

Wednesday, April 3

The officer walked up the flagstone path to the front door and rang the doorbell. A boy answered wearing a pair of purple Colorado Rockies sweats and a muscle shirt. His eyes were watery, and his nose was red. He seemed confused as to why a policeman was standing on his front step.

'I'm Officer Shane Pobiv. Isaac Wyatt?'

'Yeah, I'm Isaac. Why? Is everything okay?'

Officer Pobiv shifted from foot to foot as he avoided the boy's gaze. 'I'm afraid not, son. I'm sorry to tell you this, but your mom's been in a bad accident. Your dad and sister are already at the hospital, and they asked me if I'd get you. You're going to need to come with me right away.'

'What kind of accident? Is she going to be alright? Why didn't someone call me?' Isaac asked, his questions flying like bullets.

'I don't know a whole lot, but I promised your dad I'd hurry. I'll try to answer your questions on the way.'

Shane could see Isaac was visibly shaken; his hands trembled, and moisture pooled in his eyes as he reached up to scrub at them before the tears could spill over.

'Okay,' Isaac said. 'I've just got to grab my shoes and my phone.'

'We really need to go now. You can use mine to call your sister and let her know we're on the way.'

Isaac didn't argue as he bent low to retrieve a pair of sneakers and rushed out the door to the waiting car. When he saw it wasn't a police cruiser, he hesitated.

'It's an undercover car, but don't worry, I have my lights in the back; I'll turn 'em on and get you to the hospital before you can blink,' Pobiv explained.

Isaac accepted the explanation, climbed inside the car, and put on his already laced-up shoes before buckling his seatbelt.

As the officer backed down the driveway, he engaged the childproof locks installed in the car.

On the road, Isaac asked, 'Um. Can I call my dad now?'

'I thought... I guess I forgot to tell you; in his rush to get to the hospital, your dad forgot his phone at work. That's why I mentioned calling your sister, but I suppose you wouldn't've understood why I said that. What say you let me maneuver through these roads and when I reach the highway, I can dig my phone out. That work for you?'

'Yeah. I guess. Yeah. Okay.' Isaac's fingers began a steady tap-tap-tap against his sweats, and before long, his legs joined in, bouncing up and down in rhythm as the officer navigated his way to I-40.

Pobiv interrupted the silence by asking, 'So, you're in high school?'

Isaac stared numbly out the window as he answered, 'Um, no, eighth grade. I'll be in high school next year.' He watched the familiar scenery pass before asking, 'How long do you think it'll take to get to the hospital this way?'

'Depends on the traffic, but I'd say no more than fifteen minutes. The other way is still jammed with the investigation and clean-up. Don't worry, son; I'll get you there.' He reached over and ruffled the kid's hair. Isaac didn't actually pull away, but he came close. Pobiv dropped his hand.

Isaac chewed his thumbnails down to the quick as the streets passed by in a blur. 'Um, I think you just missed the turn for the hospital.' He hitched his thumb behind him to show the turnoff that said, 'Hospital Exit.'

Distracted, the officer looked over and said, 'What? Sorry. I was thinking about your mom.'

Isaac turned in his seat as much as the seatbelt would allow and repeated, 'The exit for the hospital? You just missed it.'

'She's not at that hospital; she's at one further down the highway.'

Isaac couldn't remember which hospital that was. 'Oh. Can I call my dad – I mean, my sister – now? I need to know how my mom's doing?' Isaac's voice was strained.

'Of course.' The officer reached into his pocket, and as he pulled out his phone, it vibrated in his hand. He answered the call. 'Officer Pobiv. Yeah. Yeah. Oh no. Okay. Yeah, I can do that. Okay, yeah, I'll tell him; I've got him right here with me now. Thanks for calling.' He disconnected.

'Hey, man. I'm real sorry, but that was one of the officers at the hospital. They're transferring your mom somewhere else, but they haven't been told where yet. Your dad wanted to know if you could just hang out with me until he finds out. Real sorry, kid; I know you want to be with your mom more than me.'

Isaac jerked his head as if he'd been slapped. 'Can you call that officer back so I can talk to my dad and at least see how my mom's doing?' His voice trembled with nerves.

'Aw, man. I'm sorry, but your dad's busy trying to find out where your mom's being taken. Officer Dante said to tell you your dad would call as soon as your sister brought his phone to him and as soon as he knew something concrete.'

'Holly's getting my dad's phone? I thought she was at the hospital already.'

'I guess your mom's partner called and asked her to swing by your dad's office to grab his phone for him.'

'Dad won't know I don't have my phone with me; I should've just grabbed it. It would've only taken a few seconds,' Isaac muttered before he nervously began biting his lips and fidgeting in his seat, his hands and feet tapping in sync. A few seconds later he asked, 'Can I call my sister then?'

'I'm afraid she's stuck in the traffic jam caused by your mom's accident. And you know it's illegal to be on the phone and drive.'

'She won't be,' Isaac said. 'She has Bluetooth, so she just has to push a button on her radio.'

Officer Pobiv reached over and touched the boy lightly on the shoulder. 'I know you're worried about your mom; so am I. As soon as I can make it happen, I'll make sure you get ahold of your dad or sister or someone close to the situation. Okay?'

He waited for Isaac to nod before removing his hand from his shoulder.

Chapter Thirty-Nine

Dog-tired from slamming into brick wall after brick wall trying to determine the whereabouts of Hunter Jenkins, Alyssa dragged herself through the door, hung her jacket on the coat-rack, and toed off her shoes. The house was unusually quiet, and she wondered where everyone was. In the kitchen, she tossed the McCormick file onto the table, set her phone and keys down, and finally removed her gun. Her back and neck hurt from being hunched over evidence folders all day. The throbbing behind her eyes told her a migraine was a strong possibility. As a matter of prevention, she headed to the medicine cabinet. The doctors told her the kind of pain reliever that worked best for her type of migraine contained caffeine. Go figure.

Though the wine begged for attention, she opted for iced tea instead. Opening the freezer, she mulled over choices for dinner. Nothing appealing jumped out at her, so she tried the pantry only to return to the freezer as if the contents might have suddenly changed, and inspiration would hit her. Julia Childs she was not, so she finally opted for some chicken breasts, pulling them out and placing them in the sink with cold water so they could defrost.

That done, she reached into the cubby hole the family jokingly nicknamed the 'dead boyfriend closet' and grabbed some potatoes which she peeled and dropped into a pot. Finally, she pulled a can of green beans out of the pantry, stared at it for a minute, then placed it back on the shelf, and replaced it with a can of the kids' favorite, cream corn. Setting everything except the chicken on the counter, she looked at her assembled masterpiece-to-be.

Not the best meal in the world, she thought, but it'd do in a pinch.

She was pulling her hair back into a ponytail when she heard the garage door open, and a few seconds later, Holly and Brock walked in.

'You're home earlier than I expected,' Brock said, kissing her cheek.

'A little bit. Where's Isaac?' she asked, looking toward the garage.

'What do you mean "Where's Isaac?" He's not home?'

'No.'

When her husband's brows furrowed to form an upside down 'v,' Alyssa said, 'What?'

'He still wasn't feeling well this morning, so I called the school to let them know he was sick and wouldn't be in. He did have a test he didn't want to have to make up, so maybe he decided to go in late for that. Though I don't know why he wouldn't have let one of us know,' Brock told her.

'Hmm. Well, maybe he's with Trevor then.'

Holly interrupted, looking up from texting, 'I saw Trevor when I drove by the school, and Isaac wasn't with him. Trevor was by himself, listening to his iPod, bopping his head.' She shrugged, grabbed an apple from the fruit bowl, and took a huge bite out of it.

'Don't ruin your appetite; I'm making dinner,' Alyssa said automatically, though her mind was elsewhere.

'I won't. I'm going to my room. I need to text Sophie and find out what she's wearing for her senior speech.' Holly groaned. 'Why English teachers feel the need to torture and bore everyone by making us write *and* listen to these speeches is beyond me. It's a conspiracy, you know?' she said, circling her apple around dramatically. 'But it must be done.' At that, she heaved her back off the counter as if it had been superglued and made her way to her room.

'See if your brother's in his room on your way, will you?' Alyssa asked.

'Sure thing.' A few seconds later, she yelled down. 'Not in here. Unless he's hiding under his bed or lost under that mountain of crap in there. In which case, there's no hope of finding him.'

Alyssa eyes wandered to the clock. It was five forty. 'I'll just send him a text and ask where he is. If he's sick, he shouldn't be out anyway.' As soon as she pushed *send* on her phone, a familiar chime came from the living room. Her head whipped around. 'He left his phone?'

She walked into the family room, Brock close behind, and sure enough, on the far end table sat Isaac's phone. Prickles of unease crawled up her spine and settled at the back of her neck. Being a detective, she was not prone to panic, but something was definitely not right with this situation. She snatched up Isaac's phone and unlocked it. The rule in their house was that she and Brock could check phones at any time for any reason. There were dozens of unread messages as well as several missed calls.

She clicked on the envelope icon. The last text was from her, of course, but most were from Trevor, and some from a few other friends. She opened Trevor's, reading them out loud.

> **Dude, whr r u? Tst today. Did u frgt?**

> **Sry, just got yer txt frm this am sucks yer sick. Test not bad. Msg me.**

> **RU feeling btr? Heard a freaking funny joke 2day. TTYL.**

> **Dude, I no yer not feeling good and all, but text me, man.**

Alyssa continued scrolling through the messages. There was one from Brock sent at around eleven thirty. *Just checking on you. On a quick break. Why don't you give your mom a call now or send her a text to let her know you stayed home. I'm heading back to my meeting in five minutes, so if you get this in time, message me back. Love you.*

'Well, obviously, he never sent me a text.' An unshakeable sense that something was wrong filled her, and her mind immediately went to Callie McCormick. *Isaac is not a young, blonde female* she told herself. *Don't borrow trouble.*

'I'm sorry, babe,' Brock said. 'I should've sent you a message to let you know. I just figured he could do it real quick since he was probably just lazing on the couch.'

'I hate to be repetitive here, but again, he didn't.'

'If he didn't go to school, I don't know where he would've gone. He had a fever of a hundred point five before I left, so I asked him if he wanted me to cancel my meeting and stay home with him, but he told me he didn't need a babysitter.' Brock's face tinged pink when he admitted, 'He asked me not to call you right away because he didn't want you to "go all mother hen" on him.' When she opened her mouth, he rushed to say, 'His words, not mine. Just, full disclosure.'

'Well, apparently he wasn't just "lazing on the couch." ' She held her palm out to silence Brock's argument – or his defense. Either way. 'Nothing we can do about it now except figure out where he is.' She lit up the screen on Isaac's phone. The last text besides hers had come in a little after five, but she hadn't heard it go off. She swiped her finger across the phone to check for voicemails, but there weren't any. She opened up the *recent* and *missed calls* log. Nothing outgoing from him after last night, and most of the missed calls, again, came from Trevor.

She pushed *return call* on the phone and impatiently tapped her fingers on her leg until Trevor answered.

'Dude,' Trevor said, drawing out the ooo sound. 'I thought you were dead. Wh –' Alyssa cut him off midsentence.

'Trevor, it's Alyssa. I take it you didn't see Isaac at school today?' She knew the answer but asked anyway.

'Oh, hey, Mrs. Detective Lady,' he said, giving his usual greeting. 'Nope, haven't seen him. Thought he was home sick. He ain't there?' After a pause, he said, 'Well, duh, he's not there, or you wouldn't be calling.'

'Any idea where he might've gone?' she asked, without much hope.

'No, ma'am. Sorry.'

'Okay. Well, do me a favor. If you happen to hear from him, let us know.'

Trevor said okay, and she disconnected the call. 'Where could he be?' she asked out loud. The headache she was hoping to stave off was back.

Keeping her voice even, she said, 'Regardless of what he wanted, I should've been told he was staying home.' And if she was being honest, she wasn't only mad at her husband; she was also mad at herself for not checking on him. Even though he was still in bed when she left this morning, she had seen that he was still feverish when she looked in on him.

Brock's hand squeezed her shoulder, and he used the other to turn her face toward him. 'I know you're mad, and you have a right to be. And I said I'm sorry. But, let's figure out where he is because this isn't like him, and then you can yell at me all you want.' He pulled her into his arms for a stiff hug.

She might be a detective, but first and foremost, she was a mom, and she was scared. Newspaper images of Timmy's body, unrecognizable from the elements, swam through her vision, and she shook her head to clear it. She refused to let her imagination go wild on her, refused to think about the last time someone important in her life had gone missing; there *had* to be a logical reason he wasn't home. And when they finally figured out where he was, they'd all laugh about it later.

Or not.

The grandfather clock in the corner chimed, and in unison, they noted the time. Six o'clock.

'Will you get Holly? We need to let her know what's going on so she doesn't freak out.'

As he walked away, Brock's words, faint but audible, filtered back to her. '*I'd* like to know what's going on so *I* don't freak out.' But he went upstairs and knocked loudly on Holly's door. Alyssa heard her daughter screech as she yelled out. 'Jeez, Dad. Scare the crap out of me, why don't you! You could knock, you know.'

'Yeah, I'll try to think of that next time. Oh, that's right, I *did* think of that. Maybe turn your music down a decibel or two and you'd hear me. So maybe you could watch your mouth and turn that rubbish off. I can hear it all the way over here. If you're not careful, you'll be deaf before you ever make it to college, much less your internship.'

'Well? Did you want something?'

'You need to come downstairs with Mom and me. We still don't know where Isaac is.'

'Wait, what? Isaac's *missing*?' Holly, wearing a pair of fuzzy monkey slippers, flew past her father as she thundered down the stairs.

'No, he's not missing; we just don't know where he is exactly,' he said.

'Isn't that the *definition of missing*?' She rushed over to her mom.

In the living room, Alyssa tried to calm Holly, to stop her from going into a full-blown anxiety attack.

'I'm sure there's a logical reason for your brother not being home. Just calm down, and let's not jump to conclusions before we even get started.' She heard herself saying the words, but she wasn't really believing them herself. Still, she didn't need her daughter panicking on top of everything else. She needed to deal with one thing at a time.

'If there's a logical reason, why do I need to be down here? Because there's nothing logical about this, that's why. My brother's missing!'

'Your brother's not missing. We just don't know where he is.'

'Oh! My! Gosh! What *is* it with you two?' Holly's head whipped back and forth between her parents. 'Not knowing where someone is *is the definition of missing!*' She enunciated each word, her voice almost a shout at the end. 'Aren't you a *detective*? Shouldn't you *know* that?'

She was so mature for her age, Alyssa sometimes forgot her daughter was still a teenager with a mouth. Even so, she understood Holly was nervous, like the rest of them.

'You know, I should call my mom and let her know what's going on,' Brock finally said, already pulling out his phone. And then his face lit up. 'That's it. I bet he's at Mom's.'

Alyssa couldn't believe they hadn't thought of that already, but even as her hopes rose, her stomach clenched, her gut telling her he wasn't at Mabel's. Still, she held her breath as Brock placed the call. When her mother-in-law finally answered, Alyssa and Holly listened to his end of the conversation.

'Yeah. Hey, Mom. No, listen. Mom…' His mom rarely bothered to ask *why* someone was calling before launching into whatever topic was on her mind when her phone rang. Alyssa fisted her hands and stopped herself from yanking the phone from her husband. 'Mom! No, I didn't watch *The Voice*.' He raised his voice over hers. 'I called to see if Isaac's with you.'

Alyssa heard him ask, but she knew what Mabel's answer was before Brock turned to her with a pained look and shook his head 'no,' pinching the bridge of his nose as he did. Isaac was *not* with her because if he was, she would've jumped right into what they were having for dinner and been indignant that they would've wanted her to call to tell them her own grandson was hanging out with her. Alyssa's chest deflated as she let out the pent-up breath she'd been holding.

Brock assured his mom she didn't need to come over, that he'd let her know as soon as they knew something, and then hung up, facing Alyssa.

She did her best to put on her professional face as she said, 'I'm going to call Cord and make a formal report.'

Holly, eyes wide, stopped chewing her fingernail and said, 'But doesn't he have to be missing twenty-four hours or something?'

'No, that's a myth, and besides, he's fourteen.' Alyssa dialed Cord, throat constricted, to report her son missing.

Chapter Forty

Wednesday, April 3

'My mom's not really in the hospital, is she?' Isaac whispered as they drove into the canyon. The trees were taller and thicker here, the road curvier and more narrow. When he didn't respond, Isaac asked, 'Was she even in an accident?' From the corner of his eye, he saw Officer Pobiv's grip tighten on the steering wheel, and Isaac reached for the door handle.

'Won't do you any good. Childproof locks. And even if you succeeded in opening the door, you'd kill yourself jumping out at this speed.'

Isaac snapped his hand back as if he'd been caught stealing cookies before dinner time. He cradled both arms around his stomach.

'What made you stay home today anyway? I was expecting to have to wait until you were walking home from school for this.' He waved his hand between them. When Isaac didn't answer, the man's hand shot out and slammed his head against the passenger window. 'I asked you a question.'

Isaac cried out and then, voice trembling, he answered, 'I was sick.'

Bishop nodded as if he understood. He drove another five minutes before he pulled onto the shoulder of the road. He turned off the engine and faced Isaac. 'Look, kid, you're a smart one, and I think you know the score here. Your mom isn't in the hospital and was never in an accident, so at least you can relax about that.' From the center console, he pulled out a blindfold and dangled it in front of his face.

Evan ignored the moisture pooling in the boy's eyes. 'I'm going to put this on you so you don't try to memorize where we are or where we're going. And then you're going to recline your seat and lie back. Do you understand?' He asked it like a question but said it like a threat.

Isaac managed to tilt his head forward in what could be taken for a nod. 'Why?' he choked out.

'Why did I take you?' When Isaac mumbled *yes*, Bishop said simply, 'I want your mom to come to me. No, don't ask me anything else. Now, hold this over your eyes,' he ordered. When Isaac obeyed, Evan shoved his head forward and tied the cloth, yanking it hard to ensure it was tight. The yelp of pain made him smile. He was already hurting *her* by hurting her son. He grabbed the kid by the hair as he pulled him back up, happy to see the boy's body quaking. He leaned in to whisper, 'Remember this: everything that happens to you now is your mother's fault. She's to blame, not me.' After Isaac was reclined as far as the seat allowed, Evan started the car and pulled back onto the interstate.

Surveilling Alyssa's house from inside the vacant house across the street this morning, he couldn't believe his luck when he realized the kid was staying home from school. Impatient to put his plan into action now that his timeline had unexpectedly moved up, he'd donned the uniform he'd too easily purchased online years ago and then gathered his belongings, looking around to ensure he left no trace behind. He walked to the house's garage where he was currently parked and threw his things into the trunk, deciding not to re-engage the cable connected to the automatic garage door.

And now here they were. Every few minutes, Bishop glanced over to make sure the blindfold was still firmly in place. He didn't expect any problems, but he was prepared for them anyway.

The unpaved road leading to his house was bumpy, and occasionally they'd hit a rut so hard, the kid's head would smack into the side of the door. When they finally came to a stop, he got out of the car and walked around, unlocking the boy's door before pulling it open. Roughly, he gripped Isaac's elbow and hauled him out, ignoring the kid's pained yelp when his head hit the top of the door frame. Keeping a tight grip as Isaac stumbled beside him, he marched the boy up the steps and entered the code to get in.

Inside, he re-engaged the lock, and guided Isaac to a small couch, pushing him into it.

It was time to implement the next step.

It was time for Alyssa to pay.

Chapter Forty-One

Wednesday, April 3, 6:30p.m.

Alyssa needed air, and she turned away with the intention of stepping outside for a few minutes, but before she could, the doorbell rang, and she and Holly both jumped. Cord was here. Feeling more than a little numb, she went to let her partner in. Behind Cord were Liz and two officers; one she knew, but the other had only been on the force a few months and wasn't someone she'd encountered before tonight.

Cord gave her arm a reassuring squeeze as he walked into the house, followed by Liz who embraced her stiff form. As the others stepped inside, Alyssa watched as her partner wrapped a blushing Holly into a strong hug. Even though the seriousness of the situation weighed heavily in the room, her daughter had just been embraced by her not-so-secret secret 'old-guy' crush as she liked to say when she was being teased.

Brock, who'd been standing in the space separating the kitchen from the living room, moved forward, arm extended for a handshake. Cord met him partway.

'Brock.' Cord inclined his head toward the two officers standing idly by the front door, the squawking of one of their radios grating loudly on everyone's nerves. 'These are Officers Finley and Alexander.' Alyssa and Brock took turns stepping forward to shake their hands.

'Thanks for coming,' Brock said.

'No problem.' Cord looked at Alyssa and said, 'You told me a little bit on the phone, but why don't we all sit down so you can fill in some of the blanks.'

Alyssa nodded and led the way to the couches so everyone could sit. Officer Finley pulled out a red notebook and a black pen. He flipped to a clean page, clicked the end of the pen, and wrote the date on the top.

Suddenly the whole thing became real, and Alyssa felt her vision blur and her body go numb. This was all too familiar. She jumped back up, startling Holly who had settled down next to her. Her fingers clenched and unclenched as she bit her bottom lip; she needed to be *doing* something. Except for that one time, the time that had irrevocably changed the path of her life, she wasn't used to being on this side of an investigation.

Only this time was different because this time it was her *son*, not her brother.

'Does anyone want something to drink? Coffee? Tea? Water? I have soda, if you prefer.' She was rambling, she knew, but couldn't stop.

Officers Finley and Alexander declined, but Cord understood her need to move, to do something active, and he said, 'I'd love some coffee – if you've got any handy.'

She forced a laugh but shook her head, appreciating his attempt at humor. 'Yeah, I'm sure I can cough up some java somewhere in this house.' She looked at the other two officers. 'You're sure you don't want anything?'

They both declined, and she strode into the kitchen to get coffee for herself, Brock, and Cord. At the last minute, she grabbed a diet soda for Holly. Brock was filling Cord in when she walked back in and set everything down on the coffee table. All eyes locked on her as she reported what she knew, and more importantly, what she didn't.

For Holly and Brock, she tried to keep it together as fear skittered along her spine.

Chapter Forty-Two

Huddled into a corner of the threadbare couch, his arms bound in front of him, his feet tied at the ankles, Isaac watched the man wear a deeper path in his already-worn carpet. On the floor was a photo album just like one he'd seen in his mom's room. It was open to a page showing a picture of two little kids. He couldn't tell much from this distance, but he thought he could make out two bikes.

Every once in a while, the crazy cop mumbled something about how she – his mom – had to pay. Pay for what? Afraid of hyperventilating, Isaac concentrated on taking even breaths and making himself as small as possible as he tried to curl into a tight ball. Aside from a headache and a sore throat, his skin was clammy in that way that usually preceded him getting the cold sweats, so he knew it wasn't only fear making his body shake. It didn't help that his heartbeat was so rapid it caused a tingling in his chest, and he was scared he might actually be having a heart attack. More than anything, he wished what was happening to him could be chalked up to nothing more than a feverish hallucination, that at any minute, his mom would walk in and pull him out of this nightmare.

And he had no one to blame but himself for allowing himself to get into this situation to begin with. Seriously, he should've known right away something was wrong when the cop, if that's what he really was – why would he have been driving an unmarked car while wearing a police uniform – talked him out of grabbing his phone. He replayed all the events leading up to this moment and easily picked out a dozen things he'd do differently. His dad always liked to say, 'Hindsight is twenty/twenty.' And every time he said it, Isaac rolled his eyes. He was now living the truth of the statement.

Suddenly the man stopped pacing and swung around so fast, Isaac flinched as he tried to burrow deeper into the couch. And before he could react, the man grabbed hold of the rope binding his hands and yanked until he landed with a thud on the floor. Isaac felt the burn in his wrists and couldn't stop from crying out. And when the man started dragging him toward the kitchen, he twisted and pulled as he tried to free himself. With a grunt, the man, keeping a grip on Isaac's bound hands, kicked him in the kidney.

He gasped, trying to catch his breath even as the man continued dragging him until they reached a door with a metal bar across it. He let Isaac drop as he wrestled with a key in the lock, jiggling it back and forth as he pushed and pulled on the door, trying to get it open. A minute later, howling in rage, with spittle flying from his mouth, he threw the key. The metallic clang as it hit the wall and landed in the sink sounded almost as scary as a bullet. Isaac was still trying to catch his breath as the man once more reached down and grabbed hold of his bound wrists, dragging him across a kitchen floor and down a hall to a windowless room where he kicked Isaac until he rolled out of the way, gasping for air. Before the man slammed the door closed, he screeched, 'You don't know anything about your mom. Everything she's ever told you is a lie. And now she'll pay!'

In the dark room, Isaac tried breathing through his nose, afraid he was going to throw up. To make things worse, he wasn't only terrified for his own life, but now he was scared for his mom, too. Because he knew she would stop at nothing to find him. And not just because she was a good detective, but because nobody messed with her kids – ever. There was mama bear protective, and then there was his mom's version of mama bear protective.

Still, he prayed she'd hurry up and find him. He even made a deal with God: when his mom rescued him, he'd never, ever raise another ruckus about cleaning his room or wearing dress clothes again. Heck, he'd throw a black-tie affair for her himself. When guilt inched its way in as he realized he was praying for his mom to walk into this guy's trap, Isaac reminded himself his mom was an officer of the law, and she knew how to protect herself.

Keeping his eyes trained on the door, he let himself daydream about his impending rescue. Mom and Cord would lead the cavalry, blowing the door off its hinges in a surprise attack. Wood from the exploding door would hit the man in the face, stunning him. Smoke from the flashbang would blind the guy, allowing Isaac the chance to knock him down while his mom came flying in all kung-Fu, ninja style.

Tears fell freely as he pictured himself wrapped safely in his mom's arms, not caring that he was fourteen and yearning for his mother.

–

Unsure how long he'd been in the room, Isaac watched as the shadow of the man's footsteps passed the door time and time again. With each pass, Isaac's muscles seized in fear. And then when they stopped, and the door was shoved open, his entire body shook uncontrollably.

In one of the man's hands was a bowl, in the other a knife. 'I'm going to untie your feet,' he said as he entered the room, 'and if you try anything at all, I'll kill you. I'll slit your throat and mail your head back to your mother. Do you understand me?'

Isaac's head nodded, but he didn't know if he was agreeing or if it was a reaction from his body shaking so hard. Pobiv set the bowl on the floor and then sliced the rope at his feet, tingles spreading from Isaac's toes up his legs as feeling returned.

'Sit up,' the man ordered, and Isaac struggled to obey, falling over several times before he was able to stay upright, using the wall to help. 'Hold your hands up.' Again, Isaac did as he was told.

The man placed a bowl of chicken noodle soup in his trembling hands, eyes narrowing as it sloshed over the sides. Isaac risked a question, his voice cracking as he spoke. 'My hands –'

'If you want to eat, you'll have to figure out a way to do it like that,' the man interrupted and walked back out, this time leaving the door opened.

Chapter Forty-Three

Wednesday, April 3, 7:30p.m.

Cord and Officers Finley and Alexander were out canvassing the neighborhood – insisting Alyssa stay home when she tried to accompany them – and Liz, in an effort to make herself useful since her forensic artist skills weren't needed at the moment, was preparing the dinner Alyssa had gotten out – though she could've told her it was going to go uneaten as the mere thought of food was enough to make her want to throw up.

Brock and Holly were in the process of calling every single one of Isaac's contacts while Alyssa was on the phone, arguing with Captain Hammond. 'No, I can't *prove* my son has been abducted...' She closed her eyes, gripping the phone until her fingers were white, as she reminded herself that throwing the phone would result in nothing but a broken phone. 'My son did *not* run away, Captain. He wouldn't do that... Yes, I'm sure you've heard that before...' Alyssa's cheek accidentally hit the speaker button and Hammond's voice filled the room.

'It would be considered an abuse of the system if I allowed you to request an Amber Alert be issued if there is not significant cause to suggest your son has been abducted or is in serious danger of great bodily harm...'

Between clenched teeth, Alyssa bit out, 'I work in law enforcement; I deal with bad guys every single day of my life, and I'm sure I've pissed off my share of people. *That* alone is enough to suggest something has happened to my son. And can you think of one single teenager who would willingly run away *without his phone?'* She was screaming at the end, and she didn't care. Until she'd said it out loud, she hadn't actually believed that her son going missing could have anything to do with her job, and her stomach twisted in on itself as fingers of fear crawled over her skin now that the thought was out there. Her mind conjured up images of first Callie McCormick's battered body and then Timmy's, and she had to bite her lip to keep herself from crying out.

'I want to help you, Detective, I do. But you've got to give me more,' the captain insisted. 'We can't even tell the public who or what to look for. Do you have a description of your suspect's car, clothing, age, race, anything?'

'Do you think I'd be arguing with you right now if I had any of that information?' She shrugged Brock's hands off her shoulders, turning away from the hurt look on his face. She couldn't deal with that right now. Finally, accepting that she was not going to budge her captain on this, she said, 'I'll call the mayor then,' and slammed her finger several times against the *end call* button, the next best thing to slamming a receiver down in his ear.

When the doorbell rang a minute later, everyone froze, and then leaped into motion at once. Brock was the first one to the door, and when he opened it, Mabel stood in the entryway, tears in her eyes as she waited for her son to step aside and let her in. Immediately, Alyssa felt the guilt creep in as her mother-in-law reached up to hug her son. She hadn't given the woman a second thought after learning Isaac wasn't with her.

Her issues with Mabel aside, Alyssa was glad she'd come because her mother-in-law loved her grandchildren, and if nothing else, she'd be a comfort to Holly. And Brock, she realized, when she saw her husband close his eyes and issue a slow, quiet exhale as he leaned his head on the top of his mother's.

In the kitchen, Liz busied herself putting the uneaten food in containers while Mabel made a fresh pot of coffee and grabbed a dust cloth and began cleaning every surface she could readily reach, every once in a while passing by her son or grand-daughter and touching them lightly on the back or shoulder as if reassuring herself they were still there. A few times Alyssa even caught her hand hovering near her, but it always dropped back to her side before actually touching her.

Again, a flush ran up Alyssa's neck as she thought of how selfish she'd been not to include the other woman right away. She was on the verge of apologizing when Holly suddenly gasped. She swung around to see what had happened. Holly's red, swollen eyes were wide as she gazed at the file scattered on the floor. The McCormick case. Alyssa had forgotten it was even on the table.

'It's okay, sweetie. I shouldn't have had it out. I'll clean it up,' she said.

But Holly was pointing at the image on the floor right next to her foot. 'I know that man,' she whispered. 'I've seen him before.'

Alyssa's eyes followed her daughter's finger, her stomach falling to her feet as her heart beat frantically inside her chest. She lifted the grainy picture of Hunter Jenkins off the floor. 'This man,' she said, holding it with a trembling hand in front of Holly's face. 'Are you sure, Holly? You need to think.'

Her daughter's eyes swung up to meet first her father's, then her mother's intense stares. 'I'm positive, Mom. He's the man I've seen at the Zeller place. He's the one I thought had purchased the house.'

Just like that, Alyssa's world collapsed into a narrow tunnel as voices flew at her from every direction. Ignoring all of them, she fumbled for her phone as she dialed Captain Hammond back. As she waited for him to answer, she asked Liz to call Cord and get him back here right away.

The second Guthrie Hammond offered a weary hello, Alyssa said, 'I need that Amber Alert issued right now. I have signi-ficant reason to believe my son has been kidnapped and his life is in imminent danger.' And then she told her captain about Hunter Jenkins being in her neighborhood, her eyes moving over Holly's stiff form: young, blonde, athletic, heart-shaped face.

Could he have been after her daughter instead?

Chapter Forty-Four

Friday, April 5

It was Friday. He'd been here since Wednesday. Isaac only knew this because the man obsessively watched the news.

Wednesday night, after he'd fed him the soup, the man had taken the bowl, retied his feet, and left without a word, locking the door behind him. When the hall light went out, the windowless room was thrown into complete darkness, and Isaac, using the wall to help, maneuvered himself into the furthest corner where he turned his face into the floor to muffle the sobs tearing through him.

He stayed that way until Pobiv opened the door, and again, without uttering a word, unbound his feet and dragged him up and into the bathroom where he shoved Isaac's sweats and boxer briefs to the floor. Isaac's stomach clenched, threatening to empty its meager contents, when Pobiv roughly shoved him until his legs hit the toilet, and he lurched forward, his bound hands barely catching himself on the wall before he fell.

'Piss or hold it, I don't really care, but I'll tell you now, if you piss all over my floor, you'll regret it.'

How he did it, he didn't know, but Isaac concentrated until he was able to go. And then he was ushered back to the room and rebound once again. He didn't see or hear the man again until Thursday. He only knew the day and time because of the morning news crew as they greeted their audience.

'I'm going to untie your hands and feet now, but I'll remind you that I won't hesitate to slice you open if you try anything.

And I won't make it quick. I'll make you beg for days before I kill you.'

Isaac swallowed the bile in his throat and nodded, rubbing his wrists where the ropes had cut in. He followed Pobiv to the kitchen where he was fed a thick mixture of dry oatmeal that he tried not to gag on. When he finished, he noticed the man staring at him, a glint in his eye.

'They've issued an Amber Alert for you, did you know that?'

Hope soared in Isaac's chest. His mom was going to find him, he knew it. His eyes followed Pobiv's to the television where his own image rested on the screen next to a grainy image of an old man. He was confused.

Then Pobiv chuckled. 'They're looking for Hunter Jenkins, but he's dead, so they won't be finding him. And they won't be finding that old man they *think* is Hunter Jenkins, either.'

Confused by what the man had said and horrified at the thought that the police and his mother were searching for the wrong guy, Isaac couldn't take his eyes off the television as his mom stood on the lawn in front of their house, speaking directly to him.

'Isaac, baby, if you're listening, be strong. We're going to find you. I promise.' Her eyes were glassy, and his chest tightened as he watched her. He leaned forward as his gaze bored into the screen, as if by doing so, he could telepathically communicate where he was being held.

His concentration was so focused on seeing his mom that he'd practically forgotten Pobiv was next to him, so his heart slammed against his ribcage, and he jumped when the man spoke again. 'Oh, she's going to find you, all right. I'm going to make sure of it,' he said, turning the news off when the journalist moved on to another story. 'Just as soon as I make sure everything's ready.' He motioned for Isaac to clean his bowl at the sink and then directed him to the door whose metal bar now rested against the wall. For a split second, he considered the possibility of lunging for it and swinging it against his captor's head, but Pobiv stood between him and it, so he knew the attempt would be a futile one which could only get him killed or beaten, so he forced his hopeful gaze away.

'Let's go,' Pobiv said. 'I want to show you something.'

Isaac drew back until the man narrowed his eyes and slowly turned his head to a wicked butcher knife resting on the counter before poking him in the back to prod him forward.

And down the stairs into a basement that housed a bare mattress with posts at the bottom, and chains draped off the sides as well as all four corners of the bed. Isaac's bladder loosened as he stammered, 'Please, please don't…'

The man laughed. 'Oh, this isn't for you. I just thought you'd like to see what I have in store for your mother.'

This time Isaac didn't have time to swallow back the oatmeal breakfast because it was out and all over the floor before he even knew it was about to happen.

Enraged, the man kicked Isaac's feet out from under him, and he went sprawling into his own mess. He rolled to the side to avoid the kicks. And just as suddenly as it began, it ended. Pobiv walked around a corner, and Isaac heard running water. A minute later, he emerged with a bucket and sponge. 'Clean it up,' he ordered.

Weakly, Isaac pushed himself to his knees, retching, tears blinding him, as he obeyed. When he finished, he was escorted back upstairs to his room where he was shoved roughly inside and the door locked behind him. He didn't see the man again until last night when he brought him out for dinner.

The same routine was followed this morning, except for the visit to the basement. And now it was evening, and for whatever reason, Pobiv had either forgotten to bind his hands or simply chose not to. Either way, Isaac was grateful for the small oversight, if that's what it was. But that wasn't the only thing different; after Isaac had finished eating, the man had ordered him to the couch instead of dragging him back to the windowless room.

This terrified him because all day the man had oscillated from conversational to bouts of rage, and while Isaac hated being in the room, at least in there, he didn't have to wonder when a fist would reach out of nowhere and punch him.

A beeping noise near the door dragged his thoughts away from the man's motives and had his heart leaping into his throat as he imagined his mom had arrived to rescue him.

But when he turned his head, all he saw was Pobiv standing near the control panel that locked all the windows and doors in the house. Earlier in the day, Isaac had heard the front door open and close several times, so he assumed the man had been running in and out, and now he was re-engaging all the locks.

Or he was, until a crash outside the window caused the man to jerk around and to the side. It took a second before Isaac became aware the code was flashing on the screen – 0684. His stomach tensed and his face tingled as he leaned his head back and stared at the ceiling so Pobiv wouldn't know he'd seen it. *Please, please let him believe the frantic pulse beating in my neck is nothing more than fear,* he prayed. Carefully, Isaac squinted his eyes in time to watch the man hit 'Enter' on the keypad. Loud clicks resounded throughout the house as locks slid into place. And then, to his surprise, Pobiv walked down the hall to his own room which was tucked in the far corner of the house, down another hall Isaac had only seen once. His heart raced as he listened to the faint clicking sounds of a keyboard.

This was his opportunity, and it would likely never present itself again. But he was afraid to move, to make any sound at all in case the man remembered he'd left him out here. His hands were sweating, and he wiped them on his sweats as he stared at the control panel, trying to convince himself this was his only chance. But when he heard movement from Pobiv's room, he knew his chance was gone. He'd blown it.

Except Pobiv didn't appear. And then a toilet flushed, and the sound of running water in the sink reached his ears. And still he didn't return to drag Isaac back to the room. He closed his eyes and inhaled deeply, placing his hands on his thighs and squeezing. *Nothing ventured, nothing gained*. The rhythmic clicking of the keyboard began once more, and Isaac told himself to move now while Pobiv was preoccupied.

Quietly, he stood and tiptoed to the hallway. He flattened his back against the wall, and cautiously poked his head around the corner, but couldn't see Pobiv from where he was. So slowly he felt a snail would beat him in a foot race, Isaac shuffled to the keypad, the sound of his heart pounding in his ears, almost drowning out the noise of the keyboard.

0684 *enter*. 0684 *enter*. He repeated the number in his mind over and over, afraid fear would cause him to forget it. He stared at the control panel, desperate to push the combination that might end this. He vowed never to make fun of the characters in scary movies ever again. *Just do it*, he ordered himself. He looked in the direction of Pobiv's room one last time and raised his finger to enter the first number.

The loud squeak of a chair had him jumping back, eyes flying in the general direction of the noise. *Oh God, I'm busted*. When the sound of footsteps headed his way never came, Isaac stepped back so he could again see down the hall, trying to tune out every sound except that which would tell him Pobiv was still preoccupied. Silence was all he heard, and he was about to admit defeat and return to the couch when the sound of the keyboard started up again, and he decided to take it as a sign from God.

He inched his way back to the panel, each step forward lasting an eternity.

Here it was – his one and only chance. He knew that if he blew this, the likelihood of him surviving the night was zero to none. Knowing that, understanding it, he was frozen, lightheaded, faint, and sick with fear. He couldn't get his hands to stop trembling long enough to push even one digit. If Pobiv suddenly decided to check on him right now, Isaac was dead, and he knew it.

You'll hear him if he gets up, Isaac lectured himself. *There's no reason the guy needs to be quiet. I mean, what would be the point? It's not like he's trying to break out of this place. You just got to do it, man. You just got to! This might be the only chance you get!*

Though he didn't go to church often, he prayed to God to let him survive this, steadied his hand the best he could, took a deep breath... and pushed the first number. The beep of the keypad was like a gunshot in his own ears, but he knew it wasn't as noisy as it seemed. After all, he'd listened to it several times now. However, when the locks actually disengaged... well, there would be no masking that cannon-like sound.

He fought down nausea, and in quick succession, entered the remaining numbers. He glanced behind him one last time before hitting *Enter*. He knew once he hit that key, he'd have to move fast, despite being sick, because his window of opportunity for a successful escape was narrow. *Here goes nothing*, he thought and jabbed the final button.

Chapter Forty-Five

Just like he figured, the unmistakable sounds of the locks opening had his captor racing down the hall. But, sick or not, Isaac's leg muscles tightened as he prepared to run, and he made a beeline for the door, yanking it open. Once outside, he had no idea which way to go – all he knew was they'd driven through the canyon, so they had to be somewhere up in the mountains because they hadn't driven long enough to have crossed the state line – so he headed for the trees, hoping he could somehow hide until he found a way to attract help. He didn't hesitate when he reached the front porch; he simply soared off the top and bolted, sprinting like his life depended on it – because it did.

His name was being yelled, but he didn't stop, and he didn't slow down, and as much as he wanted to, he didn't turn around to see how close the man was. *It doesn't matter how close he is*, he told himself. *It just matters that you're faster than him.* He let his track coach's words play in his mind, spurring him on.

He ran. And kept on running. Being sick sucked, but being sick while running was way worse. He had no idea how long he'd been running before he realized he no longer heard Pobiv's footfalls or labored breathing behind him.

Still, he raced on. He kept up the pace until his sides ached, his legs and calves were on fire, and his lungs threatened to burst from his chest. Having no other choice, he slowed to a walk. *Jell-O* would be an accurate description of how his legs felt at the moment. And he tried not to think of the blister on the back of his foot.

Unable to take another step, he stopped near a tangle of bushes and brambles. Risking a look behind him, he was both terrified and elated that he saw no sign of his kidnapper. Sucking in a breath for the pain he was about to cause himself, he forced himself into the thick of the bushes and hunkered down. When the pain from a thorn scratching up his arm threatened to make him squeal, he reminded himself how much worse it would be if his escape attempt failed.

Winded from fear, running, and the elevation, Isaac told himself he could rest for five minutes and no more before he had to go. He knew he needed to keep moving if he was going to be successful. Besides, he was afraid the sound of his own panting would give away his location.

When his heart rate slowed to as normal as could be expected, Isaac carefully moved out of the bushes. He was still clueless as to which direction to go, but he guessed *down* was as good a bet as any. Surely that would lead to a road or a house or cars or hikers or *something*.

Not running so much as walking briskly, Isaac kept a steady pace. He was parched, and his muscles cramped, letting him know exactly how much they definitely did not appreciate this abuse. He desperately needed water, and the food Pobiv had served – a slice of lunchmeat on toast – threatened to make a return. 'Ignore the pain, just keep moving,' he whispered to himself, so softly he didn't even hear his own voice. He wasn't sure how long it'd been since he'd left the safety of the bushes when he heard it – heavy breathing above the sound of snapping branches from fallen tree limbs. Someone was coming.

Isaac ran.

-

He couldn't run another step. He was lost, scared, and Pobiv was closing in on him. He didn't know how close behind he was, but no matter what, it was too close. He wanted to fall down and weep.

A voice inside his head told him not to give up, that he could do it. He had an urge to tell the voice to shut up, that it didn't know anything. There was nowhere left to run, nowhere to go, and no one to help. He was done, finished.

The sound of his mom's 'danger' advice rang loudly in his ears. If all else fails, *just run*, she always preached. Predators wanted easy prey, not someone who fought back. He knew this situation was far different, but the concept was the same: fight back no matter what.

A huge tree loomed in front of him. An idea leaped into his head, and as difficult as he knew it would be, he was determined. With a steely sense of single-mindedness, Isaac latched onto the lowest branch of the tree. He tried to pull himself up but collapsed to the ground with a thud. Refusing to give up, he went at it again and again, offering prayers to any god who would listen. After a few failed attempts, he was able to drape his arms over the limb, and carefully, painstakingly, pulled himself up.

Twice more, he made the climb until he was able to secure himself high enough to be out of imminent danger. *Beat* didn't even begin to cover what he was feeling.

He made himself as comfortable as possible, ignoring the ants traipsing up and down his arms like he was their personal playground. Though his plan was to hide only long enough for Pobiv to move on, to get far enough away that he could continue his escape, he was prepared to do what he had to if he was discovered because there was no way he was returning to that prison without a hard fight. After carefully adjusting his position a couple times, he waited for Pobiv. He didn't have to wait long.

Chapter Forty-Six

Alyssa paced, pausing at her window to peer out at the dark every time she passed it.

Isaac had gone missing on Wednesday. Now it was Friday night. No one in her family had slept for more than an hour at a time, and each time they did sleep, they woke with a start, guilt breathing down their necks that they'd fallen asleep while Isaac was in danger. Worried about his mom's health, Brock had urged Mabel to go home and get some rest last night. After arguing for more than fifteen minutes, she'd relented, promising to be back first thing in the morning. And she had been, leaving only about thirty minutes ago.

Brock, Holly, and Mabel, with Liz and even Ruby's assistance, had spent Thursday and today making posters and driving all over town, hammering them to telephone poles and taping them to store windows. Though Cord hadn't been allowed to assist, he had supervised as Officers Alexander and Finley had gone through the vacant Zeller house. But other than crushed carpet where Hunter Jenkins had walked and the disconnected cable to the garage door, there was no evidence he'd been there, not even a gum wrapper.

For the hundredth time, she wished Mabel had purchased the house after all. Anything would be better than her son being kidnapped. And every time the image of Timmy's lifeless body swam through her mind, she shoved it back. She refused to believe she'd lose her son the same way she'd lost her brother. She would find him.

Hal had come over to keep her company – or so he'd said. In reality, he'd driven his special van over to sit on her and keep her from storming over to the Zeller house herself. At least he didn't placate her by telling her everything would be fine.

In fact, he'd helped her contact the media and set up a briefing in front of her house yesterday. She clutched her fist to her heart as she remembered staring into the camera, praying her son could see her, and promising, *promising* him she'd find and bring him home safely.

Twin tears streaked down her face, and she roughly wiped them away as she continued her pacing. She went to snap the rubber band on her wrist until she remembered it had broken, and she hadn't replaced it. She stuck her thumbnail in her mouth and chewed.

She needed to do more, needed to *act*. Needed to find and kill Hunter Jenkins. Yes, that was exactly what she wanted to do. He'd taken her baby, and she wanted to hurt him. Everyone, Cord included, told her, ad nauseam, that she needed to let others help, that she was too close to the situation, that she could jeopardize evidence. As if she would be so inept when it came to her son.

She wanted him home safe; she wanted to hug him until he couldn't breathe.

She bargained with God as she weaved a worn path in her carpet from pacing. *God, if only you let us get him back, safe and alive, I swear I'll go to church on Sundays as often as I can. I'll make the whole family go.* Or, *God, if you'll just bring him home safely to us, I'll help at the soup kitchen every Thanksgiving.*

When Isaac didn't come rushing through the door after her pleas with God, she cursed Him for allowing this to even happen. *My brother wasn't enough; you need my son, too?*

And now it was Friday. Cord had called twenty minutes ago to give an update. They still hadn't been able to find the string that would unravel the whereabouts of Hunter Jenkins, nor could they trace the car, and Alyssa had wanted to hurl the phone just to see it shatter against the wall. Why couldn't they find this man?

Brock and Holly were in the kitchen, and as she glanced that way, she realized that somewhere between Wednesday evening and now, she and her daughter had switched roles; Holly had become the consoler, the calm one. Alyssa knew it was wrong, that she needed to be the one consoling her family, to seek support *with* them. But she couldn't. Because her flaws loomed like beacons inside her. She'd failed Timmy, and he'd ended up dead; she'd overlooked Hunter Jenkins on the security footage, and Callie McCormick had died – and possibly others – and now, because she'd been preoccupied with her job, her son had been abducted, quite possibly by a serial killer.

The pain in her stomach at the thought nearly doubled her over as she fought to catch her breath. She was supposed to protect Timmy. Protect her son.

No, Isaac was *not* dead. He was missing, yes, but he was still alive. She knew it. She'd feel it if he was dead.

You didn't feel it when Timmy died. Stop it! She ordered herself. Isaac *would* come home. He would be found. And no matter what, they would deal with it together, as a family. She *was* going to get her son back!

'Mom!' Holly snapped Alyssa's attention away from her disintegrating calm. She looked at her daughter with a blank look. 'Mom, your phone's ringing.' She nodded at the cell sticking out of her mom's front pocket. 'Answer; it might be about Isaac.'

Automatically, Alyssa glanced at the clock. A little after eleven p.m.

Brock appeared in the doorway as Alyssa yanked her phone out and answered. This was what happened every time someone's phone rang. Everyone gathered around. Usually it was someone asking for an update or wanting to say they were thinking of her and her family. Each time the realization hit that Isaac was still missing, faces would droop, and shoulders would sag.

249

Alyssa felt the weight of her daughter's stare, as well as her husband's.

Anxiously, she answered the call. 'Hello?'

Chapter Forty-Seven

Bishop, red-faced and sweating, swore as he kicked up leaves, making no secret of the fact that he was searching for the boy. He held a large branch he'd picked up along the way and swung it wildly, hitting all the surrounding bushes and trees. His arm throbbed from the gash caused by a low-hanging branch he hadn't seen when first chasing the boy. He wished he'd had time to grab his knife because he was surely going to kill him. But it would have to wait until he captured him and dragged him back. He'd kick him down the basement steps, and then he'd carve him up and mail the pieces to Alyssa one at a time, starting with the boy's head.

'Come on out, kid, because you know I'm. Going. To. Find. You.' He enunciated clearly, his voice reaching new levels of distress with each word. He swallowed back the roar building up in his chest. 'It'll be easier if you don't make me hunt you down. I know you can't be far; I know you can hear me.' He stopped moving and listened.

'I know these woods far better than you. You don't know what kind of wild animals are out here. Nighttime's a dangerous place to be outside in these mountains.' No, he wasn't just going to kill the kid slowly; he was going to cut his eyes out and record the whole thing so he could also send it to Alyssa for her viewing pleasure.

Bishop peeked around and in all the nearby bushes and rock outcroppings. He cursed again. How had this happened? How

251

had he *let* this happen? And how had the boy been able to move that fast? He was sick and weak, which is why when he'd remembered he'd left the boy in the living room, he'd decided to leave him be. It had never occurred to him that the kid could've seen the code to the control panel.

Finally giving in to his building anger, he let out a roar that had small animals scampering away. He never looked up.

—

Isaac shivered, from cold, from fear, and from battling the constant need to vomit. He rubbed his hands up and down his goose-pimpled arms, trying to chafe warmth back into them. He wished he had something other than his torn excuse for a shirt.

Pobiv had been directly beneath him. Directly. Screaming that he would find him. And Isaac had held his breath, willing the bile that had erupted into his throat to stay there. When tears sprang to his eyes, he'd pressed his face into the bark, afraid a teardrop might fall and land on Pobiv causing him to look up and discover him wedged in a vee of the tree. When a gust of wind picked up, Isaac had taken the opportunity to release his breath and take another.

An eternity or two passed before Pobiv had moved on. Isaac noted which way the man had gone, and then briefly considered returning to the house. He could run inside, find a phone, and call for help, while his kidnapper was out searching for him in the opposite direction.

He vacillated back and forth before ultimately deciding he couldn't risk it. There was no guarantee he could even find the place again. Besides, even if he could he had no idea where to tell his mom to go to come rescue him. And frankly he wasn't brave enough to stay inside the house long enough for someone to try to triangulate the call, or whatever it was they did.

He had to be tough; it was better to risk the cold and wet and darkness until he reached a safe place – wherever that might be – than it was to return to the lair.

After counting to sixty ten times – making sure he said 'Mississippi' after each number – he'd cautiously climbed down from the tree, biting back a scream when his ankle twisted on an exposed root, and then he trudged on for what seemed like hours. When he'd gone as far as he could before fatigue and weakness ordered him to stop, he found a ledge he hoped would keep him hidden from predators – of the animal and human kind. And then he stared up at the moon and stars, wondering how much time had elapsed since his escape. All he knew was: it was cold, dark, and getting darker fast. And he was lost in the woods somewhere. Going downhill.

He leaned back against the rock ledge and closed his eyes for just a second, his breath wheezing in and out. The snap of a twig and falling rocks had his head snapping up. He didn't move so much as a muscle, not even swatting away the mosquito buzzing around his ears, biting at him. There was a tickle below his nose, and he prayed he wouldn't sneeze, giving away his position.

Another noise almost directly above the outcropping he was sheltered beneath had him stifling a cry. He pressed himself harder against the frosty stone, wishing it was malleable so he could hide *inside* it.

He sat, alone, terrified and chilled to the bone, biting his cheeks to stop his teeth from chattering.

When two deer bounded down from the ledge and stopped mere feet from him, he couldn't hold in his frightened yelp. Both mule deer turned their heads and sniffed the air around them. He cocked his head, listening, trying to determine if something – or someone – had startled the animals. If Pobiv was nearby, they would've kept running, right?

He'd never realized until now how noisy the forest was. The wind blowing through the trees and the canyons sounded like cars passing by, so much so that he couldn't help but hope he'd see a car each time a gust of wind picked up. Squirrels and birds flitting in and out of the trees forced loose pinecones to fall and caused his heart to either stop or speed up so much he was sure it would fly out of his chest. All kinds of critters scurried across the forest floor, and they all sounded like rifle blasts.

His legs shook uncontrollably from the cold, from exhaustion, from fear, but he forced himself up. He knew he couldn't stay in this spot much longer, but he didn't know which direction to go, and he had no idea what he'd do if he didn't find help soon. Exhausted or not, he had to keep moving.

But he was weak, and he was afraid his rib was cracked where the man had kicked him, so it took several tries before he could finally stand without collapsing back down. His nose was running, and he suspected he had a fever again. Or still. And his ankle throbbed. He wanted to remove his sneakers to check it out, but he knew he'd never get his shoe back on if he did. He settled for wiggling his toes. Then, he forced one foot in front of the other, telling himself he could rest after fifteen steps, twenty. Thirty.

He sidestepped to the end of the little cliff and steeled himself for being back in the open again. *Don't think. Just go.* He took a deep breath and hobbled as quickly as his legs and lungs allowed.

It was harder to see, so he tripped over rocks sticking up from the ground and fell over fallen logs. Each time, he pushed himself up again, urging himself to keep moving.

He brushed away silent tears as he ignored the branches slapping him, cutting his arms and face, and leaving scratches that would make any cat proud. The pull on his body assured him he was still heading down, and he pushed his battered body beyond the limit.

He was fantasizing about a hot bath, a large turkey with green chile sandwich, and an ice-cold soda when he tripped, sprawling face first into a sodden pile of leaves. His ankle twisted again, and he bit back a cry of pain. He tried to push himself up, but when he put pressure on his wrist, he tumbled back to the ground, having injured it by landing the wrong way on his arm when he reached out instinctively to capture his fall.

Lying face down on the ground, his ankle and now wrist throbbing, Isaac sobbed, unable to stop, even knowing the noise could lead Pobiv to him. He just wanted his mom! Was that so much to ask?

Get up right now and move. His mom's voice came out of nowhere, and with his good hand, he used a nearby tree to help him to a sitting position. Every single cell in his body hurt like hell. He leaned against the tree, trying to convince himself to move when he heard it. He held his breath and listened.

Yes, there it was again. A car. Not the wind this time, but an honest to goodness car. That meant there had to be a road nearby. He stood, gingerly putting weight on his ankle, testing that it was only a sprain. Convinced it wasn't broken, he shuffled as quickly as he could in the direction of the approaching car.

The darkness was so thick now that he could barely make out his hand in front of his face, but he kept moving. Inch by slow, painful inch, he trudged up a small incline where he recognized the car, a little louder now, was coming from his left side. He turned his head. Yes! Bright headlights were coming his way.

Still, Isaac was a fan of scary movies, so he hesitated a fraction of a second, knowing this could be a trick, that Pobiv could be cruising the mountainside, looking for his escapee.

He counted to ten before deciding the possible benefits outweighed the risks. He couldn't sit out here all night. He needed help, and he needed it now. He had to take his chances.

Making up his mind, he made his way to the road. Just as he stepped to the shoulder, waving his arm to flag down the car, the unmistakable sound of footsteps directly behind him caused his stomach to clench. Pobiv.

He ignored the agonizing pain in his ankle and everywhere else, and not allowing himself to think of all the things that could go wrong, Isaac raced into the middle of the road, jumping up and down despite the damage to his feet, not caring if he never ran track again, and waved his arms frantically. The car would either have to stop or run him down. He prayed the driver saw him and would stop to help, not just veer around him, thinking he was some type of lunatic.

A bouncing light shone through the trees, and an enraged shout came seconds before the car slammed on its brakes, barely avoiding hitting him.

The driver yelled out, 'What the hell is wrong with you?'

That was as much as he got out before Isaac was at the driver's side, clutching the door with a death grip, yelling and crying. 'You've got to help me. Hurry. I was kidnapped, and I escaped, and he's after me. Hurry. Hurry. You have to help me. Please, please, please. He's after me.'

'Okay. Okay. Who's after you?' The man reached down to unlock the back door as Isaac was already grabbing for the handle. The lock released, and yanking open the door, Isaac fell inside, slamming the door and crying, 'Go! Go! Go!'

Something crashed into the side of the car, and both occupants swiveled their heads to see a crazed man erupting out of the forest, throwing his flashlight. A crack appeared across the passenger window, and the driver, looking through the rearview mirror at the terror on Isaac's face, hit the gas, rocketing the boy to safety.

From the backseat, Isaac watched his captor standing in the road, arms raised, shouting something into the air.

He'd done it. He was going home.

Chapter Forty-Eight

Friday, April 5, 11:00p.m.

'Alyssa Wyatt?'

Alyssa stilled. 'Yes. Who's this?'

'Ma'am, I think I have someone here who wants to speak with you. Just a second.'

There was a rustling sound and something else before another voice came on the line. Brock and Holly stared at her, eyes wide and hopeful.

'Mom?'

The breath left her body in a whoosh, and her knees gave way when she heard the voice on the other end of the line.

'Mom, are you there?' His voice cracked. 'Mom?'

'Isaac! Where are you? What happened? Where are you?' The detective in her disintegrated; in this moment, she was just a mom about to be reunited with her son. Brock and Holly crowded around her to try to listen in. Alyssa could've put him on speaker, but she didn't want to move the phone away from her ear for fear he'd disappear again.

'Can you come get me, Mom?'

The line was full of static, and only bits and pieces made it through. 'Isaac! Where are you? I can barely hear you; you're cutting out. Try to tell me where you are!'

Holly wiped her nose on her red sweater and covered her mouth with both hands. Alyssa placed a reassuring hand on her daughter's shoulder. Brock stood quietly, but anxiously, his foot tapping. He had a notepad in hand, and Alyssa wondered when he'd grabbed it.

'… at… on… just a sec…'

Was that road noise? Was he in a car? Alyssa heard Isaac say something to someone else, presumably the person who'd placed the call. He must've turned his head away from the speaker because his voice was distant and warbled. Panic reared its head again; if she couldn't hear him, she'd lose him again. She had a tenuous hold on her nerves as it was.

'Isaac? Are you still there? Isaac?'

When he came back on the line, she could hear him a little better. He sniffled, sending an ache through her heart.

'I'm here, Mom. Can you come get me? I'm so scared.' His words were whispered, almost inaudible. 'He's going to find me and take me again and I don't want to go back I just want to come home so can you please please come get me now?' Everything came out in a rush, in one long sentence.

Listening to her son's voice shake through his fear, Alyssa's detective skills kicked back in, strengthening her protective maternal instinct. She stood straighter. 'Of course, baby. Of course, we'll come get you. Just tell me where you are. Dad and I will come get you. And Holly. I need you to do something for me, okay? Can you do something for me?'

'Y-y-yeah, okay.'

'I know you're scared, baby, and I'm going to come get you, but I need you to calm down so you can tell me where you are, okay? The person you're with now, the one who called me – he's safe, right?'

'Yeah, he's safe; he, he helped me.'

'Okay, tell me where you are.'

Holly had her phone out, GPS navigation open, ready to type in whatever address Alyssa repeated. As it turned out, it was unnecessary because Isaac told her they were in a car heading to the police station located on Lomas Blvd.

She and Holly raced to the garage while Brock stopped long enough to grab the car keys. By the time he made it to the

258

garage, Alyssa already had the garage door open and Holly had opened the driver's side door for him, before sliding into the backseat. Seatbelts weren't fully locked in before Brock shot out the open garage door, racing toward their son.

'Mom? Don't hang up, okay? Don't hang up.'

Alyssa's heart broke, hearing her son's tormented cries. Whatever had happened, they would get past this, but first she had to get to her baby boy. 'I won't hang up. I'm right here. I'll stay on the line until we get there, I promise.'

'Okay. Hurry, Mom. Please hurry.'

Alyssa glanced at the tense look on her husband's face as he drove, and she pressed the speaker button on her phone. 'Baby, why didn't you call me yourself instead of whoever's driving?' She hoped to distract him with the question, but she was also curious. And despite that fact that this person was helping her son, she was suspicious.

'My hands were shaking too badly, and I kept misdialing.'

Alyssa died a little inside at the anguish in her son's words.

'We're coming, buddy. Just hold on,' Brock said, a tremor making his voice vibrate. He slammed the gas pedal down harder and accelerated well past the speed limit.

People were just going to have to get out of their way because there was absolutely no way in hell she was telling him to slow down. When he flashed his lights and ran a red light, she knew he was on the same page.

She turned her head when she heard Holly on her cell phone, talking to Cord. Holly raised her eyebrows to ask if she was doing the right thing, and Alyssa reached back to pat her daughter on the knee. She smiled, mouthing the words, 'Good thinking, sweetie.'

Fifteen long minutes later, they squealed to a stop in front of the Lomas substation nestled just a few short blocks from the Sandia Mountain foothills. The front of the building was ablaze with light.

'Isaac, baby, we're here. We're getting out of the car right now, and –' That was as far as she got before the front door crashed open, and her son came stumbling down the steps, supported on both sides by two officers who seemed to be simultaneously assisting her son while keeping an eye on the perimeter, just in case. The phone was pressed to her ear, and she shoved it into her pocket as she ran to him, wrapping her arms around him tightly as Isaac's body crumbled into her own.

Holly cried, embracing her brother from behind. Then Brock wrapped his strong arms around all of them, cocooning them together.

Alyssa glanced up to see a tall, muscular man standing on the steps, along with several officers. The man appeared to be wiping a tear from his eye as he watched the scene unfold in front of him.

Not a minute later, Cord sped into the parking lot, tires squealing, screeching to a stop, and barely turning the engine off before jumping out and running to them.

Chapter Forty-Nine

Friday, April 5, 11:30p.m.

'I shouldn't have gone with him. I know he had a uniform, but I should've asked questions. I should've known something was up when he told me to leave my phone.' The tremor in Isaac's voice twisted Alyssa's insides as he apologized for the hundredth time. His family, along with Cord, surrounded him as he tried to give a detailed statement of everything he remembered.

Cord broke in this time, placing a comforting hand on Isaac's shoulder. 'Isaac, man, like your dad said, no one's blaming you here. In fact, I would've done the exact same thing, right down to leaving my cell. You were worried about your mom, and that's what was forefront in your mind. You need to let that go, so you can help us find this guy. Okay?'

Isaac's head dropped forward, and Alyssa turned to one of the officers. 'Can we get him a blanket, please?' She asked as though it were a question, but she knew it sounded more like a demand. When one of the cops returned with a heavy wool blanket, she thanked her. 'Go on, sweetie,' she encouraged him as he gripped her hand. Since they'd walked into the police station, he hadn't let go… not that she would've let him. The only exception was when the police had pulled him into one of their conference rooms so they could photograph his injuries.

Alyssa's jaw had clenched, and her muscles had tightened as each cut, scrape, and bruise was revealed, and the blood roaring through her ears made it difficult to concentrate on what was being said. It wasn't until Brock grabbed one of her hands that she realized she'd been squeezing her fists so tightly that her fingernails had left bloody, crescent-shaped marks all over her palm.

'He said he wanted Mom to come find him.' Isaac's eyes filled with fresh tears, and she felt his pulse quicken as he rocked back and forth. 'He showed me a basement he'd prepared for you.' His choked words were barely above a whisper.

Alyssa scooted her chair in closer to her son and wrapped one arm around him, pulling back, eyes drawn together in concern when she noticed him wince. 'There were chains on the bed... and he...'

Alyssa caught Cord's gaze, and she knew he was thinking the same thing. Callie McCormick. 'I'm right here, sweetie. He's not going to get me. Or you. I promise.'

'I threw up, and he... he... kicked me, and screamed... I couldn't...' Isaac moaned as he replayed it in his own mind. He was beaten and bruised in more ways than one, Alyssa knew.

The knowledge that he was taken because of *her*, that Isaac had been tormented because of *her* left her choking and suffocating at the same time. All she wanted to do was track down the man who claimed to be Hunter Jenkins and make him suffer for what he'd done. Dual emotions of rage and heartbreak beat through her.

'Sweetie, I want you to think carefully now and describe him. Do you think you can do that?'

'He was about five ten, maybe a little taller than me. His hair looked like he was in the military.' Isaac's leg bounced up and down as he spoke. 'He was maybe about thirty or forty, I guess.'

Both Alyssa and Cord snapped back, a questioning look in their eyes. 'Are you sure about his age, Isaac?' Cord asked, placing a warning hand on Alyssa's shoulder.

'Well, I mean he could've been older, I guess, but he wasn't as old as Dad or Mom, I don't think.'

Alyssa saw a faint smile try to work its way onto her husband's face, but he, too, was struggling to keep it together, to stay strong for his son and daughter. With her arm still wrapped around Isaac's shoulder, she stretched her fingers toward Brock's until he reached out and squeezed them. They stared at each other, and their message was clear: they'd get through this, somehow, some way.

Then Isaac shocked them all. 'Mom, he was watching the news, he was proud that an Amber Alert was issued. And I saw... I saw you on television...' His teeth clacked together loudly as he said, 'He laughed because he said you were looking for Hunter Jenkins, but that Hunter Jenkins was dead. And then he said you wouldn't be finding the old man you *think* is Hunter Jenkins, either.'

Alyssa sat up straighter, her brows drawn together. They knew Hunter Jenkins was a stolen identity, at least in name – they hadn't found any record of his social security number being used after the real Hunter Jenkins' death – but, what had the kidnapper meant when he said they wouldn't find the old man they *thought* was Hunter Jenkins?

Was it possible they were dealing with two perpetrators working together? She was sure Jenkins was somehow involved; it couldn't have been a mere fluke that Holly had seen him in the neighborhood before Isaac went missing. It was far too much of a coincidence, especially when adding in the fact that Jenkins had gone missing shortly after Callie's death.

Cord excused himself to head out to his car. When he returned, Alyssa recognized the McCormick file in his hands. He pulled out an image of what she knew would be the grainy photo of Hunter Jenkins and handed it to Isaac who took it, obviously confused. She watched her son's face for any signs of recognition.

'Is this the man who claimed to be Officer Shane Pobiv?' Cord asked.

Alyssa's eyes wandered to the name written down on the police report, something tickling at her brain when Cord spoke the man's name aloud. She mentally searched through offenders she'd arrested in the past but came up empty. She wasn't familiar with the name itself, but there was something there that she needed to explore because she wanted to know why the name Shane Pobiv made the back of her neck itch.

Isaac shook his head in response to Cord's question. 'No. This man's way too old. But that's the guy whose picture was on the television.'

Alyssa caught her partner's eyes, but she couldn't tell what he was thinking.

'I have to go to the bathroom,' Isaac said suddenly, and his grip tightened on his mom's.

Brock stood, holding his son's elbow when Isaac's wobbly legs buckled beneath him. 'I'm glad you said that, son, because I have to go, too, so if you don't mind, I'll just go with you.'

As they turned to go, Alyssa said, 'I should call your mom and let her know what's going on.'

'Already done,' Holly chimed in. 'I sent her a text, giving her a brief run-down, and told her we'd call tomorrow.' She said all this while staring at Isaac. She hadn't taken her eyes off him since they'd all tumbled from the car, afraid he'd vanish into thin air again if she let him out of her sight.

Alyssa understood the feeling.

'Thanks, sweetie,' she said, relieved her daughter had taken care of that detail. She should feel like a horrible daughter-in-law for not having thought of it sooner, but she didn't have any room left.

'I'm going to talk to the guy who picked you up, okay?' she told her son. He swallowed but nodded, his head swiveling every few seconds as they headed toward the restroom, reassuring himself she was still there. As soon as he rounded the corner with his dad, she stood to go speak to Tex Rivers, the twenty-six-year-old man who'd saved Isaac, but Cord's hand settled on her shoulders.

'You know you can't question him, Lys. It's a conflict of interest, and you don't want anything standing in the way of a conviction when we catch Hunter Jenkins, or whatever his real name is.'

Her first reaction was to assure Cord there would be no trial because he wouldn't live that long, but she knew that was grief and anger speaking. She upheld the law; she didn't break it. Besides when she captured the guy who'd done this – and she would – a lifetime in solitary confinement would be better than a death sentence. 'I just want to thank him,' she said, 'not interrogate him.'

She reached the other officer's desk – Officer Sandoval, by the tag on his uniform – as Tex was explaining how he'd come across Isaac. 'I just wanted to get out on an open road and try out my new car.' He hitched his thumb over his shoulder to point outside where a shiny cherry-red Chevy sat, now with a cracked passenger window. 'When I came around the corner, the kid bolted in front of my car in the middle of the road waving and jumping like he was on fire.'

Alyssa listened with a tight stomach as Tex continued to describe the events as they unfolded, from Isaac pounding on the windows, scratching at the door and pleading to be let in, to the man who'd suddenly appeared in the road, searching for his escaped prisoner.

Officer Sandoval stopped Tex and cocked his head at Alyssa. 'Detective – your son told me you work out of 4th and Roma,' he said when she arched her brows. 'You can't be here while we're speaking to a potential witness in your son's abduction.'

'I just want to thank him,' Alyssa repeated.

Cord reached out and shook Sandoval's hand. 'Sir, do you think I can take a look at the description of our suspect? We think he might be connected to another case,' he asked, man to man.

Tex spoke up as if a question had been asked of him. 'It was dark, and it all happened so fast. I was kind of freaked, you know? Look, I'll be honest, man, I almost didn't stop at all. I've heard too many stories about people pretending they're in trouble just to trap you.'

Sandoval stopped him, staring at Alyssa until she gave a brief nod, thanked Tex Rivers again and walked off, listening as he told Cord, 'He was short for a guy, shorter than me,' Tex said. 'I'm about five ten, and he seemed smaller than that. But he was built bigger. Had a barrel chest – I call it the military or cop chest. Burly, I guess you could say. Close-cropped hair, but not crew cut, more business-cut.'

'Old, young, middle-aged?' Alyssa overheard Cord ask, and she wondered if anyone else could sense the tension in his question.

'Hard to say. Could've been any of those, but if you wanted me to guess, I'd say middle-aged.'

'Mustache, beard, any scars you could maybe see?' Cord asked, and Alyssa was surprised Sandoval was letting him get away with it. But since he wasn't family, and he *was* investigating the same person, she supposed it was okay.

'Naw, man, I'm sorry. I didn't notice anything like that, but like I said, it was nearly pitch black out, and everything happened so fast.'

Alyssa watched the time pass, counting the minutes until Brock returned with Isaac. When she saw him limping, his face twisting in pain with every step, she tried once again to convince him he needed to go to the hospital. 'Baby, you still have a fever, you're covered in bruises, and those cuts have to be looked at.' She looked pointedly at his wrists.

When his trembling resumed, and he shook his head, tears streaming like a waterfall, it was his sister who stepped up to him. 'Brother, we'll be with you the whole time.'

He wouldn't stop shaking his head. 'They'll want to take me for X-rays,' he admitted, 'and they won't let you go with me.' Alyssa could see how much the admission cost him, and she turned just as Cord was walking back over, having caught the tail end of the conversation.

Then, making sure Isaac saw him before he touched him on the shoulder, he said, 'Hey, man, you know I'm married to a pretty hot nurse, right? So how about we don't make you head to the hospital tonight, but you let Sara come and look you over? I think we'd all feel better that way.'

Isaac's shoulder dropped as the weight of the hospital was lifted off him for the time being. 'Yeah, okay,' he agreed.

Cord excused himself to call his wife. Thirty minutes later she rushed into the station and hugged Alyssa, Brock, Holly, and Isaac. 'Before I begin,' she said, 'have the police already photographed his injuries?' At everyone's nod, she said, 'I assumed they had, but I needed to ask.' She turned to Isaac. 'Ready to get started?' she asked gently. She offered a sad smile at his grumbled yes, and then began checking him for any immediate concerns. When she finished, she said, 'I want to remind you all that I'm not a doctor, and Isaac really needs to see one first thing in the morning to have his ankle and wrist looked at, at the very least. I'd feel better if he went right now…'

When Isaac started to protest, she interrupted, 'I can't force that on anyone, but I do strongly advise it. From that bruise on your side, I'd guess you have cracked or broken ribs. It probably hurts with every breath you take, right?'

Isaac nodded.

'And you might not have noticed it as much before because of the adrenaline rush. But you're feeling it now, and you'll definitely feel it in the morning. The hospital might be able to give you some pain medication that will help with that – as well as help you sleep.'

'Mom, Dad, please. I promise I'll go tomorrow. I just want to go home tonight. Please,' he choked out. The tears in his eyes and the tremble in his body won out over common sense, and Alyssa capitulated after catching Brock's eye and seeing his slight nod.

On the way home, everyone was silent, and Alyssa tried to compartmentalize all the information thrown at them that night, but all she accomplished was to replay what she'd heard about the nightmare her son had endured and his miraculous escape, thinking of all the things that could've – should've – gone wrong.

By the time they finally pulled into the garage and entered the house around two in the morning, the entire family was ready to collapse but afraid to let each other out of sight.

Alyssa draped her arm around Isaac and said, 'I know this is going to sound silly and totally *mommish*, but I think I'd sleep better tonight if you'd leave your door open.'

Brock chimed in, understanding what she was doing. 'To be honest, it'd make me feel a little better, too.'

'Me, too,' Holly piped in.

Relief flooded Isaac's eyes, and Alyssa knew her son realized his family had just given him an out, but he played it off, shrugging, and said, 'Yeah, okay.'

Alyssa hugged him and said, 'Thanks, baby.' She leaned in to kiss his scraped-up cheek and whispered so only he could hear, 'Come get me if you have trouble sleeping, okay?' He nodded, and Alyssa stepped back so the rest of the family could embrace each other and say their goodnights.

On the way up the stairs, she said, 'And tomorrow, you *are* going to the doctor to get checked out, whether you like it or not.' She gave the timeout symbol and cut him off when he started to argue. 'It's not up for debate. You're going; I don't care if you think you're okay. Tonight, you get a reprieve only because Sara was kind enough to look you over. Tomorrow, you go.'

Isaac grudgingly nodded his assent, and, footsteps heavy with fatigue, they trudged to their bedrooms, leaving their doors open, needing the illusion of being connected even though they were in separate rooms.

Chapter Fifty

'Stupid! Stupid! Stupid!' Bishop's lips pulled back, baring his teeth, and his veins strained against his neck as he yelled at the image in the mirror. His face was covered in scratches from where he'd repeatedly raked his fingernails over it, his arms wore crisscross cuts, his shirt was torn in several places where thorns had attacked and grabbed at him, and the area under his eyes was flushed a dark purplish hue. Ignoring the stinging burn, he watched blood swirl in a circle down the drain as he ran hot water over knuckles scraped raw from punching trees on his race back to his house nestled high in the mountains.

Only when the water changed from red to pinkish did Bishop shut the taps off. He wrapped a towel around his left hand, the one with the most amount of damage, and headed for the kitchen where Isaac's discarded soup bowl rested on the counter. His eyes glazed over as a roar erupted from deep in his chest, and he slammed his fist down, rattling the dishes in the cabinet. His fury piqued again, he swiped his arm across the counter, forcing anything in his arm's path to shatter against the wooden floor. And then he opened a cupboard and began hurling dishes against the wall.

How could he have made such an amateur move? Leaving the boy unbound and alone? He stomped into his living room and kicked an end table, toppling it on its side, and shattering his new lamp.

'How? How did he get the code?' he muttered to himself. In his mind, an image flashed. He'd just entered the code when

269

a noise from outside startled him, and he'd jerked around to see what it was. When he turned back, the code flashed on the screen, and he hit enter. That had to have been what happened – in that split second of inattention, the kid must have seen it. Once again, he had the urge to gouge the kid's eyes out. He picked his boot up and hurled it at the alarm, causing a flash of electricity to burst from the gadget. It'd be the first thing he did when he got him again. And he had no doubt he would. If Alyssa wasn't coming to him this way, he'd go to her.

His anger finally slowing, his gaze landed on the basement door where he had plans for Alyssa Wyatt. What were the chances the boy could pinpoint this exact location? It wasn't like he'd been able to get a good look at the place as he was fleeing. And it had been dark.

A new plan took shape, and this time, it included more than the detective and her son. It included her entire family.

As his idea grew, so did his hatred, and so he fed and nourished it. Before he killed her, she would know who had destroyed her life and taken everything from her. He imagined how he'd laugh as she pleaded for her family's lives, for her own. He'd let her believe there was a chance.

And then, he'd ignite the flame and throw gasoline on the fire as he watched her hopes die a slow death.

Chapter Fifty-One

Saturday, April 6

Alyssa let Isaac sleep until ten the next morning. She'd lain awake another hour after everyone else had fallen asleep – everyone, that was, except Isaac. He'd tossed and turned long after Holly and Brock drifted off. Finally, when she thought her eyes were made of fine sandpaper, Isaac stopped rolling around and fell into a fitful sleep.

An hour later she was woken by Isaac's thrashing and mumbling and crawled out of bed to wake him from his nightmare. The light from his bathroom shined down on him, and her insides twisted as tightly as the covers embracing his body. Even now, he kicked out with one leg while wringing the sheets in his fists. The physical ache in her heart, she knew, was nothing compared to the torment her son had endured and would relive for a very long time, if not the rest of his life. And there was nothing she could do except love him through all the necessary stages.

That and catch Hunter Jenkins, and make sure he never stepped foot outside of prison ever again.

When Isaac's moans became anguished cries, she tiptoed across the room, navigating through piles of dirty clothes, books, and miscellaneous other items. She stopped at the side of the bed, and gently placed her hand on his shoulder, hoping her touch would seep through his nightmare and into his subconscious, reminding him he was safe now.

To her surprise and relief, his body, bathed in sweat, stilled immediately upon her touch. She kept her hand there for several seconds then stroked the top of her son's head, moving his wet hair out of his eyes. He murmured something unintelligible in his sleep, but she swore she heard him say, 'I want my mom.'

'I'm here, baby,' she whispered. 'I'm not going to let anything else happen to you. I promise.' Images of Callie McCormick and Timmy flashed in her mind. Viciously, she shoved them away. She *would* protect her son and the rest of her family – the way she hadn't protected the others. And she *would* track down Hunter Jenkins, even if she had to go to her grave to do it.

It was a vow she made to her son's sleeping form and to herself. When he'd been still for ten minutes, Alyssa removed her hand and walked back to the open bedroom door, stopping to gaze at Isaac, unable to take her eyes off him quite yet.

As she watched her son, Alyssa tried to work out the puzzle. Isaac hadn't recognized Jenkins, yet she was certain he was involved, because why else would he have been in her neighborhood? Plus, his kidnapper had *known* Hunter Jenkins was dead.

Brock's familiar footsteps interrupted her thinking as he stepped up behind her, and she leaned into his strength as he laid his head on her shoulder, his cheek pressed against hers. He spoke softly into her ear, 'He's a lucky boy to have you for his mom.' He turned her in his arms and rested his chin atop her head. 'He's going to be okay. We'll make sure of it. Why don't you come back to bed now?'

She nodded her head, and together they walked down the hall to their room. She woke several more times throughout the early morning hours, listening for the sounds of Isaac's breathing before dozing off again until the next time.

Now, here it was, morning, and she was on her second cup of coffee. Brock sat at the kitchen table reading the newspaper, sipping from his own cup, a plate with toast crumbs pushed to the side.

'I called Dr. Brown's office and explained what happened. He agreed to meet us at the clinic since they're closed on the weekends. We have an appointment at eleven. It's just a couple blocks away, so we shouldn't have any trouble making that time.' Alyssa waited for Brock to look up from the article he was reading. 'I think you should go with him because he might be more comfortable talking to the doctor if his dad is there instead of his mom.'

Brock cleared his throat and then asked, 'Do you think he was hurt… in that way?' The pain in his eyes conveyed how difficult it was to even ask the question.

'No. Brock, he'd tell us something like that. I don't think he hid anything last night.'

He tipped his head forward, considering her words, then said, 'You're right. So, what will you be doing while we're gone?'

'I'll get ahold of Cord and the rest of the team. I'm going to ask Liz to contact Tex Rivers and see if she can pry out enough information for a rough sketch, and then if he's comfortable with it, I'd like Isaac to sit down with her and do the same, and then we can compare the two, and see if that shakes anything loose.' Just the thought of asking her son to willingly go through his ordeal, even for a good reason, was enough to make her sick.

A haunted look fell across her husband's face, and she knew he was no more comfortable with the idea than she was, but they really didn't have many options at this point.

When her phone rang, Brock pushed his chair back, poured himself another cup of coffee, and said, 'I'll take a quick shower, and then go wake Isaac and Holly.'

She nodded as she checked her caller ID. Guthrie Hammond. 'Captain,' she answered, wondering why he was calling.

He cleared his throat. 'Grapevine says you got your boy back. I'm glad. A couple things: first, I want to apologize for the hard stance I was forced to take on the Amber Alert issue. I hope you

273

understand that, as law enforcement officers, we walk a tenuous line sometimes, and we must be careful not to overuse or abuse the system, or it fails to work. That's why there are so many fail-safes in place.'

Alyssa *did* get it, as a member of law enforcement – but as a mother, she was still more than a little sore about it. She kept quiet as Hammond continued. 'And second, we need to find out why Jenkins is trying to draw you into a game of cat and mouse.'

You don't think that's my number one priority? My son was kidnapped! Alyssa bristled even though she'd wondered the same thing. 'That's the plan,' she said, then ended the call.

–

She replayed the conversation back as she gathered the ingredients for a ham, green chile, and cheese omelet, her son's favorite. She preheated the oven and pulled out a package of bacon, arranging it on a cookie sheet as the oven warmed. She was chopping the chile when she heard Brock singing loudly off key. Her palm covered her heart as she smiled, knowing her husband was purposely making noise to lessen the chance of frightening Isaac when he went in to wake him.

A few minutes later, their muffled voices carried down the stairs, 'Do I have to?' from Isaac and a 'Yep. Mom says, and you know what happens when Mom insists.' Grumbling, groaning, and squeaking bedsprings accompanied Isaac as he rolled out of bed. A bittersweet smile lifted the corners of her mouth as she wondered if that was what Timmy would've been like had he lived to be a teenager.

She poured another cup of coffee as Isaac walked into the kitchen and scraped a chair back. Alyssa gave him a warm smile. 'Little bit of a rough night for sleep, huh?'

Isaac looked embarrassed but mumbled a 'yeah' before he collapsed into the chair, crying out at the jolt to his body. Then he leaned forward and laid his head on the table.

'It'll get better, you know?'

He twisted his neck and regarded her doubtfully.

'Not right away, but it will. So, hey, I'm making your favorite; green chile and ham omelet with bacon on the side.' Alyssa washed and dried her hands, then ruffled her son's hair as she walked by to grab a bowl out of the cupboard.

'You're just trying to make up for forcing me to go to the doctor,' Isaac said sullenly. 'Sara said I was fine,' he said as he picked splinters from the wooden table.

'Sara said you were *fine enough* to go home last night but that you *had to make sure to go to the doctor today to get checked out.*' Alyssa refused to feel guilty for doing what was right.

'Moommm. I really *don't want* to go. I told you I'm fine.'

'Yes, you did. And you probably are, except for the probably sprained ankle, the possibly sprained wrist, the cuts, the scratches, the fever, and the possibly cracked or broken ribs. Do I need to go on?'

Isaac remained stubbornly quiet.

'Honey, I've already explained this. You need to get checked out in case any of those scratches are infected. And it wouldn't hurt to check those ribs, either.'

'They won't do anything if they are,' he mumbled. 'They don't even wrap broken ribs anymore. Trevor told me when he broke his when he got thrown from that horse last year.'

'That may be true, but you're still going. Besides, it would make me feel better, so please, I don't want to fight with you on this.'

Holly entered the kitchen at that moment, and Alyssa noticed her eyes immediately landed on her brother as her gaze went from head to toe and back again, assuring herself last night was real, that her brother was home. 'It might not happen often,' she said, 'but I agree with Mom.' She smiled as she sat next to Isaac. 'Do you want me to go with you?'

'I don't want to go with anyone. I don't want to go at all.' Tears were beginning to pool in his eyes, and Alyssa sighed.

'I know you don't want to, sweetie. But you need to, and sometimes you just have to do what you have to do.' She set her spatula on the counter and walked over, putting one finger under his chin and tilting his face up to hers. 'Kind of like you did when you took a chance to escape. You knew the possible consequences, but you did it anyway, even though you were sick, weak, and terrified beyond belief.'

'I guess.'

'Besides, that nasty bruise on your ankle is twice as big and blacker than it was last night. It looks like it's trying to catch up to the one on your ribcage,' she said softly, trying not to wince at the brightly colored bruises peppering her son's body, trying even harder not to let the helpless rage she felt at not protecting him from all this show through.

As if mentioning the ankle brought it back to his attention, Isaac leaned down and probed the tender skin, lifting his sweats to his knees so he could better see it.

Nervous in a way she wasn't accustomed to, Alyssa spoke from the heart. 'What you went through was traumatic and terrifying. But, what *you* did, escaping like you did, as sick as you were – that took courage and strength. And I'm proud of you, and so are Dad and Holly.' Holly's head bobbed up and down as her hand covered her brother's, both her children openly crying now. 'And Grandma – who will be here when you get back from the doctor's.' She cleared her throat as her own emotions threatened to choke her words. 'And you should be proud of yourself. When you accept you're safe again, concentrate on that, okay? You were, you *are* so brave. And because of that, you survived. Remember that when times get tough… because they will. But we will all be here to help navigate those deep waters, okay?'

Isaac spoke over a lump in his throat. 'Yeah, okay.'

When Alyssa looked up, Brock stood in the doorway, wiping his own eyes as he held her gaze and mouthed, 'I love you.'

Isaac scooted back from the table. 'I'm going to jump in the shower – or get in gingerly, because jumping's probably out for

276

now,' he slipped in the small joke to break the choking tension in the room. 'I'll be back before breakfast is done.'

On his way upstairs, he yelled down. 'Maybe later I can talk you into making me fudge brownies.'

Everyone laughed, but she knew she'd be baking later. Probably right alongside Mabel. She didn't need a psychiatrist to tell her she was trying to make up for self-reproach brought on by not protecting her son in the first place.

Chapter Fifty-Two

Sunday, April 7

The vacant house no longer an option – the police weren't even trying to be covert; a uniformed officer was parked outside the home at all times – Evan hunkered down in a group of bushes in Alyssa's neighbor's yard. He'd already decided that if they caught him, he'd kill them, and their blood would be on Alyssa's hands, along with those of her family. And while he preferred a full view of her front yard, he settled for a partial view of both the front and back.

Yesterday, he distracted himself from his urge to be here by planning. The first thing he did was head to the hardware store where he purchased chains, posts, and hooks and then got to work revamping his basement to accommodate four guests instead of one. Then he headed upstairs to his room, where a box sat on his bed next to the items he'd stolen from Alyssa's house, among other things. He secured one of the photos from her album to the inside, triple-checked that he hadn't forgotten anything, then sealed the box with packing tape. It was too bad he wouldn't get to see her open it. The expression on her face would be priceless.

As soon as the post office in Tijeras was open, he climbed into his car. He'd considered rebirthing Hunter Jenkins for the drive in, but since his face had been plastered all over the news, he thought it safest to leave the prosthetics behind. Unconcerned that the kid might've been able to describe him enough to get a likeness on the news so soon, he decided he'd go as himself. After all, he'd been doing it for years.

Even so, he took precautions, knowing this delivery was crucial. He had no intention of being caught before he finished this. Finished *her*.

As it was Saturday, the line was long, and Evan scooted the box in front of him until it was his turn, and then he hefted his package onto the counter. The employee was an older lady who'd seen better days. 'How can I help you today?' she asked.

'I need to overnight this.'

'I'm sorry, sir, but the mail doesn't run on Sunday. We can have it delivered by Monday, though, if you'd like.' The woman – Irene, according to the lanyard draped around her neck – glanced at the address. 'Oh,' she said, lowering her glasses to squint at him. 'You sure you want to pay for that? It's going to Albuquerque, so it'll probably get there by Monday, no later than Tuesday, I'd think. Of course, we can't *guarantee* that.'

Evan's back teeth scraped together as he resisted the urge to slap the lady. *Yes, you stupid cow, I do want to pay for overnight. I don't care if it's just going next door.* 'I want to make sure it gets there on time. It's for a special occasion, so I don't mind paying the extra cost.'

'Then I'll need you to fill this out, if you don't mind.' She grabbed a form and a pen, setting them both down in front of him while she stamped the box in several places, and after he assured her he wasn't sending weapons, money, or the like, she asked if he wanted insurance.

'Oh, I don't think you can give me the kind of insurance I'll need,' he said cryptically.

'And it looks like you forgot your return address. You'll want that in case something goes wrong with the delivery.'

'Not necessary,' he said in a tone that brooked no further argument.

'Okay, sir. Up to you,' she said in a way that promised she'd mentally added *idiot* at the end, then she weighed the box and gave him the total. He counted out some bills and handed them over, watching as another man lifted the box off the counter and set it on the floor behind him. 'Here's your change, and have a nice day,' she said.

'Oh, I intend to,' he said, turning away. 'Believe me, I intend to.'

Today, he'd set an alarm for three thirty a.m., and parked at a twenty-four-hour store, jogging the rest of the way to the detective's house. That was when he'd noticed the cop car. These bushes were the next best option, and so he'd skirted around the house and through the neighbor's yard to hide in them.

And he'd waited. When the sun finally rose, he watched as, several times, Alyssa stepped outside, her hand moving to the gun holstered at her waist as she walked to the street and observed the comings and goings of her neighborhood. Once, when her eyes flowed past her neighbor's house, right over his hiding place, he bit his cheek to stop from laughing. He'd infiltrated her safe haven time and time again, and here he was, once again, right under her nose, and she didn't have a clue. He couldn't wait to see the look on her face when he told her.

Finally, she waved to the officer and turned to go back in, and as she lifted the hair off the back of her neck, a memory of their mother – her mother – doing the same thing ignited his temper, and he dug his nails into the palms of his hands to stop himself from lunging at her and slitting her throat right there. If he did that, it would be over too quickly, and he needed her to suffer.

And though the thought of it nauseated him, he'd decided yesterday as he'd prepared his basement, that one of the first things he would do was take her precious Isaac down there, but he wouldn't gouge his eyes out first. No, first he'd do all those things that Carl had done to him when he'd first abducted him. He'd force her to watch every second, and any time she closed her eyes or looked away – any time *any* of them did – he'd start all over. But he wouldn't muffle Isaac's screams as Carl had done to him the first time. No, he'd let those screams tear at her mind as she watched helplessly.

He'd make her hell last days, weeks if he had to, before he finally ended it. And then he'd burn the cabin to the ground with them inside. Maybe he'd burn it down while they were still alive. Either way, he'd leave New Mexico and settle somewhere up north, maybe Montana or Washington. He already knew that once he finished this, he'd never take another woman. There would be no need. After killing the person who'd ruined his life, after making her pay, he would be vindicated once and for all. He only wished he hadn't stumbled upon *her* parents' obituaries because he relished the idea of making them pay, too.

Chapter Fifty-Three

Monday, April 8

Clicking keyboards, tapping fingernails, ringing phones, voices shouting over one another, screams of innocence, and dirty, smudged windows were normally great distractions, but this morning, Alyssa ignored all of it. Two composite sketches lay side by side in the conference room, and she studied them. There was a vague familiarity about him, but she couldn't really say what exactly it was.

Because Isaac had met Liz in the past, he was comfortable with her, so she'd explained that she'd be happy to sketch a profile from his description, but suggested they use another forensic artist to speak to Tex Rivers, afraid she'd be influenced by doing both, subconsciously putting in similarities that didn't belong. Alyssa had sat in the living room and watched, in awe at how Liz coaxed minute details from Isaac's memory. The same could be said for the man who'd made a composite from Tex Rivers' description, especially since Tex had barely gotten a glimpse of Isaac's kidnapper.

She picked up one sketch, then the other and held them up to the light, as if the fluorescents blinking down would provide all the answers eluding her.

Absently, she snapped at the hair band around her wrist as she glared at the drawings. Then she pulled her hair back into a messy ponytail, then immediately took it back down, and began snapping her wrist again.

'The rest of the gang's on the way.' Cord walked into the room, breaking into her thoughts.

Alyssa nodded. She hadn't wanted to leave Isaac today, had cringed when he'd announced this morning that he was returning to school. 'There's no rush. Your teachers will understand.' She'd make sure of it.

'Dad just got that big contract, and *you* have to go so you can find... so you can find him,' he'd said. And she'd heard what he wasn't saying: *I feel safer at school, surrounded by classmates and friends, keeping my mind busy.*

Reluctantly, she'd agreed because he was right.

So as soon as she arrived, she sent a text to her partner that they needed to round everyone up. Because it was no longer a matter of finding Callie McCormick's killer. It was a matter of finding the man who'd kidnapped her son. And until she was pulled from the case, she was working it. She turned the sketches toward Cord. 'Does he look familiar to you at all?'

'Not really,' he said. Then looking pointedly at her red wrist, he added, 'I think it's safe to say *that's not helping.*' A few seconds later, Hal wheeled himself in, followed by Joe.

Joe threw his thumb out like he was hitchhiking. 'Liz is talking to Ruby about something, and Tony's just putting something in the fridge.'

As she waited for the others, she thought about texting Isaac. She glanced at the clock. 10:13, which meant he'd be in Spanish class right now. He wasn't supposed to have his phone on in school, but she knew he kept it on anyway.

> **Hi, baby. How u doin? School going ok?**

She set her phone aside, not expecting a reply right away, so she was surprised when her phone chirped. She snatched it up. Not Isaac. Holly.

> **Hey, Mom. I'm in between classes.
> Talked to Isaac today?**

> **Just sent him a text. Why?**

> **No reason. Just worried about him.
> Wish he'd taken another day. You
> think he's ok?**

Alyssa smiled at the way her daughter used proper capitals and punctuation, even in her texts.

> **I'm sure he's fine, honey.**

> **I've sent him like five texts already.
> He answered my first two only
> because they were before class
> started.**

Five texts? Who was the mother here?

> **And how'd he seem to you?**

> **Said he was fine, but you know
> Isaac.**

> **He knows to call if it gets to be too
> much for him.**

Alyssa watched the ellipsis symbol appear on her screen as Holly typed out another text.

> I probably shouldn't tell you this because he'll be mad if he finds out, but last night, he told me he can't stop looking over his shoulder. He's afraid it's only a matter of time before he comes back and gets him again. And you.

Alyssa's stomach plummeted to her feet, but before she could think what to say, another text appeared from Holly.

> You think he'll be embarrassed if I'm waiting for him after school?

Her belly had dropped to her toes just as her heart leaped into her throat. As much as those two bickered, they were also fiercely protective of each other.

> I think he'd pretend to be, but secretly, I think he'd like it. But Dad's picking him up today.

> Okay. Well, I've got to get to class. Message me if you hear from him, okay?

> Ok. Love you, sweetie.

Love you.

Setting her phone to the side, she realized everyone was there, and they were all looking at her with varying degrees of concern etched on their faces, waiting expectantly. Her eyes went from the sketches in front of her to the whiteboard covered with images of missing women to the printout of Hunter Jenkins' photo. As she studied them, pieces of the puzzle began to move in her mind as something clicked, and she straightened as the idea took shape.

She looked to Cord. 'Do you remember what Isaac told us his kidnapper said when he learned about the Amber Alert?'

'He said the man told him Hunter Jenkins was dead,' Cord said.

Alyssa nodded, excited now as her theory developed. 'And what else?'

Cord's brows drew together as he tried to guess where Alyssa was leading him. 'He said we won't find the old man they think is Hunter Jenkins, either.'

'Right.' Alyssa's eyes swept the room. 'He emphasized *think*. Why would he do that?' She waited for someone else on her team to catch on.

It was Hal who first reached the same conclusion she had. 'Because Hunter Jenkins wasn't only an alias, it was an elaborate and effective disguise.'

The second he said it, everyone sat up straighter, like a puppet master had yanked on their strings, and they immediately began speaking over one another, and although Alyssa couldn't be positive she was right, her gut told her she was.

'Well, that might explain why I thought he was a strange-looking fellow,' Joe said, recalling the comment he'd made after interviewing Jenkins right after Callie McCormick's disappearance.

'Well, earlier today, I'd already put in the request to get busy pulling aerial photos based on descriptions Isaac could remember. Jenkins – or whoever he really is – has to have property somewhere in the Sandia's, so I'd already decided to start there. I'll let you know as soon as I get a hit,' Hal added.

'Thanks for getting on that already.' Now that she had a thread to pull, Alyssa was finding it difficult to stay still. She wanted to be out there hunting down the man who'd hurt her son.

Tony jumped into the conversation. 'Since we're running with the idea that Jenkins and the guy who kidnapped Isaac are the same, then we should consider the fact that Callie McCormick was found in the Jemez, quite a ways from the Crest where Isaac was rescued, so our suspect either drove all the way over there to drop the body, or he has another property out that way. I think it might be prudent to check out both areas.'

Hal nodded. 'I'll let my guy know.'

'What we need now,' Alyssa said, 'is to find a link connecting these women.' She pointed to the white board where magnets held the pictures of the women they suspected might be victims of Hunter Jenkins. 'With the exception of Rhonda Dupres and Sandra Jackson, none of these ladies even lived in the same area. And we can't base a case on blonde hair.'

'But, isn't it popular opinion that serial killers target the same type of woman?' Liz asked.

'Yes, but if that's what we're going on, then I think we'd have a hell of a lot more missing or murdered women on our hands. There *has* to be something else.'

'Playing devil's advocate here,' Cord said, 'but couldn't it be that the only link is in the killer's head?'

Everyone nodded in agreement. 'There's that,' Liz said. 'And based on what Isaac told us, we know he was trying to draw you in, make you come to him. So, the real question is why? What was it that made him choose you? Is he changing his MO, and if so, again, I ask why?'

'Well, if we could find the bastard, we could just ask him, couldn't we?' Alyssa groused, not caring that she sounded bitchy. She massaged her temples, remembering the first time she'd met Rafe McCormick, how he'd done a double take when she'd walked in, how Mearl Leroy had stared, head cocked to the side as he studied her, as if he'd seen her before. 'She reminds me of you.' 'There's a slight resemblance, back when you had blonde hair.' 'I think you remind her of Callie.' Several people had commented about the similarities between Callie and herself. So maybe it was time to delve into that.

There was a brief knock before Ruby pushed open the door. 'Alyssa, a package just arrived for you,' she said, carting a cardboard box in her arms.

'What's this?' she asked as she stood, forehead crinkling. 'Anyone have a pair of scissors or knife I can borrow?'

Liz slid a fingernail file over, and Alyssa sliced the tape, opening the box.

'What the hell?' she muttered.

'What is it?' Cord asked, already walking her way.

Alyssa, bewildered, pulled out the first item – a box of Booberry cereal – and set it on the table. Next, she grabbed a container of grape Kool-Aid and placed it beside the cereal. By then, the team had gathered around. 'What in the world? A pack of candy cigarettes? I haven't seen these things since I was a kid. They were Timmy's favorite,' she said. 'Well, except he preferred strawberry Kool-Aid over grape.' As she said it, that feeling of failure settled like a well-worn blanket around her shoulders. If they'd had strawberry that day, Timmy would've gone inside with her instead of staying… She didn't finish the thought.

Cord peered into the open box and pointed to a greeting card leaning against the side. 'What's that?' he asked.

Alyssa yanked the card out and flipped it open so she could read it aloud. *I've been thinking about you.* That's when she noticed the photo. She recognized it as one that had been taken a few weeks before Timmy had gone missing. The two of them stood next to their bikes, frozen, goofy grins on their faces.

Except now, Timmy had a jagged cut scratched across his. The image was a stark reminder of the brutal way he'd been ripped from their lives.

A sick feeling settled over her as she was drawn back to another time. 'I don't know what's going on,' she said to her team, 'but, I think Isaac's kidnapping has something to do with my brother's murder. But what? And why?'

At her words, Cord grabbed the box. 'No return address. We need to notify the captain,' he said, already throwing open the door and heading that way.

Alyssa wasn't even aware of sinking into her chair.

Chapter Fifty-Four

Monday, April 8

The package, its contents, and what it all meant was still weighing on her mind when Alyssa got home that evening. Her family was sitting around the table, and her heart ached as she watched them. She removed her gun, and then decided not to put it away just yet. 'I'm going to go change,' she told her family. 'I'll be back down in a minute to help with dinner.'

She skirted the table, avoiding her husband's eyes. It didn't work, and he followed her upstairs. 'Want to tell me what's going on?' he asked, concern evident in his voice.

'Not a matter of wanting to,' she said, trading her khakis for a pair of yoga pants. 'Just not sure *how* to tell you,' she admitted. Her eyes strayed over to the potted plant resting in the corner of her room, where one of the few pictures of Timmy she allowed out stood behind one of the giant leaves, hidden from plain view.

Finally, looking up, she said, 'We'll talk about it later, okay?' She waited for his nod, then headed back downstairs.

To her surprise, Holly walked up and hugged her mom from behind. 'What's that for?' she asked. 'Not that I don't appreciate it.'

'You just looked like you needed one.' She rested her hand on her mom's shoulder, and whispered, 'You're going to catch this guy, Mom. I know you will.'

Alyssa's heart melted into a puddle at her feet. 'How did you get so smart, my beautiful daughter?' she asked through her tears.

'I have a great female role model. She's a detective. You should meet her sometime. I could introduce you, if you'd like.'

Alyssa turned and wrapped her arms around her daughter. 'Thank you, sweetheart. I needed that today.' When she stepped away, she said, 'I'd better get dinner started before my role model status gets demoted.'

Holly laughed and said, 'I'm going to work on some homework for a while, if that's okay.'

'Yep. I'll call you when dinner's ready.'

She was replaying the contents of the box and the note in her head, trying to fit the new pieces of the puzzle in with the rest when Isaac startled her.

'Need help, Mom?' he asked as he grabbed an onion, a knife, and the cutting board.

Alyssa gasped and dropped the spatula she was holding when she whirled around. She covered her racing heart with her hand. 'Good Lord, you scared me. I didn't hear you sneak in here.'

'Sorry,' Isaac said sheepishly. 'I just wanted to see if you needed help. I could cut the vegetables for the salad, if you want.'

Wondering what he *really* had on his mind, she said, 'That would be nice, thanks.'

They worked in companionable silence for a few minutes before Isaac said, 'I think I need to see someone. But it kind of makes me feel weak.'

Alyssa watched liquid pool in his eyes as that haunted look crept back over his handsome features, relieved that he'd been the one to bring up the topic of seeking help. Every night she listened as he tossed and turned, crying out for help – for her – in his sleep. She stopped stirring the sauce on the stove and angled her body to face him. 'I know; I understand,' she whispered softly. 'I felt the same way when my college roommate convinced me to see a therapist about my... my brother.' An image of Booberry cereal and candy cigarettes danced in her mind.

'Did it help?' Isaac asked, using his shoulder to wipe away the tear that trailed down his cheek.

Alyssa let her mind go back to one day in Dr. Blanchard's office when she'd been pouring her soul into the air. When she was finished, he'd stared at her, and eyes steady on hers, asked, 'Do you wish you'd been killed instead?'

She remembered the shock she'd felt at his question. 'What? No! Why would you even ask that?'

'Then stop letting it kill you, Alyssa. You were a nine-year-old girl. Still single digits. You were dealt a crappy hand. You wanted Kool-Aid. You got it. The guy who kidnapped your brother? He's the one who killed him, not you. Do your brother a favor and instead of wallowing in your guilt, do something about it, do something to make him proud. Don't let your brother's killer kill you, too. I'm not saying forget it; I'm saying make something good come out of it.'

She'd been horrified at the thought of making *something good* come out of her little brother's murder, but she understood what Dr. Blanchard meant. And the more she thought about his words, the more certain her career path became. So, eager to escape the dark memories of the past she couldn't change, she and Brock had finished college and moved to New Mexico where she began her career in law enforcement.

She could still remember the high she'd gotten the first time she rescued a little girl who'd been snatched from the playground; how it felt to snap the cuffs on the perpetrator, the relief she'd felt when the girl was returned to her parents. She'd helped give that family the happy ending hers never got.

Now, putting her hand against her son's cheek, she answered his question. 'After a while. It wasn't easy, but I'm glad I did it. And I think you will be, too.'

'Will you tell me more about... that time... your brother? How you got through it?'

'Some day,' she said, wondering if she'd keep her word. Especially considering the fear she now held – that Timmy's murder had something to do with her son's kidnapping, which was somehow also tied to a possible serial killer.

With that, Isaac changed the subject as he threw together the salad. 'By the way, do you think you could pull out some of the old family albums? I need to rummage through some pictures for a stupid Memory Book we're being forced to make in English class,' he mumbled grumpily. 'We get bonus points if we include pictures of our parents.' He rolled his eyes.

Alyssa choked back laughter. 'One day far in the future, you'll run across that stupid Memory Book and be glad you made it.'

He rolled his eyes and groaned, 'I'm not a girl, Mom. I don't *do* scrapbooks.'

Later, after the table had been cleared and dishes stowed away in the dishwasher, she went to the closet and pulled a dusty box of old albums off a shelf and dragged it into the living room. She opened it up, grabbed the top one, and thrust it at Isaac, thunking it against his chest. 'Let's embark on your scrapbooking journey, shall we?'

To her surprise, as she flipped through the albums and boxes of loose pictures, she wasn't filled with sadness. Maybe it was because she enjoyed watching her children laugh at goofy photos. Alyssa and Holly were snorting over one particularly hideous picture of Alyssa with her hair teased high, grinning stupidly up at Brock, who sported a perm at the time, when she noticed that Isaac, picking through a separate box of photographs, had grown very quiet, a mixture of fear and something else frozen on his face.

Even as Holly inched her way closer to her brother, offering him her silent support, Alyssa leaned over to see what had caught his attention, afraid of what she'd find. Had she accidentally put some old newspaper articles about Timmy's murder in these boxes and forgotten about it?

Isaac held two pictures in his hands. The first one was bent in the corner with a fold crease down the center. It was a picture of her dad, probably when he was in his mid to late thirties. The second was an image of both her parents, in happier times. Her mom was pregnant with Timmy, and her hand lovingly cradled her belly as Alyssa burrowed between her parents. 'That's your grandfather,' she said, gently removing the pictures from her son's trembling fingers. 'What is it, baby?' Alyssa asked.

Isaac's face had gone from a pale white to a sickly shade of green. He pointed. 'That's the guy who took me. That's him!' He shoved the box away and scrambled backwards until his back hit Brock's feet.

Alyssa's heart thumped wildly in her chest as cold fingers of dread threatened to choke her. 'Sweetie,' she spoke gently, 'this is your grandpa. He couldn't have taken you, honey. He's dead. You're still safe.' She kept her voice low, like she was trying to calm a frightened animal, which in way, she was.

Isaac inhaled deeply, but kept his eyes trained on the photos. His voice shook as he stood abruptly. 'I think I've got enough pictures for now. Thanks, Mom.' Without waiting for a reply, he raced up the stairs, closing his bedroom door with a thud and then opening it once more, still afraid to be closed in.

'I'll go check on him,' Holly said.

When both her children were upstairs, Alyssa rested her head on her knees, the photos still clutched in her trembling hands. The sound of cardboard boxes scraping across the floor had her glancing back up, and she saw that Brock had gathered all the pictures, closed the lids, and moved the boxes and albums out of the way.

Quietly, she shared her suspicions with her husband, telling him about the box addressed to her and delivered to the precinct. 'I don't know how everything is connected yet, but Hunter Jenkins is the one common denominator which seems to link everything else together,' she whispered, her voice barely audible. One thing she did know was that she was even more determined to find him.

Later that night, lying in bed, her mind couldn't stop seeing Isaac's face when he'd seen the picture of her father. When she finally fell asleep, it was in the half hour before her alarm went off at four thirty.

Chapter Fifty-Five

Tuesday, April 9

Tuesday morning, Evan prepared the final touches on the basement. He'd moved his shadowbox to the center of the wall where Alyssa wouldn't be able to miss it, and he placed the items he'd stolen from her house – a scarf, hair clip, the movie *Primal Fear,* and a bottle of lotion – on one of the beds. Tonight would be the beginning of her end. He still regretted being unable to witness her expression when she'd opened the box of all Timmy's favorites – he'd considered having it delivered to her house but thought it had added a special touch to have it sent to her place of work. Another rub to show her he was right there, and she couldn't find him.

Up in his kitchen, he went over his plan, going over every detail. He couldn't afford a single mistake. He was going to have to kill a cop to get to her, but, really, why should that matter? Last night, he'd risked driving into a seedy part of Albuquerque where he'd brazenly approached a group of gang members, announcing he needed a gun. After frisking him, making sure he wasn't a cop, or wearing a wire, one of them had led him down a dark alley, where he'd rapped on the back door of a well-known, popular restaurant. When another guy popped his head out, a scowl on his face, the kid spoke rapidly in Spanish. The guy in the doorway said something in return and then shut the door in the kid's face.

'Six hundred even, if you want it. Meet me back here at eleven p.m. Not a minute later, not a minute sooner,' he'd ordered before walking away.

Evan didn't balk at the price. He would've paid double, if he'd had to. And when he arrived exactly at the designated time, the kid, surrounded by his gang buddies, asked for the money, counting it before shoving it down pants so low Evan wondered how they stayed on at all, then handed over the gun, along with a box of bullets 'on the house, man,' and then sauntered off, $600 richer. Or at least $300, as Evan assumed he'd raised the actual price asked.

Tonight, he'd creep up on the cop – he'd already scoped out another way into the vacant house – and shoot him. Then he'd sneak into the Wyatt residence, and using his gun to keep them in line, he'd secure the husband and kids with ropes and then inject them with the midazolam. Then all he'd have to do was wait for Alyssa to arrive. With her, it would be tricky because she'd still have her weapon, so he brought a tranquilizer gun with him. He'd be waiting for her the second she opened the door, and he'd take her by surprise. Then he'd load them all into the cop car, drive them to where his vehicle was parked, transfer them, and finally bring them back here.

As he imagined the fear on her face when she realized she'd failed her family, a wicked grin curved his lips. And when he made her choose which one he would torture first, well, that would really be the defining moment, wouldn't it?

He rubbed his hands together, eager for the night to arrive.

Chapter Fifty-Six

Alyssa snarled at anyone who happened to come into snapping distance of her vicinity. She was operating on little caffeine, less sleep, and entirely too much worry and stress. At some point, in the middle of biting Cord's head off, he stalked off. At least he'd lasted longer than the rest of the team, she thought as she stared down at the composite sketch of Isaac's kidnapper. The resemblance to her father was vague but definitely there. She was mildly surprised she hadn't made the connection right away, but she also knew the mind had a way of closing off things it didn't want to see.

When her partner returned twenty-five minutes later, his hand was out, extending a very large cup of black coffee.

'I come offering peace,' he half-joked.

Embarrassed and exhausted, she put her head in her hands. 'God, I've been such a bitch today, haven't I?'

'Yep, sure have,' Cord agreed, a little too vehemently, in Alyssa's estimation.

'Don't sugarcoat it or anything. Just give it to me straight.'

'Hey, you're the one who said it. I just agreed. Besides, a fact's a fact, my friend. Can't help it if you speak the truth.'

'Yeah, but you didn't have to agree so quickly, did you?' she mumbled grumpily.

Cord waved his arm to encompass the empty conference room. 'I present to you evidence A, B, C, and so on and so forth...'

As her partner made his case, Alyssa's eyes fell on a sheet of paper sticking out of one of the files. *Evan Bishop.* With everything else going on, she'd shoved him to the back burner. But there was something about his name that was scratching at her.

When she figured out what it was, she drew in a deep breath, and her nerves played bumper cars with each other as she moved the composite sketch aside and swiveled to grab Isaac's file, running her finger down the page until she found the officer's name. Muttering, she tore off a sticky note and scribbled down both names, drawing lines to matching letters. When she finished, she tossed the pen aside, and glanced over to her partner, her eyes wide. 'Officer Shane Pobiv. Cord, it's an anagram of Evan Bishop.'

Without waiting for his response, she grabbed her keys, her phone, the composite Liz had drawn from Isaac's description of his kidnapper, and raced out the door. 'Let's show this sketch to Miles Garcia at the Old Country Feed Store and see if my hunch is right,' she said.

Thirty minutes later, her suspicion was confirmed when the owner and two of its employees verified the man on the page was indeed Evan Bishop.

'Sure looks like him,' Miles said, passing the image to his workers, who each nodded their head in agreement. 'I mean, he looks a little different in the sketch… didn't have that scar there when he worked here, I don't think. But definitely think it's the same man.'

Alyssa thanked him and headed back to her vehicle, her mind swimming in so many directions at once that she had a difficult time focusing on any one thing. As soon as Cord was buckled in, he said, 'I'll call Hammond and fill him in, and then I'll send a message to the team to meet us back in the conference room asap.'

She nodded as she merged onto the interstate. Half of her listened to her partner's end of the conversation while the other half tried to connect the dots. Was it possible Hunter Jenkins and Evan Bishop were the same person? As she mentally moved the pieces around, something else tumbled into place. She shook her head hard in an attempt to erase the thought, her brain instinctively trying to swerve away from it, and in doing so, she yanked the steering wheel on the car, nearly cutting off an eighteen wheeler, who laid on its horn, scaring her back into her own lane.

'Lys?' Cord asked, having finished his conversation with the captain. He had one hand braced against the dash while the other reached for the handle above his head.

In that moment, she wanted nothing more than to squeeze her eyes shut and close out the possibility of what she was about to say. Instead, she tightened her fingers and said out loud what she'd been thinking. 'Remember how I said I believed Timmy's murder was somehow related to Isaac's kidnapping?'

'Yes,' her partner said, obviously confused.

'Timmy's full name was Timothy *Evan* Archer.' She paused to let that sink in. 'I don't know who this Bishop person is, but I think he must've known my brother,' she said at the same time another thought jarred her. 'Pull that sketch out,' she said, and when Cord did, she took her eyes off the road to glance over at it, her stomach tightening. 'Isaac said he thought the guy was in his thirties or forties, remember?' she asked.

'Yes,' her partner said slowly.

'Even though Carl Freeman – Timmy's murderer,' she reminded him, 'was never caught, the authorities believed he always targeted boys with the same look and of the same age range, from four to seven.' She choked as she thought about how truly young her brother had been when he was ripped from their family.

'So, you're thinking Evan Bishop is about the same age as Timmy would've been, and that he was one of Freeman's victims?' Cord clarified.

She pursed her lips tightly and tipped her head forward in acknowledgement. Aside from the noise of traffic, the car was silent for a moment as the two of them tried digesting what this could mean. Finally, she broke the silence and said, 'But what I don't understand is *how* Bishop survived. Why didn't Freeman murder him like he did the others?'

Cord had a pen in his hand, and he tapped it rhythmically against his leg. 'Not all the boys were found though, right?'

Alyssa nodded. 'Since Freeman was never caught, and the kidnappings and murders matching his MO just stopped, the authorities ran with the theory that he was likely dead.' She peeked over at her partner. 'Serial killers don't just quit. They're either captured, killed, or die.'

'Okay, let's say Evan Bishop was one of Freeman's victims,' Cord said.

She winced at the word. As a mother, she found it difficult to picture the man who'd tortured her son as anything but an evil being.

Cord continued. 'If we go on the theory that the authorities were right, and that Freeman died... maybe Evan Bishop simply outlived him.' From the mesh pocket in the car's door, he pulled out a notebook, flipped to a new page, and began writing as he spoke trying to put all the pieces of each of the puzzles together: Callie McCormick's murder, the missing women cases, Evan Bishop/Hunter Jenkins, and Isaac's kidnapping.

'Okay, let's start at the beginning. We now have a few common factors threaded through these events,' he said as much to himself as to her. He drummed the pen against his jawline as he thought out loud. 'We know Evan Bishop worked at the Old Country Feed Store where Evelyn Martin was headed the night she went missing. We also know he matches the composite sketch of Isaac's kidnapper, and he and your brother have the name "Evan" in common.'

Alyssa temporarily removed one hand from the wheel to press against her stomach but added to Cord's train of thought. 'We know Hunter Jenkins was an alias we now believe was taken on by Evan Bishop, and his fingerprint was lifted off Callie

McCormick's vehicle when he should've had no way to come into contact with it – unless he was involved in her kidnapping. And if he was involved with that,' she said, 'then it stands to reason he was also involved in her murder.'

From the corner of her eye, she saw her partner's hand hover over the page. Then he said, 'Which leads us to Isaac's kidnapping. From Holly, we know Jenkins – or Bishop – was in your neighborhood more than once before Isaac was taken, so…'

Alyssa's right foot pressed down harder on the accelerator, and she turned on her blinker before going around a slow-moving vehicle driving in the fast lane, barely resisting the urge to blast her horn.

They made it back to the precinct in record time, and she and Cord had no sooner unlocked the door to the conference room and stepped inside with Liz and Tony than Joe came running up, Hal right on his heels.

'We have a hit!' Joe said, face red, his chest making wheezing sounds as he tried to catch his breath. 'A hit?' she asked, her heart thumping so wildly, she was certain everyone could see it. It was Hal who answered. 'We ran some property searches of houses in Sandia Park, the Crest, and the surrounding areas based on Isaac's description of the woods and where Tex Rivers said he picked him up.'

Joe interrupted, waving a piece of paper in his hand. 'Evan Bishop purchased that property nearly six months before Evelyn Martin went missing.' His eyes wide, he glanced first at Alyssa, then the rest of the team. 'Thing is, on paper, Bishop doesn't exist until this property was purchased *in cash*.' He rattled the paper again, as if that would shake the answers out.

Hal wheeled his chair over so he could unroll a map squished beneath his arm. 'Right here.' He circled his finger around a highlighted area.

Was it possible that Evan Bishop was yet another alias? Alyssa's face felt flushed, and her fingers tingled. 'I want a search warrant ordered for this place like yesterday!' she snapped out.

'Already called it in. Just have to head over to the courthouse to grab it,' Joe said.

'Then let's go,' she said, already heading for the door before Cord's words sank in.

'Do you think it's wise for you to go, Alyssa?'

She pulled up short. 'Why wouldn't it be?' she asked, genuinely confused.

'Think about it. This is the guy who took Isaac...' Cord began.

'Kidnapped. Kidnapped Isaac,' Alyssa interrupted.

'Okay, the guy who *kidnapped* Isaac... Do you want to jeopardize the entire case? They could say you contaminated evidence, even planted it.'

Exasperated because a part of her knew he was right, she said, 'I'm not going to jeopardize the case, Cord. I'm not stupid. Now, let's go.'

Chapter Fifty-Seven

Evan swayed on his feet, watching in horror as two SUVs emblazoned with the APD logo pulled up next to his house. He'd been out walking off his nervous energy when they'd arrived. And now he stood behind a tree and listened as eight people rolled out of the vehicles. He could barely make out what was being said because of the blood rushing through his head. He moved a little closer, making sure he stayed hidden by the trees. And then he heard *her* as she hollered out, 'Everyone, make sure your lapel cameras are on. I don't want there to be any questions as to my whereabouts or what I was doing during the course of this investigation. We clear?'

Alyssa! That selfish bitch was invading his sanctuary. How dare she! Rage flew through him, and it was all he could do to force himself to stand still. He knew if he'd had the gun, he would've shot her dead on the spot, not caring what happened next.

Pounding footsteps as several officers went to the front door echoed through the trees, and Evan noticed the others stood off to the side and watched their surroundings.

'Evan Bishop, this is the Albuquerque Police Department. We have a warrant to search these premises. Open up.' A minute ticked by before they pounded again, repeating the same thing, but this time, adding, 'Open up or we *will* use force.' Silence greeted the warning, and so the officer announced, 'We're counting to ten, and then we're coming in.'

A female officer began the countdown as Evan watched Alyssa Wyatt's steady gaze turn from the front door to scan the area, and he imagined she was thinking about her son's escape.

A few seconds later, a thundering boom echoed through the trees as two burly officers took a battering ram to his front door, crashing into it repeatedly until it fell inward.

Observing the destruction of his property, and more importantly, his plans for revenge, Evan's breath heaved in and out. Hatred stronger than anything he'd ever felt before rushed through his veins, making his vision cloudy. When the officers swarmed inside, he backed quietly down the hill. The only thing this changed was how he would make her pay. He was already conjuring up a new plan when he heard someone call out. 'Detective, I think you need to see what we found in the basement.'

Earlier that day, he'd pulled out his journal – the one detailing each of his women's time in captivity. He'd planned on reading it to her, watching the horror wash over her face when she realized what he was capable of – how much worse he planned on making it for her and her family. But there was nothing that could be done about it now, so he slipped quietly away.

'Detective, I think you need to see what we found in the basement,' an officer Alyssa knew as Hermosa called out to her.

Without thinking, she stepped forward and then stopped. 'I'd better not. Why don't you tell me?' she hollered back.

Hermosa's face was ashen as she came down the steps. 'Vials of midazolam, syringes. Rolls of rope and duct tape. A gun. Your picture's sitting on top of one of the mattresses in the basement. But that's not all. There's a shadowbox that contains some very disturbing items. I took a picture. I'll show you.'

Alyssa took the phone from the officer and used her fingers to enlarge the image. Her eyes fell to the items Hermosa had mentioned. 'Is that a severed hand?' she gasped, her stomach turning. At Hermosa's nod, she pointed to the image of a jar. 'What is *that*? Is – is that an eye?' But before Hermosa could respond, something else in the picture drew her attention. Items that had gone missing from her home, things she'd assumed Holly had borrowed and not returned: her hair clip, her favorite lotion, a pink scarf – now sliced into ribbons – and a couple other of her belongings she hadn't noticed were gone – were lined up neatly in a row on a mattress.

Her jaw tightened as she realized the implication. 'That bastard's been in my house!' She tossed Hermosa's phone back to her and yanked her own out of her pocket. 'Could you send Cord out, please?' she asked at the same time she dialed her husband.

As soon as Brock answered, she took a deep, steadying breath and said, 'Listen, I'm about to tell you something, and it's going to freak you out a little – or a lot, really.'

'Oh-kay,' he said, drawing out the word. 'Do I do that a lot – freak out?' Before she could answer, her husband said, 'Wait, you found out something about Isaac's kidnapper, didn't you?'

'Yes. But that's not why I'm calling. We need to make sure the kids are *never* alone in the house.' She forged ahead. 'I can't go into details now, but I have every reason to believe the kidnapper was in our house before he ever took Isaac.'

'What? I'm on my way home now,' he said.

Alyssa heard a crash, and she imagined her husband had probably exploded from his chair with such force, it had hit the wall. 'As soon as I hang up, I'm placing a call to Hammond. I want police guards stationed at both schools' front and back entrances, as well as the house security beefed up. In fact, I'd feel better if you went and picked them up from school and went somewhere safe… maybe even your mom's… until I can get home.'

'Was already planning it,' Brock said.

'Let me know when you're all together,' she said and then ended the call, looking over to her partner who'd come out as

306

soon as Hermosa had let him know. He hadn't overheard the entire conversation, but he'd heard enough.

He wiped one hand over his face. 'Jesus,' he said. 'Well, I've got some more news for you. I really wish I had a chair to give you right now because I think you're going to need it.' He took a deep breath before he broke the news, so Alyssa knew it was going to be big.

'There's a box of photos in the master bedroom. Callie McCormick and the women from the other cases are all in it.' It was Cord's turn to pull out his phone, and he handed it over to her, tapping on the screen until an image appeared.

Her brows knit together in confusion. 'What is that?' she asked.

'That,' Cord said, 'is a prosthetic. If you zoom in, what you'll see are a few other props that can transform a middle-aged man into a much older man.'

'So, we were right. Evan Bishop and Hunter Jenkins are the same person,' she said.

Cord nodded. 'Yep.' He reached over and swiped to the next image. 'And those,' he tapped his finger, 'are articles about your brother's murder wallpapering Evan Bishop's bedroom.'

Alyssa tried to process everything flying at her. She itched to be inside, needing to see all this for herself. What did it all mean?

A noise behind her distracted her, and she snapped her head around as she peered into the trees. Hand on her gun, she swept her gaze around, and just as she took a step in that direction, a large deer jumped out and took off. She removed her hand from the gun and placed it over her pounding heart. 'Good lord, that scared the hell out of me,' she muttered.

At the same time, her phone rang. She glanced down to see who was calling. The medical examiner's name flashed on the screen. 'It's Lynn Sharp,' she told Cord when he asked. 'Maybe she got the results back from the DNA profile.' She swiped to answer. 'Hello.'

Hearing nothing but static mixed in with incomprehensible words, Alyssa held her phone out to check her signal. Two bars. It was fine when she'd called Brock, so why was she having an issue now? She moved a few steps closer to the house and tried again. 'Hello?'

Lynn still cut in and out, but she could hear her better. '...results... I... tell you this.'

'I'm sorry, Lynn. You're cutting out. Say that again?'

This time the medical examiner's words came in clearly. 'Alyssa, the DNA we extracted from the skin cells found beneath Callie McCormick's fingernails came back.'

'And?' she asked when Lynn paused.

'And I think you should be sitting down for this.'

Chapter Fifty-Eight

Tuesday, April 9, 4:00 p.m.

Alyssa raced home, barreling through her door as Lynn Sharp's words replayed on a loop in her mind.

'We ran the profile through a national database. There's a 99.9% probability that Callie McCormick's killer is related to you.' She'd paused. 'As in a sibling.'

Suddenly, recent events began to take on a new light, even as she denied what was right in front of her. She wanted there to be a logical, more reasonable – more acceptable – answer.

Upstairs, she pulled out the articles outlining the day Timmy's body had been found. Over and over she read them. But other than the items which had belonged to her brother, there was nothing definitive in saying the *body* had belonged to him. They had all just assumed.

Her breathing came heavier as she sank onto her bed, her eyes landing on the nightstand. She leaned over and pulled open the drawer... and found the photo album she kept in there missing. Further proof *he'd* been in her house before Isaac had been kidnapped.

Her skin felt tight as wave after wave of remorse and regret and anger washed over her. When her phone rang, she glanced down to see it was Brock. 'Hello,' she said.

'Hi. Is everything okay?' he asked. 'I just saw I missed a call from you.'

Alyssa pressed a fist to her chest. 'Yes, everything's fine,' she lied. 'I was mostly just checking on you and the kids, making sure you're all at your mom's.' She longed to tell him what she now suspected... she refused to say *knew*, longed for him to be there and help hold her together as she tried to sort out this puzzle that had turned into a nightmare.

'We're all here,' Brock said now. 'Mom's about to make meatloaf. Mmmm.'

She couldn't help it. She laughed a little. 'You know, it would probably make your life so much easier if you just told her how much you hate it?'

'True. But unlike you, I'm kind of a coward.'

'Only when it comes to your mother,' she said. And then, 'All right, babe. I've got to go. I'll call you when I... finish... up here.' She hesitated. 'I love you. All of you.'

She knew she'd alarmed her husband because his voice turned serious. 'Lys? Are you sure everything's okay?'

She let her eyes wander around their room as she lied once again. 'Yes. Just tired. But I really do have to go now.'

They said their goodbyes, and a few minutes later, Alyssa heard a noise downstairs. Rising off the bed, she slowly descended the steps, hand ready as it rested on her gun.

When she rounded the corner into the kitchen, thunder pounded in her ears as Evan Bishop stood with his back against her counter, grinning, the smile falling far short of his eyes.

'Hello, sister. I guess you couldn't get rid of me after all.'

Stars swam in front of her eyes as the blood rushed from her face. She didn't want to believe what she was seeing, what was right in front of her. It couldn't be; it just wasn't possible.

Lynn Sharp's words echoed in her head again. *99.9% chance Callie McCormick's murderer is your sibling.*

Alyssa swallowed. She watched his eyes follow her hand as she moved it from her gun to her pocket. 'Timmy?' She couldn't stop the tremor in her voice. 'You – you're supposed to be dead.' Less than ten feet separated her from the brother she'd believed had been murdered.

Evan laughed, a humorless sound. 'Yes, I know. But *supposed to be* and actually being are two different things, aren't they?' A dark cloud covered his face. 'And don't ever call me Timmy. My name's Evan now.'

'I don't understand,' she said, shaking. 'They found your body. Your bike, your clothes.'

'No, they found Woody Pentel. Carl told me later what he'd done. He was trying to protect me.'

'What? Protect you? No, Ti – Evan. He *kidnapped* you, *murdered*... we thought you were dead. It destroyed Mama. Your death left a hole in our family that could never be filled. We grieved.' Alyssa's voice was ragged, and she realized she was crying. Her fingers moved blindly in her pocket.

Evan advanced two steps before stopping, and that's when she noticed the backpack on the counter behind him. His eyes followed hers, and he smiled again. 'Don't worry. We'll get to that.' This time he cocked one hip against the table, looking for all the world to be relaxed while Alyssa felt as if her world were crumbling all around her. Again.

'Tell me something,' he said conversationally. 'Did you ever laugh about how easy it was? Did you, Mama, and Daddy have Kool-Aid toasts after Carl took me away? How long did it take before you cleaned out my room and erased all memories of me?'

More than anything, Alyssa wished this not to be happening, for this to be nothing more than a bad movie script. She changed the subject. 'Those women you kidnapped and killed,' she began. 'Were they supposed to be me?'

Evan laughed. 'Figured that out on your own, did you? I guess that's what makes you an okay detective. Not a great one, obviously, seeing as how I broke into your house more than once – you and your boy were even here. I could've killed you then, but it would've been too quick,' he said, his eyes narrowing.

Nausea rose up her throat at his words. 'So, you kidnapped my son, too?'

'I think you already know that answer,' he said. Then he waved his hand around the room. 'If he hadn't escaped, I would've made sure you knew where to find him. I had it all planned out, how you would come to me, how I'd kill your precious boy in front of you the same way Carl killed that boy in front of me. Sliced his throat wide open and made me watch, forced me to stand there as that warm, sticky blood sprayed my face.'

It was harder to keep the bile down this time, but Alyssa managed. 'I'm so sorry that happened to you,' she began, stunned when Evan's fist reached out and hit her.

'Shut up,' he roared. 'Just shut up.' Spittle flew from his mouth as he yelled. 'After your kid got away, I came up with a better plan, one that would keep you alive long after I'd killed your precious little family,' he sneered.

There was no way Alyssa would let this man harm her family, no matter what had happened to him. She pulled her hand from her pocket and moved it back to her weapon, but she was too late. Evan Bishop's gun was already drawn and pointed directly at her chest.

'Look at the bright side, *sister*,' he sneered. 'You'll get to die much more quickly than I'd hoped.' He shoved off the table and advanced slowly. 'But, don't worry. I'll make sure I get your family, too.'

Alyssa's training kicked in, and without conscious thought, her right leg kicked out, sweeping both his legs from underneath him. He wasn't expecting the move, and as his weight carried him to the ground, he automatically reached out an arm to protect his face from the fall, and his grip on the gun loosened.

Her body still acting on instinct, she kicked the gun away with her foot and then moved in before he could roll over, pressing one knee into his back as she struggled to wrest his arms behind him. Seconds that felt like hours later, Cord was gently pulling her up as he and several officers rushed through the doors, weapons drawn.

As she stood staring down at Evan Bishop, her eyes clouded with tears, and she was grateful her partner supported her weight as her knees threatened to crumble beneath her. 'It worked. I got it all,' she whispered, pulling a mini recorder from her pocket and handing it over to Cord.

'You bitch! I'll kill you for this. Do you hear me? I'll kill you?' Evan roared, his enraged face turning purple as veins popped out on his temples. He was still screaming as Joe read him his rights and hauled him out to the police cruisers that had pulled in after watching him 'sneak' into Alyssa's home.

Only when Joe pulled away did she allow herself to collapse to her knees and release the gut-wrenching agony that held her hostage.

Chapter Fifty-Nine

Breaking news cut into scheduled programs at seven thirty that night. Alyssa stood alongside her team, squeezing her fists tight, pushing her nails into the palms of her hands to avoid smashing them into the television that broadcast today's events like it was a must-see movie. She watched the reporter breathlessly discussing the capture of the man they'd nicknamed the 'Two-Faced Killer.' It was stupid and insulting, but there was no stopping the media when it came to grabbing headlines, regardless of whom it might affect. Behind her, Cord growled, 'I'd like to get my hands on the jackass who leaked this.'

A chorus of 'Get in line' and 'After me' reverberated throughout the room. The fact that their jobs had just got infinitely more difficult because someone had a big mouth and wanted to show everyone he or she was *in the know* was irritating. The circus parked outside the precinct doors, blocking too many cars from coming or going, was frustrating.

Yet, as unpleasant as all this was, it wasn't nearly as tough as getting the angry call from Rafe McCormick. He'd raged, yelled, and cried for half an hour. He went from one end of the spectrum to the other, varying between bouts of name-calling to blubbering how grateful he was that authorities hadn't rested until his wife's murderer was caught. And Alyssa had taken it all, feeling each word like a barb in the heart.

As if that wasn't headache-inducing enough, that wasn't even the worst part. Someone had dredged up all the old articles about Timmy's murder and shared them for the world to see. Social media had taken the story and run with it. Now that was the cherry on top, the icing on the cake.

Now everyone she worked with, save her team and the captain, snuck pitying glances her way, feeling sorry for poor little Alyssa. And she couldn't even go for a drive to clear her head because the media vultures had every exit cornered. She was only mildly surprised they didn't have reporters hanging off the window.

No longer able to stand being in the midst of all the raw emotion swirling about, Alyssa headed for the ladies' room. Inside, she repeatedly slammed the stall door until she felt a tiny bit better. Finally, she washed her hands and splashed water on her face, not caring if her make-up streaked. When she stepped out of the security of the restroom, she stopped short. Cord waited for her outside the door.

'That must've been quite a show,' he said, nodding toward the restroom. 'Kind of wish I could've seen it.'

'Shut up,' she bit out as she stalked away.

Cord fell into step beside her. Wordlessly, they headed to the snack machine. 'I *hate* the looks people keep giving me,' she whispered angrily. Tears of frustration sprang into her eyes. Between that and the alternating numbness she felt, she didn't know how she was supposed to behave.

'They just care, Alyssa.' Cord held up his palm to stave off her argument. 'I'm not saying it doesn't suck. I'm just explaining why they're doing it.'

She stalked past him and entered a small room where she watched through the two-way mirror, listening as Evan Bishop was interrogated. Her emotions were raw and conflicted. As a wife and mother, first and foremost, she wanted to storm the room, lunge across the table, and choke this man for what he had done to Isaac and the rest of her family. What he had *wanted* to do, what he had *planned*. The meager contents of her stomach threatened to reappear as her mind filled itself with images of what he'd threatened to do to Isaac.

As an officer of the law, she wanted to see him sent away for good for murdering all those women she now knew represented her and his hatred for her, even if he hadn't realized at first that was why he was doing it. Shrinks across the state were going to have a field day with this. And Indiana was officially in on the action now, too. It was never-ending.

As nine-year-old Alyssa, she wanted to wrap her arms around this tortured man and promise to protect him this time.

She didn't know if he knew she was watching, or if he'd just guessed, but he stared at the glass separating them, even as the officers in the room threw question after question at him. He hadn't yet requested a lawyer, though they all knew it was coming. He looked simultaneously sad and confused while still filled with rage.

She couldn't help it; her heart was ripped to shreds as it broke all over again. So much lost innocence. It was so unfair. For the first time, Alyssa was glad both her parents were dead and didn't have to see this.

She watched as Evan slowly raised his cuffed hands and brought them to his face. He touched the bridge of his nose near the scar he had. He rubbed it, as if trying to send her a message of some kind. His nose was slightly bent, like it'd been broken at least once. Then, as Alyssa watched, he brought his fingers to his mouth and puffed on an imaginary cigarette.

Memories crashed through her, images of causing mischief and mayhem with Timmy, catching lightning bugs in jars with holes in the lid, watching them as they lit up the night sky, scolding him for pulling lights off their butts when he got bored of chasing the little insects.

She didn't realize she was shaking or that Liz had arrived until she placed her arms around Alyssa and gently guided her from the room.

-

Not ten minutes after Liz pulled her from watching the interview, Alyssa's family descended on the precinct like avenging angels, with Brock leading the charge, followed by Holly, then Isaac, and finally Mabel bringing up the rear as they all rushed into the conference room, now vacant except Alyssa, Cord, Liz, and Hal who had run everyone else out when she had returned to the room.

When the door opened, Alyssa's head jerked that way, the sight of her family making her eyes film over with tears. She stood to meet them partway. 'What are you doing here?' she asked. She'd managed to find a window of opportunity to call Brock explaining what had happened – leaving out the part where Bishop wanted to torture her family before killing them – shortly before the story broke on the news, but when he asked her if she wanted him to come to the precinct to be with her, she insisted she was fine, that she didn't need him there, and she'd feel better if he stayed with the kids. She promised she'd head over to Mabel's as soon as she could.

Clearly, his solution was to gather up everyone and drive here anyway. And thank goodness for that because she realized she really did need him. Unconcerned that anyone outside her team may view it as weak, she went willingly into her husband's arms, closing her eyes briefly as she welcomed his strength, feeling it seep into her.

As she rested her head against his chest, Holly slid up beside her to nestle her head onto Alyssa's shoulder as she hugged her. Alyssa opened her eyes and turned her head, catching Isaac's gaze. His face was splotchy, the way it got whenever he was angry or upset, and his eyes were so red they appeared bloodshot. His arms and legs trembled as he met her stare, and when his bottom lip began to quiver, she pushed herself out of her husband's arms, and went to him, enclosing as much of him in her embrace as she could.

Tears immediately began soaking through her shirt as sobs quaked through his body, and Alyssa held her son tighter until his cries became less severe. When he finally stepped back, he looked everywhere but at her, so she reached up to gently grasp his chin – when had he grown another two inches? – and tilted his head down toward her.

'Isaac, please look at me,' she whispered.

He sniffled but obeyed, his eyes once again filling with moisture. 'I'm so sorry, Mom. I don't know how I'm supposed to feel right now.' His words were broken and full of anguish, much like her own heart.

'Oh sweetie. Come here.' She led him to a chair and gently pushed him into it before rearranging her own so that it was facing him. Then she leaned in and enveloped him once more in her arms, rocking him back and forth as his emotions spilled over yet again.

She remained silent as he cried himself out, glancing every few seconds at Brock, Holly, and Mabel. Holly had turned into her father's arms as Mabel wrapped as much of herself around both of them as she could. And though tears fell freely from her mother-in-law's eyes, the fierce protective look on her face had Alyssa's heart thawing a bit for the woman who'd so long been a thorn in her side.

Finally, when Isaac's tears had subsided into hiccups, Alyssa scooted back enough to give him space, but kept her hands on his shoulders as she said, 'You have nothing to be sorry for, son. Nothing at all.' She touched one finger to his cheek to bring his face back to hers when he turned away. She needed him to see she was speaking the truth when she admitted, 'I don't know how I'm supposed to feel, either.'

Isaac pulled back slightly, tilting his head as he absorbed her words. 'You don't?' he murmured.

She shook her head and swallowed so she could speak past the lump in her throat. 'No. I'm very confused right now.' And then she shared another confession. 'As your mother, I want nothing more than to go in there and…' she forced back the word 'strangle,' and replaced it with, 'hurt him for what he did to you. And if anything, I'm the one who should be apologizing to *you*.' Her voice, like her heart, cracked. 'If only I'd never gone inside that day, Timmy never would've been taken, and none of this would've ever happened.'

Much to everyone's surprise, it was Mabel who spoke up. 'No, Alyssa, that's not true. If you had been outside with Timmy that day, at that time, it's much more likely both of you would've been taken – and then we all would've missed out on this beautiful family of ours.'

Alyssa brushed tears away as they fell down her cheeks, but before she could respond, the conference room door opened again, revealing Captain Hammond. She hadn't noticed when the others had stepped out, leaving them their privacy. Yet, they hadn't gone far because she saw her teammates, joined now by Joe and Tony, standing just outside looking in, all of them wearing identical masks of concern. It was Cord's eyes she caught as he arched one eyebrow and mouthed the words, 'Are you okay?' She shrugged and then turned her attention to the captain.

In a manner very uncharacteristic of his personality, Hammond bounced on the balls of his feet and held his hands stiffly together in front of him, almost as if he were choking an imaginary chicken. He cleared his throat, looking uncomfortable as he observed Alyssa's family. 'I'm sorry to interrupt,' he said. 'You know that granting your request for this interview was against my better judgement, but I've cleared it with the district attorney's office. Even so, certain conditions will have to be met.'

From the corner of her eye, Alyssa watched Brock and Holly stiffen. But she ignored that as Hammond continued. 'There will be cameras recording every second to avoid any conflict of interest issues. And as this might be our one and only chance to find out how many other women there were, I need your reassurance that you'll remain levelheaded and professional at all times.' The captain's eyes shifted to Isaac and back.

Alyssa bristled that Hammond would question her professionalism, but she also understood the reasons behind the warning, so she held her tongue, feeling the weight of everyone's stares, but especially her family's.

Holly was the first to voice her objection. 'I don't like it, Mom. Why do you need to be the one to interview him?'

She didn't get a chance to respond before Brock added his two cents. 'Holly's right. You need to let someone else do this. You already told Isaac you were confused. Do you really think you're the best person to question him?'

Alyssa's eyes narrowed at that last part, even if she did understand their concerns. 'I may be the only one who *can* get him to talk. I'm the one he has a connection with,' she countered.

Finally, Isaac offered his input. 'Mom's right.' He looked at his dad, sister, and grandmother before turning to her. 'You're a detective. Go do your job. We'll be waiting for you when you're finished.'

Alyssa's heart swelled with pride for her son, knowing how difficult this must be for him – to be present in the same building with the man who'd not only kidnapped and tortured him, but who had also vowed to kill her. All she wanted to do was go to Isaac, hug him to her, and never let go, but Hammond was already moving to the door.

'As an extra precaution, we'll have a guard stationed inside with you, as well as one outside,' he said.

'Wait, won't he be shackled?' Brock interrupted, stepping forward with one arm outstretched as if he would yank Alyssa back himself.

The captain's head bobbed up and down. 'Of course, of course. I assure you, the guards are strictly a precautionary measure.'

'And I'll be in there with her,' Cord said. When Alyssa opened her mouth to argue, he cut her off before she could begin. 'Save it. I'll stand in the corner behind Bishop so I'm as unobtrusive as possible, but you'd better believe I'll be in that room.' His gaze was unwavering.

'That's a fine idea,' Hammond agreed, clapping his hands as he led the way down the hall.

'Will we be able to watch?' Brock asked as everyone filed after the captain.

Alyssa's head snapped back to stare at her husband even as the captain answered. 'Unfortunately, no, I can't allow that.' He stopped at the door where Evan Bishop was still being held and then looked at Alyssa. 'At any time you think you need out of there, for whatever reason, say the word, and this ends. You don't have to be any more of the hero than you already are.'

She forced a smile she knew didn't come close to reaching her eyes. 'I'll be okay.' She turned to her family. 'Why don't you all go on home now?' she suggested, knowing it wouldn't happen but mentioning it just the same.

'We'll wait right here,' Brock said, crossing his arms across his chest.

'Well, I'd like something to snack on, so I think Isaac and I are going to go hunt down a vending machine,' Mabel said. 'We'll meet you back here in just a bit.'

Isaac's head swiveled back and forth, conflicting emotions flashing across his face as he struggled with his desire to go with his grandmother against the need to know – to see – his mother was safe.

Alyssa smiled gratefully at her mother-in-law and then pulled Isaac to her one more time. 'I bet if you talk to Hal, he'll show you where there's a secret stash of strawberry pop tarts,' she whispered softly into his ear. He nodded once and only after he rounded the corner did she allow herself to briefly touch her husband's face and then finally turn to the officer perched in front of the door. 'Okay,' she said. 'Let's do this.' She inhaled deeply, hoping no one noticed her trembling hands. As the guard unlocked and shoved open the door, she steeled herself before stepping forward into a past she thought was dead.

The first thing Alyssa noticed as she and Cord stepped into the room was the coldness of Evan Bishop's eyes as he followed her movement across the room. It brought to mind the popular saying *If looks could kill*.

She refused to allow her eyes to waver as she approached the table where he sat with his hands shackled in front of him. She pulled out a chair across from his, and once she was settled, she began. 'Evan Bishop, I need to make you aware this interview is being recorded. Your consent is not important, but you do need to understand. Do you?'

He leaned forward, and Alyssa fought the urge to lean away. 'Oh, I understand, *sister*,' he sneered.

'If you'd like me to stay in here, you'll address me as Detective,' she said in return. She was glad no one could see her insides as they seemed to tumble across one another. In so many ways, she wanted to search deep into his soul to see if any part of the little brother she'd loved and missed for so long was still there.

He laughed, a mirthless sound. 'I guess some things never change. Your heart is still as cold as it was when Carl kidnapped me.'

Alyssa wanted to close her eyes, to shut out his words as she lost the battle to protect her heart, leaving her feeling raw and exposed. Only decades of practice allowed her to hide her emotions as she forced herself to stare directly at the man who, genetically speaking, was the brother she'd mourned the loss of. She opened her mouth, but he spoke over her.

'Tell me something,' he said. 'How did you do it? How did you know I would show up?'

With each question fired at her, Evan's voice grew louder and more shrill, but Alyssa kept her gaze steady as she admitted the truth. 'When the medical examiner called to give me the DNA results, things clicked into place,' she said even as she thought: *crashed into place was more accurate*. 'I called my captain and reassembled my team. We – I – suspected since you weren't

322

at your house when we arrived to search it, that you may be watching mine.' She watched his face carefully as she continued.

'So, I had the captain pull the patrol units from the house and come back on foot, so they could watch and wait.' She shrugged. 'It was a hunch really. I wasn't sure you'd act so quickly.'

Evan tilted his head sideways as he considered what she'd said, and the move sent a rush of memory through her as it reminded her so much of their father. 'What would you have done if I hadn't shown up?' he asked.

Once again, Alyssa forced herself to hold his gaze. 'Then I would've found another way. But, understand this… I *would've* caught you, if that's what you're wondering. I'd hunt you to the ends of the earth if I had to, but you would *not* have gotten near my family ever again.'

The seconds ticked by as silence filled the room. And then Evan shocked her by asking, 'Is it true Mama and Daddy paid him to take me?'

Alyssa was thankful when her voice came out strong and clear instead of wobbly, the way she felt. *How could he think that, even now?* 'Tim… Evan, whatever Carl Freeman told you, they were lies. Our family was forever changed when… Timmy… was ripped from our lives. It changed us.' This time her voice did crack, but she needed this man in front of her to understand he'd been lied to his entire life.

She jumped when he suddenly slammed his head against the table once and then glared up at her, spittle flying from his mouth as he growled, 'Don't you dare lie to me! You think I don't know the truth already? You don't think he told me about your little plan, how you refused to take me back?' Evan's face turned a violent shade of red and purple. 'I didn't believe him right away. But one night, he locked me in the basement while he went to try to talk to all of you. And when he returned, he told me how you all laughed and closed the door in his face.' His words broke at the end, and Alyssa wondered if maybe, just maybe, she was seeing a glimpse of the little boy she'd called brother.

She moved her hands to her lap and clenched them together so she wouldn't reach across the table and grasp his fingers between hers. 'Don't you see? Carl Freeman *lied* to you. He wanted your cooperation, so he brainwashed you into believing we didn't want you, that we didn't love you anymore. But, that's just it. Nothing he told you was true.' She stared into his eyes, trying to reach whatever part of him she could. 'I don't pretend to understand why people like Freeman exist in the first place. But Timmy's murder is the reason I became a detective, why I fight to give families the happy ending ours never had.' She swallowed. 'And because I blamed myself for so long for leaving Timmy alone.'

She purposely used Timmy's name in order to keep the two men separate in her mind. Evan Bishop was a serial killer, someone who had probably murdered at least eight women, and who had tortured her son. Timmy was the brother she'd lost.

Evan's voice and eyes went flat as he said, 'You should've blamed yourself. It was your fault.'

In that moment, Alyssa realized that Carl Freeman's hold on the man in front of her was strong and deep-seated, and nothing she could say right now would change his mind. In fact, everything she said would be twisted to fit what he already believed. So instead she asked the question that had been niggling at the back of her mind. 'How did you end up with the name Bishop instead of Freeman?'

He glared murderously at her, his lips pursed together in a tight line for so long she was surprised when he actually answered.

'Carl opened the phone book one day, ran his finger down the page until I said stop. It landed on Bishop.' He said it as if that was a completely normal thing for one to do.

'How many others… like you… were there?' Alyssa asked now, not sure she really wanted to know. But, if there was any way to bring closure to those families whose sons went missing, not knowing what had happened to their loved ones, she needed to find out.

He shrugged. 'I lost count. A dozen. Two? More? Who knows? As long as he brought them in, he left me alone.'

Alyssa's nails dug deeper into her palms. 'Did he keep others alive, like he kept you?' *Why didn't he kill you, too?* was the question she really wanted to ask. And maybe some distant time in the future she would, when he was willing to listen to the truth.

Sounding almost proud, he said, 'No. I was the only one.'

'Is Freeman dead now?' she asked.

Chills ran down her spine when Evan laughed, his eyes bright as he nodded. 'He got cancer, and when he got too weak to provide for the two of us, I rowed him out into Lake Michigan and watched him drown.'

Alyssa watched as he closed his eyes for just a moment, and the faintest of smiles flitted over his face, making her realize he was replaying the memory in his mind. 'You know he begged me to save him? To bring him back into the boat? Of course, I ignored him.' He opened his eyes again. 'It wasn't a quick death, either. Watching him struggle to keep his head above water, watching him gasp for air over and over again made me happy.' He tilted his head to the side and studied Alyssa. 'And then I left and ended up here – like it was fate. Destiny.

'When I realized who you were, who *I* was, when I remembered how you stole everything from me, all I wanted was to return the favor.' He leaned forward as if he wanted to share a secret. 'Before the police showed up on my doorstep, I was even going to let you choose who I killed first. But not until you watched me break in your little boy the way Carl did me. And I would've made you watch and listen to his screams, made you watch as he begged you to save him. And I would've relished in the fact that you *couldn't* save him. I would've made you beg for your family's life, and then I would've slowly killed them all in front of you. But you? I would've kept you alive. Every day, I would've forced you to watch the recordings of your perfect little family being tortured, and I would've cherished every moment you had to live with the knowledge that it was you who killed them, not me.'

From the corner of her eye, Alyssa saw Cord stiffen while the guard near the door stepped forward, but she shook her head no, and the man returned to the corner, but kept his eyes glued to Bishop.

Slowly she moved her hands from her lap to the table. She had to move the subject away from her family because she didn't trust herself not to leap across the table at him. 'Is that why you killed Callie McCormick and all those other women?' she asked. 'Because you thought you were getting back at me?' He'd already answered this question, but as an officer of the law, she needed more.

Evan sat back, a sly grin tugging up the corners of his lips. 'Why, *Detective*, I'm sure I don't know what you're talking about.'

'Evelyn Martin, Jill Lawry, Mary Terra, Alice Winslow, Debra Hyatt, Rhonda Dupres, Sandra Jackson.' She paused. 'Callie McCormick.' With each name she watched his eyes narrow and his jaw tighten, and she knew she was finally touching a nerve. 'Are there…' She didn't get a chance to finish her question because Evan broke in.

'I'd like to speak to a lawyer now,' he said, effectively ending the interview.

Alyssa kept her emotions in check she pushed back from the table and stood without saying a word, staring down at Evan Bishop, his eyes as frosty as a winter's day, and then on wooden legs, she walked to the door, Cord close behind her.

'When will you be back?' he asked, his voice sounding almost panicked, as the guard moved to let them out.

She didn't turn around. 'I won't,' she said and left the room.

His face flushed with her rejection, Evan watched Alyssa Wyatt walk out, the door clanging shut with finality as she did, and roared his anger to the room, his howls filling the air until he was hoarse. She had the nerve to come in here and lie to his face and then refuse to return? He vowed then and there that he'd find a way to escape, and when he did, he'd make sure she never turned her back on him again.

Chapter Sixty

Friday, April 12

Alyssa's heart pounded inside her chest as she concentrated on taking steady breaths in and out. Her legs muscles were on the verge of feeling like melted marshmallows, but she welcomed every throb, every ache, and every sensation because it helped keep her mind off everything else, things that tormented her in the night as well as her waking hours.

Finding out Timmy had not only been alive all along, but that he'd been living right in her backyard, so to speak, was simply one more checkmark she had to place in her personal box of failures. The list seemed to be growing. How could she not have known? Why hadn't she *felt* that he was still out there, just waiting to be rescued? *Because you were nine years old,* she reminded herself, not that it ever helped.

To exorcise these demons that clawed at her brain, she'd forced herself out of bed predawn every morning, punishing and pushing herself with vigorous runs through the bosque, replaying her life like a movie reel; from the time Mama and Daddy had brought Timmy home from the hospital, how she remembered staring down at his tiny little body, placing her finger inside his little fist as it flailed in the air, and promising she'd always be there to protect him; to the day he'd been kidnapped, the fear she'd felt when she realized she'd screwed up in the biggest way possible; to the moment she realized her brother was not only alive but a serial killer; and then to that second when she had stood up and walked out of that inter-rogation room, mentally offering her final goodbye, thinking as she stood that she'd been wrong all along. She'd always told herself to move on from the tragedy of her brother's murder, that the past could not be changed.

But it had. And she didn't know how to process her thoughts on it.

Especially since today was the day Timothy Evan Archer, aka Hunter Jenkins, aka Evan Bishop, was scheduled to appear before the judge for his bond hearing, and she had every intention of being there, despite protests from her family and her teammates. She tried to pretend it was like any other case of hers, but she knew it was far more than that.

'Are we done yet?' Holly's voice beside her dragged Alyssa back to the here and now. Glancing over, she noticed most of her daughter's hastily done French braid had come loose, and sweaty tendrils of hair framed her face, red with exertion. 'Seriously. Wondering. Why. I. Wanted. To. Come. With. You,' she panted. 'Had I known you were planning a solid five-mile run, I might've reconsidered.'

But mother and daughter both knew that wasn't true. Holly had offered to come along because she was worried about Alyssa, about what all this was doing to her emotionally.

Together, they rounded the corner onto their street and slowed their gait to a jog until they reached the sidewalk in front of the house. There they continued walking, both of them with hands on hips, sucking in huge gulps of air. And even though the morning had been on the cool side, they were both hot and sticky from their exercise.

On the front lawn, Alyssa bent over, stretching her legs and flattening her palms on the green grass. Beside her, Holly collapsed onto her stomach and sprawled out, and Alyssa decided it looked like an awfully good idea, so she let herself drop down next to her daughter, ignoring the dampness of the dew soaking into her already wet tank top. Holly groaned before flopping to her back.

'Ay-yi-yi, I hurt all over,' Alyssa panted. 'I'm pretty sure even my eyeballs hate me right now.'

'I'd laugh, but that would take up way too much oxygen that I need to breathe,' Holly said, her chest rising and falling with each breath. 'Oh, sweet, precious air, come into my lungs and fill me with your life-giving sustenance.'

Alyssa snorted out a chuckle, then grabbed her middle and groaned. 'Stop. It hurts too much.'

She laid there with her daughter until she heard a tap on the window, and like two puppets on the same string, they twisted their necks toward the noise. Brock waved to them from inside the house, motioning for them to come in. When neither of them moved, he turned his palms up and shrugged, nonverbally asking what was going on.

'You s'pose he really expects us to move?' Holly asked.

'I think he does,' Alyssa said.

'Think he'd be willing to wheelbarrow us in? And I'm only half joking, by the way.'

Alyssa pretended to consider her question. 'Well, you are his favorite daughter, so maybe if you bat those ridiculously long lashes and those beautiful eyes at him…'

'Maybe,' Holly said, 'but that still takes too much energy. But you put out for him, so…'

Alyssa choked and slapped her daughter weakly. 'Holly Renee! Did you really just say that to me?'

Her daughter tapped her index finger to her forehead in a poor imitation of Winnie-the-Pooh and said, 'Yes. Yes, I believe I did. Oh, look, Dad's coming out. He thinks you're beating me, and he's racing to my rescue.'

A second later, Brock poked his head out the screen door and yelled, 'You two going to lay there all day or what?'

'Thinking about it, why?' Alyssa asked. When he tapped his watch, she mumbled under her breath, 'Ugh. Guilt trips; they work every time.' To her husband, she said, 'All right, give us another minute.' And as soon as he went back in, she pushed herself to sitting, but when she reached back to help Holly up, her daughter's face turned serious.

'Mom, I didn't just want to go with you this morning because I'm worried about you. I mean, we all are. I also wanted to let you know that Grandma and I talked a couple nights ago, and we decided it might be best to put off the Europe trip for now.'

The relief that flowed through Alyssa was swift and immediate, but she held her tongue and let Holly finish. Now sitting up, her daughter stared off, and Alyssa followed her daughter's gaze to the Zeller house.

'I just think I need to be with my family right now,' she said. 'And Grandma agrees. In fact, you'll probably find this hard to believe, but she was actually the one who brought it up, asking how I'd feel going later, maybe even next summer or something.'

Holly was right – Alyssa was a bit shocked the idea had come from Mabel. Maybe she hadn't given the other woman enough credit over the years.

What her daughter said next brought guilt crashing back down on her, though she managed to hide it. 'I'm just afraid Isaac's going to blame himself when we tell him,' she admitted.

Alyssa reached out to squeeze her daughter's arm. 'You, my darling, are a wonderful sister, and a kind, caring daughter and granddaughter. Your brother is going to be okay because the rest of us are going to make sure of it. And while you can't worry about how all of your decisions will affect him – or even the rest of us – I have to admit you've eased a lot of my worries by coming to this decision on your own – or at least without Dad and me asking it of you.'

'Europe will always be there, so like I said, maybe next year.' With a grunt and a moan, Holly pushed herself to her feet, and then reached down to help her mother. As soon as she was standing, Alyssa pulled her daughter in and held her tightly.

'Also, since we're riding the honesty train,' Holly said, 'I may as well confess that Dad and I are going to the courthouse with you today.'

Alyssa jerked back, ready to protest, but her daughter covered her mouth with her hand. 'Nope. Don't waste your breath arguing. We've already discussed it, and it's going to happen. Isaac cried because he feels like he's letting you down, but Dad made sure he understood that wasn't true, that you'd probably feel better and worry less if he didn't go.'

Alyssa nodded her head because Brock was right.

'Anyway,' Holly continued, 'he's just not... ready... yet, so Grandma's going to pick him up, and they'll spend the day together.'

Without any warning, tears suddenly burst from Alyssa's eyes like a broken dam, and as she stepped back, she placed a palm against her daughter's cheek. 'I love my family, you know that?'

'I do. And we love you, too, and that's why we're going,' Holly said, linking their arms together as they walked into the house.

–

Three hours later, Evan Bishop was being escorted from the jailhouse van to the courthouse, shackled at the ankles and wrists.

Because news crews filled every available spot and some that weren't, parking was at a premium, even for the authorities. It seemed like the entire city had shown up for this. Lights flashed as cameras went off. They were surrounded by questions being shouted from all sides.

Alyssa, Holly, and Brock, along with Cord, had already pushed their way through the throngs of people, Cord being none too gentle about shoving people who wound up in their path.

As they made their way to the top step, Alyssa pulled back, ignoring her husband's hand on her waist as he tried to guide her forward. She was unable to stop herself from turning around to get a glimpse of Evan Bishop, still wondering if she could glean just a trace of the carefree little boy Timmy had once been. But even she didn't know if it was to assuage her own guilt or because she wanted to keep that promise, that vow to protect, she'd made to her little brother forty years ago. And maybe it was a little of both, and that was okay, too.

And then suddenly he was there, ten feet from the stairs, two officers on either side of him as another used his long arms to push through the crowds, creating a pathway for their prisoner. Alyssa's eyes locked with Evan Bishop's as his gaze swept up, and she thought he froze for just a second, but she couldn't be sure.

His gaze swept away from her for just a moment, and she knew he'd spotted Holly because he jerked a little and shook his head as if dislodging a memory. When he turned her way once more, he held her stare, and she thought she saw a familiar spark. Was it regret or something else? When she saw his mouth move, she realized he was speaking to her, and her feet automatically moved forward.

It took her a second before she understood what he was saying. 'I will come for you.'

Chills raced up and down her spine as her heart fell to her toes, and she knew she'd been kidding herself thinking she still had a chance of saving the little boy. The man in front of her was nothing more than a sadistic killer, and she had to accept that and somehow move on, even if it meant she could never forgive herself for the part she played in it.

Suddenly, there was a huge commotion as someone forced his way to the front. The man's face was red, his eyes cold, his teeth bared. He shouted something that got lost in the wind, jabbing the air to accentuate every single word.

A sound halted time for a split second. Then panic and pandemonium erupted with people screaming, pushing, shoving, and trampling each other to find safety.

'Shots fired at Civic Plaza. I repeat, shots fired.'

Alyssa whipped her head around, automatically reaching for the weapon she didn't have. 'Get her inside,' she ordered Brock, gesturing to Holly as she moved swiftly down the stairs.

Someone shouted. 'We need an ambulance! He's been hit.'

Who? Who'd been hit? She looked around her wildly. Then she saw it; the orange jumpsuit, the handcuffed wrists and chained ankles lying entirely too still on the ground, blood flowing from his mouth, eyes now vacant.

She heard herself screaming as Cord pulled her away. Several officers surrounded a man, guns pointed. 'Get down! Drop the weapon! Get down!' they yelled.

Alyssa saw a weapon fall from the man's hands as he sank to his knees, hands up in surrender. One of the officers moved and she got a close look at his face.

Rafe McCormick.

He'd fired the shot that killed Timmy for real this time, completely ripping away any last lingering hope she might've had of saving him.

A LETTER FROM CHARLY

Hello!

Thank you so much for choosing to read my debut novel, *All His Pretty Girls*. The road from initial thought to final product has been exhilarating, frightening, tear-inducing, and exciting, sometimes one at a time and sometimes all at once.

The topic of serial killers and what makes them that way has always fascinated me, so it was no surprise the idea for this story came to me a few years ago when I took my vehicle in for a tune up, and a man sat down next to me, and just like Mearl Leroy in this book, began talking to me about all kinds of random things. And while he was quite friendly, the writer in me couldn't help but create a story from this situation, and I began to wonder: what would happen if this grandfatherly-type person was actually a serial killer? And from there, the story grew, and I couldn't wait to get home to begin writing it down. Of course, my cast of characters grew, evolved, and steered me in several different directions, surprising even me a few times. Writing *All His Pretty Girls* taught me characters really do talk to me, and they won't be quiet until I listen, even when I don't want to. In fact, they can be quite insistent.

So, I truly hope you enjoyed meeting Alyssa, her family, and her team as much as I enjoyed writing about them. If you did, I'd love to hear from you and would appreciate if you would take a few minutes to write a review and share your thoughts... and tell your friends and family, too. Readers like you help authors like me continue to create the stories that weave through our minds on a regular basis.

If you'd like to learn more about me or would like to contact me, you can find me at:

www.clcox-author.com
www.twitter.com/Charlylynncox
www.facebook.com/charlycoxauthor
charlycoxauthor@gmail.com
charlycox@clcox-author.com
Sincerely,
Charly

ACKNOWLEDGMENTS

Writing a book is a journey that takes an author on many ups, downs, and curves, and there are so many people that I want to thank. Without you, the path I took to this point may have been very different. I only wish I could name every single person ever who played some part in getting me here.

I'd first like to begin by thanking all those authors out there who gave me places to escape to in my mind and who first gave me a reason to love reading. You've taken me on more journeys to more places and introduced me to more people than I ever could've managed on my own.

Next, I'd like to thank my husband Kevin – my biggest cheerleader and the person who has to listen to me cry when I'm sure nothing sounds right, and I'm positive I've written nothing but drivel, and who never ever allowed me to give up, and who never failed to tell me he believed – and my son Timothee – who not only reads and pokes holes in my plots, but who's willing to tell me about them, laugh at me when needed, encourages me every step of the way, and more importantly, who helps me untangle the knots, even if that means taking my calls when he's with his friends. (One of these days, you'll finish one of your own books and set the reading world on fire.) Without the two of you, my world would be a far lonelier place.

To Dad and Uncle Al – you were both taken far too soon, and I wish you could be here now to share in this moment.

To my friends (and fellow authors) Patrice Locke and Jennifer Bohnhoff for being the very first readers of the very first version of this story. If it hadn't been for the two of you,

I'm not sure I would've been brave enough to share my writing with anyone, much less the world. You showed me critique is nothing but encouragement to improve.

For Drew Dooley, dear friend and fellow writer, for so many things, but mostly for reminding me why the gremlins are there and for helping to pick me up during those times it got to be too much, for reminding me to step back and take a breath, for pushing me to always be my best, and for just being you. I can't wait for the world to discover your writing – and not just because I want to go to Bora Bora. (And for her wife Deb who makes me homemade salsa straight from her garden. I'm convinced it helps my creative side. Hint hint.)

For my awesome friends and neighbors, Theresa and Kevin, for cheering and crying with me with every up and down, and not just in my writing travels, either.

For my sisters, Kim and Kerri, and my sisters and brothers-in-law – you make my heart smile.

For Dawn – thank you for letting me borrow Wyatt's name and for answering some of my initial questions when I first began traveling this road toward this dream of mine. Also, thank you for reading one of the earliest versions of this story – and encouraging me to keep going.

For Aunt Lucy who has never once stopped believing in me or in *any* of my dreams.

For Bud and Ray Wolfenbarger for answering endless questions, texts, and phone calls regarding police and investigative procedures. Thank you for not disowning me and blocking my number. You are, by far, my favorite law enforcement guys in the entire world.

For my forever best friends who are the kind of people who drop anything (including birthday parties in their honor) to show their unending love and support: Tammie (bfflylas to the end) – there is not enough room to thank you for all the things I should. You've been with me through more ups and downs and helped me back up more times than I can count, and who

338

has laughed and made lasting memories with me since we were teenagers. Who knew all those years ago, fate would land us in all the same classes, connecting us for life? Angie – if there's a more fiercely loyal, honest, protective, and giving person out there – never mind, there's not. You are the glue that holds us together. Tracy – who knew when we met in junior high that decades later, you'd be helping me nurse my husband back to health after his 'seat belt broke,' and then as if that wasn't enough, answering all my strange medical questions and then making sure I got them right… without openly laughing; and finally to Ro and Annette – thank you for reminding me that you're always there for me, even when I don't know I need it. I wish everyone could be as lucky to have a group like you. After this long, we're kind of Gorilla-glued together now. And thank God for that. I never want to navigate this world without a single one of you.

For all those people out there in the large writing community who've become my friends along the way (Stephanie S., and Jodi L-S., to name just a couple). Thank you for reminding me my panicky moments are completely normal.

And I'd be remiss if I didn't thank Hera Books, Lindsey Mooney, and especially Keshini Naidoo – editorial and literary genius extraordinaire – for seeing to the heart of this story and for being willing to help drag out of me the vision you saw. Your insight is awe-inspiring, so thank you for your unending support and encouragement and for answering my many millions of questions and emails (only slightly exaggerated) when I felt the task was impossible. I'm sending cyber hugs your way.

And finally, to all the readers out there. Without you, there would be no need for authors to share the stories that crawl through our minds itching to get out into the world.